# THE WAR OF THE LORDS VEIL

# THE WAR

## of the

# LORDS VEIL

*Adam Nichols*

**MILLENNIUM**
An Orion Book
LONDON

The right of Adam Nichols to be identified as the author of this work has been asserted by
him in accordance with the Copyright, Designs and Patents Act 1988.

First published in 1994
by Millennium
An imprint of Orion Books Ltd
Orion House, 5 Upper St Martin's Lane
London WC2H 9EA

A CIP catalogue record for this book is
available from the British Library

ISBN: (Csd) 1 85798 187 1
(Ppr) 1 85798 188 X

Millennium
Book Fifty One

Typeset by Deltatype Ltd, Ellesmere Port, Cheshire
Printed and bound in Great Britain by
Clays Ltd, St Ives plc.

This book is for Nick and Barbara, my parents. It is sometimes said that, as nascent souls, we choose the man and woman to whom we are born in this world. If that is so, it was the very best choice I could ever have made.

And for Steve Jones, without whom it would never have happened.

No book is ever finished without help. I'd like to say thanks to:

Juliet King, who cheerfully lent me a home when I needed one.

Jane O'Connor, my sister, who first made me feel the story was coming alive.

Bernadette English, literary midwife extraordinaire, who helped nurse the whole thing into life.

Marley Morris, who kept me thinking about character.

Catherine Hennessy, who lent me both her German and her home.

Jeff Green, who lent me his technology.

Vera Wells, who kindly lent me her house.

Tad Williams, who very tactfully began the process of teaching me how to perform major surgery.

Caroline Oakley, whose patience and sanity were a balm.

Mia, who was never without a word of encouragement.

Ellen Shizgal, who read an early version of the manuscript and *liked* it (and who gave me a dozen roses on the sale of my first short story and assured me, straight faced, that this was only the beginning).

Thanks, all!

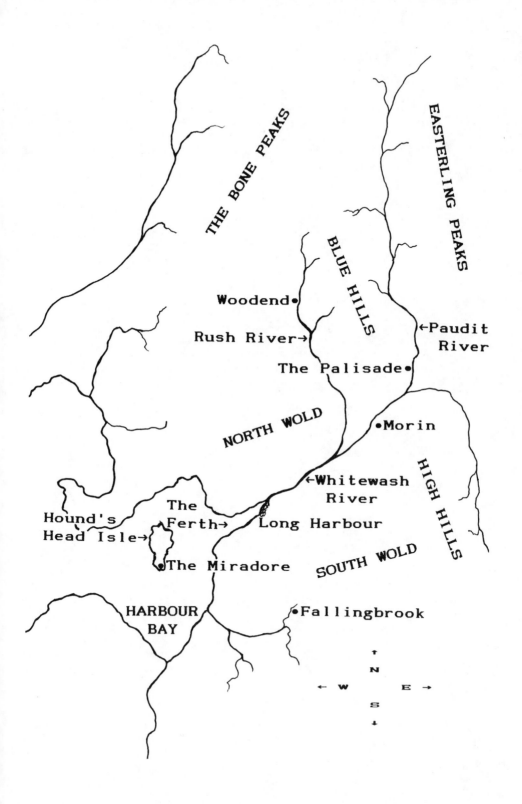

# PART ONE

# ENDINGS

# I

# On the Upper Slopes of
# the High Hills, in the South Wold

Young Tai was wrenched awake in the dark just before dawn, his heart racing.

He felt it happening to him again.

The familiar solidity of the world about him fell away into confusion. His senses were obliterated by the awful rush of it, his eyes blinded in their sockets, his ears torn to deafness. He could feel nothing but the terrible, squirming chaos all about. His belly clenched up like a fist, and he lay aquiver in fear, struggling, praying for it to pass quickly, as sometimes these fits did, all the while feeling the ordinary solidity of the world shredding away inexorably.

And then there was only a dark, moving confusion, pulsing sickeningly without and within him. He screamed, or thought to scream, but could feel no mouth to scream with, no ears to hear. He felt himself being torn apart, ruptured into chaos like the very world itself.

This was worse than he had ever experienced before. In panic, he tried to thrash free of it. It was killing him. Killing him . . . But he could do nothing. He could no more resist this dreadful, rushing chaos than a tumbling leaf could resist the autumn gale.

And then, distantly, there was . . . movement.

Tai sensed it, though never had he understood how he could sense anything when the world went like this about him. Murky and unclear it was, like the half-glimpsed movement of hidden beasts at the bottom of some deep pool. He could not see, could not hear, yet he was aware, somehow, of the surge and shift of that movement.

Drawing nigh with terrible, predatory ease.

Towards him.

Tai recoiled instinctively from this menacing presence. A rush of terror went through him. He felt like a hapless fieldmouse faced with the gathering deadly coils of some great serpent, and he struggled to break away, to flee. But the chaos reeled sickeningly about him, gripping him. He only floundered, helpless. The terror filled him, like liquid fills a gourd, until he felt he must rupture apart with the sheer, terrible force of it.

And nearer came the deadly . . . *something*.

But then, as if bursting from turbulent waters, Tai felt himself suddenly rising out of it.

The haunted chaos fell away, and the world began to congeal again about him. He felt himself coalesce.

It was over.

Tai lurched half up from the tangled folds of his blanket roll, his heart drumming frantically. His breath came in heaving gasps. Shaking, he cast anxiously about to see if anyone had seen the fit take him, but all nearby seemed soundly asleep.

The quiet, and the coolness of the night air in his lungs, were soothing. In a little, he let himself back down to the ground with a sigh and lay there unmoving.

Only streaming tatters of cloud remained overhead, remnants of the storm that had raged most of the past day. The sky was quiet now, but the air had the smell of more rain in it, more storm yet to come. The moon was gone full. Long fingers of silvered light lay over the camp. Through the intricate, dark shapes of the oaks that hung over the camp clearing, Tai saw the flickering glamour of the stars. He lay still, trying to obliterate the memory of what he had just undergone.

Slowly, he felt his breathing began to ease, his heartbeat slow.

The sky was pre-dawn dark, the air cold, and everything wet from the storm just passed, but under the blanket roll Tai was sticky with fear-sweat. What had he ever done to bring this strange and terrible affliction down upon himself? He loathed it. It made him sick in his guts with terror every time the fit struck. It had stalked him all the years of his young life, like some fell hunter, striking with its own unfathomable rhythm. One moment the world was solid and sane and familiar. The next, he was ripped away into that dreadful, soul-tormenting chaos. It was like being plunged into a boiling cauldron, an agony of terrifying dissolution; like a death, each time. Torn apart . . .

Never, *never* could he grow used to it!

Tormenting and terrifying him, making of him a drooling, gibbering fool so that any who witnessed it laughed or drew away in disgust.

These fits of his were a shameful affliction: his good right arm would he give to be free of them. He clenched his teeth till his jaw ached, fighting the remembrance, denying it. There was something desperately wrong with him, that he could not stay in the world like other men but must fall out of it into that terrible, formless chaos. And this fit had been worse than any previous. They were getting worse. The very thought made him shudder sickly.

Stiffly, Tai levered himself up on an elbow. There would be no more

4

sleep for him this night. He knew that well enough from past experience. Unrolling from his blanket roll, he stood there shivering in the cold bite of the pre-dawn breeze. He reached up the blade that lay on the ground next the blanket. The thing felt heavy and awkward in his hand. But none of them moved now without some such weapon, the times being what they were.

Buckling the scabbard round his waist, Tai studied the slumbering forms near him. All lay still. He could hardly credit it, but none seemed to have noticed the fit taking him, and he was thus spared the mortification of witnesses. Thankful, he stepped carefully over Colby, who lay snuffling softly in sleep, and picked a slow way through the others. Tai felt shaky and nauseous, and his legs moved clumsily under him. The blade in its scabbard dangled like an ungainly extra limb, and he shifted its position, giving somebody an inadvertent prod in passing. The man cursed him sleepily.

Casting about, Tai made out the dim shape of one of the night-watch near the tangled, dark mass of trees at the verge of the clearing. He moved slowly in that direction, needing the company.

'Can't sleep, lad?' the man asked. Wrapped in a blanket against the chill, he stood propped against the belly of an old oak, his attention on the moon dappled dark beyond the camp.

'Cold woke me,' Tai said after a little.

'Aye.' The man wrapped his blanket tighter. 'Cursed cold it gets up here in the High Hills. And true wild country like this . . .' He gave a little shudder. 'The Fey Folk do not take kindly to visitors, men say.'

Tai stood, shivering in the damp air, wishing he had thought to bring his own blanket. He hardly listened to the man, his attention instead on the world, on how dark the gnarly oak above him was, and blessedly solid under his fingers when he reached to it. In the camp clearing behind, a sleeping man snorted softly. The faintest of breezes whispered in the trees round about.

'Still and all,' the watchman went on, ''tis not the Fey Folk we need be watching for this night, is it? Nothing moving out there in any case, far as I can see.'

The words brought back to Tai sudden recollection of what he had experienced when the fit was upon him. *Movement.* Some predatory . . . *presence* drawing nigh him. He shuddered, remembering. He had never experienced anything of this sort before. Sometimes, there were things he could *sense* somehow amidst the shifting chaos: vague movements, like distant ripples in far-off, dark water. But this had been different, clearer, terrifying.

Could it mean anything?

Should he say something?

But he could not bring himself to speak of it. The years of his childhood were all too clearly etched in his memory, and the torment he had endured at the hands of his foster-brothers: they had panto-mimed his fits, flinging themselves to the ground, flopping about like dying fish, making weird gobbling sounds, laughing at him with childish cruelty until they had reduced him to helpless, hopeless tears.

The memory burned.

The man before him Tai knew only slightly, as he knew most of the company here only slightly. What could he say? 'I have fits, friend. And I . . . *sensed* something.'

Some few persons were gifted with the Sight, yes. Though un-common, it was not unknown. But these fits of his were no gift. Curse, rather; and all that went with them suspect. The watchman would only back away if Tai said anything, and shake his head at such pitiful insanity. Or laugh at a foolish boy imagining things in the dark. He had been laughed at too much already in his young life, had Tai.

So he kept his silence.

'Should be dawn soon,' the watchman said. 'Cannot come soon enough for me.'

Tai hugged himself, gazing at the dark, tangled oaks round about. Their branches were all but naked, for winter was still hardly gone, even in the lowlands. Under the moonlight, the trees looked like a throng of enormous, wrinkle-jointed old men, caught in the very midst of some queer dance and held immobile. The queerness of it put Tai in mind of the Fey Folk, and a little shiver ran up his spine. He sketched a quick warding sign with a hand.

Seeing Tai make the sign, the watchman chuckled softly. 'Gives one the wobbles, night like this does. But 'tis years and years since any saw the Fey in these parts. I do not think we need worry on that score.'

'Let us hope not,' Tai said. 'Touch wood.' He pressed his palm flat against the oak, feeling the wet coldness of moss against the rumpled bark, thankful that the world continued to hold solid and comforting about him.

'Cursed, thankless work, this night-duty,' the watchman muttered. 'And a long day tomorrow ahorse.' He sighed. 'Our Olivor's a good man, but he sees trouble everywhere. I'll bet you a pint of good brown ale that there is nobody within leagues of here. Grim folk and mighty, these cursed invaders from the south may be, but they don't know the country hereabouts as Olivor does. We outran them well enough, mark my words, lad. We've no more to fear from *them* this night than we do from the Fey. Quiet as a grave plot out there it is.'

'Aye,' Tai replied. 'Quiet it seems.' He eased himself down next the man, put his back against the oak, the awkward length of the blade across his hip, and wrapped his arms about his knees for warmth. 'How far,' he asked, 'do you think we need travel tomorrow before – '

But Tai never had a chance to finish the question.

There came a sudden crashing from the darkness under the oaks, a wild, blood-chilling howl.

'Powers preserve us,' Tai heard from the man next him. ''Tis *them*!'

The small glade of their encampment was suddenly filled with dark, leaping shapes. Near the camp's rear verge, the horses screamed, thrashing at their pickets. Men cursed, crying out, voices still thick with sleep.

Tai scrambled desperately away from the leaping, howling shapes that surged from the woods. He tripped over some unseen thing in the dark, fell sprawling to the ground, struggled up, staring about him, stricken. To his left, he made out a surge of moving figures, the cold glint of iron in moonlight. He skittered a few paces, turned, befuddled by the howling confusion, stumbled back, and found himself suddenly caught amidst a chaotic struggle of bodies in the dark. He felt the terror in his guts as he tried desperately to cut at one of them, only to have his blade skitter uselessly across stone-hard armour. A sudden, bright, blinding pain lit the back of his skull.

And then there was nothing at all.

Tai came back to himself with a start, his face pressed into cold, wet sod. Hands gripped him, and he struggled despairingly, trying to wrench free.

'Easy, lad,' a voice said softly. 'Easy. You're with friends.'

Tai settled a little, and the thumping of his heart eased some. Twisting round, he saw he was sprawled amongst a ragged huddle of men. His skull throbbed like a rotten tooth. Somebody helped him sit up, and he crouched there, hands to his head, shivering miserably. Dawn-light silvered the horizon, making of the surrounding trees a dark lattice-work, and showing the grim shapes of guards that stood round them. Like the rest, Tai kept his head down, eyes averted from the fell shapes of those guards.

The men huddled together, some only half clad, drawn near for warmth and what little comfort they could gain one from another. There were no more than a dozen or so, all battered, some moaning with wounds. Tai searched faces as best he could, but there was no sign of Colby, no sign of any of the few men he knew from his own district. He shivered, holding himself tighter. 'What of the . . . the others?' he asked of the man nearest him.

'Dead,' came the reply.

Somewhere off back amongst the trees on the other side of the clearing, somebody screamed, shrill and terrible. Then the sound ceased, cut short.

'Or dying,' the man next to Tai added bleakly.

'How did *they* find us up here in the Hills?' somebody demanded.

'And why spare us now?'

To these questions, none seemed to have any answer.

Tai hung his head. This was the end then. The end of all their hopes, and a bitter end indeed.

He heard the death litany being recited for some poor soul. 'A scathless journey in the darkness, friend,' a hoarse voice whispered. 'A scathless journey and a fruitful end. Gone from the world of living ken. Into the Shadowlands . . . to begin again.' Tai sketched a blessing sign with his fingers, as did others about him.

A man lying next to him moaned, clutching his belly. Tai reached a hand out supportingly. He could do little else. With a belly wound like that, this man, too, was not like to live much longer.

None of them, most probably, was like to live much longer.

Tai shivered, thinking on the presence he had sensed drawing nigh when the fit had been upon him.

*Them?*

Could it be? No! He could not credit such a thing. There was no sense to his fits. They revealed nothing.

And yet . . . What if it *were* so? And what if he had spoken up and given the alarm? For a moment, he imagined what it would have been like: escaping to safety in the dark, ahead of *them*, nobody dead or dying. Olivor himself saying, 'Good work, lad. Clever of you to notice *them* so quick. Don't know what we would have done without you . . .'

But no.

Tai hung his head and cursed. They were naught but an affliction, these fits of his.

And everything now was taken.

A last few wounded were hauled up and dumped amongst the huddled group of survivors. Among these newcomers, Tai saw Colby. He felt a rush of relief. The men about Tai were from other villages, other parts of the Wold. A rag-tag bunch indeed, with only the one common bond: the desperate struggle to resist *them* as *they* overran the land with fire and blade. But Colby was kin.

Tai slunk the little distance that separated him from where Colby lay, moving slow and quiet so as not to draw notice of the guards.

'Sister's son,' Colby greeted him, in a voice hardly more than a croak.

Colby was a brawny man, grey haired, prone to easy laughter. There was little laughter in him now. He lay on his back, white-faced and gasping. His face was battered and swollen, and he spat blood from torn lips, and more blood drooled down his bearded chin. At first, Tai could see no other sign of a wound, but then he spotted the long, wet red rent along the right-hand side of Colby's rib-cage.

'Uncle . . .' Tai moaned in grief. Not entirely true, that 'uncle', nor the 'sister's son', for Tai was only foster-son to Colby's sister, taken in after his own mother died at his birthing. But Colby had always been readier than most to accept him, and dear to Tai's heart for that.

Colby lifted his head and smiled crookedly. 'Good to . . . see . . . you,' he gasped. 'How be you, lad?'

Tai scarce knew how to answer. 'Alive. But you . . .'

'Aye,' Colby agreed. 'Me . . .'

Tai wrung his hands helplessly. Colby's swollen face was cramped with pain, but his light eyes were as clear as ever, and he smiled a rueful smile. Tai could not help but think of the days passed.

They had run and hid and struck out when they could, this rag-tag group he and Colby had become a part of. Most of them were farmers, with farms now in ruins and families dead or scattered, who were learning the terrible craft of war as they went. Cold nights, hard travel, aching joints, fear like a live thing in Tai's belly, the last of his boyhood left behind in the smoking ruin of what had been his home. And small hope indeed of ever bringing one of *them* down, deadly creatures that they were. Yet through it all had Colby been there, with his familiar laugh and solid strength. Tai's anchor. The last of his kin, and the most dear to him. Tai felt his heart was like to break, seeing his foster-uncle as he now was.

Colby reached a hand up to one of Tai's. He coughed again, gagging, wiped away the blood with the back of his other hand. ''Tis good to be next a kinsman . . . at the end of all.'

Tai blinked back sudden tears. 'Aye,' he replied, clutching Colby's cold hand in his.

The man with the belly wound dragged himself over, gasping. 'Not perhaps the . . . end of . . . all.'

Colby elbowed himself painfully up so as to see the man. 'What . . . ?'

'Some managed to flee. I saw it. In the first instants when *they* attacked. In the confusion. Olivor. Quick of thought as ever. Olivor is escaped! And some of the others: Jordie and Hawl, a couple dozen all told, perhaps. Perhaps more . . . 'twas too dark to see clear. Escaped northwards by horse.'

'Truly?'

The man groaned softly, holding his torn belly in with his hands. 'I . . . saw it true.'

Tai felt the faintest surge of something. Not hope perhaps, but something akin to it. Some had got free! And if Olivor yet lived . . . Heart and mind of all they had tried to do was Olivor. A tough, sharp-thinking man, brave and canny. A man to rally others against *them*.

'The best of news, that,' Colby said. He slumped back to the ground, gasping. 'If they have escaped indeed . . .'

Tai swallowed. The day was growing, and he could see the pain writ more clearly now on Colby's battered face. And not a plaint did he make. Tai ached to do something, anything, to help ease him.

But there was naught he could do.

Sudden movement made Tai start, his bruised skull throbbing at the shock. Two of *them* came up, fell-faced and hideous, plucked a man out from the small group of survivors and began to haul him away. Those nearby tried impulsively to go to his aid, but the circle of guards beat them back. The taken man was dragged, struggling helplessly, across to the far verge of the clearing.

'What . . . ?' somebody began.

But it was all too clear what *they* were about now.

The man screamed.

Tai had one glimpse, saw the man's eyes white and staring in his haggard face, the blade in the hands of one of *them* coming away webbed with bleeding flesh. After that, Tai had to turn aside, shuddering.

But he could not shut out the man's choking, helpless screams at each new touch of the blade, as the interrogation proceeded and *they* carved answers from the poor soul.

The men huddled closer together, shaken. The same thought could be seen clearly on each face: Who would be next?

Near Tai, somebody groaned, 'A curse on *them* for all *they* have wrought!'

The screaming rose to a shattering wail. The poor soul . . . Tai closed his eyes tight, shuddering, covered his ears with his hands, helpless to do anything else. *They* were too powerful. Tai felt tears fill his eyes. An impotent rage flooded through him. What had his people ever done to bring such creatures down upon them? *They* raged up from the south, burned and killed and destroyed, coming from the Powers alone knew what grim place, indestructible in armour, hideous, fearsome, implacable and deadly. Men died, and women, and small children. Farms burned. That was the all of it. No reason given. Death, and more death, and he and his helpless to stop it.

*They* plucked another from the huddled group of survivors and dragged him away. This time the interrogation, and the screams, lasted longer.

The rage in Tai congealed into a cold lump in his belly, and he slumped in upon himself, shuddering.

The screams went on. And on.

Nearby, he heard somebody being sick into the grass. He felt his own belly surge in response.

'You all right, lad?' Colby asked of him.

Tai shrugged, wincing as a flare of pain lit his battered skull.

Colby reached out and squeezed Tai's hand. 'Would that you had – ' he gasped, swallowed – 'had escaped this, lad.'

To that, Tai could find nothing at all to say.

The last of the screams died away.

Tai glanced up. *They* stood near, all too clearly visible now in the growing light. The morning sun glittered coldly on a blade-edge.

A terrible silence.

Tai waited, shivering. He tried to keep his eyes downcast. Unnatural creatures, *they* were. Look one direct in the eyes, men said, and your balls shrivelled up like winter berries.

'Separate the ones least damaged,' a voice ordered finally, ordinary-sounding enough. Tai chanced a quick glance, then looked immediately away again. With shaking fingers, he made a warding sign, scant protection though it might afford. The features of the rest were bad enough, but this one seemed to have no face at all, just a pale, shimmering orb, eyeless, lipless.

'Those least damaged,' the voice continued, 'shall provide us with . . . *sport*, later.' There was a pause. Then: 'For the rest . . . dispose of them. We have what information we need. They are of no further use.'

Some of *them* waded in amongst the huddled survivors. Men tried to squirm away, but there was no place to take refuge. A hard hand grasped Tai by the arm, wrenched him up, and began pulling him away.

He heard screams. Beside him, a pike-blade slashed out at the man with the belly wound. The intricate, razor edge of the blade took the poor soul across the throat, opening him to the spine. Tai clung determinedly to his hold on Colby. When the creature pulling at him would have kicked Colby away, Tai turned on it. 'No! He's not so badly off. He can walk!' He fended the creature away desperately, trying to gather Colby up.

'Leave me, lad,' Colby gasped. 'Look to yourself.' He tried to push Tai's hands away. 'Leave me!'

'No,' Tai said. 'No! That I shall not.' Dragging Colby to his feet, Tai forced his way somehow past the creature before him and stumbled off along the dew-slicked grass, Colby's arm across his shoulder. A handful of others hobbled beside them, driven by *them*. Behind, the cries of the dying reached a crescendo, then tapered away to a dreadful silence. Tai did not look back, could not look back. He held on to Colby, who was coughing weakly. 'Walk,' he urged his foster-uncle. 'Walk!'

A pike butt slammed into Tai's shoulder with bruising suddenness. He gasped, faltered, forced himself on at a quicker pace, hauling Colby along.

Down the slope they straggled, those of them who had been culled. A man slipped on the wet grass, scrambled up again, panting. Another collapsed to his knees, doubled over with retching, until one of the dread-featured guards kicked him onwards.

Tai felt muscles burn with the strain of supporting Colby's weight. His foster-uncle was a head taller and thick of build, and Tai's slim frame sagged under the weight. His heart and head beat painfully. But he struggled on.

Towards what, Tai knew not, save that he still lived, and Colby still lived, and he had nothing but that left to cling to now.

# II

# On the Southern Verge
# of the Bone Peaks

Old Crane stood on the chill, stony spine of Mount Stroud, high as any eagle, the voice of the uneasy wind crying through the ancient stone crests about her. She gazed southwards through the twilight, shivering. Stroud was the last of the true Peaks. Beyond him lay the tangled backs of the foothills, thick with beech and mountain oak, green-furred in the distance with spring growth, and then the lowlands, falling away to the far southern horizon. Dark clouds lay humped and twisted on that horizon. A rumbling of thunder rode the mountain air, distant and low, felt in the bones more than the ears.

The growing storm-wind tore at Crane's hair, making a white, streaming banner of it. Thunder echoed again darkly from the south.

The world seemed to shudder.

It was distant still, but coming closer.

That-Which-Broke-All-Patterns.

Crane's old heart stuttered.

The southern lowlands stretched far off before her, lush and green. But she had seen this same landscape in Dream, blackened and shattered by the passage of some terrible, dark thing.

The Dreams gave her no rest now. Green meadows slimed with blood. A yellow-eyed, snarling mountain cat. An auburn-haired woman, eyes flooded with tears. A great, bloodied axe hewing wet flesh. The flickering of torchlight on some gleaming, faceless thing. Blue wings and brown fur and weeping.

Fragmentary, confused, shudderingly powerful, not like anything she had ever before experienced.

Though she was a Dreamwalker and wise, Crane could make no clear sense of this. The simple memory of it was enough to make her belly cramp.

But perched here in this special place high on old Stroud's Peak, a place where earth and sky met, Crane sensed it, alive as she was to echoes of the deep pattern of things, the shift and balance of the Powers that moved through the world. This was like a long pulling, from the south. Some terrible thing coming, and she to be a part of it.

Old Crane shivered. She wanted no part of this thing, whatever it proved to be. Storm was loose in the world. A time of breaking. And she was one of the things to be broken.

Here on Stroud's bleak summit, there was no mistaking it.

Crane had daughters, granddaughters, and daughters of grand-daughters now. She had outlived most of her age-mates. It was almost time for her to slip away into the Shadowlands and let others take up the tasks she had performed for so long. She had thought it time to leave this life in peace, to settle her soul for the final journey. But it seemed that was not to be.

The Dreams said it. The knot in her belly said it. The rumble of distant thunder said it too.

She was Dreamwalker, she dreamed Dreams. She was what she was.

A sudden gust of storm-wind took her breath from her in a spiralling white veil. Chill dark had crept into the world as she stood here. Crane sighed. It was a lengthy walk down again, and downslope walking was no easier on her old knees than up, even with the ash walking stick that was never far from her hand these days. She wrapped the long white rope of her hair about a blue-veined hand, knotting the hair up to keep it clear for the walk, and started down.

The camp was alive when Crane returned, knees aching from the long downwards tramp. In the night's darkness, fires crackled and leaped brightly. The people danced, long-shadowed, leaping high as the flames. Children and dogs were boisterous with excitement. The wild of spring was in their blood. Wild clouds raced past the moon above. The trees *shurooshed* in the pelting wind.

Leaning one-legged and comfortable on the length of her walking stick, the palm of her left foot snug up against the inside of her right knee, Crane stood watching them and smiled, remembering how her own young blood had sung in her veins on nights like this, with the long winter gone and the world alive again and bright summer nigh as the next breath, it seemed.

But she could not join in, not this night. Too much weighed upon her.

From the south, a distant *crump* of thunder echoed.

Crane felt the world move under her. It was cusp time, when patterns changed. And somebody must link the old and the new together so that their union did as little damage as possible. Like midwifing some great creature mating with itself, seeing that it did neither itself nor those about it unnecessary harm.

Crane sighed. She did not wish to be the one to meet this

dark something that came from the south. She very much did not wish it.

But she was Dreamwalker, and she had no choice.

Moving quietly through the camp's verge, she retrieved a sleeping skin, then slipped away amongst the trees. Few noticed her coming or going, for old Crane could make herself most difficult to see when she so wished.

But old Moss was sharper of vision than most, for all that he had only the one eye. He stood waiting for her, leaning against a dark oak bole at the edge of the fires' light, his lined, broad face dead serious. 'I see thee, Dreamwalker,' he said in the formal way.

'I see thee, old friend,' Crane replied.

Moss regarded her with his one good eye, bright as a crow's. The other was only a wrinkled socket. 'What has thou found, up on Stroud's stony shoulders?'

Crane shrugged uneasily. Moss was no Dreamer, but he was more sensitive than most to the world's deep patterns. 'It comes.'

'*It?*'

'That which comes, comes.'

'And thou?'

Again Crane shrugged. 'I do not know. I await the Dream's bequest.'

Moss said nothing, merely nodded thoughtfully. He pushed away from the oak, placed a hand on her shoulder for a moment, and then walked off quietly back to the camp.

Crane watched him go, tempted, momentarily, to call him back. But it was not human company she needed this night. Turning, she continued deeper in amongst the trees until the boisterous camp sounds dwindled into nothing behind her.

In the dark, it took her a time to find what she needed. It was an oak she had known from her girlhood, ancient and huge and battered, but sound of heart still.

'I see thee, Grandfather,' Crane said in greeting.

Above her, the old tree creaked and groaned in the wind.

'Watch over me,' Crane asked, 'If it pleases thee.' Below the comforting spread of his old and gnarly limbs, she settled herself in the sleeping robe she had brought.

For a long time she lay listening to the *shuroosh* of the trees in the wind, staring up at the here-and-gone face of the moon through the latticework of oak branches. Then she took a deep, slow breath, breathing in the world, slipped gently into sleep, and fell away to the Dream.

No shuddering confusion of images this time.

She found herself walking along a rocky Dream-path towards the edge of a high precipice. Standing on that edge, she looked out southwards at an endless tumble of open Dream-land, filled with scurrying, milling, shouting, struggling shapes, some human, some with men's limbs but great unhuman tusks and glowing eyes.

Crane felt herself drawn irrevocably to the edge, balanced there, gazing out at the tumult below. A Dream-wind blew at her back, pushing her. Moved by the completeness of certainty that the Dream sometimes gave, she leaped into the empty air, letting the Dream-wind take her, and swooped bird-like towards the unknown south.

III

# On the Outskirts of
# the Village of Woodend

Egil sat bolt upright in the big bed and stared into the darkness about
him. Somewhere, something was not right. He had come out of sleep
suddenly, with no clear idea of what had awakened him. But
somewhere there was something . . .

The night echoed and crashed as a great beast of a storm thundered
through overhead. But it was not simply that which had awakened
him. Such spring storms were not uncommon, and the weather lately
had been disordered and unpredictable in any case. A particularly close
crump of thunder might bring him momentarily awake, but he would
soon curl up again next to Shawna, his wife, warm and comforting
beside him in the bed, and let the storm rage its fury in the open sky as it
liked. This storm, which had come rumbling up across the horizon just
after sunset, was nearly spent now anyway. No, it was not simply the
storm. There was something else. What voice had called him from
sleep?

From outside, through the shuttered cabin windows, an actinic
splash of lightning flared, followed by growling thunder and then
momentary silence. And then he heard it, or thought he heard it. The
sound of human voices. Or was it only the voice of the storm-wind?
Shawna still slept soundly beside him, her long dark hair a half-
glimpsed cascade across the bolster. Egil was loath to leave the warmth
of the bed, but again he thought he heard the sound of voices from
outside. Times were not as they once had been; strangers had been seen
in the hill country, homeless wayfarers with terrible tales of fire and
demons and death in the South Wold. Most folk deemed them naught
but tales. Still . . .

Softly, so as not to awaken Shawna, Egil eased himself off the bed,
drew on a pair of homespun breeches and a sleeveless undershirt that
lay draped over a nearby stool, and padded across the rough planked
floor to the shuttered window.

Nothing. No more voices. Nothing but the sounds of rain and wind
and the storm dying slowly away into the night. But he felt a tightening
in his belly that would not go, and stood where he was, listening, trying

to unravel the sounds, pick out anything that did not belong. Perhaps it was the demon-talk that made him so skittish. Or perhaps it was just the night itself, for it was a night in which Powers moved, this. He could sense the blind strength and the ferment at the heart of the storm as it stomped through the sky overhead, and he felt an echo in his own breast of that same ferment, a deep unease, for it seemed to him suddenly that the smell of change was in the air, change as violent and unpredictable as the storm itself.

'Skittish as a kitten,' Egil murmured to himself, shaking his head. There was nothing out there, nothing but night feys and flitters and the disquieting echo of the storm in his own spirit. 'Flitters of the night,' he whispered, 'Spirits dark in flight. Safe am I against your wiles, safe and sound against your guiles. Oak and ash and thorn protect me, you are powerless to affect me . . . Flit away and fall away and fade into the darkness.' He smiled, feeling an absurd and foolish sense of security from reciting the old charm.

Still smiling, Egil had turned back to bed when, suddenly, he heard the latch that secured the entrance door go *tlickk*. Frozen in mid stride, he stared as the door swung open, admitting a spluttering cascade of rain and cold night air. A lightning flash created a momentary, sharp rectangle of light in the shuttered darkness of the cabin's interior, and the shadow of a man-shape lay framed in the sudden brightness.

Egil took two paces towards the door, a wooden plank creaked loudly under his foot, and suddenly he found himself tumbled on the floor, struggling against rain-soaked assailants, whom he could only half see in the darkness.

Egil was a big man, a very big man, standing head and shoulders above anybody else in the district. His arms were thick and strong from ploughing and the hewing of timber for firewood and trade. He hit out now, blindly, instinctively, and his fist connected with a solid jolt against bone. He felt a flair of pain in his knuckles. One of his attackers slid off him.

But a wet hand hauled him back by the hair, and he felt the cold touch of metal against his throat. In his ear, a voice hissed, 'Enough! Lie still, farmer, or I will open your throat here and now.'

Sounds of movement came from the loft above, where Thomae, Egil's only son, slept. 'Father,' Thomae called. 'Father, what *is* it?'

'Stay where you are,' the man holding Egil called. 'I have a knife held at your father's throat. Stay where you are or your father dies!'

Lightning flared and crashed in a sudden, rapid barrage outside. Rain swirled in through the open door. Egil could hear quick, skittering sounds from the loft as his son made for the ladder that let down into the main room of the cabin. Egil tried to move, to open his mouth, but the cold blade of the knife pressed more tightly against his throat.

'Do as he bids, Thomae,' Shawna called from the bed, her voice tight with tension. 'Stay where you are.'

'Nobody is to move,' the man holding Egil ordered loudly. And then, 'Bring Alton in and close the door against that cursed storm,' he hissed to his companion, the one whom Egil had hit. The only response in the flickering dark was a groan. 'Do it. Hurry up! And then bring the fire to life.'

Egil could only lie there, helpless, the knife at his throat, while the second intruder fetched a third from outside the cabin, carried him in, propped him up against a wall, then kicked the door shut. The sound of the storm receded and the cabin was suddenly black and silent.

In the light that flared finally from the rekindled fire, Egil could see these intruders for the first time. They were dirty and exhausted-looking, soaked through. The man who had been carried in lay against the wall without moving, a wide, blood-sodden, ragged bandage across his middle.

'Who are you?' Egil demanded of the man holding him. 'What do you want with us?'

He received no reply.

The man who had lit the fire held a longbow in his hand now, an arrow nocked to the string. He limped awkwardly, one thigh bound up in a scabbed bandage. The left side of his face was swollen and puffy and blood trickled in a steady, wet flow from the corner of his mouth. He drew the arrow back and aimed it at Egil's belly, the razorhead point of the shaft glimmering coldly in the firelight.

A cold fury showed in the man's battered face. Egil shivered, defenceless, belly up on the floor.

'Not unless I tell you to,' said the one holding Egil.

The bowman kept the arrow anchored against his cheek. He gestured to one side, a quick movement of his chin. 'Move away from him, Olivor.'

Egil felt the hand gripping his hair tighten involuntarily, but the blade at his throat stayed still and the man's voice, when he spoke, was calm. 'No. Not until I see you ease up. I do *not* want any here harmed needlessly.'

The two men faced each other in tense silence, Egil between them. In the cabin, nothing moved. Egil took a breath, another, his eyes fixed on the uneasy dance of the firelight on the arrow's razorhead blade.

Then the bowman shrugged, eased up so that the bow was only half drawn, and nodded. But the arrow did not waver, and remained still aimed directly at Egil's belly.

The grip on Egil's hair loosened, the knife was removed, and the man slid himself up and away towards the fireplace. Egil lay unmoving for a long, uncomfortable moment, waiting to see what the bowman would do.

The man eyed him coldly, but made no move.

Egil breathed a quiet sigh. Above, at the edge of the loft, he made out the pale oval of his son's face as Thomae leaned over and down, staring into the main room that took up the whole of the ground floor of the cabin and which served as kitchen, sitting room and bedroom. Shawna was still on the bed, but in a halfway crouch now, her hands gripping the coverlet fiercely, glaring at these intruders into her home.

Watching his wife, Egil felt a shiver of special unease. He was an easy man, was Egil, calm in his own strength, and as slow to anger as an ox. But not so Shawna. She had her mother's black temper. Hair like a raven's wing and eyes like a hawk's. A woman with iron in her soul, who loved fiercely and hated fiercely and forgave'nothing. He was not certain what she might be capable of doing in a situation such as this. And these men . . .

From where he still lay on the floor, Egil motioned at her with a hand: *stay where you are.*

She only looked at him, unblinking, uncowed. He felt a surge of quick pride. She was no ordinary woman, this wife of his.

The intruder standing by the fireplace, the man Egil had heard called Olivor, broke the lengthening silence. 'We intend you and yours no harm, farmer . . .'

Egil felt his hands shaking with delayed reaction. 'You come in here in the dark of the night like *this* and you—'

The other gestured Egil impatiently into silence with the knife he held still in his hand. He was not particularly tall, this man, but he was heavy-boned and thick across the arms and shoulders. A fringe of untidy, greying hair rimmed the back of his otherwise bald head, and he had a long, tangled beard. He stood propped tiredly against the stone lintel of the fireplace, close to the flames' heat. His face was white and strained, and his eyes moved constantly, flicking from one part of the cabin to another, from one face to another. 'We must have food and drink and warmth, and the opportunity to dry ourselves and to rest out the time till dawn.' He sighed and ran his free hand over his eyes. His voice was hoarse and low. 'It has not been a . . . good day, farmer. We are tired and short of temper. So do not try us. Do as I say and nobody will be hurt.'

20

Egil eased himself slowly to his feet. The bowman followed his movement. Olivor ran a hand across his bald head and whistled quietly through his teeth. Egil's hair was long and tangled, the hot colour of red plums, streaked with grey. His eyes glinted in the firelight, and he towered head and shoulders above both the interlopers. Left bared by the sleeveless, homespun undershirt he wore, the muscles of Egil's arms and shoulders – muscles acquired during long days of chopping and hauling wood so as to supplement the meagre income derived from the field crops – stood out in stark relief under the shifting light of the fire.

The bowman hissed involuntarily, seeing Egil's size.

'Stand by the bed, big man, with your woman,' Olivor said. He gestured at the bowman. 'And forget not Bram here.'

Egil walked slowly to the side of the bed. Shawna reached up a hand and he took it. He could feel the raw outrage in her, as if it flowed to him through her touch. He held her hand tightly, worried. When the temper was on her, Shawna had no common sense whatsoever.

'This is the way of it,' the one by the fire said. 'We need a hot meal, now, and we need food to take with us on the trail. Nothing more.'

Shawna started to respond, but the man motioned her impatiently to silence. 'No talk. We have little enough time at best. Just do as I say, *exactly* as I say, and you will be none the worse but for the loss of a little food.' He looked directly at Egil, eye to eye, from his position by the fireplace. 'I mean you and yours no harm, farmer, truly. This I promise you. But if you try to stop us, to interfere with what we need, I will let Bram here put his arrow through you as he wished to earlier. Or if not you, then your son. Or your woman. Is that understood?'

Egil felt Shawna stir at his side and squeezed her hand warningly. This man Olivor had thus talked only to him, ignoring his wife entirely. Not the sort of thing, that, to make Shawna sweet-tempered, even at the best of times. Well . . . but perhaps he could still keep everybody calm enough so none received hurt. That was all he wished, that none of his were hurt.

'Well?' Olivor persisted.

Egil looked at Bram, who held the arrow still unwaveringly aimed at him, looked back to the knife in Olivor's hand, and nodded once, slowly. He did not know what these men were about, but there was clearly nothing to be gained by contesting them.

'Good,' the bald man said after a little. Then, looking around the room, he sighed once again. 'You are lucky, farmer. You have a nice holding here. I only hope you are able to keep it.'

Egil shook his head, confused, not understanding any of this.

'The world changes, farmer. Have you heard no rumours of what is happening southwards?'

Egil nodded. 'Some.'

'And?'

'They are only rumours.'

Olivor snorted. 'Rumours! Worse things than you can imagine are coming, farmer.' He turned his gaze abruptly upwards to the edge of the loft where Thomae, Egil's son, still squatted. 'You, boy, come down here.'

After a moment's pause, Thomae shimmied down the steeply inclined ladder that led from the loft where he slept. Thomae was a tall, gangling lad, almost come to full manhood, with his father's height but his mother's slimness of build. He had inherited his mother's temper, too. His hands were like big square shovels, and he kneaded them together angrily as he stood at the front of the ladder glaring at the man by the fireplace. 'Who are you to be giving orders here? A coward with a weapon in his hand thinks himself a Lord, they say. Put the knife down, Olivor-no-hair, and we shall see whether you be coward or Lord! A coward, I doubt not.'

The bald man sighed. He ignored Thomae entirely and, instead, looked at Egil. 'Tell him to be quiet. I want no trouble with muscle-brained boys! Just tell him to keep quiet and to stay out of our way.'

'How can you let him give you orders like that, Father?' Thomae demanded bitterly.

'Thomae!' cried Shawna, her voice like a whip.

The boy ignored her. 'This is *your* house, Father, not his! How can you . . . ?'

'Shut your face, boy,' Bram the bowman snapped.

Thomae whirled on him. Before Egil or anybody else could move, Thomae had hurled himself at the man, swept the bow away to one side, where it landed with a clatter on the planked flooring, and was pummelling furiously at the man's face with his fists.

Bram dumped the boy heavily to the floor.

Egil leaped from the side of the bed, but not quickly enough. Olivor had already snatched the bow from where it lay on the floor and nocked the arrow once again to the string. 'Stand where you are!' he hissed.

Egil skidded to a halt.

Thomae had leapt back up, oblivious of all else, and charged into Bram again. His momentum carried the two of them crashing up against the wall next to the shuttered windows. They struggled there, forming a single, dark, interlocked and moving shape in the firelight, then split apart. Groaning, Thomae rose to his knees, then fell, rag-dolled and still, on to the planks of the floor. The bowman, breathing hard, struggled to his feet. In the man's hand, Egil saw the hard gleam of a knife-blade.

Shawna leaped from the bed. In an instant she was across the room and had flung herself at Bram, sending him crashing to the floor. But as she bent over Thomae, he staggered back to his feet and came for her. Once, he swung at her, hard, hitting her with the pummel of the knife across her temple, and she dropped without a'sound.

'Do not move,' the bald man commanded Egil, his voice a harsh whisper. 'Stay exactly as you are or I will drop you where you stand.'

Egil stood unmoving, held immobile by the terrible shock of it all as much as the weapon trained on him. He stared at the still forms of his wife and son. Things had happened with such frightening, disorientating quickness.

Bram shook himself slowly. His face was battered, one eye swollen almost shut now. He coughed, spat a long, bloody ribbon of mucus on to the floor, coughed again, and came slowly towards Egil. The bandage about his thigh had been ripped apart, and blood soaked his leg. He hobbled forwards, the knife in his hand weaving it in and out through the air before him. The blade had a dark, glimmering sheen of blood on it.

'Enough!' the bald man called. 'I told you I wanted no needless slaying here, Bram. Enough, I say.'

For a moment, it seemed that the two men would go for each other. Bram, his good eye wide with fury, the knife still held before him, veered towards Olivor. Olivor, in turn, trained the bow on Bram.

And then, in the silence, through the still shuttered window, there came the distant wail of hounds baying in the night.

'Bloody oath!' Olivor cursed. 'How could they have followed us in this storm?' He looked around him quickly, shook his head, cursed under his breath some more. 'I'll keep the farmer covered,' he ordered his companion. 'See if you can rouse Alton. Quickly!'

Without a word, Bram limped over to where the still form of the third man lay propped up against the wall. He shook him gently at first, then harder. There was no response. Kneeling awkwardly down, Bram put his ear to the other's chest. After a moment, he hauled himself upright again. 'He's dead, Olivor.' There was a sob to his voice as he said this, and he leaned against the wall as if suddenly exhausted.

Olivor muttered something Egil could not hear and kicked at the stone fireplace, once, hard. 'Leave him, then,' he said after a moment. 'We must save ourselves as best we can now.'

Bram hesitated, staring down at his dead companion.

'There's nothing we can do for him now,' Olivor said softly.

In the distance, the frenetic baying of the hounds came more loudly.

'Hurry!' Olivor said, backing towards the door, still keeping Egil covered with the bow. 'We must be off before they draw too close.'

Bram lifted a scabbarded sword and harness from beside the dead man. 'Goodbye, old friend,' he said quietly, looking down. He touched the pommel of the sword to the dead man's lips, then touched it to his own. 'A scathless journey in the darkness, friend,' he intoned softly. 'A scathless journey and a fruitful end. Gone from the world of living ken. Into the Shadowlands . . . to begin again.'

'And may his next life bring him more joy than this one,' Olivor added.

Bram nodded silent agreement. He stood looking down at his dead comrade for a moment, then he turned and, one hand to his thigh, stumbled painfully out through the door and into the night.

Olivor backed slowly to the doorway, the bow still held in his hand. 'Farmer,' he began with a sigh, 'I would not have wished it this way. These are . . . bad times.' He stood there, uncertain, as if trying to find something more to say. Then, with an uncomfortable shrug, he too was gone into the night.

It seemed long before Egil could find the strength to do anything but stand there, stricken. Then he stumbled forward and tried to gather both his wife and his son into his arms. Thomae felt cold and sticky with blood, but he still breathed. Shawna moaned softly as Egil hugged her clumsily to him with one arm. They were alive. Both alive!

The wailing of the hounds came again from without the cabin, much closer now. Egil rose, went to the cabin's back corner and picked up the heavy, double-bladed axe that he used for splitting timber. He moved to the open doorway, his hands white-knuckled where he gripped the haft of the axe. There would be no more intrusions this night . . .

But what he saw coming across the dark fields staggered him.

Overhead, the storm had broken up into twisted tatters of racing cloud, and the moon hung low in the sky. Coursing through the rain-soaked fields that rimmed the cabin came loping shapes in the eerie, quicksilver dance of the moonlight. But such shapes! Like things out of childhood nightmare they seemed. Demon faces lent an eerie radiance by the moon. Glittering, inhumanly huge eyes. Bared tusks the length of a grown man's fingers.

They were man-shaped, clad in coldly glittering war-mail and armed with long, intricately bladed pikes, and they ran like men. But those terrible demon-faces had nothing in common with humankind.

And before them ranged ... Egil did not know what manner of creature, but true hounds they were not. Great leaping shapes, long and lean and skeletal, skittering along upright on spidery legs, then bounding down on all fours again, all the while baying like lost souls.

Egil shuddered in dread, and made a warding sign with one hand. What manner of fell creatures had come upon him?

The uncanny demon pack rushed onwards breaking like a noisy wave, and came to rest in a crescent about the cabin. The hounds yelped and whined, postured and reared. Egil held his spot in the cabin's entranceway, keeping them back with the swinging threat of the axe. His hands were clammy with cold sweat and his heart beat hard. Their eyes were not beasts' eyes, but human, with the light of human will in them.

Then there came a sudden strident, wailing horn-blast, and the beasts went still.

Behind the demon pack a rider appeared. This one was man-shaped too, but it had the head of a silvered hawk, with a darkly curved, vicious beak and yellow glinting eyes. It pulled up, the horse blowing and stamping, and the hounds – or whatever manner of creatures they were – turned and set up a barking chorus, gesturing with their spidery forelimbs first to the cabin and then beyond, towards where the two fugitives had fled. At the nape of Egil's neck, the little hairs prickled. The sound they made was nigh on to human speech. And the hawk-faced creature seemed to understand.

Hawk-face spurred his horse closer. He was clad for war like the rest, in scale armour and mail, as was his horse. In one hand he carried a naked, black-pommelled war-sword.

Staring up into that cruel, inhuman face, moonlit and eerily gleaming, Egil swallowed and clutched his axe more tightly. *Spirits of the night*, he thought. *Spirits dread and drear ...*

'Farmer,' the creature said, turning the word somehow into an insult, and laughed, a chill shudder of sound in the moonlight. The glinting hawk-eyes stared unblinkingly. The dark beak opened wide, then closed with a *clakk*. 'You think to *threaten* me, farmer?'

Egil felt a shiver go through him. The creature's voice vibrated with a kind of rasping power, but it was human-sounding for all that, and could be clearly understood.

Hawk-face gestured with the war-sword to a section of the demon company he commanded. 'Those we hunt have been here. Search the house! Then fire it. Raze it to the ground! And take that foolish tool away from this farmer and kill him.' The horse danced under the creature's rein, armour rattling coldly. 'Leave a lesson here that others of his kind will remember. Do it quickly as may be and follow after!' With that, he whirled and drove his horse onwards. The hound-creatures leaped off and away, howling. Most of the demon pack followed. But not all.

Egil stood where he was, barring the cabin's doorway, breathing hard, the axe raised.

The demon-faced pack moved in on him.

Egil struck out, but though he smote one of them, heard the creature grunt, the axe blade skittered across scale armour instead of biting. The axe was torn out of Egil's hold. Something hit him heavily on the side of his head. Something else smashed hard into the pit of his stomach, driving the breath out of him, and he was dragged down in a heaving swirl of bodies.

Egil struggled frantically, but he might as well have been a little child for all the good it did him. *Their* strength proved inhuman, incontestable, and he found himself pinned helplessly to the ground, held there by iron hands.

The creatures laughed then, a guttural, chilling sound. They hung over him like figures from a nightmare, tusks agleam, great unhuman eyes glowing like lanterns in the running moonlight. One raised a coldly gleaming blade. Egil shrieked, feeling the iron cut into his flesh. *They* laughed louder. The blade bit again and again, each stroke an agony, tearing bloody ribbons from his arms and chest and face.

Then, from inside the cabin, Egil heard Shawna scream. The sound was all blind, outraged fury at first, but it changed into an agonizing wail.

Egil thrashed desperately, trying to shake the iron grip on him, but it was no use.

'Forget this farmer,' one of the creatures growled to its companions. Its voice was a guttural rasp, but the words were clear enough. 'I want my turn with the woman.'

'*No!*' Egil gasped, struggling. 'No . . .' The butt of a war-pike smashed across his lips, filling his mouth with blood.

'Forget him,' the creature repeated. 'Or finish him now.'

One of the others turned. 'The Sub-Commander's orders were to make a lesson of him and then hurry so that—'

Shawna's scream cut the air.

'Damn the Sub-Commander. He's not here. And that *woman* is!'

Egil felt the hands holding him loosen. He struggled to haul himself free, succeeded in rising to his knees until an iron foot drove into his midriff, crumpling him.

'Do what you like with this farmer. But *I* want the woman!' With that, the creature was off into the cabin.

Egil laboured desperately for breath, his vision pulsing sickeningly. Pain tore through him. His limbs quivered, useless, blood-soaked, lacerated. He heard argument break out amongst the demon-faced pack about him, but it was dim. Everything about him was beginning to dim. Only poor Shawna's wailing remained clear, a terrible sound, tearing at him, more agonizing than any blade *they* wielded ever could be.

He fought to rise, struggling up to his knees once again, but fell heavily on to his face. He could raise himself no more, and only floundered helplessly, bleeding into the wet ground, sobbing, his heart broken. Shawna's cries burned him, and *their* terrible laughter. From where he lay he could see clearly the dark bulk of the cabin. Flickering firelight glowed through the open doorway. 'Shawna!' he cried. '*Shawna!*'

There came a crash from inside. Shawna's voice rose in a sudden hysteria of rage. Flames leaped up through the building. Egil heard the hungry roar of them as they caught.

He saw demon creatures tumble out of the cabin, bolting the door behind, and scatter into the night, dark silhouettes against the blood-red light of the flames. He heard shouting and curses. One of the creatures thrust a war-pike at him in passing, a hasty jab, sliding across his ribs and thudding into the ground. He waited for the next, killing thrust, helpless. But it never came.

His wife shrieked, trapped inside as the leaping flames devoured all.

He dragged himself towards the cabin, each movement of his limbs a torment. Under his groping hand, he felt something hard and cold. The axe! It lay on the ground where it had fallen when the demon-creatures wrenched it from his grasp. He clutched at it desperately, climbing to his knees. 'Shawna! I'm coming . . .'

But his lacerated limbs proved useless quivering things, and he toppled awkwardly over. 'Shawna,' he sobbed, struggling unsuccessfully to rise. '*Shawna . . .*' He lay sprawled beyond the cabin's door, blood-soaked ground pressing against his ruined face, the taste of dirt in his mouth, helpless, while his wife's screams cut the dark night air and the flames danced their terrible, triumphant dance.

# IV

# Coming Down Out of
# the Bone Peaks

The beeches danced their slow dance in the wind. They were sisters, and old and, like all their kind, too deeply immersed in the earth to have overmuch interest in her, but in their own manner they knew Crane was there, welcomed her as they welcomed any of the life that flitted and flew about them and that did them no harm. They dipped and swayed, limbs swishing. Crane smiled. They were old and peaceful and, in their own green way, wise. Though she was away now from her own lands, she felt at home amongst them.

Crane composed herself at the thick base of one of them, patting the wrinkled trunk as she did so. 'Watch over me, old sister,' she asked softly. 'If it pleases thee.' Above, the night sky hummed with stars, a glittering cascade beyond the dancing branches. Crane's blood sang in her ears. The world sang. The great dance was danced, and she was a part of all. She took a deep, slow breath, breathing in the world. Then, with the skill of long years, she slipped gently into sleep and . . . away.

Stretching out her arms, Crane revelled as always in the freedom of the Dream. Her old joints did not creak here. Her age did not matter. She whirled and danced with the beech sisters for a moment, giving herself over to their creaky joy. This was a good place, a safe place. She need not worry about the other part of her, left behind and vulnerable, while she voyaged in the Dream.

She gave the beeches formal thanks for their goodwill and protection. Then, moving easily, she slid away and out beyond.

Standing in the open, arms outstretched once again, she waited. She knew not what for, but her need, she knew, would call something forth for her.

But what came was unexpected and strange. One of the Fey, the elder folk, who lived always between the two worlds of Dreaming and Waking. He stood before her, a tall, silent figure, a man and yet not a man. He had human enough hands, feet, face, but with the extreme slimness of limb, the paleness of flesh that marked all the Fey. The eyes in that pale face were huge and dark, and gazed at her, unblinking.

He moved then, raising his arms in a graceful, encompassing gesture.

When they came down, those arms had become wings, white and sweeping, and he stood before her on one long, slim leg, the other tucked up underneath him. He turned a liquid dark eye towards her. The white feathers about his neck and head were fine and intricate as the lace of foam in a waterfall. Crane's dream-heart beat more quickly. She moved towards him and ran her fingers gently along his long, pointed beak. Then, with the wonder of the Dream, the great wings enfurled her.

They lifted from the ground, air whistling through pinions, and soared, swift as the wind, outwards and beyond, casting about.

And then an expanse of water lay below, restless and deep. Submerged in those depths lay a rocky outcrop. A lone figure stood there, clear to see for all the depth of intervening water, tall and thin, shrouded in a long, dark cloak, his face hidden and shadowed by the cloak's hood. His head lifted as he gazed upwards at them through the water, the dark hood of the cloak falling away momentarily to reveal eyes like twin, glittering black marbles in a skull-like face.

They dropped suddenly out of the air, diving down towards the surface of the water. When they struck, it shattered like crystal. The figure below was one man, two men, many men, a series of identical images in that shattered crystal water. The figure raised one hand, slowly. Many hands, slowly, were raised. The hands dropped, the crystal water whirled . . .

And Crane found herself gasping into sudden wakefulness amongst the beeches.

She shook her head, blinked, levered herself up, her old joints creaking. The beeches rustled, murmuring in their comforting way, but she felt a shiver of unease sweep through her. She had never been . . . *evicted* from the Dream like that.

It was as if, by the raising of his hand, that figure had banished them. Or was that all part of the true Dream, and the strangeness of this abrupt ending simply a part of the strangeness of the times in which she now lived and moved?

To enter the Dream was to experience reflections of the hidden, deep pattern of the world. But sometimes it was not easy to interpret those reflections. The shattering of the water into many images of that hooded and cloaked figure . . . Though she could not grasp it yet, she felt in her bones that those images held meaning, that the whole was true to the Dream. But that abrupt ending of it all had left her aching.

One accepted what was given. That was the way of it. The Powers moved the world in their great, vital way, and the Dream was a gift, the Dreamer a channel through which it moved. But instead of granting

29

some glimpse of what it was that came upon them from the south, this Dreaming had brought her only more questions, more mysteries. Nothing was clear any more.

Blind times.

Crane shook her head. Let it be, she thought. Let it be. It is not time yet.

Slowly, she moved away from the beeches, dizzy and a little uncertain on her feet. Leaning on her ash walking stick, she eased down through the lesser trees that stood near the beeches. Only a little way further, and she would come to where the others lay sleeping.

But in the darkness she saw a pale glimmer of movement, and there stood the Fey, silent, barring her way.

It was the same one, she felt it in her bones. Crane swallowed. The Fey were unpredictable, unknowable. Their world and the human world overlapped, yes, but the two were not the same, for the Fey lived closer to the land, closer to the Powers than human people could.

They had been here long and long before human people came to this land and accepted human presence grudgingly. Crane did not understand why this one had sought her out. 'I see thee, Guide-of-My-Dreaming,' she said, greeting him formally.

The only reply was silence.

'What is it thou wishes of me?'

His hand made a quick movement, impossibly slim fingers flashing in the dimness. Crane flinched but stood where she was. He had not touched her. The movement might have been a dismissal, a beckoning, an anything. But it seemed to her an angry gesture.

'What does thou wish of me?' she repeated.

He reached a hand to her, fingers brushing her face, soft as a spider's web. But the anger was there, she was sure now. 'Who?' she asked. 'What is thou angry with?' for she felt equally sure, somehow, it was not her.

He stood before her, silent, inscrutable. For an instant, Crane had a flash of sudden vision, seeing what seemed a great black creature, crouched spider-like at the centre of a monstrously large web, the web's strands stretching out from the south to entangle all.

And then the Fey was gone, a quick movement, a breath, nothing.

Crane shivered, staring at where he had been. It was a *strange* time in which she lived now.

Shaking herself into motion, Crane continued slowly on.

She entered the camp softly, so as not to disturb the sleepers, their slumbering forms radiating from the banked coals of the cookfire like petals from a flower's centre. Only old Moss-one-eye was awake, squatting at the watchfire on the camp's verge, seeing to the fletching of an arrow while he kept the watch. He looked a question at her as she drew close, aware of what she had gone to do.

Crane hesitated, then sighed and shook her head. 'Nothing is made clearer,' she said in a whispering breath.

Moss shrugged, shifted his haunches. He twirled the arrow in his hand slowly. Satisfied, he put it back and reached for another. Inspecting this one, he found something amiss with the delicate, fluted flint-head. 'The young ones do not take enough care,' he said softly, tugging at the sinew thread that held the sharp stone head in place. 'I tell them, but they only laugh. They are blind.'

Crane put down her walking stick and hunkered down next to him. 'Blindness can be a gift of sorts, sometimes.'

Moss sighed. 'Perhaps.'

In silence, they stared at the little dance of the watchfire coals.

Crane was Dreamwalker, and walked the Dream along paths others could not, was sensitive in ways that others were not. But Moss and each of the others here had felt a southwards calling. As she had. Four hands of people: women, men, old and young. Each beckoned somehow by the Dreaming, each feeling the call too strongly in her or his own heart to resist.

Into what?

And for how long?

None of them knew, least of all her. This night's Dreaming was typical, fragmentary and confusing, as it mostly had been ever since the first inklings of this dark presence southwards. But there was little choice but to continue on. To refuse the Dream was like a kind of death, cutting oneself off from the deeper currents of the world, like a fish flinging itself out of the water that gave it life.

But, like the fish, they could have no notion of where the current might take them.

Crane sighed. And now it seemed the Fey were somehow involved, in whatever deep way the Fey might involve themselves in human affairs. She recalled the sudden, brief vision she had been given: some dark being southwards, web weaving, entangling all in its mesh. It was a man, she felt sure of that, for all the terribleness of the vision-shape. But what sort of man was powerful enough to disturb the Fey?

And what had the Fey been trying to convey to her with that vision? Prediction? Warning? Bridging the differences between Fey and human thinking was never simple. How did that vision fit with the Dream he had guided her through? Crane shook her head and sighed once more.

Moss, by her side, squinted at her through his one good eye. Reaching across, he put a hand on Crane's shoulder. 'Sleep,' he said in his quiet way. 'Thou needs rest, old woman.'

Crane smiled. 'So does thee, old man.'

He snorted at that, but said nothing, only pointed to her vacant spot amongst the sleepers. Softly, he resumed work on the arrow shaft in his hands.

Crane lay for a long time in her sleeping robe, gazing up into the heavens. Moonlight washed the lower sky, but the stars were still a glittering magnificence overhead. She lay quiet, gazing upwards, until gradually, her mind calmed by the stars' great, still grandeur, she drifted off into a sleep in which she dreamed not at all.

V

# In the Blue Hills

Egil lived the screams again, staring in helpless horror at the leaping flames, hearing the tumble and crash of the cabin's rafters collapsing, and the terrible, wailing cries of his wife, trapped in the cabin by the devouring fire.

The poor soul.

He felt it all pass through him again: the heart-breaking sound of Shawna's screams; the triumphant roar of the leaping, hungry flames; demon-faced figures loping off hastily into the night; him sprawled outside in the dark, helpless.

And later, wet with blood and chilling rain, the cabin only smoking remnants. In his mouth had been the taste of blood, and he shook with pain. But worse, far worse, was the reek of the fire. With every breath he took, the stink of it assailed him, the suffocating odour of wet, charred wood; the horrible pungency of burnt meat.

All he ever loved, dead and burnt.

Egil blinked, struggling out of memory back into the world. He lay, exhausted against the side of a boulder, the rough, mossy surface of it hard and cool against him. He groaned. Every movement was a kind of torture; the whole of his body seemed one throbbing bruise, and his face and torso were a torment of lacerations where the demon-pack had cut him, cuts that bled and scabbed and twisted open and bled again when he moved.

Fever gripped him like a live thing, making him sweat and shiver by turns. He hardly knew where he was, or how he had got here. Like a wounded animal, he had crawled away to die. Only hazy recollections remained to him of a long, half-crawling, half-stumbling journey, gusts of frigid rain and darkness, streaming clouds, a cruelly cold dawn wind. Daylight. Chill darkness once more. And now the sun beat down upon him in momentary warmth.

He felt himself sliding across the rough surface at the rock at his back, and groaned at the pain the movement caused. His face lay pressed against prickly grass. The green blades hurt the wounds on his cheeks, but he did not have the wherewithal to move.

He wanted to die.

Sometime during the darkness, during the painful, crawling journey that had brought him here, he had died. He felt that in his bones.

A sickening vertigo had seized him, and he had felt himself falling, or rising – he could not tell which – tumbling like a leaf in slow, dark air. And then a dim, strange landscape enfolded about him. Grey slopes, the humped, dry backs of distant hills, black spikes of thorn, ash and cinders, the cracked spines of dead leaves underfoot. Dull radiance all about. For one long, terrible instant he seemed frozen there, stricken, helpless and terrified, while the knowledge of where he was had seeped into him: the Shadowlands, the place of the dead, where the newly sundered spirits of the dead wandered until reborn once more into the world.

Then Egil had seen his wife before him, pale and insubstantial, her and yet not her. And behind her another, his son Thomae. Shawna's mouth was open in a gaping scream. She writhed and thrashed furiously. Flames seemed to leap about her. She screamed and screamed and screamed.

It cut through him like a razor, that screaming. 'Shawna!' he cried, stretching sore arms out to her. '*Shawna*!'

But he could not come to her.

And she screamed, and went on screaming, hysterical, unreachable, wild and terrible, as if the agony of the flames had torn her mind clean from her, leaving in death only that strong, strong will of hers leaping in vain and desperate fury.

Behind her, the dim figure of Thomae was silent, dwindling. He tugged at his mother, trying to pull her away with him. Shawna shrugged him off. Beckoning fruitlessly, Thomae dwindled towards the distant, darkling hills as he ought, into whatever realms lay beyond, towards the inevitable. But Shawna only seemed to grow nearer and clearer, twisting in tortured fury before Egil, screaming still.

Egil struggled desperately to calm her, to reach her, but could not. Could not. Try as he might.

The dim Shadowland landscape had faded then. All he could make out was Shawna's face, contorted with rage and agony, the hot flicker of translucent flame about her, and then he had found himself in the world of the living once more, crawling through the dark, the haunting echo of his wife's wailings loud in his mind.

Egil cried out where he lay sprawled against the boulder. He envisioned Shawna and his dying, unconscious son, crisping into burnt meat. He heard her terrible cries.

He could not bear it.

What had he and his ever done to bring such a fate upon themselves? And why should *he* be lying here now, alive?

His son. His wife. The poor soul: trapped, eaten by the flames. He could *not* bear it.

Sobbing, he curled himself into a foetal ball against the boulder, trying to drop away into darkness. He wanted to die and have done, and be with Shawna, to comfort her, to ease the pain and the rage that consumed her. His limbs thrummed with pain. The fever gripped him. Flashes of hurtful memory jagged through him still, uncontrollably. He yearned for the Shadowland dark and the blind comfort it seemed to hold . . .

But it was not to be. Whether he willed it or no.

Egil came back to himself slowly. Looking through a fanned-out intricacy of grass stems, he saw the sun, a burning white coal, sink into a hedge of dark cloud. Great spattering drops of cold rain skirled upon him in a sudden wind. He tipped his head back, trying to drink, for he was parched, his tongue like a piece of old leather in his mouth. His vision had a strange, unnatural sharpness to it. The green of the grass near him seemed to glow and the moving sky to dance.

He wanted nothing to do with the world. He wanted only Shawna. Holding her tightly in his mind, Egil heard the echo of her haunting cries, and, for a moment, it seemed to him he saw a wavery figure hovering near him. He raised himself up on one elbow, reaching for her, joints creaking, all his effort and strength gone suddenly into this one, simple movement. But the figure had gone.

In the silence about him, a voice was sobbing softly. Only after what seemed a long, long time did he recognize it as his own.

Lying there, propped against the rough side of the boulder, panting like a hound, Egil tried to rouse himself once more. In his bruised right hand, he still clutched the double-bladed timber-axe with which he had tried to fend off the demons. He did not know why he had lugged the heavy thing along. It had been scant use to him. Using the axe as a crutch, he levered himself to his knees and looked about him. A steep, grassy slope lay before, strewn with pale blue flowers. The verge of a forest loomed dark and thick nearby, its tumbled, green contour dipping down into the distance.

Egil knew where he must be: the upper western slope of some part of the Blue Hills.

He did not wish to be here. He did not wish to be anywhere. Groaning, he slumped back to the ground. 'Shawna,' he breathed. 'My poor Shawna . . .'

Something moved through him like a chord of fire, and Shawna flickered in his awareness, there and gone, and there again. Wailing. Gone.

Gripped by the fever, Egil lay there, shivering miserably, dazed and beaten and paralysed with grief, gazing blindly into the day. Then, from the corner of his eye, he saw sudden movement. A tall, silent figure came ghosting out of the forest that lay nearby, a man and yet not a man. Human hands, feet, face, but impossibly narrow of limb. The apparition looked backwards towards the trees out of which it had come, turned and stared acaross the blue-flowered meadow at Egil, huge, unblinking dark eyes in a pale face, then flitted away with uncanny, silent speed across the brow of the hill.

Unexpectedly, Egil heard the sound of men. Blinking back the fever-sweat, he saw a ragged group come spilling up out of the forest into the meadow. There they faltered, came to stumbling halts amidst the scattered rocks of the hillslope, stood with heads hanging, exhausted. A rag-tag group they were, perhaps two dozen in all, bleak-eyed, wounded and weary, men with the haggard look of those who had lost too much too suddenly.

Egil stayed quiet where he was, curled down on his side, and watched through the grass. Though he lay scarce twenty paces from them, the men did not notice him.

'What now, Jordie?' Egil heard one of them say.

The group all stared at one man, grey-haired, haggard-faced, who stood a little off from the rest. This man gazed into the forest from which they had just come, his back to the group. His shoulders slumped wearily, and wordlessly he settled himself on the grass, stretching one leg painfully out in front of him.

A youngster with a face covered in blond peach fuzz, and with a huge, mottled bruise discolouring the side of his face, moved forwards. 'Jordie,' he said. 'Jordie! What do we do now?'

The grey-haired man looked round. He took a deep, ragged breath. 'There's nowhere left to go,' he said, his voice hoarse and tired. 'We're dead men, Petry. Olivor's dead too, I don't doubt. Everybody's dead. We're *dead* . . .'

The youngster stared, stricken. His lower lip trembled. 'Don't do this, Jordie. Don't! You're all we have left now. Don't *do* this!'

The man named Jordie shrugged, turned away from the boy's accusing stare. He sighed a long, weary sigh.

At the sound of the name 'Olivor', Egil had tensed. That was the name of the bald man who had come slipping into the cabin during the storm, who had brought the demon-pack after him. Who *were* these men?

'Well?' the boy named Petry demanded. He ran a hand over the purplish swelling that marked his young face. 'What do we *do*?'

'Jordie's got the right of it,' one of the others muttered. 'It's over for us. We're all dead men. *They* will catch us up soon enough.'

As if in response to this, the wavering wail of hounds sounded from the thick forest that lay below them.

'Bastards,' one of them spat.

'Loosens my bowels every time I hear that,' another said.

The man called Jordie stared down into the depths of the forest. He massaged his thigh with one hand, wincing.

'We'll never make it,' wheezed a stout man with his left arm in a makeshift sling, dirty and crusted with stains. He slumped backwards on the grass, groaned, and lay there propped on his right elbow, cradling his injured arm. 'I'm too bloody exhausted to go on. Riding non-stop from the High Hills since yesterday dawn with *them* up our arse. And all through the bloody night. We killed the poor horses under us, we did . . .'

'He's got the right of it,' another added. 'Worn thin to the bone we are, and half of us cut up so bad we can't hardly walk. We shan't make it into the mountains in time, I don't reckon.'

'What did we ever do to bring such a fate down upon us that these creatures should appear from nowhere and—'

'Aye,' said some one else, 'Against such . . . *creatures*, we never stood a ghost of a chance.'

A long, uncomfortable silence followed.

'You make me sick,' one of the men snapped, getting up from where he sat at the edge of the group on the rock. 'Whining like small boys, the lot of you.' The man's left ear was nothing but a torn flap of flesh, and the whole left side of his head was purpled with bruising. He glared at them. 'We're all going to die! The terrible demons will get us!' His voice had suddenly become high and whiny, a travesty of some frightened pubescent boy's. 'We're all going to die. Oh, it's *so* terrible . . .' His voice dropped back down to normal. 'And *he*, the fearless Jordie, close personal friend of the great Olivor himself, *he* is the first one to lead you in the chorus of moans and groans.' The man spat disgustedly into the grass and sat back down on the rock, his back to them all.

Jordie stayed silent, head down.

'That's unjust, Hawl,' Petry, the youngster with the battered face, retorted hotly. 'And you know it!'

Hawl swivelled off the rock. In his hand, he held a short, slim-bladed dagger. 'Shut your face, you adolescent *shit*!'

Petry paled, but he held his ground. 'Jordie's allowed to have his bad moments, Hawl. He's – '

'Look at him, boy!' Hawl pointed with the knife. 'He's so scared, running is all he can think of. Is that the sort of man we wish to lead us? Punky as a rotten log, he is!'

Jordie struggled to his feet. He looked searchingly at the gathered men, at Hawl, then let out a long, slow breath.

Nobody said anything.

'All right,' Jordie said. 'All *right*! We are come now to hard choices, it seems.' He held up a finger. 'One, we can scatter and take our chances as best we may singly.'

There was a disquiet murmur at this.

'But most of us have nowhere to go,' he continued. 'The wold is taken, our farms and villages burnt or overrun by *them*. No place to shelter, no one to look to for help.' He shrugged. 'Little enough choice, that.'

Jordie paused, ran a hand wearily across his eyes, continued. 'Our second choice is to keep running as we have been and trust to luck and whatever Powers may move to our aid.'

Hawl muttered. The man with his arm in a sling groaned. Several others followed suit.

Jordie nodded. 'Aye . . . it seems we're done with running. The Easterling Peaks are too far anyway, and we're too worn to make them without being caught from behind . . .'

'Which leaves what?' Hawl asked in the silence that followed.

Jordie still looked down at the forest. 'We can try to take some of *them* with us.' He went on quickly before any could speak. 'Do any of you fancy being taken prisoner by the likes of *them*? Some of the others were taken alive when the creatures attacked us in the High Hills. I saw it. What do you imagine *they* do with prisoners?'

An uncomfortable muttering greeted this.

'Die we will,' Jordie went on quickly, 'one way or another. Slowly, under *their* hands, or . . .'

'What are you suggesting, Jordie?'

'Why do we not – ' Jordie grinned a tight, humourless little grin – 'try to take some of *them* with us into the Shadowlands?'

Silence.

'We've reached the end,' Jordie said quietly.

Louder now, the sound of the hounds wavered up from the forest.

'How do we know those . . . *things* can even die?' somebody demanded querulously.

'They die all right,' came the response. 'I vouch for that.'

'They did cursed little dying yesterday dawn,' a third pointed out.

Jordie held up a hand. 'Whatever manner of creature *they* be, they *can* die.' He pointed down towards the forest below them. 'We might lay an ambush at the rim of the trees. Send out a few into the woods to decoy them back to the rest of us.'

There was a slow, scattered muttering from the gathered men, but there was a different tone to the voices now. In some strange way, the mood had been lightened.

'Too simple, perhaps,' Jordie said. 'But 'tis a chance to strike a final blow at *them . . .*'

'We've got three longbows still,' a man said. 'About a dozen arrows, perhaps.'

'Good,' Jordie responded. 'We can feather those sodding hound creatures at least . . .' He stood there, hands on hips, looking at them challengingly. 'Well? Shall we?'

The men about him muttered their assent.

The cry of the hounds came once again from below them.

'Let's to it, then. Who knows how near they may be? I reckon we have little enough time at best.' Jordie turned and limped downslope towards the skirts of the forest. Hawl, the man with the bloodied ear, was the first to go after him. Then, in a body, the others rose from the grass and followed.

Egil rubbed at his cut and swollen face. He had been lying in one position so long, his whole body seemed locked tight in a painful knot. He groaned, stretching his limbs, and tried to stand. It took him three attempts.

Leaning against the boulder for support, he gazed down the slope at the verge of the forest into which the men had disappeared. It had been strange, witnessing all that had just passed between them, like some bizarre theatre played out for his benefit. And though he did not know who they were, or what, exactly, had happened to them, he knew enough. They had lost everything, as had he, and at the hands of the same fell creatures. Nothing was left them in this life now but the leaving of it. Egil felt an undeniable bond with such men.

Reaching down, he picked up the axe, then worked his way unsteadily downslope after them.

As he moved, his limbs eased a little. The attention of the men before him was focused downwards, in the direction from which they expected the force they awaited to appear, so it was easy enough for Egil to come upon them unnoticed from behind. It had begun to rain again, cold drops spattering the leaves, and the sound of it helped cover his own movements. He found the men crouched up, waiting, scattered in a horseshoe shape around a small, partial clearing surrounded by thick bush, the prongs of the horseshoe poking deeper into the forest.

Egil hunkered down nearby and waited with them.

The wailing of the hounds came closer.

Egil shifted position gingerly, trying to ease his cramped limbs. Every joint in his body ached and, because of the network of slashes about his face and arms and chest, he could not seem to find any position to ease the constant, nagging hurt. In his hand, the axe felt unbearably heavy. The fever burned through him. His tongue was parched and swollen. Flies came buzzing about, drawn by the dried blood on him.

Egil gazed at the forest, at what he could see of the clouded sun through the webbery of branches about him. He felt light-headed and dizzy. All the hopes he had once had. All the plans . . . But the person with those hopes had been another man entirely; the man he was now had none. All his life, then, came down to this one moment, this one timeless moment of waiting, waiting to take as many of *them* with him into the Shadowlands as he might, waiting for the crash of bodies that would end it all.

Waiting . . .

A clamouring howl sounded from the wood before him. Two men came skidding up the slope through the trees. Egil recognized one as the youngster with the battered face, Petry. 'They come,' the boy panted, his face drawn and pale. He slipped into concealment with his companion.

The deep forest was empty, and then, suddenly, Egil could see the loping, unnatural shapes of the hounds, three of them. He shivered to see such beasts once again. Behind them came demon-faced, pike-wielding creatures like the ones that had come upon him at the cabin. Crouching there, Egil quivered with instinctive dread, gazing with horror at their boar-like tusks, their great, glowing, unhuman eyes.

A bowstring twanged. One of the hounds squalled, an arrow through its guts. The demon pack surged forwards. Again came the twanging of bowstrings. The remaining hounds went down, wailing. But against the demons themselves, the arrows proved useless, skittering off their scale armour as off a rock.

Then, screaming like demons themselves, the ambushers sprang desperately from their concealment.

Egil struggled up, weak and awkward. His pulse thumped painfully in his ears. For a long, anxious moment he thought he would not have the strength to do anything but fall flat on his face. Grunting with the effort, he staggered, axe held high. The fever was playing tricks with his vision. Bodies swirled about him in spastic jags of motion and sound. He caught a flickering glimpse of some man being cut down to his left, of another hacking uselessly at a demon who skewered him with its pike. And then Egil was swallowed into the swirl and duck and grunt of the fighting. He kicked a pike-blade desperately aside as it was swung up, aimed for his belly, and chopped down with the axe. He felt the blade shiver along armour and fetch up, gratingly, on something unyielding as stone.

Egil hauled back, just in time to awkwardly fend off a slash from a blade that seemed to come from nowhere. He parried the blow, the other's weapon jittering against the wooden haft of the axe. He swung the axe in a great sweep. The creature before him leaped backwards and away. Egil shivered and looked about him. More demons were boiling up from downslope. Too many.

Something hit Egil's head from the side, hard. He went down, his skull ringing like a bell. A body tumbled across him. He squirmed desperately, pushing and gouging against the weight upon him until he realized that the body atop him was a man, a sticky mess, dead or dying.

Egil heaved himself to his feet, panting, his vision filled with crimson squiggles of light. The terrible ghost-screams of his wife rang in his head, suddenly clear and loud, obscuring the confusion and noise of the fighting, filling him. He felt a blind, hysterical rage pour into him like a live thing, like liquid fire. A terrible strength powered through him as he swung the axe in great, wild, deadly arcs against the creatures before him, felling them like so much wet wood. The ghost-wailing filled him, flowed through him. He lost his sense of himself, of what he did. The rage and the strength filled him, blotting out all else, and he hewed his way through the creatures before him like the terrible Power of death itself. Nothing could withstand him. *Nothing*!

And then, abruptly, it was over.

Silence.

'Bloody oath!' a voice said softly from behind.

Egil blinked. The forest floor about him was an impossible carnage heap of butchered creatures, twisted scraps of scale-armour and shattered bodies. Egil shuddered, coming back to himself. In the silence, he could hear a wet dripping from the leaves of the bushes and tangled undergrowth that had given them cover. He turned, the axe still gripped stickily in his hand, and saw one of the ambushers, his face bone-pale, staring about at the sodden wreckage. Behind this one were others. Egil recognized the man named Jordie, the youngster Petry, Hawl with the bloodied ear, the man with his arm in a sling, more than a few of the rest, glassy-eyed, awkward on their feet, staring about them as if not quite believing what had happened.

Jordie stared at Egil where he stood amidst the dead. 'Who . . . ?' he started, but his voice came out a mere croak and he had to cough, swallow, start again. 'Who *are* you?'

'Where did he come from?' someone else said to a companion.

Egil swallowed. He did not understand what had happened, or how. He could still hear the faint echoes of the ghost-wails, fading now. Looking around at the bloody ruins at his feet, he felt a surge of nausea go through him and he gagged. Haltingly, he hobbled over towards a tree bole, slid down against it, breathing hard. He let the axe drop, and hung his head wearily. He pressed a hand gingerly over his face. The hand came away bloody. The cuts across his face had begun to bleed again. Remembering who had given him those wounds, Egil looked across at the havoc he had wrought and smiled a bleak, vicious smile.

'But who – '

'What happened to – '

'– *is* he?'

' – your face?'

The questions came simultaneously.

Egil looked up to see a ring of flushed, confused faces surrounding him.

'Did you see him wield that axe?' somebody said.

There was a general muttering of amazed agreement.

'Nothing could stand against him. *Nothing*!'

The one named Jordie limped over to stand before Egil. 'Who are you?' he demanded. 'Who *are* you?'

Jordie's face was white and staring. With a start, Egil realized how he must appear to these men: clothes in tatters, bruised and battered, ribboned with bleeding scars from the cuts across his face, arms, and upper body. No wonder they stared. 'Egil,' he said in response to Jordie's question, his voice coming out like a crow's croak. 'My name is Egil.'

Jordie stared, ran a hand through his greyed hair, shook his head. 'We owe you our lives . . . Egil.'

'We're alive,' somebody muttered, as if it had taken Jordie's statement to make the fact sink in. 'It's a bloody *miracle*!'

'Aye, perhaps the Powers move for us now.'

'If he had been with us yesterday . . .'

Egil saw the same look of expectation on each of their faces. They gathered closer to him.

He shifted uneasily. What did these men expect from him?

'Here,' somebody said, handing him a water-flask. 'Drink.'

The water was blood warm and tasted of leather, but he drank greedily.

'Chopped those demon creatures apart like so much wet kindling,' somebody was saying.

'The fell things *can* die. Didn't I tell you so? Demons they may be, but beneath it all they're mortal as you and I.'

'Look!' a voice cried suddenly.

All eyes turned.

Out amidst the carnage that Egil had wrought stood young Petry, pointing with a shaking hand down at one of the slain demons.

Demon it was not.

The huge-eyed, fanged visage flickered and died, revealing an ordinary human face in a battered, demon-formed war helm. And all over the sodden ground the same flickering change was occurring.

'Human, they be,' somebody breathed. 'Some dread enspellment . . .'

'Human and *dead*,' somebody else added.

Petry let out a whoop. 'Do you see what this means? Do you *see*?'

'Aye, lad,' Jordie said. 'We see.' His voice shook with emotion.

'No!' somebody called suddenly. 'Petry, don't!'

But it was too late. The boy had plucked up one of the helms. 'It's . . . warm,' he said. The huge, translucent yellow membranes that were the eyes of the demon-visaged helm seemed to flicker for a moment, as if with a life of their own, then went still.

'Put it down, boy. Put it *down!*'

Petry shrugged. 'Seems harmless enough now.' But he dropped the thing to the ground nonetheless and walked away, wiping his hands.

Hawl came up to Egil, knelt at his side. 'Perhaps the Powers *do* move for us now. Out of nowhere you come to us in our moment of need . . .' He faltered self-consciously, reached a hand out and placed it upon Egil's arm. 'You *are* a man. I . . . I just had to . . .'

Egil shrugged himself uneasily free of Hawl's grasp. The men clustered about him, eyes bright with expectation. He still did not truly understand what had happened to him here this day, but the moment of his death had come and gone and left him stranded here, like flotsam, still alive, as it had with these men. And now, now they looked to him with hope burning in their eyes.

Egil stood up, grunting at the pain the movement caused him. He tried to move away from the tree, but his head throbbed and his vision clouded. He did not wish to be here. The hope in these men's eyes was all wrong. It was not life he had fought for here, but death. He had wanted only death and the slipping away into darkness. He had wanted only reunion with his poor Shawna, and peace.

He tried to step away from the men crowded about, away from what burned in their eyes, but his legs gave way suddenly. 'No!' he cried, fending their hands away. 'No . . .'

The last thing he saw was their hands reaching for him. And then he sank away.

# VI

# At the Confluence of
# the Paudit and Whitewash Rivers

Sub-Commander Gerrid reined his horse to a sharp halt in front of the Field Command Pavilion of the Lords Veil. He dismounted slowly and handed his steed into the hands of a waiting groom. 'Sub-Commander,' the groom said, bowing to one knee in respect before taking the reins.

Gerrid waved him off distractedly. A runner stepped out from between the guards at the Pavilion's entrance, a rolled dispatch tucked conspicuously into his belt, and loped off through the tents and horse corrals, field smithies and cook yards of the camp. The Sub-Commander stared at the canvas Pavilion. He was not at all looking forward to the audience that lay before him. The Lords Veil did not take kindly to failure. And, worse, he would have to face them unhelmed.

With a sigh, he reached up and removed the spell-helm from his head.

A great wash of exhaustion hit him so that he staggered under it, his heart suddenly labouring. It had been three days since he had last slept. He was *tired*. With the spell-helm on, such tiredness meant nothing. But with it removed . . .

He gazed down at the thing as he held it in his hands – a solid, warm weight, bronze and iron and bone, snarling fangs, great golden eyes, raised feline ears. A shiver went through him. As always, looking upon it, he experienced a complex mix of desire and distaste. It was a cruel thing with a strange life of its own. He could feel the soft, living *thrum* of it vibrating the bones in his hands. The eyes that gazed blindly at him were golden membranes through which, when he donned the helm, the world appeared brighter, purer, as if lit with an inner radiance. Wearing it was an exaltation: the thrill of strength flowing through him, the world dancing bright and throbbing with life about him; and he bright and strong and invincible.

But now the world was dulled to its normal condition. As was he. His back ached. His shoulders hurt where the armour always galled him, and his thighs burned from too many days in the saddle.

He felt cast adrift, and part of him longed to put the helm on once more, to feel the exaltation it brought flow through him again. It felt always like this, the first moments after removal. The helm was addictive as a drug. And like a drug, it exacted its price. Deprived of it, he felt dizzy and nauseous, weary in both mind and spirit.

It could possess a man's soul, this thing, if the man's will was not strong enough. He looked down at it. Ally and threat, feeding upon him yet feeding him . . .

Gerrid tore his gaze from it, focusing once more on the Command Pavilion before him, waiting for the intensity of the withdrawal to wear off. Best to face the Lords Veil now, before they called him in for an accounting. He took a long breath in an effort to clear his head, then another. There was no point in delaying.

The Sub-Commander strode towards the guards at the Pavilion's entrance. They made as if to stop him at first, but recognizing him for who and what he was, they saluted, clenched fist to shoulder. Gerrid handed his sword and knife over to them, along with the spell-helm, for none might enter the Pavilion of the Lords Veil armed in any fashion. He gave the helm to the guards uneasily – was never comfortable when parted from it – and strode past them. They were only ordinary men-at-arms, both wearing the impersonal, demon-tusked visages of their common helms – so inferior to the individual-ized, snarling-puma visage of his own officer's spell-helm. Mindful of his rank and dignity, Gerrid spoke not a word to them.

Inside the canvas dimness of the Pavilion's entranceway, Gerrid paused, trying to throw off the weariness that gripped him. He straightened his aching back and flexed his arms to ease the weight of the armour across his chafed shoulders.

Four small statuettes stood aligned against the canvas wall before him, finely cast in gleaming bronze. First came the Hunter, poised and alert, bow drawn. Next was the Warrior, brandishing his great sword. Then came the Lord of Hosts, cloaked and hooded and faceless. Finally, there were the twin, interlocking forms of the Victor and the Vanquished. Gerrid paused. There were still those who placed offerings before statues such as these. And the Lords Veil, though above practices of that sort, still kept such things about them for the morale of the common soldiers in their force. Old customs died hard.

Self-consciously, Gerrid went through the familiar ritual from the rural days of his youth, when he had been a simpler soul than he was now: hand against his forehead before the Hunter, the clever one; hand over his heart before the Warrior, the brave one; both hands clasped before the Lord of Hosts, the all-knowing; a solemn bow before the figures of Victor and Vanquished, locked forever in their endless struggle.

Before leaving, Gerrid turned back briefly to the figure of the Warrior. 'Wish me luck, Great Heart,' he whispered. 'I shall need it.'

Finished then, Gerrid straightened and ran a hand over his tired eyes. He was not sure what he could say to the Lords Veil. He had failed, and how was he to explain that failure? This northern hinterland was a wild, strange place indeed in comparison with the cultivated south he knew so well. This was a lonely land, all storm and wind and ragged hill and deep forest, with the stony crests of the mountains looming over everything. He did not like it.

It should have been simple enough to run the fugitives down. But squalls of cold rain had obscured the spoor. Their quarry, helpless, exhausted, horseless, had somehow slipped away northwards, as if swallowed up by the wild land itself. And then to find the hounds and the entire advanced party butchered up in the hills. He had never seen anything like it . . . No, he did not like this land. There was something more than uncanny about such butchery of spell-helmed troops.

Gerrid shook himself. Whatever the explanation, it was a failure for which he must take responsibility. Squaring his shoulders, he continued determinedly on.

The interior of the Pavilion was bare of furniture but for a field desk, a few scattered folding chairs, and the bronze standing lamps that would be lit come nightfall. The early evening light, bright enough outside, was here cut by the canvas walls to a kind of dimly pervasive ochre glow. Seated in chairs behind the desk were two figures, identical in dress, identical in feature. Both had long, dark hair ribboned with grey, slate-grey eyes, and broad, cleanly shaven faces, deeply lined about the mouth and eyes. Hard faces, hard eyes; hard men. Before them on the desk top rested two silvery gleaming ovoids – the Lords Veil's spellhelms: eyeless, mouthless, unlike any other men's.

They looked up as he entered.

Gerrid bent down on one knee, head bowed, and waited for them to acknowledge him.

'So, Sub-Commander, it is done?'

Gerrid was not sure which of them had asked the question. He had always found it difficult to tell which of the twin Lords Veil he was dealing with, and this difficulty he found strangely unnerving. It felt almost as if he were dealing with the same man, incarnated somehow in multiple bodies.

Lifting his head, Gerrid blinked tired eyes, opened his mouth to answer their question. But the words never came. It had taken several minutes for his eyes to adjust properly to the tent's ochre gloom. Now he suddenly noticed the figure standing motionless at the back of the tent behind the Veils' desk: Tancred, the Lords' Seer, tall and skeletal and shrouded in a long, dark cloak, his face hidden and shadowed by the cloak's hood. Gerrid stiffened. The thought of the kind of power that Tancred held made his stomach twist up. What was Tancred doing here? Gerrid could not help but feel that the Seer's presence did not bode well for him.

For a moment, Gerrid was gripped by a sense that it was not the Lords Veil and their Seer before him at all. The two men at the camp desk, so alike in feature, seemed suddenly to embody for him the figures of the Hunter and the Warrior, cunning and courage. And behind them, dark and brooding, Tancred seemed the very Lord of Hosts himself. Gerrid felt a superstitious shiver run through him, a complex mix of fear and awe and exultant pride that he served men like these. For the Lords Veil were men such as could conquer any land, order it to their own designs, subdue it and shape it as they willed. As they were doing now in this northern hinterland.

And he, Gerrid, would shape it with them.

Or not, perhaps: it was far from sure what the outcome of this audience would be.

'Well?' one of the Lords Veil demanded. 'You have not answered our question, Sub-Commander. Is it done?'

Gerrid blinked, shifted uncomfortably, took a breath. The kneeling position he was still in made his sore back ache, but he could not rise until they had given him permission. 'We . . . I . . . I did not get them, Lord.'

The Lords Veil exchanged a quick glance. But when they looked at him, Gerrid could tell nothing from their closed faces. Their thoughts ran deep and quick, and it was seldom that a man could know what was in their minds. Behind them, Tancred stood silent.

'And how did this happen, Sub-Commander?'

The question came from behind him, in a voice that had the guttural resonance of one wearing a spell-helm. Gerrid twisted about and saw a new figure, dressed in the same dark clothing as the two Lords Veil, wearing a featureless, silvered spell-helm identical to theirs. Wide-eyed, Gerrid stared as this newcomer removed his helm, revealing identical dark hair and eyes, the same broad, tanned, lined face as the two Lords Veil at the desk.

Gerrid tried to hide his shock, but all three Veils smiled. He had heard rumours, the usual interminable camp rumours, but had never given them any credence. This seeing of a *third* Lord Veil, real and in the flesh, rocked him.

'I repeat the question, Sub-Commander,' said the Veil behind him, drawing up a folding chair and sitting, still behind, arms crossed, spellhelm hooked now to his belt. 'How did this happen?'

'You may rise,' instructed one of the Veils seated at the desk.

Gerrid levered himself to his feet. He glanced behind at the lone seated figure, then at the two in front. Awkwardly, he tried to turn, to position himself so that he could see all three at once, but he found it impossible.

Again, all three smiled.

'I have nothing against your keeping your back to me, Sub-Commander,' said the one behind him. 'Tell us how you managed to let them get away.'

Gerrid swallowed uncomfortably, feeling the eyes at his back. His own eyes felt as if someone had rubbed rock salt into them, and he sagged momentarily with exhaustion. 'There were – ' his shoulders hunched unconsciously – 'difficulties, Lords.'

The two Veils seated at the field desk said nothing, merely gazed at him.

'Difficulties?' the voice from behind him put in. 'And just what were these . . . *difficulties*?'

This talking to someone he could not see rasped away further at Gerrid's already over-tired nerves. He longed for his spell-helm and the confident strength it gave to him. The two before him might have been carved of wood for all the response he could read on their faces. And he could feel the hard eyes of silent Tancred on him. Gerrid took a long, slow breath. 'It was difficult tracking, after they scattered into the bush. In the rain, the hounds lost the scent more than once.' Gerrid shrugged unhappily.

'It is a wild land, and these rebels know it well. They rode their horses to death, Lords, and put distance between us. Then they split into two groups and continued on foot. Sub-Commander Chayne took one of these groups, I the other. My squad hounded them all that day and through the night, but they managed to elude us. And then – how I do not know, Lords – they managed to ambush and destroy my advance party.'

One of the Veils at the table raised an eyebrow. '*Destroy?*'

Gerrid swallowed uncomfortably. 'We . . . came upon them late in the evening. The hounds were all dead. The men were . . . we found them butchered, stripped of arms and armour and helms. How these rebels accomplished it, Lords, I have no idea.'

'And those that did this?' inquired the Veil from behind Gerrid. 'What of them?'

'Gone, Lord. Without the hounds we had no sure means of tracking them.'

The Lords Veil gazed at Gerrid in an ominous silence. This failure could very well mean the end of his career, and worse. The Lords Veil were not patient with failure. But the Lord of Hosts alone knew what they might be thinking: Gerrid could read nothing from them.

'They know this wild land, Lords,' he began. 'They know its hidden places and . . .'

At the look on the faces before him, Gerrid fell silent. He felt suddenly so weary that, for a moment, he truly did not care. He just wanted this to be over. Putting a hand to his lower back, massaging the sore muscles there, he cursed to himself.

'And why, Sub-Commander, did this happen? Why did you fail us?' It was the voice from behind him once more.

Gerrid was silent for a moment. Then, with a sigh, he said, 'They know this northern hinterland better than I do. They have had more experience than I in this wild country. And they must have some hidden power, some hidden ally . . .'

Two pairs of eyes gazed at him, dark and hard as grey slate. 'They outfought you. It is as simple as that, is it not?'

Gerrid bit his lip and shrugged. He tried to keep his back straight, his eyes resolutely on the two blank faces before him, but he was too weary to make more than a token effort. 'As you wish, Lords. I am merely trying to tell you the truth, an unpleasant truth, as best I can.'

There was a long silence. Tancred stood unmoving, as still as one of the bronze figures that lined the tent's entranceway. Still, Gerrid could make nothing of what the two Lords Veil before him might be thinking. He heard the scraping of wood on ground as the Lord Veil behind him got up from the chair.

'And that is all, Sub-Commander?' this one said as he ambled round in front of Gerrid. He halted there, a few paces away, hands clasped loosely behind his back, swaying in an easy, rocking motion from foot to foot. 'You have nothing more to say for yourself? No further explanation than that for why you have failed us?'

Gerrid shrugged, remaining silent. Another great wave of tiredness swept over him.

The rocking stopped. One hand unclasped from behind his back, the Lord Veil paced up to Gerrid, gripped the hand on Gerrid's left shoulder, and stared him directly in the eyes. Gerrid could feel the big thumb dig uncomfortably into the hollow under the armour near his collar-bone. 'You have failed us. And what shall we do with you now?'

Gerrid stared straight back into the slate-grey eyes before him. He could feel himself beginning to sweat uncomfortably. 'All men fail at some time or other, Lord Veil.'

Those slaty eyes blinked, once, slowly, then the hand fell away from him and the Lord Veil sauntered crabwise over to stand next to the other two at the field desk, both hands clasped behind his back once more.

Gerrid found himself facing three entirely blank faces. He had a sudden, irrelevant feeling that, if he were to turn his back on them for a moment, and if they were to change places amongst themselves, he would have no idea as to which was which. What were they going to do with him? Strip him of his Sub-Commander's rank? Take away his officer's helm and relegate him to the status of a common man-at-arms? Or something far worse? He shuddered at the thought.

Gerrid faced the three Veils squarely, refusing to flinch from their cold, assessing gaze. He might lose his Command here, but he had no intention of losing honour as well.

For the first time, Tancred moved. Gliding out from behind the Veils' desk, he came to stand before Gerrid. The Seer's face was disconcertingly skull-like, entirely devoid of any hair, skin stretched tight over bone. For a long, uncomfortable moment, his dark, hard eyes stared into Gerrid's, like twin, glittering black marbles. His stare was like a groping invasion; Gerrid tried to shift away from the Seer's unblinking gaze but found that he could not. He was held there while something – *penetrated* him.

It *hurt*.

He struggled, trying to fend away this vile intrusion, but he was held like some hapless insect, pinned and struggling. Nothing he did was of any use. It was like a great gouging hand reaching into him, tearing at his psyche.

And then, abruptly, it was over.

The Seer smiled at him coldly.

Gerrid shuddered. He felt fouled. His limbs shook weakly and he had difficulty getting a clean breath. A connection of some sort must have been briefly created between him and the Seer for, as he stood there shaking, Gerrid had a sudden, disturbing flash of perception. The Seer could have prevented the pain caused by his intrusion, but it did not matter to him. To Tancred, Gerrid was of no importance, a tool to be used and discarded if he should prove flawed. It did not even matter that Gerrid should catch a glimpse of this disquieting fact. Tancred had other concerns, larger concerns, compared to which the fate of one struggling Sub-Commander was of laughably little –

Like a door closing, Gerrid's perception shut off.

The Seer turned from him, nodded once to the Lords Veil. 'He is hiding nothing.'

'And the helms that are stolen?' one of them asked.

'It takes a man of power to activate them once their original wearers are dead,' the Seer replied. 'There is no such man in this forsaken, wild hinterland.'

'You are certain?'

'I would *know*.'

'Then the helms . . .'

'With nothing to feed on, the helms will fade. I deem you have no worry on that score.'

Without a word further, Tancred turned his back on the Veils and stalked out of the Pavilion, his cloak swirling about him. He asked no permission and took no leave.

Gerrid shivered, watching him go.

For long moments the Lords Veil remained silent. Gerrid could see no shadow of anger on those three identical faces, but he felt the crackle of it in the air. Tancred's abrupt departure had been a calculated affront.

But all the Lords Veil said was, 'This destruction of your men-at-arms must be looked into, Sub-Commander. A small thing, perhaps, but it is a mystery. We do not like such mysteries.'

'And we shall speak more of this failure of yours, Sub-Commander,' another continued.

Gerrid's belly twisted up. Now he would hear what sentence they had decided to pass upon him.

But instead of that, one of the Veils simply said, 'For now, we shall let that issue lie fallow.'

Gerrid blinked, uncertain as to what this announcement might portend.

'You are right,' the voice continued. 'All men fail at some time or other. Even the best of men.'

'You would be no use to us if you could not admit your failures,' said one of the others.

'If you had tried to shuffle out of this, or blame others,' the one standing said, 'you would have died right here and right now.' From behind his back he brought out a needle-bladed stiletto.

Gerrid felt a sudden flat, metallic taste in his mouth as he stood there looking at the blue-gold sheen of the blade. Then words passed with unnerving rapidity from one to the other of the three Lords Veil, each uttering a sentence, or part of a sentence, only to have it picked up by another, who in turn continued.

'A man who cannot look his superior directly in the eye and admit to failure is one with wiles and weaknesses in his heart rather than a man's courage . . .'

'And a Sub-Commander who will not admit failure to us is a man we cannot trust . . .'

'You know too much now to be simply dismissed . . .'

'So, Sub-Commander, we either trust you or kill you. As long as we trust you, you live and prosper as we live and prosper.'

'But should we cease to trust you . . .'

'Should we see you shift about, see your eyes flick away from ours when we look at you . . .'

'That will be the day of your death.'

'Is that clear?'

Gerrid nodded, unable at the moment to find the proper words to reply to this piecemeal ultimatum.

'You are young yet. We expect a Sub-Commander not yet into his third decade to make some mistakes . . .'

'But not too many!'

'More important still is that we know you do not lie to us.'

Gerrid bristled. 'Lords, I lie to *nobody!*'

'And that is what saved you here. If you had, we would have known. And if, somehow, we did not know – our Seer would.' The Lord Veil who was speaking grinned a humourless grin. 'He is not someone from whom it is easy to conceal things.'

Gerrid shivered, remembering.

'Remember well what we have told you here, Sub-Commander. Serve us well, serve us so that we can *trust* you and, as we prosper, so will you too.'

'The tide of Destiny is with us,' said one of the other Veils, his voice ringing with a sudden vigour. 'The power and the strength is ours. We will conquer this northern land. And with the resources we gain here, we will return southwards and sweep all before us. We will triumph over all. We cannot fail!'

Gerrid felt another shiver of awe go through him. He could well believe that the very forces of Destiny did move through them, were embodied in them somehow.

'Enough, then, for the present,' the Lord Veil who was standing said. He beckoned Gerrid closer. 'We have other matters to discuss.'

Gerrid blinked. The abruptness of this shift caught him momentarily off-balance. After an awkward moment, he moved towards the field desk. It was all right. He had weathered it. The tension in him began to ebb. But he could not shake the suspicion that there were things left unexplained here. Why should the Lords Veil allow his error to go unpunished? This was not like them at all.

A map scroll was uncased and placed across the desk. It showed their camp, the eastern portion of the North Wold, and the long, forked shape of the join between the Whitewash and its tributary rivers snaking north and south up into the mountains that gave them their birth. The north branch was called the Paudit. The south branch had no name on the map.

'With the shattering of the rebel group led by this Olivor,' one of the Lords Veil began, 'we have eliminated what remained of organized resistance, and so the first part of this northern campaign is finished.'

Gerrid nodded. He was finding it difficult to concentrate. His eyes kept closing of their own accord. And he still felt the aftershock of seeing three Lords Veil before him instead of two. He shook himself, trying to get his mind thinking straight once more. 'Is there any word on this rebel leader's whereabouts, Lords?' he asked.

'He has been taken,' one of them replied.

Gerrid blinked. 'Taken?'

'Others had better success than you in the hunt.'

Gerrid swallowed that in silence. There was nothing for him to say.

'And now that we have broken the back of the resistance offered by those cursed rebels, there are events in the south to think on. We are sending the bulk of our strength back southwards, to garrison Sofala and Minmi City. Things southwards are . . . complicated.'

'And am I to join that force?' Gerrid asked eagerly.

'No,' came the reply. 'You will be staying here in this northern hinterland.'

Gerrid bit back on the quick disappointment that rose in him and kept his face carefully blank. So this was to be his punishment for failure. With the focus of things shifting southwards once more, there would be scant chance of preferment here in the north. He had made the rank of sub-Commander by volunteering himself for hazardous duties, had created a reputation as being a daring man. But now . . .

'Our Seer has made demands of us,' one of the Veils was saying. 'Tancred wishes to establish a camp, of sorts, north of the river, where he can perform certain trials and test new discoveries which he claims will aid us in coming campaigns.'

Another of the Veils pointed to the map and continued. 'Your Company, Sub-Commander, is to move north of here, to act as part of a pacification force. You will empty the remaining villages, conscript their inhabitants, and help establish this camp.'

Gerrid stared at them in dismay.

'You have some objection?'

'Lord,' Gerrid said, 'will I be under Seer Tancred's command?'

The Veil he had addressed smiled. 'No. You will be under Commander Chayne's command.'

'You mean *Sub*-Commander Chayne, Lords.'

'We have already told you that others had better success in the hunt than you. Commander Chayne ran down this Olivor, this rebel leader. We reward success.'

Gerrid took a breath, let it out. 'This rebel leader was in the group Chayne pursued?'

'Yes. Commander Chayne ran them down. First the main group itself, then, during the night, he flushed this Olivor from a farmer's cabin and ran him down as well.'

Gerrid could feel the eyes of the Lords Veil upon him. 'I . . . I am pleased he met with success, Lords. Chayne is a competent man.'

'We are glad you think so, Sub-Commander. You will be taking orders directly from him.'

Gerrid swallowed. So much for weathering this failure of his unscathed. Not only was he to be tucked away out of any possible action, and thus possible preferment, but he was to suffer the humilation of taking orders from Chayne as well. He bit back on the sudden outrage that burned in him. He and Chayne were of an age. They had been newly commissioned Sub-Commanders together in the great push that launched this northern campaign. But now – *Commander* Chayne. Chayne had all the advantages that Gerrid lacked. He came from a noble family, had privileged connections. And now luck. It was insupportable.

'You do not look pleased, Sub-Commander,' one of the Veils said.

Gerrid could think of nothing to say.

The Lord Veil smiled at him, a thin, cold smile. 'We reward failure as well as success. Each as it deserves.'

'Yes, Lord,' Gerrid said, sketching a bow of submission.

'We have reason to believe,' said one of the Veils, 'that Chayne has begun to shelter himself under the wing of our Seer. It was at Tancred's request that Commander Chayne be placed in charge of this camp that Tancred plans.'

A different Veil leaned towards Gerrid. 'How do *you* feel about our Seer, Sub-Commander?'

Gerrid blinked confusedly. 'Lords, I—'

'Would you trust him? Remember what we have said about trusting *you*, Sub-Commander. Speak truthfully!'

Gerrid stared at the three of them, swallowed uncomfortably. 'Lords, I do not trust him. He . . . he makes me sick in the pit of my belly.'

To Gerrid's surprise, the three Veils laughed.

'Good, Sub-Commander. You confirm our trust in you.'

'In many ways Tancred is a good servant. But he has hidden depths to him that make us wonder. Yes, they do indeed make us wonder.'

'It would be,' continued another, '*most* useful to us if we had a trusted man near him to inform us should anything untoward begin to occur.'

'Do you take our meaning, Sub-Commander?' finished the third.

Gerrid bristled. 'I may not be of noble birth, Lords, but I am an officer, and an honourable man. You wish me to – to *spy* upon him, Lords?'

The Veils laughed softly. 'Let us say that we wish to have somebody in this camp of Tancred's whom we can trust. If you are fastidious about such things, Sub-Commander, there are other officers we could use . . .'

Gerrid shook his head quickly. He had no choice here, and the Lords Veil knew that well enough. 'I am your man, Lords. I will do as you ask, whatever you ask.'

'You are part of a select group, Sub-Commander. Let that be a consolation to you. Only those we deem entirely trustworthy are allowed to know that there are more than two of us. And you will not be kept in isolation overlong.'

Gerrid nodded gratefully. 'I thank you, Lords, for your trust.'

'Good, then. For now, leave us. We will sort out details later.'

Gerrid bowed low, 'By your leave.'

They waved him off, the three of them already bent low over the desk in conference over some new matter, and Gerrid backed respectfully out.

In the evening air, reunited with helm and weapons, Gerrid stood for long moments simply breathing. He had weathered it. He had survived. Shaking his head, he marvelled at the subtlety of what the Lords Veil had arranged for him. They had punished him all right, banishing him to this camp of the Seer's and placing him under Chayne's command. And then making a common *spy* of him. Adding insult to injury, that. He felt a flush of anger, thinking what it was going to be like taking orders from the newly promoted Chayne. And the prospect of rounding up stupid villagers and herding them into this camp of the Seer's was repellent to him. He was a warrior, not a herdsman.

Yes, he was punished right enough. But it was subtle punishment. And beyond lay the promise of preferment. The proverbial stick and turnip.

The waiting groom brought up Gerrid's horse, but Gerrid chose to walk rather than ride, hoping to work off a little of the stiffness in his limbs. He hung his sword and helm from the saddle. It was tempting to put the helm on, but there were limits: though his was an officer's helm, and far above those of the common ranks, it could still kill a man if he wore it for too long, burn him out like a guttered candle. So Gerrid walked, sore and exhausted, weaving a meandering way through the ordered chaos of the big camp.

Overhead, the bowl of the sky was still clear, but the setting sun buried itself in a dark mass of clouds humped along the western horizon. More clouds, more cold rain. A curse on it, Gerrid thought. He had had enough of this forsaken northern land. He would round up the stupid villagers, do what he must in this camp of Tancred's as quickly as could be, and then be done and back southwards.

The quicker the better.

# VII

# The Village of Woodend

Jonaquil leaned tiredly against the front doorway of Guthrie's small house. It had been a long, long night, bringing young Inda through the delivery, and Jonaquil was very weary. But all had gone well. Now, inside, mother and newborn were both resting easy on their first morning together. And Guthrie, the new father, was aglow with pride, as if *he* had been responsible for it all. Jonaquil yawned and stretched, trying to rid the kinks from her back. Untying her long auburn hair, she let it fall loosely down her back. She watched the sun ease itself up from behind the far crests of the Eastering Peaks. The village was astir, cooking fires lit. Twists of smoke curled gently away from chimneys into the morning air.

Jonaquil ought to have been content. The delivery, though long, had in no way been dangerous, and she could foresee no complications in the coming weeks. But she could not relax. Her stomach was knotted up tight with unreasonable dread. She shifted uneasily where she stood in the doorway. The dawn breeze, cool as mountain water, was filled with an intricate tapestry of birdsong, human voices, and the soft lowing of cows on their way to pasture after the morning milking. All seemed well.

Yet the formless dread gripped her and would not lessen.

Jonaquil had known this feeling before. It was a part of her Healer's gift, and of her Healer's burden, this sometime sensitivity. And now it was painfully strong in her. But it was a thing of the belly, not the mind, and she had no idea of what it might presage.

Old Tirry came tramping by on his way to the fields. 'Morning, Healer,' he called.

Soft though his greeting was, it started Jonaquil.

Tirry doffed his field cap respectfully, ran a hand through his scraggly grey hair. He scanned the house, his eyes alert as a bird's. 'All well within?'

Jonaquil nodded tiredly and smiled. 'All well.'

Tirry hesitated. 'Yet you seem worried, Healer. You sure nothing is wrong?'

'All's well inside,' Jonaquil assured him. 'Truly.'

'Is it a boy-child, then? Young Guthrie was bragging about how it would be a boy-child.'

She nodded and leaned back wearily against the support of the door-jamb. 'A lazy boy-child it is, determined to stay comfortably where he was, thank you very much.'

Tirry chuckled softly.

'But there is something . . .' Jonaquil began, and then stopped, staring.

Behind Tirry's back, in the distance, a figure appeared on the bluff on the eastern bank of the River Rush, beyond where the village bordered the water. The figure was joined by another, then another still, until the bluff grew thick with them.

Jonaquil shivered. All the village had heard rumours of calamity southwards. And a few days days back, during the night of the storm, some terrible thing had happened out at Big Egil's steading beyond the village proper, leaving nothing there but a smoking ruin.

Jonaquil shaded her eyes with her hands, trying to see more clearly into the distance. The figures on the river's far bluff were only silhouettes, back-lit by the rising light of the sun and difficult to make out clearly, but she thought she could discern the bristle of weapons. Her heart turned in her breast with dread.

Tirry, seeing Jonaquil stare, whirled about. 'Powers preserve us,' he murmured, sketching a warding sign with his fingers. 'Who are *they*?' He went a few steps off, looking beyond the corner of Guthrie's house and across to the fields that bordered the outskirts of the village. His face paled and he beckoned, shakily, to Jonaquil.

Moving away from the doorway, Jonaquil looked to where Tirry was pointing and saw in the distance a group of figures methodically destroying the village crops, scything viciously at the green sprouts of young spring barley, as if butchering crowds of helpless children.

At first, Jonaquil took these crop-killers to be armed men, for they were clearly man-shaped, clad in coldly glittering armour and wielding long, intricately bladed pikes. But then one of them looked up and she saw its face full in the thin morning light. She gasped. It was an impossible, savage demon face, with glittering and inhumanly huge eyes, and tusks long and bared as a wild beast's. And all the others were the same.

Jonaquil felt a dizzy terror sweep through her. What manner of terrible creatures had come upon them?

Tirry stood frozen, his face white with dread and fury, as he watched the destruction.

'The fields,' a voice wailed from somewhere. 'The fields!'

Suddenly, the whole village was moving.

The door behind Jonaquil banged open and Guthrie came tumbling out. 'What is it?' he demanded. 'What's wrong?'

Tolke, Guthrie's older brother, came panting up. 'Stop them. We've got to *stop* them!' Tolke was tall and rangy as a hound, with straw-blond hair, a long, toothy face, and a mean temper that all in the village knew and avoided. He stood now, fists clenched, face flushed with fury. 'They're bloody *destroying* everything!'

People gathered, staring.

'Don't just *stand* there!' Tolke yelled. 'We've got to stop them. Come *on!*'

Nobody moved.

Tolke started forwards, stopped, swivelled to face the people who had begun to gather in a confused clump before Guthrie's house. 'You look like a flock of stupid, startled geese,' he said acidly. 'Mouths agape, *stupid* geese. Come *on!* Will you just stand and watch while our livelihood is destroyed?'

'What can we do, Tolke?' somebody said. 'Look at them! *Look at them!* They're demons! Demons are come upon us!'

Tolke scowled, a feral, toothy grimace that made those near him back away. He turned from the crowd about him and looked towards Guthrie, his brother. Guthrie glanced back uncomfortably into his house, stood poised and awkward for a moment, then pushed forwards past Jonaquil to stand by his brother's side.

'Good!' Tolke snapped. 'There's at least *one* man amongst you. Who else? Who else is with me?'

But from the small window near the floor of the house, a voice called, 'Guthrie.' Inda's pale face showed there. 'Guthrie!'

Guthrie stopped, torn.

Tolke glared coldly at Inda. 'Shut up, woman! Get back in your house.'

But Guthrie was already shuffling back to the veranda.

To Jonaquil's surprise, Old Tirry said, '*I'm* with you,' and came to stand beside Tolke. 'And I,' said another, younger man. More folk were gathering now, drawn by Tolke's loud and angry voice. 'Me too, I'm with you . . .'

'Good,' Tolke responded, frowning at his brother's retreating back. 'Does anybody have weapons? Knives, scythes, anything with an edge!'

Goll, the village smithy, raised one beefy fist above his head. 'Hammers! My hammers will beat skulls as well as horseshoes!'

The growing crowd began to jostle itself into movement. 'To the fields! To the fields!' some of the younger men shouted, their voices shrill and breathless.

Jonaquil, exhausted from the long night just past, had fallen into a sort of numbing daze. She had watched the crops being destroyed, listened to Tolke harangue the people about her, but it had all held the unreality of an uneasy dream. She blinked now, ran a shaking hand over her eyes. Tolke shouted something. People in the crowd shouted back.

Beyond the villagers, Jonaquil saw the figures from the river's buff come splashing across the ford. They were savage, demon-faced creatures, armed and armoured like those destroying the crops. Clad for war.

The shouting crowd had not noticed their approach.

'No!' Jonaquil cried, coming out of her daze. 'This is not the way!'

Tolke's face was a mask of fury. She stood herself before him. 'Fighting is *not* the way. You'll only get yourselves killed!'

'They're destroying our fields!' Tolke snapped. His anger, clear in his rigid stance and clenched face, had bled into those gathered about him. A sullen, communal murmur of assent greeted his remark.

'No!' Jonaquil said again. 'It's madness!' She could feel the group before her coalescing. Somehow, she had to stop them. She knew Tolke, knew the viciousness of his temper. He could whip everybody up into a mindless fury. And then . . . then who knew what disaster might ensue? They would be scythed down like the barley in the fields.

She stared into the crowd of faces before her, looking for somebody to appeal to, somebody with enough common sense to help her deflect the crowd from this mad course they were set on. Off to one side, she spotted the podgy face of Dara, Woodend's Mayor. But Dara's eyes skittered away from hers and he slipped back, hiding himself in the crowd.

And then, suddenly, demons came clashing up the laneway leading from the river. There must have been three dozen of them, maybe more, amounting to fully half the adult population of Woodend itself. They formed a crescent about the group gathered in front of Guthrie's small house, silent and terrible.

The Woodenders had gone into a shocked hush, frozen where they stood, staring.

The silence lasted, tense and nerve-rasping, until a rider cantered up from behind the ring of demons. This one was different from the rest. Whilst they all wore the same demonic, tusked visage, he was a snarling hunting cat, with great golden eyes.

Jonaquil stared, her heart thudding in in her breast.

The cat-creature vaulted to the ground, lithe and powerful. He stood there surveying them with great, unhuman eyes. 'Gather what possessions you can carry on your backs. Then be ready to leave.' It was a guttural, raspy voice.

Nobody moved. Nobody spoke.

The creature's hands were covered with leather gauntlets, and he wore high leather riding boots with thick heels and spurs that clinked metallically in the silence when he moved. A war-sword swung in a scabbard at his side, hung from a wide leather strap that crossed diagonally over the scale-mail armour that covered his torso. All this was human enough. But that face – the snarling, feral face from which no human voice should come – was enough to keep the villagers transfixed, like so many hapless rabbits in the presence of some great, predatory creature.

Raising a gauntleted hand, he stabbed a finger at them. 'Do you hear me?'

The crowd remained frozen, stricken, only Tolke moved. 'And who,' he said, sidling up to the stranger, bristling like a hound preparing itself for a fight, 'who are you to be giving us *commands?*' Tolke's voice was tight. He moved stiffly, fists clenched at his sides.

'No, Tolke!' Jonaquil cried. 'Don't . . .'

But Tolke was too far gone in his own fury to listen.

The cat-creature, arms crossed, watched Tolke advance upon him in silence.

'Who are *you*,' Tolke demanded, 'to come riding into our village, destroy our crops, commanding . . . *commanding* us to—'

The cat-creature struck in a quick blur of motion, his gauntleted hand hitting Tolke, hard, full in the face.

Jonaquil recoiled involuntarily, her Healer's sensitivity making her own flesh react to the blow. Tolke tumbled backwards with the force of it and lay on the ground, moaning.

The cat-creature stared across Tolke's crumpled form at the villagers. He crossed his arms once again. 'Collect only what possessions you each can carry on your back. And be quick about it!'

A murmur of dismay went through the group of villagers. They stood, shaken, staring at the ring of demon creatures about them, at bruised Tolke, at the distant havoc wrought in what had once been their carefully tended fields.

The cat-creature beckoned two of the demons to him. 'Keep your squads in loose formation here, but be prepared. I want no hesitation, no confusion if we need to sweep the village. Clear?'

'Yes, Sub-Commander,' the demons replied, thumping their shoulders with armoured fists before rejoining the ranks of the others.

Jonaquil, meanwhile, had turned Tolke over. Seeing the shape he was in, she let out an involuntary gasp. His nose had been broken by the blow, and the rest of his face was bloodied and swollen and pulpy like an overripe fruit. As she looked on, Tolke spat a mouthful of saliva ribboned with blood and the splintered remnants of a tooth.

Jonaquil felt the bile rise in her throat. As village Healer, she had tended some nasty injuries over the years, badly broken limbs, ragged cuts where axe or scythe had accidentally hewn flesh instead of wood or grain. But none of these had been the intentional result of calculated violence. It sickened her to witness such an act.

And the echo in her own sensitive flesh of the pain of Tolke's injury set Jonaquil's face to throbbing so badly that she gasped for breath. Healer's gift and Healer's curse, such sensitivity.

She tried to reach out to Tolke, but he straight-armed her viciously away and staggered to his feet, facing the cat-creature once again.

'Walk away, little man,' the creature said. He gestured to the ring of pike-armed demons. 'Or you shall die.' Then he shifted his attention away from Tolke, ignoring him completely, and addressed the group of villagers once more. 'Are you all deaf and stupid? You are leaving this sorry little village of yours. Do you understand?'

'But,' a small voice said, 'but . . . why? Where are you taking us?'

'Southwards,' the creature replied.

A ragged chorus of questions and muttered confusion followed this statement. Somewhere at the back of the group, a child began to wail.

Tolke was livid. He glared at the cat-creature, his whole body shaking with impotent fury. 'You have no *right!*'

The cat-creature swung his head and turned those great, inhuman, golden eyes upon him. His silent stare was unblinking, terrible in its cold intensity.

Tolke backed down, shuffling away into the anonymity of the crowd. Jonaquil moved over to him, putting an arm about him for comfort, but he thrust her aside and stumbled on alone, a hand to his poor, broken teeth, his face white and stricken.

By now, Dara had moved to the fore of the group of villagers and stood facing the cat-creature uneasily. Jonaquil looked up, surprised. Though he was not a brave man, their Mayor now stood, lower lip quivering, pudgy fingers intertwined nervously over his ample belly, facing these armed, terrible-faced demons and their hard-eyed, inhuman leader. Jonaquil felt a little surge of admiration for him.

The cat-creature eyed him. 'And who might you be, fat man?'

Dara winced. The rolls of fat that nestled under his chin quivered. Self-consciously, he tried to straighten himself, suck in the bulge of his belly. 'I . . . I am the Mayor here. I speak for this village.' His voice came out as an incongruous squeak. Jonaquil could see the sweat sheen on his podgy face.

The cat-creature made no reply, merely looked at him.

Dara coughed nervously. 'We . . . we have done nothing.' His voice was beginning to resume its normal, deeper resonance. 'We have harmed no one. Whatever may be happening out in the rest of the world, we have had no part in it. We just want to be left alone . . .'

'You are wasting my time, fat man,' the cat-creature responded. 'And your own.'

'But we *can't* just leave here!' The squeak was back in Dara's voice now. 'This is our home. There are children. And the old ones. Where are you *taking* us?'

The cat-creature shrugged, an entirely human gesture. 'The world changes, village man. A new order is upon you.' He gestured impatiently. 'Time is wasting. Collect your belongings. There is a resettlement camp two days' march south. You will be taken there.'

The villagers only stared at him, unmoving, still in shocked silence.

'My patience wears thin. I will *not* repeat this again. Go!'

Jonaquil felt her heart sink. She could not believe that this was actually happening: impossible demons from some fell foreign place, and this inhuman and unbending leader, part man and part feral creature. Her mind reeled.

The cat-creature gestured, and a rank of demons moved forwards. With the butts of their war-pikes they scattered the crowd, beating children and women and men indiscriminately. Jonaquil stood overwhelmed, immobilized, surrounded by shrieks and wails, flailing pike-hafts and stumbling bodies, until a fellow villager grabbed her by the arm and hauled her away. She was torn raw by the panic and the pain about her, and could only stumble along, half blind, gasping for breath.

'You all right, Healer?' It was old Tirry, hand on her arm, worried.

Jonaquil nodded, too painfully breathless to speak. She braced herself against a building, head down, panting, trying to calm her shaking heart.

'Bastards!' Tirry hissed.

Looking up, Jonaquil saw that the village square lay empty now. The demons were returned to their ranks. And from the fields came the others, finished with their task there. The two groups joined with silent, grim efficiency. None paid any further attention to the village or its inhabitants.

It meant nothing to them, this thing they did here, Jonaquil suddenly realized. Nothing at all.

But it was the end of *everything* for Woodend.

Wearily, Jonaquil drew herself up. Tirry looked at her questioningly. 'I am all right,' she said. 'Thanks to you.'

'Sure?'

'Yes. Now go. See to your belongings. They will not brook delay kindly.'

'And you?'

'I shall see to mine.'

Tirry left her then, though not without a few backward glances of concern. Jonaquil waved him on and began to trudge towards her own small house. She felt sick, her limbs quivery, her heart thumping painfully. but she made what speed she could.

At her home, she unlatched the door and slipped inside. The familiar interior was comfortably dim. The house had only two rooms, a small bedroom, and a kitchen with a large, open fireplace that also served as a dispensary. Jonaquil stood for a long moment, panting. Drying herbs dangled in bunches from the wooden rafters, the good smell of them filling the room.

It was all her life, this room, this house. How could she leave it?

From a shelf along the back wall of the kitchen, she reached down a carved wooden box, opened it, and brought out the small, egg-shaped, translucent nugget of clear golden amber that the box contained. Blinking back tears, she cupped it in her hands. Idris had worn this, hung from a slim gold chain about her neck, for all the years Jonaquil had known her. At her death, the old Healer had bequeathed it to her apprentice. Jonaquil had never known if Idris might have put some manner of charm upon the small cobble, or if it was just memory and association and strength of feeling on her part, but, holding it as she did now, she always felt, or thought she felt, her teacher as a sort of presence.

Clutching the amber stone, Jonaquil looked at her home and shivered. Weeping or raging over what was happening would serve nothing. There was no gainsaying such creatures. But, oh, it was hard ... *hard* to have everything taken from her in this cruelly abrupt manner.

'Be practical, girl,' an old, familiar voice in her memory said. 'What can you take? See what is portable. See what is irreplaceable. Get *to* it!' Jonaquil smiled through her tears, remembering Idris, who had moved through the turmoil of the world like a cloud through blue sky.

Jonaquil slid the chain over her head and slipped the amber inside her linen shirt. The cobble hung between her breasts, cool against her skin at first and then comfortingly warm. In the five years since Idris's death, she had handled it often, but this was the first time she had ever worn it herself. That felt eerily fitting now, somehow, as if the cobble had stayed there in its box for so long only so that she might don it now, when the need was upon her.

Shaking herself, Jonaquil took up a shoulder-bag and began to cull hastily through her supplies, following Idris's imagined advice and choosing only those things that seemed most easily packed and most irreplaceable. Her precious glass vials must stay; they were far too fragile to transport. Much could be packed in small sacks, though, and she set quickly about doing that and transferring them into the shoulder-bag.

She stuffed in some spare clothing. From a hook by the door she lifted down a dark-coloured travelling cloak and stuffed that in as well. The bag bulged a bit, but it would do.

Standing there, she made a single, long plait of her auburn hair, to keep it out of her eyes for the walk which lay ahead, the Powers alone knew where. And that made an end to her preparations.

She took a last long look at the house, at all the things, little and big, that she must abandon; then, wet with tears, she turned and left.

Outside, the laneways of the village were filled with frightened, bustling people. Children skittered about, wide-eyed and uncertain, some helping, most too miserably confused to do anything but get in the way. Jonaquil tried to gather together as many as she could, talking softly to them and to their parents, shepherding the children in a confused group up to the open square near the river, by Guthrie's house, where the village had been told to congregate.

'My Daddy says some's not going,' one of the older boys told her, detaching himself from the gaggle of children. He stood in front of her, hands on hips. 'If some's not going, I'm not going neither!'

'Of course everybody is going,' Jonaquil told him. 'We are all going together.' She took him by the shoulders, turned him round, and gave him a gentle push towards the others.

'But my Daddy says—'

'Hush,' she scolded him. 'Get along now.'

She herded the children along to the meeting place and waited there, trying, with only marginal success, to keep them in some sort of order, and out from under the feet of the adults. She looked for Tolke but could see no sign of his poor battered face in the growing crowd of nervous villagers collecting here. Most people had arrived by now, and the children began to scatter to their various families.

Spotting Guthrie and Inda, Jonaquil went over to them. Young Inda was pale-faced and shaking but, though the babe fretted some, he seemed well enough, all things considered. Having satisfied herself, Jonaquil turned her attention back to the crowd around her. She felt a shiver of unease go through her belly. Most of the village was here, yes, but there were still some missing. She put her shoulder-bag down and stood there, her hands twisting in indecision. Those she marked as absent were mostly single men, mostly young. And there was still no sign of Tolke.

Others about her had begun to notice too. 'Where is young Pol?' she heard somebody whisper. 'And Ben, where has he got to?'

Dara came puffing up to her out of the crowd. 'Have you seen Tirry, Healer?' he asked. Tirry, a widower of some years now, leased a room in Dara's rambling, thatch-roofed house. 'His room is untouched. No sign of him. Brought a couple of his things along . . .' Dara ran out of breath and stood there, his pudgy hands flapping clumsily across his stomach.

'Tirry too?' Jonaquil said.

Dara looked at her worriedly. 'You've noticed, then?'

Jonaquil nodded.

'What do we—?' Dara began, but was cut short by the startling bray of a bronze trumpet. The rush and whir of movement and talk among the collected villagers dwindled into nothing.

Astride his horse, the cat-creature called to them. 'Gather yourselves in some kind of order. We will ford the river and then work our way southwards. I want *no* stragglers. Do you hear?' He guided the horse forwards, to the edge of the clustered villagers. 'Where is the fat man, the Mayor?'

'Here,' Dara called, leaving Jonaquil's side and approaching the horse nervously.

'Is everybody here and accounted for?'

Dara hesitated. His eyes skittered away from the cat-creature's face and then back again.

'Don't fool with me, fat man,' the creature said. 'If we have to comb through this miserable little village of yours looking for stragglers, there will be trouble. Serious trouble. Do you understand?'

Dara shuffled about uncomfortably. 'There are, perhaps . . . perhaps one or two still missing.'

'Perhaps?'

'The packing . . . perhaps they still have things they are packing.'

'Fool!' the cat-creature snapped. He reined his horse about, nearly knocking Dara flat in the process, and gestured to a squad of demons. 'Scour the village!'

A dozen tusk-visaged demons detached themselves from the larger group and began to lope through the village.

Dara came puffing back towards Jonaquil, sweating, his face white as bone. 'What are those idiots up to? They could get us *all* killed!'

At that moment, one of the demons called out.

All eyes turned. A group of young men appeared at the village's far end, armed with sickles, hammers, whatever they had been able to find. Tolke led them, clutching a wood-axe, his battered face taut with fury. The little group came forward, then hesitated, seeing the demons arrayed before them. They bunched together, arguing suddenly amongst themselves.

Jonaquil felt sick. 'No!' she cried. '*No!*'

A brief scuffle broke out amongst the men. Several threw down their weapons and would have abandoned the rest, but were knocked to the ground by the others, who stood there gripping their feeble defences. Their voices could still be heard, shrill in argument, when the demons hit them.

It was one-sided butchery, pure and terrible, iron against flesh in a wet, deadly flurry. In mere moments the poor souls were scythed down, just as the barley in the fields had been. Not even those who had thrown down their weapons and lay huddled on the ground were spared. The street ran with blood like a charnel-house floor.

With her Healer's sensitivity Jonaquil doubled over, blind and retching with the sudden, terrible intensity of it.

The Woodenders stared, horror-struck.

A stricken silence overcame the village.

Jonaquil wiped her mouth, tried to spit out the last of the foul-tasting stuff. She felt unexpected hands steadying her, glanced weakly up, and saw it was grey-haired Tirry.

'Changed my mind at the last moment,' he said softly.

The cat-creature had stared coldly at the massacre, silent. Now, he gestured his demons back, then called out, 'Form up by squads! Get these villagers moving. We have a long march ahead of us.'

A wail of anguish went up from the Woodenders, but leaping demons were upon them, beating them out of the village, wielding the butt-ends of the war-pikes with vicious efficiency. Still shaken and weak, Jonaquil stumbled along in the midst of it all, Tirry's arm about her for support, trapped in the mindless rush of it, a madness of terror and shouting and stumbling bodies.

Only on the far side of the river, on the bluff above the Rush's eastern bank, were they able to recover themselves a little and look back. Black smoke rose from the village at half a dozen points. Flames danced and crackled.

And then they were herded over the other side of the bluff and Woodend was gone. All Jonaquil could see before her was the rolling, empty expanse of the Wold, the humped backs of the Blue Hills, and the far, rocky teeth of the Easterling peaks beyond that. She felt sick and stricken, and her heart beat in a flurry of unease. Where were they being taken? And for what dark purpose?

'Faster!' one of the demons ordered. 'No straggling.'

Panting, numbed, sobbing, clinging to each other, the Woodenders stumbled onwards as best they could.

# VIII

# Coming Down Out of
# the High Hills

Down from the High Hills they struggled, Tai and Colby and the others, battered and wretched. They had endured a cold, wet night, sleeping only fitfully, and now they moved, heavy-limbed and stiff, awkward with fatigue. Tai had lost count of how many days they had been marching; each blurred into the next. He recalled one blessed halt, a half-day's wait while a new squad of demons arrived. Then, in the ungentle hands of this new lot, they had again been forced onwards.

Poor Colby had taken a fever in his lungs and staggered along weakly, racked with sudden, violent spasms of coughing. Tai urged him on, one arm about the older man's shoulder in support, careful not to put strain on the livid wound along Colby's ribs. A gust of frigid rain hit them, increasing their misery. Such squalls had come and gone all morning. Tai's teeth chattered. He wiped wet hair out of his eyes with a muddied hand. Under his hold, Colby nearly went down, his feet skidding from under him.

'How . . . how much further must we—' Tai heard somebody behind begin to ask of one of the demon-faced guards that flanked them silently. The answer the man got was a pike-butt in the belly. Tai heard the grunt the poor fellow made at the sudden pain of it.

Tai slowed. He could feel Colby's tremors. His foster-uncle could not endure more of this. Tai trembled, facing the baleful-eyed, boar-tusked demon guard nearest him, but he let his foster-uncle go for a moment and forced himself to confront that guard. 'We must have rest!'

The pike-butt took him across the shoulder, sending him to his knees. Tai scrambled up again. 'You are like to kill us all with this pace. We *must* have rest.'

With one gauntleted hand, the creature smacked him across the face. Tai's head rocked and the old pain flared again in his bruised skull. He tasted blood. But he stood his ground desperately, panting. 'We must . . . have . . . *rest*!'

The demon raised his arm for a second blow.

Tai held his ground, his heart thumping. 'I thought we were to provide sport at the end of this march. Little enough *sport* will we be as dead men.' He took a ragged breath, another. 'And dead are we like to be if you give us no rest!'

The inhuman yellow eyes stared at him but, after a little, the creature nodded. 'Rest, then, little man.'

They had been trudging across a sloping, grassy hillside layered with upthrusts of stone. The demon guard gestured now to the lee of one of these rocky upthrusts. 'There.'

The little band of weary men huddled thankfully against the cold stone, sheltered from the worst of the rain squall. A leathern water-flask went round, and some stale barley-cakes. Tai tried to get Colby to eat one of the cakes, but his foster-uncle refused, though he took a little water. Tai felt Colby's forehead anxiously. The older man was badly fevered and wracked with shivering. 'Uncle?' Tai said. 'Uncle?'

Colby blinked up at him, uncertain. He struggled to a more upright position, back hunched against the stone, and stared dazedly about. He shook his head, groaned, hugged himself. Looking across at Tai, he grinned a small, stale grin. 'Never was much . . . much good at walking. Always liefer have a horse under me.' A coughing fit took him then, and he doubled up under it.

Tai held him through the fit.

'Thank you, lad,' Colby murmured weakly when it was finished.

'Here,' Tai said, offering the barley-cake once more. 'Eat.'

Colby shook his head.

'Eat!' Tai insisted. 'You need your strength.'

Colby laughed hollowly. 'For what? I'll never see the end of this march, lad.'

Tai said nothing, only pushed the cake into his hands.

'I'm a dead man,' Colby said softly.

'No! You're not going to die. I won't . . . *won't* . . . permit it.'

Colby arched an eyebrow. *'Permit?'*

'Eat,' Tai ordered. 'Don't argue with me.'

Colby looked at him for a long moment, then nodded wearily. 'Aye. All right, then. Eat I shall.' He chewed on the cake, swallowed, chewed some more. 'You always were a good lad. None of the rest ever gave you credit enough. Little Scarecrow, they used to call you. Remember?'

'Aye,' Tai said softly. 'I remember.'

'Little black-haired skinny thing you were, too. Pale as a peeled potato. And Mari's boys tormented you something terrible over those fits you used to have.' Colby ran a hand vaguely over his face. 'Grew out of those, didn't you, lad?'

'Aye,' Tai lied.

71

'Good thing, too. I remember well how you used to—' But another fit of coughing cut off what Colby was trying to say.

'Lie back,' Tai told him when it was passed. 'Rest yourself.'

'Aye, lad. 'Tis best, perhaps. A little sleep, now, that would do me proper good.' Colby stretched out against the rock, shoulder to shoulder with Tai for warmth. In a little, he began to nod. Tai put his arms about him to keep him warm as possible. Head against Tai's shoulder, Colby snuffled into an uneasy doze.

Tai sat, blinking tired eyes. He knotted his hair back, away from his face. It was greasy with filth and tangled as a bird's nest. His head ached fiercely, the thump he had just taken from the guard having re-awakened the old pain in his skull. Though he felt weary beyond belief, he forced himself to stay awake, keeping an eye on their demon guards. He did not wish poor Colby awakened rudely by a hard foot or a pike-butt in his belly.

'Foul, unnatural creatures!' Tai heard a man mutter nearby. 'Why is it that the Powers do not snuff them out entire?'

'The Powers are not in the world to do your bidding or mine, man,' a companion answered.

'The world is gone mad,' said a third, 'that it has such *things* in it.'

Tai licked swollen lips where the guard had struck him. Unnatural things indeed. They stood nearby, some in the lee of the rock, some out in the rain, as if it discomforted them not at all. They had strode steadily along all yesterday and today, immune, it seemed, to fatigue or hunger or any of the weaknesses of men. They were silent most of the time, and baleful-faced enough, with those tusks and eerie yellow orbs of eyes, to give a grown man the shakes. Tai made a quick warding sign with his fingers, but it was from old habit rather than conviction. Such a sign held force against ill-wish charms; against ill-luck and the small witcheries of life; even, some insisted, against the Fey Folk on moonlit nights. But no warding sign held any protection against creatures such as these.

In a world balanced by Power and Power, how could *they* exist?

Tai felt the hatred rise inside him, like a draught of sour acid in his belly. He cherished that hate, using it against the fear. He tried not to think on what fate might await Colby and him and the rest at the end of this march, tried not to imagine what such creatures would consider *sport*. Tai shuddered. It did not bear dwelling on.

They were still alive. That was all he had to cling to for the moment.

Colby groaned in his sleep, and Tai glanced worriedly down at his face. It was pinched and pale, with a bluish cast to the pale skin. It seemed no more than a shadow of the familiar, hearty face of the man he had known and loved for all his young life.

Gazing on poor Colby, Tai harkened back to his boyhood, recalling the excitement he had always felt, seeing his foster-uncle riding in from the wild country. Colby had ever been a wanderer, visiting his sister's family when the mood was upon him, but never staying. A big, boisterous man, full of wild life and stories.

Recollections of Colby brought Mari, Tai's foster-mother, to mind, and he saw her in his mind's eye as he had seen her so many times: arms crossed, thin-lipped and disapproving, berating her brother for his loose life and his unhealthy influence on boy-Tai. An unremittingly practical woman Mari was, with a farm to run, no time for frivolities, and burdened with a skinny foster-son prone to fits.

Tai remembered it all with painful clarity: how he used to hang on Colby's every word, currying his horse, oiling harnesses, accompanying him at every chance he could into the hills to hunt or fish or just to wander. Foster-uncle Colby might be, but he had been the only one of Tai's foster-kin never to remind him of that fosterage, the only one to accept him, fits and all, as if he truly belonged. Tai had loved Colby with all his boy's heart, and lived for the times Colby came visiting.

He had caught his first fish with Colby, received his first bow from him. The two of them had been out in the hills, hunting, when the demon troops came. Returning, he and Colby had found the village of Fallingbrook naught but a terrible, smoking ruin, and Mari's farm no better. He owed his very life to Colby and that hunting trip.

Colby had given him so much. He had been a strong man and generous, full of laughter. And now the poor soul lay like this.

Because of *them*.

Tai clenched his fists, feeling the anger knot up inside him. He would *not* lose Colby, would *not* let the last of his kin fall away into the Shadowlands. This he vowed to himself, voice a half-whisper, arms crossed over his breast in the formal manner: 'By bone and blood I do swear . . .'

Somehow, he would keep Colby alive.

And, who knew, perhaps they might find some way to escape from their demon captors. They could flee to the wild lands beyond the North Wold. Enough of fighting. There was nothing left to fight for now in any case. Yes: escape and flee northwards and never, ever have anything to do with *them* again.

But the world had gone wrong, and everything in it, and there seemed small chance of his even being able to keep such an oath.

Tai sighed wearily. He shifted position to ease aching muscles, but carefully, so as not to rouse Colby.

The men round about were hunkered down against the rock, wet and shivering, bleak-eyed and exhausted. There was little talk. Like Tai, they lay unmoving, staring blankly at nothing.

In a little, though, one of them got shakily to his feet. It was Brie, a long-legged man from the village of Thornton away to the south and west. Tai knew naught about him but his name. Aside from Colby, there was no one here that he knew well.

Brie stumbled over towards the guards, hardly able to walk, it seemed. Tai could not imagine what the man thought he was doing. Neither could the demons, apparently, for they gazed at him in obvious curiosity.

Brie drew close to them, stumbled, went down on one knee, and then was suddenly up and running through the rain in a desperate try at freedom, skittering downslope like a rabbit.

A thrill went through the huddled men as they watched.

But the demon guards merely laughed, barking laughter that made the small hairs on Tai's neck prickle. Two bounded after Brie, like hounds chasing a hare, catching him up easily. Though how they moved so swift and easy in the armour they wore, none could fathom. The two guards drove poor Brie back, clubbing him with their iron fists, herding him over to the upthrust of rock that gave the men shelter. There he stumbled to a halt, panting, bruised and shivering.

'You are under protection, man,' the guard said, his voice, like all their voices, guttural and deep, vibrating with a kind of rasping power. 'You are the Lords Veil's meat. Otherwise . . .'

The creature glared at Brie with its unhuman yellow eyes. Then, swift and sudden, it seized one of Brie's hands. Like a normal man might yank a small twig from a tree limb, it ripped the little finger from the hand with one quick, deadly twist.

Brie screamed. The creature laughed and flattened Brie with a casual kick. It held the bloodied finger up for all to see, then flipped the thing over its shoulder into the sod and stalked off.

Brie lay where he was, gasping, clutching at his multilated hand, doubled over with pain.

The guards said nothing further. There was no need.

Late in the day they were straggling along a muddied and treacherous footpath, the slopes of the High Hills well behind them. The muscles in Tai's legs burned, and his skull lit up with pain at each beat of his pulse. The most he could make now was a clumsy stagger. And Colby seemed like to drop at any moment.

The footpath along which they struggled made a dip around a shelf of rock and opened out abruptly on to an unexpected vista. They had come to the border of the wild country, and before them lay the great, open, rolling expanse of the South Wold, lush with spring growth. Beyond, the sky was crimsoned by sunset. Off to the right, Tai could see the glinting curve of a river – the Whitewash, must be. Close by the shore stood the smouldering ruin of what had been a town once. Black and drear it looked, set against red-gold sky and green land.

'Aiee . . .' murmured a voice at Tai's shoulder. 'Breaks my heart, it does. That I should live to see this.'

Tai looked round. A tall, beak-nosed man stood there. Tai did not know his name. 'Do you know the place?' he asked, gesturing to the sad ruin below.

'Aye,' the man replied. 'That I do.' He wrapped his arms disconsolately about his thin chest. 'Morin it is. Or was. A thriving little port town, once. I grew up hereabouts.'

Tai felt a cold grief come over him. This was not his home, but it was the same everywhere, destruction and ruin. No more would he ever sit outside his foster-mother's house in the evenings and watch in the distance the bright dance of the white-water stream that gave his own village its name – Fallingbrook. His past life was stolen from him entire, destroyed in fire and blood.

The blackened ruin before him seemed suddenly more than just a single town; it was every town and every village, and a symbol of everyone's grief.

He could see the bruise such a sight dealt the spirit of the man next to him, could see it in the man's eyes. Tai reached a hand to him in brief, silent sympathy.

'Move,' a demon guard ordered from behind.

The men continued dispiritedly onwards. It was easier walking now, though, along rock-free, gently sloping meadowland. Since they no longer needed to traipse single-file along a rutted path, the men moved in a clump, limping on as best they could, helping one another where possible. The demon guards had fanned out a little distance about them, and for the first time since the morning there was a chance to exchange a few words.

'My poor feet are like to drop off!'

'Is there no end to this march?'

'Where are we being taken?'

'Aye, that's what I wish to know. I don't like to think on what *they* may be leading us to.'

At this, there was silence for a little.

'Most like 'tis the end for us,' one man said then. 'But Olivor and the others may have made good their escape. And if Olivor's still alive, there's hope left.'

'Aye,' agreed another. 'The demons'll not catch him easy. He's too canny, is our Olivor. He got a good start the morning of *their* ambush. I saw him make off successfully on horseback with Jordie and the others.'

'If he and the rest managed to cross the river northwards, they'd have the Blue Hills and the wild land beyond to hide in. These demons don't know the country.'

'And there's villages up there that still haven't yet felt *their* presence. They could get food and help, and maybe fresh horses.'

'Olivor's alive,' a dark-haired, burly man said with conviction. 'I've no doubt of it.'

The very thought of it seemed to brace them all.

'Keep your eyes sharp about you,' the burly man went on. 'Some chance may yet present itself to us.'

'With *them* so near?' somebody else replied querulously.

'Aye, even with *them* so near. Strange things happen. Would you waste our only chance, if it comes, by not being 'ware?'

'There'll be precious little chance, I reckon,' one remarked bitterly. 'You saw what they did to poor Brie when he tried that dash.'

'Aye,' Brie groaned. 'We're not like to outrun *them*.'

'But still, there may be *some* chance,' the burly man insisted. 'And with Olivor free, we have reason to run.'

A new spirit seemed to take hold at this thought. The men looked about them with brighter eyes, gauging the terrain, casting glances here and there as they descended towards the Whitewash.

But no chance presented itself: the guards herded them along through the mutilated stubble of the fields – the spring crops had been destroyed – and on to the outskirts of what remained of Morin. The walking was hard indeed through the trampled furrows of the fields; they could move at no more than a slug's slow crawl. Which earned them more than a few hard knocks, for the guards seemed eager to press on now.

The ruined town was a litterpit of rubble, and quiet as a death-yard save for the small sounds of their own progress. They saw nothing move save, once, the flapping shape of a lone crow they startled into flight. What lay about them was a grim, drear sight indeed. Charred beam-ends, the cracked remains of a chimney piece, stark yellow shards of human bone protruding from the wreckage. The brief flare of vigour that the thought of Olivor being free had given them dwindled into nothing.

'Why?' somebody moaned. '*Why*? What profit for them is there in senseless destruction such as this?'

No one had an answer.

They pressed on because they must, and soon, from ahead, came the sound of voices.

'Something's alive here then,' one of the men said with relief.

They all shared that sense, for the silent, charred deadness of this place weighed heavily upon them.

The guards drove them stumbling onwards towards what turned out to be the town quays. The dock was intact, the unburnt wood glistening white and clean. They saw movement next to a small, twin-sailed cutter that lay moored there. Men. For a moment their hearts lifted, until they saw more of *them* there as well, overseeing the labouring humans.

As the weary group drew closer still, they saw something else that stopped them dead where they stood, staring.

Along the edge of the quay, next to where the cutter lay docked, a row of wood spikes had been set. Thrust on to the sharpened point of each spike was a severed human head.

Hearts beating hard, the men drew nearer. They saw familiar faces, former comrades, the dead mouths of some opened as if in a silent scream, staring eyes, flies buzzing in swarms. Tai stood, immobilized with the very horror of it.

Someone pointed with a shaking hand to what topped the last spike. A bald head showed pale as bone above a dark beard, matted with old blood.

'Olivor,' somebody groaned.

Along the quay the guards herded them, past each sad head in turn. The sickly-sweet smell of dead flesh hit them now, and the sound of the flies.

Stricken, they let themselves be driven aboard the cutter where they were manacled side by side against the gunwale on the open foredeck. None had said a word. There was naught to say. They crouched, heads down, broken. Tai felt Colby, fettered next to him, grasp weakly for his hand. He squeezed back, but could not meet his foster-uncle's eyes. He felt empty as a discarded shoe, and no less battered.

When the cutter cast off and bobbed away into the river's current, none so much as lifted his head.

## IX

# In the Easterling Peaks

There was fire all about him, leaping sheets of flame and thick smoke. He heard his wife's screaming voice.

'Shawna!' Egil cried. '*Shawna!*'

Frantic terror in her cries there was, and mindless, seething rage.

Egil ran, stumbling first this way and then that, dodging flames that seemed to reach for him like fiery hands, plunging through walls of acrid black smoke, trying to follow the terrible sound of his wife's callings.

But he faltered amidst the miasma of smoke and flame that balked him at every turn. It was no use. He could not come to her. Crouched there on his knees, the horrible taint of burning meat clogging his nostrils, he cried out, a long, wailing cry of helpless despair.

Egil awoke covered in cold sweat, shivering, his heart hammering wildly under his ribs. Grey dawn light lay over the rough trunks of the big, gnarly mountain pines about him. A bird called, faintly, in the distance. He lay there for a time, shaking, disorientated, not entirely sure if he were awake or still caught in the dream. The air was icy and damp, and coldness seeped from the ground through his sleeping roll, making him shiver in uncontrollable, teeth-jarring fits.

Men were beginning to stir in the encampment, hugging themselves for warmth, muttering and grumbling, their breaths steaming about their faces as they tried to coax fires into life. Levering himself up on one elbow, Egil looked about. He could recall naught but vague flickers of the journey here from the Blue Hills. He had lain here for days, the time shrouded in a shivering delirium of fever. And all the while, stitching his fevered dreams together, haunting his waking mind, were the flames and the continuous, furious ghost-keening of his dead wife.

Near Egil lay the soggy remnants of an old cookfire the men had abandoned, nothing now but a puddle of ash surrounded by rain-slicked stones, cold and dark. That was how he felt, cold and dark and congealed inside, with no chance of coaxing any fire into life inside him. The ground's coldness went right through his spirit.

Listlessly, Egil stared about him. From the far side of the encampment, he heard voices raised in argument. The day had hardly begun and already they were at it. From where he lay, he could see the men clustered together, with more drifting in from different corners of the camp. 'And I say we must *do* something, and that soon!' somebody cried.

Grey-haired Jordie stood facing this growing group, arms crossed, his jaw clenched with aggravation. 'And just what,' he demanded, 'do you intend that we do?'

'Fire that palisade down there by the river!' came the quick reply. 'That for starters!'

'Oh aye? And what of the villagers inside?'

'Them? To blazes with them fellahs! Those *traitors*! We've seen them cutting down trees to build that palisade, working for *them* like good little lads . . . *collaborating*, that's what 'tis called. And we just stay up here in the Peaks, freezing our arses and doing nothing, while the *enemy* has free run of the—'

The voice was drowned by a garbled, angry chorus from the men gathered about.

A sudden gust of wind shuddered the trees, splattering everything with icy water. The men cursed irritably, shaking themselves like so many hounds.

A fit of the shivers took Egil, and he wrapped his sodden blanket roll more tightly about himself, wet and fever-aching. But the ache in him was not just in his joints. It was in his belly, his marrow, his spirit. He ached for Shawna, ached for his wife as she had once been, for the softness and the strength of her, ached for her and for his lost son and lost life and the peace of mind he had once taken so for granted.

But there was nothing for him now save this cold, miserable, argument-ridden camp.

'Are we going to remain here and do *nothing?*' he heard somebody shout. 'I say we march down there and fire that palisade. Burn it to the ground and all that's in it!'

One of the men let out a ragged, hooting cheer, 'Aie-ee-*haa!*' Others took it up. 'Aie-ee-*haa!* Aie-ee-*haa!*'

Grey-haired Jordie shouted them into silence. 'What's wrong with you all? Have you forgotten what manner of creatures these southern demons are?'

'Just scared, you are,' a voice said.

One of the men stepped forward to confront Jordie. It was Joff the Miller, a lanky, wild-eyed fellow with a long scar marring the left side of his face. 'Just scared,' Joff repeated loudly, turning to the men about him, his arms weaving an active counterpoint to his words. 'Scared the big bad demons will get him. Well – ' he pointed to the heap of weapons, armour, and queer, demon-faced helmets that lay stashed under a rough tarpaulin at the camp's verge – '*they* can die just like men! But Jordie here says no. Scared! That's what you are, Jordie. Scared, scared, *scared!*'

Joff pivoted, turning his back on Jordie, and turned towards where Egil lay. 'Who's leader here?' Joff called. 'You? Or this Jordie-scaredy-britches?'

Egil blinked, not expecting this.

'Well?' Joff demanded. 'Are you leader or not? Will you lead us down there?'

Egil could see Jordie's face behind the others, drawn and worried, and twisted up with frustration. 'You undo everything we try to accomplish here, Miller,' Jordie said, but nobody seemed to hear.

They looked towards Egil now, like so many hungry children, a mass of pale faces, eager, hopeful, questioning.

Egil did not feel he could bear it, the intensity of those looks. All he wanted was to turn away from them, to bury himself somewhere away from all of this. But they would not let him.

Crawling stiffly to his feet, he made a slow way towards them. His bones ached. His limbs felt wooden. The cuts across his arms and torso and face, now a network of itching, ripping scabs, sent little shivers of fiery pain through him any time he moved too quickly. Fetching up against the rough bark of one of the gnarly old mountain pines, he stood there panting, arms clutched with ginger care over his scarred chest.

'Look!' the Miller said, pointing to the collection of helms and weapons. 'That was Egil's work. Egil's not a man to let *fear* guide him. And he is on his feet now. Look! Look at the size of him! With him to lead us we cannot fail! Down to that palisade, I say! *They've* had the upper hand long enough. 'Tis time for us to strike back! Down to the palisade and destroy it with fire and sword!'

The cheer erupted again: 'Aie-ee-*haa!* Aie-ee-*haa!*'

Egil stood, wordless. For a moment he felt a dim, flickering echo of the men's eagerness in his own breast. But he was too weary. He could recall the madness that had gripped him in the Blue Hills only imperfectly: the noise, the frantic movement, the ghost-wails of Shawna and the wet hewing of the axe. It made him shudder. He missed the hot brightness of the fury that had gripped him then, for it had warmed him in some strange manner. But it was gone from him now.

All his life he had lived by the long rhythms of soil and sun and season, wedded with a farmer's ties to the demands of the land, and held in the crucible of his family. But now he was cast adrift from all that. All the makings of his life had been stripped from him, as if some great, taloned beast had ripped open his insides, leaving him hollow and bleeding.

The cheering dwindled away. The men waited, expectant, all eyes upon him.

But Egil had nothing for them. He wanted only to be done with the cold and the fever and the pain, to have peace, to no longer hear the haunting sound of his dead wife that nagged and nagged at his mind. He had nothing to say to these men, save to leave him be.

'Well, well,' a voice said suddenly, breaking into the awkward quiet that had fallen. From the far edge of the clearing Hawl came striding in, a longbow in one hand, a brace of rabbits in the other. Putting the bow and the rabbits down, he stood there looking at the gathered men, fingering the cauliflower mess of his tattered left ear. 'What have we here?' He looked questioningly at Jordie.

Jordie shrugged, weary and disheartened.

'I suppose the Miller's been trying to get you all to go storming off down there to that palisade by the river?' Hawl said.

There was a mutter of assent. 'Jordie here tried to stop it,' somebody said.

'He *always* tries to stop us from doing anything,' another put in sullenly.

Hawl scowled at them. ''Tis Jordie who's got the right of it. If the Miller here would only use his brain as much as he uses his mouth . . .'

Several of the gathered men chuckled at this remark, but mutters of general dissatisfaction drowned them out.

'Have you not learned *anything*?' Hawl demanded of them. He spat disgustedly. 'Listen to the Miller, go storming down there into that palisade like a pack of fools, and all it will get you is a fast entry into the Shadowlands. Or worse, you'll wind up being taken prisoner! Like the poor souls we had to leave behind in the High Hills.'

'But all we're doing is freezing our arses off up here,' somebody grumbled. 'We've got to do *something*.'

'Yes. But doing something *stupid* gets us nowhere at all!'

'Look!' One of them pointed to the pile of weapons and helms. 'We know what *they* are. We can *kill* the creatures!'

Hawl shook his head. 'We do *not* know what *they* are. Were you there in the Blue Hills?'

The man whom Hawl addressed shrugged self-consciously and shook his head.

'No,' Hawl said. 'Of course not! You have no notion at all of what happened. And the loud-mouthed Miller here neither. None of you has who wasn't there. You see a few trophies, hear a few stories, and think suddenly that all you need do is go running down there in one glorious charge.'

'You're just scared as Jordie is!' Joff the Miller cried.

'Shut up, Miller!' Hawl shouted. 'Just *shut up!* Will any one of you accuse me, *me* of being frightened?'

The men muttered uneasily.

''Tis not fear that moves me, but good sense. We do not know at all what deadly secret strengths these creatures may possess.' Hawl pointed to the pile of demon weapons. 'Do any of you understand what those queer helms are?

'Have you not learned *anything*? You don't know these creatures, those of you who want to go charging down there. We need time. There's too few of us yet. We need to gather more men. There's more filtering in every day as word gets out. We need to plan and to think and to find out more about *their* weaknesses before we act. Yes, we killed some of *them* . . .' Hawl pointed to Egil. '*He* killed them. But we lose everything if we go rushing into things unthinkingly. It's as I've told you! Charge down there in to that palisade and you'll end up dead or a prisoner. We've left too many dead behind us already, and I don't like to think on the fate of the poor souls we had to abandon to *them* the morning of the ambush in the High Hills.

'We are the last hope, those of us here, and we must be canny and smart now. Surely that ought to be clear to all of you?'

There was a grumbled acquiescence to this.

'But meanwhile,' somebody complained, 'we just sit here in the rain and do *nothing*!'

'Wrong!' Jordie put in, coming to stand next Hawl now. 'We've sent two parties down there already to—'

'Ha!' the Miller snorted. ''Tis always the same men. And they don't do nothing more than look about a bit and maybe steal a couple of tools if they find them lying about. 'Tis like poking a bull with a twig, that. Won't do more'n annoy *them* if we continue just doing that!'

'But that is just what we *will* continue to do,' Hawl said. 'Sending small groups down like that is the only sensible course. It lets us learn more about these creatures, and it lets us create trouble for them without losing any of our own men.'

'What makes you think you can tell us all what to do?' the Miller demanded petulantly.

Hawl turned on him angrily. 'Miller, haven't you been listening? Have you no sense at all?'

'Sense enough to want to destroy *them*? My village, my family, my sons, they're all dead and gone. I have a score to settle. And now that we have a chance to destroy these creatures, you tell us to hold back. Well, I say – ' the Miller turned – 'I say we put the question to Egil Bloodaxe. With him at our head, we'll bring ruination down upon these man-demons and smash them for good and all. *He's* not a man to let fear guide him!'

Once more, cheers erupted. 'Aie-ee-*haa!* Aie-ee-*haa!* Aie-ee-*haa!*'

Every face turned to Egil. Like so many windows, those faces seemed, windows opening on a naked intensity of hope. It made his belly curdle.

'Lead us down there, Egil Bloodaxe!' the Miller cried. 'With you in our lead we cannot fail!' The cheering began again.

Shaking, Egil turned from them all and shuffled back to his dank sleeping roll. He felt the keening of his dead wife rise within him once more, a furious, mad sound. Egil groaned, covering his ears with his hands, trying to shut it out. But it made no difference. The sound was within him.

One glance he cast backwards at the men. They stood in confusion, staring and stricken. He could not face them, could not face the agony that the betrayal of their hopes wrote so clearly upon their faces. He heard more argument break out amongst them then. He did not care. It was over for him. He wanted only to die away and have done. Nothing more. For ever.

# X

# Across the Blue Hills

Jonaquil wiped the sweat from her eyes with a forearm. Next to her, an older woman stumbled and went down with a little cry. Jonaquil helped her back to her feet, panting, and together they floundered up to the top of the next stony hummock above them. Ahead lay only more of the same, a series of jagged, steep ascents. Jonaquil looked back along the rock-strewn slope up which the villagers struggled in a long, ragged column. All were staggering in a daze of exhaustion now. The time for the day's-end camp had come and gone. The sun hung low in the west. The old ones and the younger children were near the end of their strength. All were near the end of their strength, truth be known.

Dara, as Mayor, and as their self-appointed spokesman, hailed the cat-creature where he rode at the front of the wedge of demons that flanked their slow-moving column. The creature reined in his horse, waiting, but did not turn back. Poor Dara, red-faced and sweating, shaking with fatigue, hurried upslope as best he could. 'It is time for camp,' he said, panting. 'We . . . we cannot go on any further.'

Astride his horse, the cat-creature looked down at Dara with unhuman eyes. 'You will continue walking until I say otherwise.'

'We cannot. I . . . we are exhausted!'

'We continue onwards. Tell the rest.'

Dara stared, his face stricken, chest still heaving.

'Go!'

Dara turned and stumbled back to pass the word along. The creature spurred his horse onwards, paying no further heed.

Jonaquil let out a long, weary breath, almost a sob. Her feet ached fiercely. Her whole body throbbed with the reflected misery of those about her. And no rest was in sight.

'Bastard!' somebody hissed at her shoulder. 'Cold-eyed bastard.'

Turning, she saw it was Guthrie, with Inda and the babe at his side.

'No woman should be made to walk like this so soon after giving birth!' Guthrie fumed.

'Don't they ever feel weary, those . . . *things?*' Inda asked, staring at the demons that ringed them round.

Jonaquil looked at the girl. Inda was young, with all the resilience of youth, but she showed the unmistakable signs of the strain of this forced journey: dark smudges under her eyes, her face pale and crimped into tight lines of weary anxiousness. She tried to smile a little at Jonaquil. 'The babe does well, Healer. Better than I.'

'And you? No bleeding?'

Inda shrugged. 'Just weary.'

Jonaquil ran a hand gently along Inda's arm in reassurance. She could think of nothing to say.

'Bastards,' Guthrie repeated.

Jonaquil watched the demons round about. There was something . . . *wrong* about them. In the full healing-trance, she could see clearly the coloured halo of radiance, the life-light that shone from all living things. Even out of the trance she could catch glimpses of it. And what she could see of these creatures was all wrong. Like nothing she had ever witnessed before. It was a kind of double glow, as if each creature were really two rather than one being. And from the corner of her eye she would catch gouts of radiance whirling about their heads, as if some powerful fountain were gushing forth.

It was unnatural. It made her stomach cramp uncomfortably and her heart tremble. These demons seemed like great stoves of radiant energy. She had never sensed anything like this before. The power of them shuddered through her like a blistering wind.

'Healer?' she heard somebody ask. It was old Tirry, leaning over her, concerned. 'Healer, are you all right?'

'Aye,' she replied, blinking, coming back. Looking at Tirry's lined, worried face, and Guthrie and Inda behind, Jonaquil tried to smile. She could not tell them what she was feeling. They would not understand, and, not understanding, would put either too much or too little belief in it. 'I'm just tired. Like us all.'

'Too bloody right!' Tirry agreed. 'Two days' march to nowhere . . .'

'Where are they leading us?' Inda asked. 'Why are they so silent? Is it such a terrible place we are being taken to, that they must keep it secret from us?'

'A settlement camp,' Guthrie said, trying to soothe her. '*He* said we were to be taken to a settlement camp in the south.'

'We're being taken to our deaths,' Inda moaned. 'That . . . that *creature* is going to have us all killed!'

'Don't be silly, girl. If they were going to kill us, they would have done it back in the village.'

'Tirry is right,' Jonaquil said, taking the girl's face gently in her hands. 'It would be senseless. We will be all right.'

But she could not believe her own words. Jonaquil had seen little of this cat-visaged demon leader in the past days, knew nothing of him but what she had gleaned from the short time in the village; his orders to continue marching were almost the first words he had spoken to them since leaving Woodend. But one thing seemed clear enough about him. The creature's inhuman eyes had no more compassion in them than a snake's.

The march continued. They limped along slowly, weighed down by uncertainties as much as baggage. Children cried, the sun dipped slowly behind them, flooding the western sky with crimson. They passed the crest of the hills up which they had been toiling, wading through the blue sea of flowers that covered those crests and gave the Hills their name. Then they were over and on the far side and the walking was easier. In the distance, they could see the upthrust teeth of the Easterling Peaks, thickly forested at their base, their high crests glowing in the sunset. The air began to cool off as evening approached. Still they walked.

And then, in the creeping dimness of the twilight, they saw it. They had struggled over a short, sharp slope, panting again, helping each other where they could. Coming over the top of the rise, they saw the winding glimmer of the Paudit below them. On its western bank, the near bank, sprawled a village. But it was unlike any village Jonaquil had ever seen.

On all sides, it was surrounded by the beginnings of a palisade made of felled trees, sunk into the ground vertically, forming a wall of sorts. Only the skeleton of it was in place, but the overall form was clear enough. Around the perimeter lay trees newly cut and trimmed, ready to be positioned along with those already up. As she watched, Jonaquil could see a group of men setting one of the trimmed trees at the wall's far edge, levering it into place, sinking it down firmly into the hole prepared for it. The bark of these felled trees had been left on, but the upper tips were hewn to sharp points, the raw wood glinting whitely in the growing twilight.

A confusing cluster of tents and log buildings filled the inside of the palisade perimeter. There was movement everywhere, people everywhere. Jonaquil had never seen so many people in one place before.

'What kind of place *is* this?' somebody near her said.

They were herded downslope, quickly now. The villagers moved with nervous anticipation. They had arrived; the long walk was over. But what had they arrived at?

They were herded in through a wide opening in the palisade,

huddled together like a flock of nervous geese. It was darker inside, with the walls towering above them on all sides. There was noise and confusion and people everywhere. The place stank.

There were demons, yes, but the most of the population here seemed to be village folk like themselves. Some scuttled about, carting various sorts of bundles. Most, though, sat quiet, unmoving. All were pale-faced, weary, dirty as beggars, some dressed in mere rags. Their eyes skittered nervously to the Woodenders as they arrived, but no one approached the new arrivals.

The entirety of it hit Jonaquil like a fist in the belly, her Healer's flesh cringing at the palpable solidity of the misery here. It was a great, searing bonfire of pain, and she quailed before it, faltering to her knees.

The cat-creature was talking with a demon that had come out of a log building. The demon shook his head and pointed to the confusion round about. The cat-creature gestured impatiently back over his shoulder with a thumb, towards where the Woodenders stood in uncertain silence. The demon held his hands out and shrugged. With obvious irritation, the cat-creature spurred his horse back through the confusion and conferred with some of his own demon group.

'You will bed down inside this enclosure, up by the far wall,' he called out to the villagers, his voiced raised against the noise and confusion round about.

Dara, once again their spokesman, placed himself to the fore. 'What about shelter? What about food? Why have we been brought to this place?'

'Do not bother me with useless questions, fat man,' the cat-creature snapped. 'You are here and you are alive. Let that satisfy you for the present.'

But fatigue, perhaps, gave Dara a fortitude he normally lacked. Placing his pudgy hands on his hips, he glared up at the creature. 'We have—' he began, but was cut short by a sudden commotion.

A squad of armed demons came marching along from the far end of the enclosure. In their midst stumbled a young man. He was pale and thin, stripped to the waist, barefoot. Purple bruises mottled his face and torso. His movements had an awkward shakiness to them, as if his legs would barely hold him. His hands were securely bound before him with tight leather thongs.

Voices rose in a confused clamour. The people crowding the enclosure shifted like a flock of awkward fowl.

The squad of demons marched the young man to a wooden post driven solidly into the ground nearby, shifted the crowd back and away. They took his bound hands and hooked them over an iron spike driven into the post, so high above his head that the man dangled helplessly on the tips of his toes.

Torches were lit, contributing a flickering glow to the twilight. One of the demons produced a long, leather bullwhip.

From the far side of the enclosure, a creature with the face of a hawk appeared on a grey stallion. He wore no armour, only dark leather and a long, dark cloak. His hands were covered with metal-studded, leathern gauntlets, the metal studs glinting in the torchlight. He had the same cold, unhuman eyes as the cat-creature. The hawk's visage swivelled, the eyes blinking slowly. In the uncertain light, that hawk's face seemed to glow eerily. 'You may begin,' he called out, gesturing to the demon holding the whip.

'Yes, Commander Chayne,' the demon responded.

The first lash brought a grunt of pain from the man at the stake. The second, a moan. After several more the poor soul began to scream, wailing hopelessly like a terrified child.

Jonaquil turned away, sick to her bones. Everything had gone deathly still. Through the man's screams, she could hear the hiss and crack of the whip as it bit into him.

After a time, it was over. Hawk-face turned and cantered off, and the demons marched away. The young man was left hanging there, moaning incoherently, blood dribbling wetly from the ragged welts across his back.

'Let this be a warning,' the cat-creature said then. 'This man tried to escape.' He looked the Woodenders over, his eerie cold eyes passing from one to another. 'There is no escape.'

Jonaquil flinched when those eyes met hers. He seemed altogether untouched by what had just happened, while she knelt, white-faced and gasping, shaken to her very marrow.

She did not know how she was ever going to endure this terrible place.

Near her, a child was weeping, separated somehow from her mother. Jonaquil struggled to her feet and took the child in her arms, letting the poor thing sob piteously into her shoulder. She felt tears flood her own eyes as she petted the little head soothingly. Just one small hurt amongst many.

'Move!' a demon orderd from behind.

Falteringly, the villagers shuffled forwards into the dark compound before them.

# XI

# Hound's Head Isle

The heave and lurch of the cutter made Tai's stomach queasy. He sat scrunched miserably up against the gunwale with the others on the open foredeck, manacled hands over his knees. His skull still beat with pain, though a little less now, but his belly was one great, knotted ache. With sore muscles, he braced himself as the boat surged up and then down again, the bow slapping against the water, the two curved sails billowing and snapping like bat's wings overhead, as they had all through the length of this westward sail.

Down the River Whitewash had they come, the rolling green shoreline marred all too frequently by sad, blackened ruins, then through Whitewash Ferth and past the crowded quays of Long Harbour (for whatever reasons, *they* seemed to have left the city intact), and so out eventually on to the open expanse of water beyond in Harbour Bay. Late afternoon sun shone down upon them now. All about was glinting, heaving water. Tai felt a surge of nausea and gagged, but there was nothing left in his stomach. He was parched and tormentingly thirsty. There would be nothing to drink, though, until one of *them* ordered it.

Tai looked to Colby anxiously. His foster-uncle had not said a word all this day. Stretching, he put a hand softly on Colby's shoulder. At first he could see no response, and Tai's heart clenched. But then Colby grunted softly. Quickly, Tai withdrew his hand; unconsciousness here was a boon, and he had no wish to rouse his foster-uncle unnecessarily.

Tai had lost track of the days since that disastrous dawn battle in the High Hills. Bad days indeed: scant food, little rest, fitful sleep. Olivor killed – the remembrance of Olivor's poor, spiked head made Tai shudder still. About him, the others huddled as silent and worn as he, each hunched miserably, head down, enduring as best he might.

Hunkered against the gunwale, staring blindly at the deck under his own feet, Tai felt the cutter make a turn into the wind, sharp enough to set his stomach aquiver. Though demons commanded the cutter, men managed it, ignoring their manacled cargo. Now these men began to move about, shortening sail, busying themselves in ways they had not since leaving the Ferth.

Tai craned his neck wearily and looked out. Ahead lay an isle, rocky and sheer. At the near end, the southern end, the stone rose in a huge upthrust, forming the craggy and improbable outline of a giant hound's head. It stood in sharp profile against the sky, the lowering sun behind it, long snout extended as if snuffling the sea air. Gulls soared about it, as flies might circle a real hound. Beneath this image, in shadow, sat a massive Keep. Tai knew of it − the Miradore, built by the original founders of Long Harbour, many and many a long year ago. It had lain deserted and unused in living memory, but Tai had heard the rumours about it, they all had, about how *they* occupied it now.

Looking at it, Tai suddenly shuddered. An inexplicable fear choked him. It seemed a palpably physical thing, like an overdose of some terrible potion that made his heart race, his abused belly knot into a hard, painful lump, his limbs go stiff and clumsy and trembling.

It was the fit coming upon him once again. He knew.

In a terrible wave, the chaos hit, shredding the familiar, solid world into nothing. This was even worse than the last time. A monstrous terror roared through Tai, like nothing he had ever experienced. The sheer, awful weight of it smothered him. His mind almost gave way entirely. But, then, like a wave, it receded as abruptly as it had come, leaving him utterly stricken. He thought his heart would burst, it pounded so. If not for the manacles, he would have scrabbled up, hurled himself into the sea: something, anything.

Tai gulped air, trying to cling to the solidity of the moving deck under him. A great thrust of pure terror it had been, going through him like water through a sieve, like—

Suddenly, with a strange, blood-deep certainty, Tai knew it was not his own fear he had felt. How he could know such a thing he could not conceive, but know it he did.

But whose fear, then? Tai shuddered. How could he possibly feel another's fear? And what was it that could produce terror of the sort he had just experienced?

It was all terrible and uncanny. And not the least of the uncanniness was that, in some queer way, he seemed able to sense the source of what he had felt: the isle ahead.

Their destination.

Tai felt himself sprawled upon the deck, his head jammed uncomfortably against the gunwale. He tried to sit up, panting for breath, his skull flaring into agony. About him, some of the human crew of the cutter had gathered, staring. One of them shook his head pityingly. Another pointed, muttered something, then sketched a quick warding sign. A third laughed.

Tai hung his head in mortification. No telling what sort of disgusting idiot he had seemed while the fit was upon him, gibbering and drooling. He heard the sneering laughter and buried his head in his hands, mortified beyond reprieve. A bitter curse indeed, these fits. As if he did not have enough to contend with!

'Tai,' he heard a voice say then. 'Tai . . .'

It was Colby's hoarse voice. But Tai could not face him.

'Tai! Look at me, lad.'

Tai dragged himself to a sitting position against the gunwale. He ran his hands wearily over his face, the manacle chains clattering with the movement.

'Tai!' Colby insisted.

Tai looked up then, fearing what he would see on Colby's face, but no longer able to resist the other's call.

'All right now, lad?' Colby leaned weakly against the gunwale, his voice a mere croak. There was no questioning the lie Tai had told about having outgrown the fits, none of the pity Tai had feared to see, no trace of disgust on Colby's face, no pulling away. Only genuine, true concern.

Tai felt a warmth come over him and found himself blinking back sudden tears. He did not know what to say.

Colby reached a manacled hand to Tai's shoulder. The effort started him coughing. So weak was he that he nearly toppled on his face with it. 'All's right again now,' he wheezed. ''Tis passed now.' He shifted as close as the chains permitted, wincing involuntarily at the pain the movement caused him, coughing worse now. 'Here, lad . . . *keough keough* . . . lean on me. I'll . . . *keough keough keough* . . . see if we can get some water.'

Tai took a snuffling breath, put out a hand to Colby, weakly, gratefully. He tried to smile. 'Lean on *you*? You're like to collapse on your face any moment!'

Colby smiled back. 'Not yet, lad.' He coughed again, spat. 'Not yet.' Then, 'Hoi!' he called hoarsely, gesturing to the human crew who still stood staring. 'Stop your gawking and give us water here.' At first, none seemed inclined to do so, but Colby insisted, shaking his manacies, raising his voice in a hoarse, croaking shout, coughing and spluttering until a sailor drew the attention of the demons and eventually complied, hauling a bucket and dipper over.

Tai drank in great, gulping draughts from the dipper.

'Easy, lad, easy,' Colby warned. 'Too much and you'll sick it back up again.'

Tai took a last swallow, feeling the wonderful, soothing coolness of it right down in his belly, then passed the dipper to Colby.

The drink soothed Colby's coughing, and he too settled back relievedly. 'Feel better now?'

'I . . . I shall be all right, Uncle. These *cursed* fits . . .'

'Don't fret so, lad. 'Tis over.' Colby lifted the dipper to his lips again, drank with a sigh.

'But what if—'

'Shush now, Tai lad. 'Tis over.'

'But you do not—'

''Tis *over*, I say. Leave it be.'

Tai sighed. 'Aye . . . All right.'

Colby pushed the bucket along to the man chained next him, turned back wearily. They sat in companionable silence, then, leaned tiredly shoulder to shoulder, supporting each other. The water sloshed uneasily in Tai's stomach, but it stayed there. He felt the world solid about him once more, Colby's shoulder a warm brace against his own. Even the throbbing ache in his skull was something to cling to. He let out a long, shuddering breath. He did not wish to think on what he had just experienced. He did not wish to remember. He focused only on the hardness of the deck under his haunches, and on Colby, hearing his foster-uncle's raspy breathing, feeling the comforting little shift and give of bone against his own shoulder as the boat rocked on the heaving water.

It felt strangely like old times, him as a boy, Colby and he sitting like this on a rock in the hills, watching the sun set perhaps, or just sitting quietly together. A pang of homesickness went through Tai then. Gone, all gone; only Colby left.

'Uncle . . .' he began, but did not know how to say what he was feeling.

'Good times, we had,' Colby replied, as if he had been thinking the same as Tai. 'At least we had that, lad. Good times and good memories.'

'Aye,' Tai agreed after a moment. 'Aye. Good times indeed . . .' He clasped Colby's hand and squeezed.

'You've been like a son to me,' Colby said softly. 'The best of sons.'

Tai blinked self-consciously, feeling tears come to his eyes. 'Do you remember the time when . . .'

They began to reminisce then, and for a brief, blessed time the chains and their own hurts and the sickening heave of the boat were as nothing to them.

The cutter docked at a stone quay at the base of the Keep. Tai and Colby were unmanacled along with the other captives and then herded ashore. They shuffled along like cripples, lame and weary. Tai's first steps were an agony of stiff limbs and aching bones; poor Colby could hardly move at all. The solid feel of the ground under his feet steadied Tai's sea-tormented stomach, but the best he could manage was a staggering lurch, half carrying the feebly coughing Colby, his bruised skull throbbing with the effort of each step.

With a sudden, sickening rush, Tai felt the terror reach for him again, felt the world about him begin to dissolve away into chaos once more. 'No,' he hissed, feeling his heart kick in his breast. '*No!*'

He fought it, clinging to Colby beside him, resisting it with every fibre of his spirit, pushing the chaos from him, refusing it, rejecting it. He would *not* allow this thing to take him. Not now. Not here. Colby needed him too much . . .

Like a wave from the shore, it receded from him.

Tai felt a little thrill of victory. He had pushed it back, denied it. He had won that much, small though it might be.

He lifted his head, taking a long breath. The air was filled with the salty tang of seaweed, and he shivered in the chill of it; evening was well advanced now. Over the sound of the breakers, the sea-wind carried with it the crying of the gulls. Away and above, some circled the great stone hound's head but, closer to hand, a mass of them dipped and squabbled over something at the lee of the Keep near the shore. They pulled and picked at it in a struggling, squawking throng. At first the press of the birds was too great for Tai to make out what it was. Some dead thing . . .

Then he saw a torn, flopping form, a queer, limbless, mutilated body. It took a long moment for him to recognize it was a man. No arms, no legs, the gulls tearing at what remained of the torso. Tai looked away quickly, shuddering, and tried to steer Colby off from the sight. He was not quick enough, though. By the stricken set of his wan face, Colby had seen it too.

The demon-faced guards paid no notice at all.

Up a pathway leading to an iron gate set in the wall of the Miradore's stone surround, the weary men were driven. The Keep loomed dark and silent, like some great stone creature hunched before them. Tai felt his heart stutter as they passed through the narrow opening of the gateway. The walls seemed to close tight, and a sudden, claustrophobic terror hit him like a fist. His own fear, this time. He hesitated, staring about him in the desperate, impossible hope of some last instant's escape. But there was only the sheer stone of the walls, the demon-faced, invulnerable guards, and a painful thwack from a pike-butt to move him forwards.

Through the gateway, they entered an open, flagstone courtyard.

The iron gate clanged solidly shut behind. There was nothing for Tai to do save stumble onwards at the guards' prodding, head down, heart hammering, helping Colby onwards as best he might, staring at his own feet as he plodded shakily along over slate-grey flagstones.

They were steered across the courtyard, down a winding flight of stone steps, and through into a low-ceilinged, darksome corridor. The walls were lined with thick wooden doors, each door shut tight by a large wooden bar cradled in iron brackets. With rough speed, the demon-faced guards thrust the men into separate cells.

Colby was wrenched abruptly from his hold, and though Tai struggled, he was flung through one of the doorways so that he landed on his face, sprawled across cold stone. Tai heard the solid *thunk* of the cell door closing behind him, and the thud of the bar as it was rammed into place. Absolute darkness closed in on him. The air was dank and chill, smelling of old corruption and mould. Tai stumbled back to the door, pounded on the unyielding wood, howling, thinking only of poor Colby alone and prostrate in the dark. But it availed him nothing, and after a time he slumped down, collapsing in utter, dispirited exhaustion to the floor.

The next thing that Tai grew aware of – how much later he knew not – was the flickering, painful glare of a torch in his eyes. He blinked groggily, raised his left hand up in a protective gesture against the glare.

Something grabbed the hand.

Several figures moved about him in the confines of the cell, demon faces rendered even more terrible by the torch's uneven light. A voice said something, abrupt and harsh. Tai saw a figure stoop near him. This one was different from the others, taller, shrouded in a long dark cloak, face hidden and shadowed by the cloak's hood so that only an eerie glitter of eyes showed. Tai felt a pair of hands upon him, bony as bird's claws. The hooded face hovered in front of his, the half-hidden eyes staring. Tai shuddered and tried to twist away, but found himself held fast while something penetrated his mind like a quick, cold, groping touch. It *hurt*.

He struggled, trying to push it frantically away, but to no avail.

And then, abruptly, it was gone, and he was left, shuddering.

He heard the voice again, though the words were too low for him to be able to understand.

Something clanked metallically against the stone of the cell floor. Tai first saw the glow, then felt the heat from a small charcoal brazier.

His heart began to thud. What were *they* about?

Tai's left hand was kept in an unbreakable clasp. The creature pulled his arm taut, setting one of its knees against his breast to keep him down. He felt his hand pressed, palm flat, against a large wooden block of some sort. Then, to his horror, he saw a blade shimmer in the torchlight as it was raised for a moment before coming down in a quick, deadly arc.

He screamed and tried to pull away, but the creature gripping him was strong enough to have held a bull immobile. Tai felt a sharp, blinding pain, shooting up from the hand and through his arm like fire. Then came the hiss of a cautery iron, the sudden stench of seared meat, and a great wash of agony that overwhelmed him entirely.

It was pain that brought him back. At first, lying there in the dark, he could not bring himself to feel at what it was *they* had done to him. He feared his left hand and had been taken from off his arm entire.

But the pain told him otherwise.

Gingerly, he reached down with his right hand. The left was intact, all but for the little finger. Nothing of that remained but a cauterized nub.

Tai fell back with a groan. Was this the beginning? Was this the 'sport' the faceless demon in the High Hills had promised? He had a sudden vision of them coming back, time and again, till all the fingers from both his hands were gone. And after that, what?

He did not think he could endure it.

He lay there, shuddering in the dank cold, sick with pain. His throat was raw, his tongue so parched it felt like a piece of shoe leather in his mouth. He cradled the injured hand against him, rocking in misery while the pain of it came and went in jagged surges.

His mind dimmed, cleared, dimmed again. Time passed, though he was hardly aware. And then, through the haze of pain, he heard the cell door open once more.

Terror flashed through him. It was too much. He could not bear it again. He scrabbled backwards until his shoulders fetched up jarringly against cold stone. But there was nothing he could do, no place he could hide. With horror, he watched as two figures entered the cell. A torch was lifted, as before. He saw the inhumanly huge yellow eyes in the demon faces gaze at him. One of the creatures gestured.

Tai flinched back against the wall.

'Come, little man,' it said. When Tai would not, it strode forwards and dragged him bodily from out of his corner.

Tai tried to gather himself up, but his limbs quivered so he could hardly rise. A hard hand cuffed him once, twice. 'Up. Up!'

Shaking, Tai tried to stand. The creature struck him again, harder this time, and his bruised skull exploded into darkness.

\*

The next thing Tai grew aware of was light. He blinked, tried to rub his eyes, and found that he could not. In a sudden panic, he tried to turn, to rise, to do something, anything . . .

But could not.

He was held immobile, upright, limbs stretched tight and chained fast to some kind of iron framework. A wad of cloth had been stuffed painfully into his mouth and bound there, gagging him. His heart beating in panic, Tai arched his back, inadvertently thumping his head against the unyielding frame. His skull rang with pain. He tried his hands, but succeeded only in rasping the nub of the amputated finger against something, hard enough to make him choke.

When he could focus properly again, Tai stared shakily about. He was in a large room, the air warm and close. Curls of strangely pungent smoke hung in the air. Long candles flickered and danced in brass holders. In a massive open fireplce on the right-hand wall, flame cracked softly. The other three walls were hung with woven tapestries. Tai took one glimpse of the images depicted, and it was enough – they were intricately stitched scenes of men and *un*-men; strange creatures part human and part animal; bladed weapons raised; impossibly scarlet blood; twisted, agonized faces. In the wavering light they seemed almost alive. Tai looked away with a shudder.

Sound caught his attention. At the far end of the room, a human harper perched on a stool, plucking at a six-stringed lap-harp, chanting. On a large, ornately worked divan, a lone man in a dark satin robe reclined. He had long black hair and a wide-boned, clean-shaven face. One of his hands rested on a glimmering object in his lap: it was slightly larger than a man's head, but featureless; an asymmetrical globe, like a queer kind of helmet, perhaps. The man's eyes were shut and his head partially tilted back, supported by his other hand, as he listened to the chanting of the harper.

Tai stared. He did not understood this at all. What was such a man doing here in the heart of *their* holding?

The man remained where he was, unmoving, eyes closed, listening while the harper chanted on, plucking an accompaniment on the harp that was more rhythmical than melodic:

> '. . . And the battle did rage and shudder and shake
> With the man-tearing spears they held in their hands.
> Their eyes they were blind in the blood-dazzled brightness
> That glittered on helms and bright-burnished swordblades
> And shone forth from shields as men came together
> And died in the trampling press.

'As when in the mountains the winds wail and bluster
And snow lies deepest on the fast frozen ground,
When snow flies in clouds, in constant confusion,
Like this was the battle, so bitter and furious,
As men sought to slaughter and vanquish each other
Or die on the blood-sodden ground.

'And there arrived Great Heart, the bold one, the brave one,
A youth newly come to the rumour of war,
He did not flee from the furious fighting
But threw swift his spear, of iron and ash made,
And laid low a foeman with sudden quick spearcast
Who fell in the trampling press.

'The spear it struck true in the throat of his foeman,
The swift speeding iron drove sheer through the bone.
And as when an oak tree, so tall and so towering,
Is blown by the storm-wind and shudders and tumbles,
So down fell his foeman, the spear sliding through him,
To die on the blood-sodden ground . . .'

'Enough!' a voice called. 'We will hear the rest later, Harper. Leave us now.'

Without a word, the harper bowed and hastily withdrew.

Gazing toward Tai, the man on the divan made a beckoning gesture. 'Bring him closer.'

'Yes, Lord Veil,' a voice said from beside Tai, and the frame to which he was chained trundled forward with a creaking of wheels. Startled, Tai twisted round and saw two demon-faced guards, hands to the struts of the framework, pushing.

The fingers of the man on the divan drummed hollowly on the globe-thing in his lap as he regarded Tai. His eyes were slate-grey and cold as ice. After a little, he reached a silvered goblet from a table next to the divan and sipped from it. 'Bring him closer yet. We wish a better look at him.'

Obediently, the demon guards pushed the frame closer.

Tai did not know what to make of this. A *man* giving orders to *them*? What could it mean?

'So . . .' The man on the divan gazed at Tai as if he were some specimen or other, about to be picked apart, bit by slow bit.

Tai shivered under that cold stare, feeling the nub of his finger throb with agony at each frightened beat of his heart and desperately dreading what might be to come.

Long moments went by. In the room's silence, Tai heard his own pulse throbbing in his ears. He heard the snappling of the fire and, beyond that, a strange, soft peeping sound he had not noticed before. His glance flickered uncertainly from the man before him to the back corner of the room whence the sound came. A dark velvet drapery hung there.

Seeing Tai's gaze, the man on the divan smiled thinly. He reached to a tasselled chord that dangled near the divan. Slowly, as if pulling back a curtain on a stage, he tugged on the chord and the drapery was drawn aside.

A large gilt-work construction hung behind, a complex thing of bars and curves and gleaming ornamentation. A chorus of loud peeping greeted the removal of the drapery, and the occupants burst into sudden movement. At first, all Tai saw within was a confusing multitude of small, moving bodies. Then he realized they were birds, shuffling and preening and shooting about within the gilt bars. They were about the size of starlings, perhaps, but of a brilliant orange and blue plumage that scintillated in the room's candlelight; they were unlike any birds Tai had ever seen, and there seemed something *strange* about them.

'Our aviary,' the man on the divan said, sipping from the silvered goblet he stil held in one hand. 'A *special* collection.' He beckoned the demon-guards to push Tai nearer. 'Look closely.'

Tai stared at the gleaming shapes as they flitted about. One of them settled, clutching the gilt bars with small bird-feet, staring back at him. Tai gasped.

The head of the 'bird' looking at him was beakless, and impossibly, unmistakeably human. And the rest, he realized, were the same. Wings and backs were blue, breasts and faces a glowing orange; from out of the smooth orange plumage of each bird-face, small human eyes stared.

Tai shuddered, stretched though he was on the iron frame. How could such an unnatural thing be possible?

From the divan, the man smiled.

Then, through the double doors behind, somebody padded into the room, a tall figure, shrouded in a long dark cloak, the hood of which hid his face.

The man on the divan flipped the chord, closing the drapery once again over the 'aviary'. He acknowledged the newcomer with a curt nod, then gestured to Tai with the goblet. 'This is the one you spoke to us of, Seer?'

98

'Yes.'

Stepping close to Tai, the man – for he was no demon – flung back the the hood of his cloak. His face appeared disconcertingly skull-like, parchment skin stretched tight over bone, entirely devoid of hair, and his eyes were like twin, glittering black marbles. 'He is such a one as I could have . . . use for.'

It was the eyes that Tai recognized, the same glittering dark eyes of he who had *penetrated* Tai somehow in the cell. He shuddered, remembering the vile feeling of it. The very presence of the man made Tai's belly quiver.

The cloaked Seer waved the demon guards off and put a bony hand possessively on Tai's shoulder. 'He would be wasted in the Pit. There are others . . .'

'So have you said,' returned the man on the divan. 'But this one is young. And it looks as though there might be a certain resilience to him. He seems the best of the lot, and shall provide us with better sport, perhaps, than the others he arrived with.'

Tai understood nothing of this, least of all why two of *them* stood calmly by while these men discussed what would be done with him. But he knew nothing here boded him any good. He shivered under the skull-faced Seer's bony clutch, would have flinched away but for the frame which held him fast. And the other's mention of 'sport' made his heart clench up in dread. He felt like the rabbit in the old tale, caught between fox and falcon.

'I tell you again,' the Seer said, 'he would be wasted in the Pit.'

'Perhaps,' came the reply. 'But we shall put him to the test nonetheless. It has been too long since last we had new blood amongst the Pit folk. We begin to grow bored.'

Tai felt the hold on his shoulder tighten. 'This is such a one as—'

'Enough! You have heard, Seer. Would you gainsay us?'

The other stood for a moment, his hard black eyes glinting in the room's candlelight. Then he bowed his head in stiff acquiescence. 'No.'

'No, what?'

'No . . . Lord.' The hand on Tai's shoulder gripped with painful force for a moment, then released him, reluctantly.

The man in the robe eased up from the divan, put down the goblet and the queer, featureless globe-thing that had rested on his lap, and strode over. 'He is *ours*, Seer.' From out of his sleeve he suddenly produced a needle-bladed stiletto. 'To do with as we wish.'

Tai shivered, staring helplessly at the blue-gold sheen of the narrow blade.

The man slotted the stiletto's point under Tai's chin. 'An easy thing,

Seer, to kill a man. This man. Any man.' He forced Tai's head back, the sharp point biting into his skin, until the back of his skull was pressed painfully against the iron of the frame. 'Perhaps he is not so necessary for the Pit after all. Perhaps we shall just eliminate him here and now.'

Tancred stood silent, his skull-like face blank of any readable human feeling.

'What do you say, Seer?'

Tancred made a slight, stiff bow. 'As you have said, Lord Veil, he is yours. To do with as you wish.'

The other nodded. 'Exactly so.' Withdrawing the stiletto, he reached to Tai's chained left hand and purposefully ground the cauterized stub of the amputated finger against the iron of the frame.

Tai groaned around the gag, his eyes watering.

The cold, slate-grey eyes stared, unblinking as a snake's. Then the man turned and walked back to the divan, sliding the stiletto back into his sleeve. Reclining, he sipped at the goblet again, smiling coldly at the Seer. 'The necessary preparations *have* been put into effect?'

'Yes . . . Lord.'

'See to it, then.' He gestured with the goblet. 'Begin.'

The Seer turned to Tai, eyes hard as glass, his expression still unreadable. He produced what seemed to be a small bronze bird's claw from out his robe, a wicked-looking little thing with needle-pointed talons, each needle tip darkly stained. Gripping this in one hand, he yanked Tai's head back to expose his throat.

Tai tried desperately to jerk away, but the frame held him fast. He felt the bite of the metal talons along his throat, felt the warmth of blood running. The Seer chanted low in his throat, harsh monosyllables, over and over in a mesmerizing cadence. Tai tried to cry out, but the gag choked him. He struggled and writhed against the chains but it was no use. The thought of poor Colby flashed through his mind, left entirely friendless now, while he died here in this terrible place, throat torn out for the pleasure of this cruel foreign Lord.

But it was not death the Seer brought to him.

A sort of frigid numbness was spreading from Tai's neck now. He felt it go across his face, like a freezing tide. Down his torso. Along the back of his skull. His limbs tingled uncomfortably. His breath, rasping in and out, seemed to echo monstrously. He had one last, clear moment of helpless panic, and then felt as if he were falling, drifting downwards like a brittle autumn leaf, tumbling through slow air . . .

Tai blinked. His eyelids felt scratchy, and a dull, painful ache beat at the back of his eyeballs. He blinked again, looking blearily about, and found that he lay in a sort of clearing, rimmed by high, rustling plants.

No room. No chains or iron frame. No cold-eyed Lord or Seer.

The plants about him were tall as any oak, but they were not ordinary trees. Fleshy purple stems drooped down from the main trunks; from these solid and waxy leaves dangled, wide as his outstretched arms, and as long – some of them – as he was tall.

Rising shakily to his feet, Tai stared. This was like no place he had ever seen.

The light was a queer, diffused radiance, leaving no clear shadows. The sky overhead seemed a solid bank of formless cloud, a mother-of-pearl ceiling that somehow obscured the sun, yet at the same time glowed with light. Apart from the whispering rustle of the plants, everything was dead silent. No sound of the sea in the distance. No wind. No sea-birds calling. Nothing.

For long, frightened moments, Tai stood unmoving. He could not understand where he was or what this place might be. One step back he stumbled, two, and then halted. His whole body felt wooden and disjointed, his joints creaking and crackling as he moved. And the motion made him sick and dizzy.

What *was* this place? What had they *done* to him?

Unthinking, he sketched a warding sign. In mid-motion, though, he stopped, astounded. His hand! All the fingers were intact on his left hand. And, he realized, his skull did not hurt at all.

What could it mean?

Tai stood there in shock, flexing the now whole hand before him. He felt odd: shivery and stiff and sickly. His limbs behaved in this strange wooden manner. Yet was he whole again. Impossibly whole. How could such things be? He did not understand . . .

The huge-leafed plants about him whispered softly. They were festooned with a network of creeping vines, Tai now saw, which hung down, heavy with white flowers.

Across the clearing a sudden rustling sounded.

Tai froze.

Something came into sight amongst the web of creepers. Like a bony-limbed, wingless bat it seemed: big-eared, furred, moving along the vines with the easy agility of a squirrel. Tai stared, his heart suddenly beating hard. The creature was the size of a large child, with a pointed, bat-like face, and huge dark eyes that glistened brightly.

Moving along the vines, gripping with both feet and hands, it muttered softly to itself in a high-pitched, squeaking voice. It reached a deft hand into one of the white flowers, then sucked the sticky residue from its knobbly fingers with a long pink tongue.

Partway through the second flower, it suddenly froze and went silent, head cocked as if listening. It glanced about nervously and saw Tai, standing motionless, for the first time. Hanging upside down on a vine, it stared at him, dark eyes very wide. Then, with an agile flip, it disappeared into the foliage.

Tai shook his head, ran a hand over his tired eyes. He could hear nothing, see no sign of anything that might have startled the queer creature.

He did not know what to think.

Though he still felt clumsily wooden of limb, the sick dizziness that had accompanied his first movements seemed to be going. He took an experimental step, another, found that walking was easier now.

A shaking in the branches above his head made him whirl awkwardly. He could see nothing, but the sense that unseen eyes were watching made him fidget uneasily. Suddenly, he wanted out of here, away from this enclosure of huge-leafed, inexplicable plants and their queer inhabitants.

He had to worm a way through, the leaves waxy under his hands, slippery, and warm. He did not like the feel of them one bit. The whole place made the small hairs along the base of his scalp quiver. He managed to push through without mishap, though, working uphill, and came out into the open.

He found himself upon a height. The land about was rocky and bare, with outcroppings of coarse grey stone – like the one upon which he perched – interspersed with tangles of strange greenery. Below Tai stretched a long, rocky slope, at the bottom of which lay the sea. But it was a weirdly calm, flat sea, silvery under the reflected light of the massed clouds overhead. And those clouds seemed, somehow, to encase the horizon so that landscape and seascape, as Tai saw them, appeared as if covered by an enormous, inverted cloud-bowl. The dead silence of everything about remained unbroken. A cold shudder went through him.

Where were the gulls? The rocky hound's head?

Where the Keep?

Tai swallowed uneasily. He did not know what to make of any of this.

In the distance, a sudden clamour broke out, the noise jarring in the still air. It was like the far-off crying of hounds, coming from beyond the greenery at his back, yet no true hound ever made sound like that. Tai glanced about nervously, but could see nothing beyond the green tangle through which he had come.

It seemed to him, though, that the sound was drawing closer.

He started off down the slope ahead. Much of it was loose rock with little vegetation, and he skidded clumsily down on his heels, his legs awkward still. Halfway down he stumbled, fetching up jarringly on hands and knees. Panting, he pulled himself to his feet and glanced back.

On the ledge upon which he had been standing, he saw the pack: dark, bony creatures, hairless and thin as spiders. At sight of him, they set up a wild howling.

Tai shivered. They had yellow fangs, and dripping pink tongues, and their eyes . . . Their eyes were human as his own.

With a cry, they came bounding down after him.

Tai turned and fled, his heart pounding, running blind and rabbit-scared. It was like a dream, almost, his legs clumsy and stiff, the hounds drawing closer and closer, he panting and wheezing, struggling, unable to increase his speed no matter how hard he tried.

The slope in front of Tai levelled to a gradual, sideways curve and then suddenly dropped off. The crest of it caught him completely unawares. One moment he was running. The next he was tumbling head over heels through coarse grass and gravelly sand.

He fetched up at the bottom, winded, his ribs aching painfully, his mouth and eyes filled with sand. Struggling to his feet, he looked up and saw the dark form of the first hound appear over the crest of the slope above. The creature hesitated, spotted Tai below, and began to plough a way down towards him, firmer on its four legs than Tai had been on his two. The rest of the pack, in full cry, came scrambling behind.

About a fifty paces ahead, Tai saw a rise of jagged, weather-splintered rock. He stumbled towards it, desperately pumping his unresponsive legs.

The rock rise stood about fifteen paces tall, very nearly sheer, but full of splits and cracks. Tai hauled himself up the splintered face of it, clutching frantically for handholds, his heart pounding with exertion and terror. The howling of the pack, loud and wild and very close behind, sent uncontrollable shivers through him. He could hear the scrabble of claws on rock below him. Something slammed against his left foot. He felt a stab of pain, kicked out, and the something fell away noisily beneath him.

Panting, Tai made it to the top of the rise and collapsed there.

The hounds milled about below, faces tilted up at him, mouths open, showing teeth and tongue as they snarled and bayed. Huge beasts, they were, larger than any hounds he had ever seen, but hairless, spidery thin of limb, and all sinew and bone, knobbly spines, and ribs showing starkly against grainy dark, sweat-sheened skin. And their faces:

yellow-fanged hound's faces, yes, but only just. And the eyes were men's eyes, glaring up at him with malevolent purpose.

And from his vantage point now, Tai saw that they moved not like true hounds. They were as like to walk on their hind legs, in a sort of skittering prance, as move on all fours. His stomach twisted up at the sight.

As he lay there taking great heaving breaths, Tai saw one of them leap and scrabble up the splintered face of the rock. Its paws had nubs, like stubby fingers, and it gripped the stone with these as best it could. It got very nearly halfway up before slipping and falling back down again. Another tried, and yet another.

Beneath one of his hands, Tai felt a crumble of loose rock. He dragged himself to his knees and pitched the hand-sized piece of stone at the nearest climbing animal. The stone missed, bouncing away off an outcrop that jutted out from the face of the rise, but continued downwards to thump into the ribs of one of the pack milling about on the ground beneath. The animal let out a startled yelp and skipped away. Tai cast about hysterically for every loose piece of rock he could find within reaching distance, frantically pelting the pack below. After a few moments of noisy, yelping confusion, they retreated out of throwing range.

Tai toppled over backwards from the kneeling position in which he had been throwing. He lay there on the rough stone, staring up at the mother-of-pearl sky, his lungs heaving. His mouth was dry and raw, his tongue swollen, and he could hardly swallow. His shoulder and ribs had begun to ache fiercely from the tumble down the slope he had taken; his heel, where the hound had bitten him, throbbed.

He heard noises coming from the pack below. Struggling over, he propped himself on his elbows and peered down. The beasts barked and yammered at each other. Words it was not, but, with a shiver, Tai realized they were somehow talking amongst themselves. Spidery limbs moved and gesticulated. Then the pack bounded away, moving parallel to the rocky rise on which he lay, working their way along its base. What were they doing?

Tai peered over the edge. In the direction the hounds were following he could see that the ground rose in a long, transverse, gradual slope. The rocky rise itself continued straight back from where he was, until the top of it was no more than a few paces above the level of the ragged grass that covered the rising slope. Once they had scrambled over the edge, it would be only a short while indeed before the pack could come upon him along the surface of the rise on which he now lay.

Tai pushed himself awkwardly to his feet. His injured heel left a bleeding trail behind him. He tried to run, limping along the uneven, littered surface of the rise, but after only a few steps he stumbled and fell heavily, smashing his right elbow against an out-thrust shard of rock, so hard that his whole arm was numbed. The pack was baying again now. He stood up, shakily, rubbing at his injured arm, and looked ahead. Running would not help him, he realized despairingly after a moment. A hundred paces or so ahead, the rise ended in a high, overhung cliff-face. He was on a kind of spine of rock, he now saw, about ten paces across, that ran out from the base of the cliff at a sloping angle until it eventually reached the same level as the ground a considerable way behind him. He turned and saw the first of the hounds scramble into sight in the distance and begin to lope towards him.

He was standing near the edge, along the side of the rise up which he had first clambered. He flexed his hurt arm, thinking to climb back down again. By the time the hounds arrived up here he would be below, and they would not be able to climb down after him. But two members of the pack had remained behind. Their heads came up eagerly when he drew near the edge of the drop.

No escape that way.

The rest of the pack was on the top of the rise now, coming fast, no more than a couple of hundred paces from him.

Tai looked around despairingly. There were pieces of rock aplenty littered about, but throwing stones was simply not enough of a defence. And it was his right arm, his throwing arm, that was hurt. He dithered about in panicky rushes, first one way and then another, tripping, stumbling, getting nowhere.

The hounds were very close now. Tai found himself teetering on the opposite edge of the rise. He glanced down and saw that there was much more of a drop on this side, twenty paces at least. On this side, however, instead of grassy sand below, there was a large pool of dark water, ringed by reeds and sedge along the further shores, but abutting right up against the base of the cliff below him. As he looked down, he could see the water ripple and surge near the weedy shore as some large creature moved just beneath the surface.

Tai turned and took one quick glance, saw the pack almost upon him, and leaped.

The water was cold and dark as it closed over him, but mercifully deep and free of rocks. He threshed his way clumsily back up to the surface, his hurt right arm of little use, and tried to flounder as best he could for the further shore. Behind and above him, he could hear the hounds whining and panting. He turned awkwardly in the water and looked up. The pack was bunched above, staring hungrily down at him. As he watched, a sudden ruckus broke out, two of the beasts snapping and snarling at another. They rolled about and, in the process, thumped into one of the pack perched right at the very edge, attention locked on Tai. The beast let out a startled yelp, scrambled desperately at the edge for a second, then tumbled down to land splashing in the water.

It rose to the surface, growling and shaking its huge head. Then it saw Tai, and the uncannily human eyes lit with fury. No more than twenty paces or so away in the water from him, it now began to churn purposefully in his direction. Above, the rest of the pack looked on, in silence now.

For a long moment, Tai could only stare at the beast coming towards him, too shaken to move. Belatedly, he tried to turn and swim away, but foundered helplessly, swallowing water instead of air. Coughing and spluttering, it was all he could do to keep his head up and breathe. The hound drew closer, swimming strongly, only the great head showing above the dark surface of the water.

Tai sagged. His ribs hurt. His heel felt sore and torn. His right arm dangled uselessly, sending flashes of pain up into his shoulder now. His limbs still had that strange, wooden climsiness to them. He felt utterly exhausted . . .

The hound was near enough now that Tai could see the mottled pink of its gums above the yellow fangs as it snarled at him. He made one last, desperate rush to push himself away from it, but succeeded only in sinking himself, gasping and struggling, beneath the surface of the water.

Below him, Tai felt a body move through the water. A furred limb brushed across his calf. Tai thrashed upwards, trying desperately to escape this new menace, only to find himself face to face with the hound, so close that he could smell the beast's damp, odorous breath.

Tai's sudden surfacing just in front of it brought the hound to a momentary, startled halt. Then, snarling, it lunged for his throat. Tai tried to fend it off clumsily and felt himself going under once again. The water seemed to close over him like a solid thing. Struggling with the last shreds of his strength, he came up, half dazed and barely conscious.

The hound was nowhere to be seen.

Water roiled and splashed off to his left, as if some large body were thrashing about beneath the surface. Tai lay in the water, keeping afloat as best he could, too exhausted to do anything else for the moment. Across from him, the water went still, then boiled up once again. He caught a glimpse of shapes moving under the surface, and then they were gone once more, sinking down into the depths.

Tai floundered away towards the reed-rimmed shoreline, thrashing clumsily until he felt the bottom with his feet. Gasping, he stood and stared back.

At first he could see nothing at all, dark water. Then, in a slow heave, the hound reappeared. It rolled up and over, water runnelling off it, coming to rest eventually with only its narrow, knobbly-spined, naked back showing, head and limbs sunk beneath the surface.

Another form surged up from the depths of the water near the hound's side. A sleek, furred thing surfaced, taking in a noisy lungful of air. Man-sized it was, and man-shaped in arms, head, body. But no man. Great dark eyes, a snub of a nose, ears slicked back against the wet skull, short, sharp teeth showing through the purple-dark line of the lips, furred hands with obvious webbing between the outstretched fingers.

It stared appraisingly at him, then submerged once more, sinking into the dark water with hardly a ripple.

Tai backed away as fast as might be, trying to make the shore. But he felt strong hands clutch at him from underwater before he was more than halfway there. He thrashed away from that grip, kicking out, and scrambled shorewards.

Ankle deep in mud, he gripped a handful of reeds and began to tug himself clear. But the same strong hands took him from behind, dragging him back into the water. A kind of hysterical strength filled Tai for an instant, and he kicked out blindly, feeling his foot connect solidly with bone.

The hands slipped off him, and he scrambled away into the reeds where he collapsed exhaustedly on to his knees, his injured arm across his chest, gasping for breath.

He felt altogether numbed and undone. It seemed like a dream, this, some mad dream . . .

He heard the crying of the hounds then, saw their dark shapes come loping along the reedy shoreline.

Tai floundered desperately to his feet, but he tripped in the reeds and fell with a splash into shallow water. Spluttering and gagging, his mouth full of slimy mud, he tried to lever himself up to his knees. There was a skittering splash from the reeds behind him, and out came the tumbling, dark forms of the hounds. A growling, solid weight landed on his legs. He struck out desperately, felt his fist glance against something. Water sprayed and burst about him. Something gripped him from the deeper water, tugging hard at his arm.

Then his leg was clamped tight, the hound's jaws closing on his calf like a saw-edged vice. He screamed, threshing the water into foam. The thing in the water pulled him one way, the hound the other. Tai felt the muscles of his calf tear as the hound's teeth slipped a little. More heavy bodies tumbled upon him and the water-thing gave up its hold.

Struggling helplessly, Tai was dragged shoreward. He felt a sharp pain in his shoulder as one of the pack wrenched him suddenly across a clump of reeds. Another tore a chunk from his thigh. Something chewed agonizingly into his belly, ripping away skin and flesh. He was jerked and shaken this way and that as they worried at him.

The beast still at his shoulder let go and, in an instant, had sunk its teeth in Tai's throat. Hysterically, he tried to fend it off.

But he was too spent, his right arm all but useless, and he could not prise away those jaws. Horrified, he felt his throat come away suddenly in the hound's jaws. For one terrible moment, Tai saw his own flesh hanging in bloody ribbons from the beast's muzzle. Then he was overwhelmed by a flood of pain and wet, choking blood, and he collapsed backwards into the reeds, riven by the swarming pack.

PART TWO

# BEGINNINGS

# XII

# The Palisade

'It is not,' Sub-Commander Gerrid insisted, 'necessary to do this.'

Commander Chayne smiled coldly. 'Your opinion on this matter, *Sub*-Commander, is not required.'

Gerrid took a breath, let it out, trying to keep rein on his temper. It was grey-dark pre-dawn, starless and chill. In the smoky torchlight, the guard squad the Commander had ordered out stood near the wall, waiting, silent spectators to the dispute that had arisen suddenly here. Gerrid felt the helm-vigour course through him, a goad to action.

'Commander, *look* at him!' Gerrid stabbed a finger at the young man who lay twitching in the mud between them. 'He is hardly more than a boy. It takes time to learn the use of the helm properly. You know that as well as I! This one will make a good enough man-at-arms. Only give him *time.*'

The boy moaned, sprawled where he lay in the mud. His eyes stared wide and unseeing, glittering like blank stones in the uncertain torchlight, and his limbs quivered. As Gerrid watched, the quivering escalated into another spasm.

Commander Chayne gestured disdainfully to the common, demon-faced helm that lay in the mud near his black-booted foot. 'Gone by forfeiture.'

'No!' Gerrid responded. 'It is *not* necessary to do this!'

Which only brought him back full circle once more, uselessly.

The Commander looked at Gerrid in silence, a cold, assessing stare. Gone was Chayne's officer's field-dress. Instead, he clothed himself now all in dramatic black and flashing silver: a costly new black cloak, an ornate belt that glistened like silver fish-scales, metal-studded, black leather gauntlets. Chayne cradled his own spell-helm in his hands, the bone and silver, beaked falcon's visage of it glowing softly in the torchlight against the dark, oiled leather of his gauntlets. In that torchlight, his scalp shone whitely where it had been partially shaved, the rest of his black hair roached into the intricate topknot favoured by the younger men of noble rank.

Gerrid removed his own helm. It was not done to keep it on in the presence of an un-helmed superior officer, and he had already pushed things almost to the point of outright insolence.

Helm off, he returned Commander Chayne's cold-eyed appraisal, refusing to flinch in the least bit. Chayne was taller than he, thinner boned, with a studied grace of movement Gerrid lacked. Chayne was nobility, from a family that traced its records back five generations. But he was a second son, and Gerrid knew that type all too well; the Lords Veil's officer corps was full of them, proud and preening as thoroughbred fighting cocks, ambitious, with small means but vaulting expectations.

The man's arrogance made Gerrid's teeth ache.

Not the best way to start a morning, this. After a long two days spent shepherding brainless, stumbling villagers, Gerrid was irritable. And now, un-helmed, he felt a wash of weariness and hunger go through him.

But this extremeness of Chayne's could not be allowed to go unchallenged.

'Commander,' he tried again, striving to put all the reasonableness possible into his voice, 'if you will only listen to me for a moment . . .'

'Enough!' Chayne snapped. 'I will have no more insolence from—'

'Is there a problem here, Commander?' a voice said suddenly. Tancred the Seer it was, come quietly from around the corner building.

'No problem, Lord Seer,' Chayne responded quickly. He made a formal bow of obeisance. 'I . . . I thought you had left already, Sire.'

'Not yet, as you can see. What is happening here?'

'This man-at-arms – ' Chayne pointed with a boot at the helmless boy sprawled in the mud – 'has mis-worn his helm. See the spasms?' In the flickering torchlight, the boy's limbs jerked spastically.

The Seer nodded, a mere half-guess movement under the shadow of his hood. 'And so?'

'I was about to administer sentence when my Sub-Commander tried to intervene.'

Tancred padded across the muddy enclosure to stand before Chayne, slipping back his hood as he did so to reveal his hairless, skull-like face and black, staring eyes. 'And do you usually brook such quibbling from a Sub-Commander?'

Chayne paled, bowing once again. 'I have the situation in hand, Lord Seer.'

Tancred looked about him, but said nothing. He turned to Gerrid. 'What of you, Sub-Commander?'

Gerrid swallowed. Ordinarily, he stayed as far from the Seer as possible. The man could curdle milk with a look. But there was no hope of avoiding him now. He bowed, as was required, but made it as shallow a bow as he dared. 'I was making my pre-dawn rounds, Lord Seer,' he began, feeling a shiver along his spine as Tancred's black gaze centred upon him. 'Hearing a commotion, I came here and found the Commander and this squad . . . and this poor fellow.'

'And?' the Seer prompted.

'This is an execution squad.'

'So?'

'You don't *execute* a man for wearing a helm improperly! Start doing that, and half our new recruits will end up dead and gone within the first month. It takes time to learn the proper way to—'

The Seer held up a bony white hand, silencing Gerrid. 'The Commander is perfectly within his rights. Discipline must be maintained.'

Gerrid stared. He stepped forward, a hot reply on his lips, but then stopped himself. He swallowed his anger and kept his face carefully blank. The Lords Veil would want to know of this. Though he had little liking for the dishonourable role of spy that had been thrust upon him, the situation here made him uncomfortably aware that perhaps such a one was necessary. Seeing Chayne with Tancred, Gerrid seriously doubted the man's continuing loyalty to the Lords Veil. With a patron as powerful as the Seer, who knew what secret ambitions Chayne might now be harbouring?

'Be careful, Sub-Commander,' Tancred warned.

Gerrid shivered involuntarily, feeling Tancred's black gaze upon him. Could the man know what he was thinking? He remembered the painful scrutiny Tancred had performed upon him in the Lords Veil's Command Pavilion.

But the Seer came no nearer, merely stared at him. 'If I were Commander Chayne, I might find your quibbling attitude . . . inconvenient, Sub-Commander. I might even find it a source of embarrassment before my superior. If I were Commander Chayne, I might find myself having to do something to teach you proper respect and demonstrate that I was a Commander fit for my position . . .'

Tancred smiled thinly and turned to Chayne. 'I leave now, Commander. Dawn will be here soon.'

'Lord Seer,' Chayne returned, bowing carefully. There was a cold glimmer in his eyes, and his face had gone pale and intent.

Tancred made no move to leave. Instead, he stood calmly where he was, arms folded across his chest. 'I would see how you do this, Commander.'

Gerrid saw Chayne swallow. He felt a little flare of vindictive joy at the other's discomfort.

Chayne beckoned forward the guard squad he had brought with him here. They moved up silently, expectantly, demon faces glittering in the torchlight.

'Take him to the wall.'

Two of the squad dragged the boy through the mud and braced him against the log wall.

The Commander waved them back.

'Sub-Commander Gerrid,' he said then, but though he spoke to Gerrid, his eyes never left the Seer's face, 'would you like that I put the life of this man in your hands?'

Gerrid blinked, startled. 'Yes, Commander, certainly.'

'Good. Then you will accept full responsibility for his fate?'

'Yes, Commander.' Gerrid looked at Chayne, who still kept his gaze locked on the Seer, then at the boy huddled against the Palisade wall, and finally back to Chayne again. 'Commander, I would—'

'Kill him,' Chayne said then.

Gerrid stared.

Chayne took his gaze from the Seer and looked at Gerrid. 'You have accepted the responsibility. Would you now disobey a direct order?'

Gerrid looked at the youngster, sudden anger nearly choking him. Already, the worst of the spasms were over, and the boy was beginning to come round. Gerrid had seen it before. For some, the helms were too much temptation. Some never put them off, revelling in the helm-feeling until it killed them. But this boy was not one of those. He would come round. Would have come round . . .

The boy lifted his head groggily and looked about him, only half aware, as yet, of where he was.

Gerrid donned his own helm. Best to do the thing quickly, before the boy knew properly what was to happen. Feeling the surge of helm-vigour light him, Gerrid drew his sword. He strode over and in one quick, flashing motion, brought the blade down upon the boy's exposed neck, severing the tousled head.

The mud blackened with blood, the poor head wobbled, face up, eyes staring, forever sightless now.

The Seer nodded approvingly. 'Nicely arranged, Commander. You justify my confidence in you.'

Commander Chayne smiled. 'My thanks, Sire.' He turned to Gerrid, pointing to the boy's spell-helm.

That was next. The helm would stay alive – with such strange life as it knew – for some weeks after the boy's death, dwindling slowly. Man and helm were wedded, the helm feeding off the man, the man gaining helm-vigour in return. There were rumours that a person of special power might reinvigorate the helm of a dead man, but they were just rumours, wild camp talk. Though it would take time, the helm in the mud before Gerrid was as doomed as the boy who had worn it. Best shatter it quickly.

Using the solid hilt of his sword, Gerrid smashed down on the helm's crest. It was a tough thing and resisted the first blows. Finally, though, it began to break, the bone and bronze frame splintering across the middle. Out of the splinters, something white and gelid slithered, like a thin, boneless, eight-fingered hand. Gerrid brought the heel of his boot down, grinding helm and all into the mud. He had little liking for being reminded of what lived inside the helms.

'And now,' Tancred said, 'I leave you, Commander. The camp is in your capable hands.' With that, he glided away past the nearby building and was gone.

Gerrid stood, panting, staring down at what he had done.

Chayne said nothing at all, merely smiled thinly and walked away, gesturing the guard squad after. They followed, dragging the dead boy with them, leaving Gerrid alone in the blood-soaked mud and flickering torchlight.

Gerrid tried to smother the anger that burned in him. He felt the solid heft of the sword still in his hand and imagined what the feel of it would be as it ripped through Chayne's guts. But that was the helm speaking through him as much as anything, and this was not a situation in which the helm should have sway. Hands shaking with repressed fury, he carefully wiped the sword clean and sheathed it, then spun on his heel and stalked off through the mud.

In the east, the first faint glimmer of dawn was showing. In the twilight of the Palisade's enclosure before him, he could see Chayne and the guard squad forcing a way through the listless mass of camp inmates, using pike-butts and boots on those who were too slow to move. The sight sickened Gerrid. He hated this foul place where he must play shepherd to stupid villagers, desk-bound orderly to an untrustworthy Commander, spy, anything but the warrior.

The sight of Chayne lording his way through the camp so provoked him that Gerrid had to stop and remove his helm lest it tempt him into actions he would later regret. He stood there, panting, trying to let the chill morning air clear his mind.

Chayne and the guards disappeared round the corner of the Palisade's main building – Tancred's building, a solid log structure. Gerrid had no inkling of what the Seer did inside that building. He did not wish to know; merely thinking on it brought an uncomfortable shiver to his spine.

He turned then and strode away towards where his own quarters lay, outside the log walls. He must send word by messenger to the Lords Veil, and that quickly. As he walked, he tried to phrase what he might write, but the anger still quivered in him.

Power, that was what fuelled Chayne's moves. Power and more power. There was no honour to the man. He would as soon stab one in the back as not, so long as it profited him. And now that he was under Tancred's wing, he was trebly dangerous.

And the Seer? Gerrid did not know. Tancred was not like other men. He had his own dark ways, his own dark knowledge. But power he had – this whole dismal camp was his to order – and power must be at the heart of his thinking too. It was said in the camp that nobody had ever gainsaid the Seer and lived to tell of it.

Except the Lords Veil, of course, whose power none could resist.

But they were far from here at the moment, and he was left to cope as best he might alone.

'A curse on all of it,' Gerrid muttered, wishing he were out of here and southwards, where things, however more complex they might be, were somehow *cleaner*.

# XIII

# The Palisade

Jonaquil stood, trying to stretch the cramp out of her shoulders and neck, watching the pale light of dawn seep slowly into the Palisade compound. The air held a damp chill and she shivered and wrapped her soggy cloak more tightly about her, trying to draw as much warmth from it as she could. Her long hair was a tangled bird's nest of knots and snarls, the auburn colour of it gone dull with dirt. She smelled of stale sweat. She desperately wanted a bath.

It had been a miserable night, the Woodenders forced to sleep in the open against the inside of one corner of the rough log enclosure, supperless, exposed to a cold rain that had soaked them all during the dark hours. Jonaquil could hear coughing and groans as the villagers about her shifted and started in troubled slumber.

She might have slept through all of that, though, so exhausted was she, save for the dream.

It had been a great jumble of shuddering images: battle and screaming and the hideous, demon-tusked faces of *them*, mud puddled with blood. Yet it was each other they seemed to fight, not ordinary mortal men; an old woman – long rope of white hair, moss-green eyes in a face wrinkled as an dried apple – lifting a hand to which clung a bird with an oddly human face; a young man, dark-haired, glowing like a torch in dark air . . .

Jonaquil wrapped her arms more tightly about herself, shivering with memory and the chill morning damp. A queer dream indeed, it was, with neither the unquestionable clarity of a prescient sending, nor the simple vagueness of an ordinary dream. Demons fighting each other, a bird with a human face, a young man with a life-glow so strong it flamed like a torch.

Jonaquil shook her head. Best to put it out of her mind. She had no skill with dreams. And this one was, most like, no more than the rising vapours of her own disturbed spirit.

She stretched her arms above her head, trying to ease the cramps along her back. She was no longer young enough to be able to sleep rough on the open ground and not suffer for it. Her shoulders and neck ached miserably. Her legs, too, for she had stood here since well into the dark pre-dawn, unable to return to sleep, her belly knotted in unease, waiting for the wan light of her first dawn here.

The compound was beginning to stir now. Cookfires sputtered into life. People moved about sluggishly, hardly more than vague shapes where they shuffled through the dark blocks of shadow cast by the log walls. The night rain had soaked the ground, and the compound was a sticky morass of mud. People skidded and slipped, cursing, as they went about. And the wetness of the rain had brought out the stink of the place – a soggy, permeating mix of organic decay, laced with the burning smell of the fires, that made her gag. But it was the bleakness on the faces that shook Jonaquil. They were grey, pinched faces, tired faces, faces empty of mirth or energy, of everything but an occasional gleam of bleak cunning. And at the edge of it all stood demons, on guard, staring in silence at the halting proceedings of the morning. Looking at these silent, brooding, inhuman figures, Jonaquil shuddered.

A sudden altercation broke out next to a cookfire nearby. Two ragged men went at each other, tooth and nail, a confusion of limbs and grunting in the dawn's half-light. It was over as quickly as it had begun. One of the men lay sprawled in the mud, groaning, and the other stood over him brandishing the spoils – a heel of muddied bread.

Jonaquil felt sick, her Healer's flesh quivering with the reflected suffering all around her. It was a terrible place, this. The number of souls crammed in here amazed and dismayed her. What manner of creatures were *they*, to force people to live crowded together like this, like so many ants in a nest? And for what purpose were they gathering them together?

For a moment, looking about her, Jonaquil saw the pooling water everywhere turned to blood, as it had been in the dream, thick crimson puddles in the mud, churned by iron-shod boots as the demons fought against each other. Shuddering, she shook the image off.

'Well . . .' a voice said unexpectedly from beside her. 'Good morning. And 'tis a miserable, cold, dismal morning, too. Welcome to the Palisade.'

Jonaquil pivoted round, startled. A woman stood there, long-limbed and thin, with short hair, grey as a badger's. Her face had the same pinched, weary look as all the rest Jonaquil had seen here, but her eyes were bright and sharp for all that.

'Good . . . good morning,' Jonaquil said uncertainly, keeping her voice low so as not to disturb the villagers' fitful slumbers.

'Didn't mean to startle you.' The grey-haired woman also kept her voice soft, hardly above a whisper. She indicated the huddled Woodenders. 'All from the same village, are you?'

Jonaquil nodded. She beckoned the woman a little way off from the sleepers. 'Woodend. On the River Rush.'

The woman scowled. 'So they've worked themselves that far north. *Damn* them!'

'What . . . what *is* this terrible place?' Jonaquil asked her, looking again at the dirt and confusion and muddy squalor.

The woman's face stiffened. 'Terrible place indeed. This is the Seer Tancred's camp. And we – ' she gestured with her arm in a broad sweep that took in the entire enclosure about them – 'we are the Seer's *creatures*. His and the Lords Veil's.' The woman lifted her fingers in a vee and spat bitterly between them. 'And an ill death may *they* die.'

'The Lords Veil?' said Jonaquil.

'From the far south. Lords of some grim domain or other in the south, now come here to extend their realm by fire and sword. The Seer serves them. Black magicians they must be, or some such.'

'These . . .' Jonaquil hesitated. 'These demon-creatures are spell-created, then?'

'Aye,' the other replied. 'Creatures of black sorcery indeed. Though not such as you think, perhaps.'

Jonaquil cocked her head questioningly.

'It's the helms. They're men right enough underneath.'

Jonaquil stared at a demon nearby. Baleful yellow eyes, tusks, a shock of coarse dark hair along a narrow skull.

'They wear helms that are enspelled,' the woman continued. 'Turns them into the *creatures* we see. Though they like it little for that secret to be known.'

Jonaquil stared. *Men.* It did not seem possible. 'How . . . how can you be sure?'

'We live too near the bastards here. Folk see things. Word gets out. One of them demons was executed just before dawn today by the Sub-Commander. His helm lay shattered in the mud for all to see, until a guard removed it.' The grey-haired woman shook her head grimly. ''Tis the girls who learned it first, though. The hard way. They are men right enough, these outland bastards.'

Jonaquil swallowed, digesting that. She stared at the nearest man-demon. The creature blinked his eerie eyes, ran a thick tongue wetly over his tusks. So the wrongness she had already sensed in them was sorcery. And fell sorcery indeed, she thought with a shudder. Even though she was not now in trance, her Healer's eyes could still make out the queer glow of *their* double life-lights, spinning gouts of faint, whirling radiance twinned with a more normal life-light glow. The helms were *alive* in some queer, unwholesome manner. She perceived it clearly, now that she knew what she was observing.

She felt ill, her flesh tingling painfully with the unresolved hurt that surrounded her here. The thought of sorcery made her shudder.

The older woman put a hand out, concerned. 'Are you all right, girl?'

Jonaquil nodded, striving to keep her mind clear, lest the sickness in her blot out all else. 'What manner of man is this Seer?'

'This is his camp,' the other replied, her face gone stiff. She pointed to a large, low-slung log structure that dominated the back portion of the Palisade. ''Tis his building, that. The Powers alone know what he does in there. None of those who have entered that building ever returned to tell about it . . .' The woman shuddered. 'I've seen men and women dragged away screaming. Even small children. When *they* come to take you, there is naught to be done. *That* is what we are here for: to be fodder for whatever dark designs the Seer has.'

Jonaquil stared, hardly believing.

'Cursed heartless, these southern outlanders,' the woman went on. 'Men or no. A cursed *hard* lot.' She paused for a moment and shook her head. 'Let's not talk about it.'

Reaching out, she put a hand gently on Jonaquil's arm. 'My name is Tishta. One time Stablemaster of the Willow Inn, in the town of Sunnyside, now of this . . . place.'

'Jonaquil,' Jonaquil responded. She squinted at Tishta, seeing the woman's life-light pulse. It was faint, but clear and unsullied, like a slight lantern lightening the gloom. Jonaquil smiled, grateful. 'I am Woodend's Healer.'

Tishta's eyebrows went up. 'A Healer?'

Jonaquil nodded.

The other woman fell silent for a moment. 'That would be good news indeed. If it were true.'

'You doubt me?' Jonaquil bristled, unused to having her word questioned.

Tishta held up her hands. 'Let us say that, like all sensible women, I am suspicious of unlooked-for good fortune.' She ran her fingers through her short grey hair and shrugged. 'If you are indeed a Healer, then it will go well for you here.'

Jonaquil looked at her quizzically.

'We may be Seer Tancred's meat, but in the meantime they work us from dawn to sunset, logging timber to build the walls – and back-breaking work that is, too, hauling the logs from out of the forest beyond the river. Everything you see here was built by us. Everything that gets done in this camp is done by us. Those cursed man-demons do nothing at all!

'As a Healer, you can avoid most of the wretched tasks you might otherwise be stuck with. Latrine duty, for instance. And, more importantly, as a Healer you can avoid becoming one of that cursed Seer's playthings. You can be a person of some substance and position here, Jonaquil-the-Healer.'

Tishta put a hand on Jonaquil's arm. 'Come along with me. I can introduce you to the Sub-Commander. No point in approaching Commander Chayne. He keeps himself well beyond the reach of the likes of you or me. But the Sub-Commander is approachable, if you handle him right. Seeing him is the first thing you need do to establish yourself.'

Jonaquil hung back, uneasy with the turn the conversation had taken, resisting the pull of Tishta's hand on her. 'I will not just walk off and leave my people.'

Tishta looked at her closely, as if gauging the extent of her scruples. 'That's exactly what you will do if you are smart. Right now, before they wake up properly. Life is far from easy here. Anything you can do to help yourself . . . well, you do it. And think about it afterwards.'

Jonaquil didn't at all like what Tishta seemed to be suggesting. 'There is more to my life than simply trying to make things *easy*,' she snapped. 'And I will *not* abandon my people.'

'Come with me now, before they awake and complicate matters. Let me try to get you introduced to the Sub-Commander. Once you've been set up as a Healer under his sanction, you can use whatever privileges the position carries to help those around you, if you like. Don't you see? The only way to survive here is to use the way things are set up to your own advantage.'

'At the expense of others?'

Unexpectedly, a smile lit Tishta's face at this sharp retort of Jonaquil's. 'Forgive me for pressing you,' the older woman said. 'I felt I had to try and prod you a bit, in my own clumsy way, and see what I got in return. 'Tis just that . . . Well, we *need* Healers here, you see. Proper Healers. Need them very badly. Too many people crowded in here. Too much filth. Too much misery. Too much sickness.'

Tishta shook her head, paused, then looked straight at Jonaquil, searchingly. 'How much have you lost?'

This sudden shift took Jonaquil by surprise. 'Look around me,' she replied, gesturing to the mud, the peeling bark of the palisade logs, and to the huddled group of Woodenders. 'They marched us here from Woodend. We could take nothing but what we could carry.'

'Did they kill many of you?'

Jonaquil blinked. She hugged herself, shivering, recalling all too clearly the butchery of poor Tolke and the others. 'A few of the younger men tried to stand against the demon soldiers when they came to the village to take us away.'

Tishta snorted. 'Poor fools!' She eyed the huddled mass of the sleeping Woodenders. 'Looks like most are still alive, though. You and yours seem to have been fortunate, girl. Others have not been.' Tishta's voice was soft, still not much more than a whisper, but, as she talked, her eyes glinted with a suppressed outrage. 'Can you imagine having *everything* taken from you; not just goods, but people, your husband, your mother, friends, shivering their life out on the end of the iron blade while you watched, helpless . . . so that all you have left is hate for those who took it all from you? Hate that is utterly hopeless, utterly powerless, that burns so strong in your guts that you can't eat, can't sleep, can't do a thing but feel it eat through you?'

Tishta sighed wearily. 'It changes a person, that. When everything is taken from you, when hunger becomes a constant, nagging torment, and nothing is left you but the hate . . . Well, the niceties of whether or not you do things at the expense of others become . . . irrelevant. I have seen too much of it of recent; seen too many people, men and women, climb to comfort on the backs of others. I had to try and test you, to see . . . to see how much . . . integrity had been left you.'

'And did I pass this "test" of yours?'

'Truth? I don't know. You can't truly gauge a human being by a few questions. But I'm willing to credit the fact that you aren't one of those whose only concern is herself.'

'Very generous of you.'

'I'm not playing any *game* here, girl,' Tishta snapped, suddenly irate. 'Life is *hard* here. It wears a person to the bone. Trust is something you give very, very carefully.'

Tishta pivoted, gesturing to the moving mass of people in the Palisade enclosure. 'Do not expect anybody here to be considerate of your welfare, girl.'

'Except you?' Jonaquil said. It had been a long time since anybody called her 'girl'. She felt a flush of resentment. She was nobody's 'girl'.

'Except me.' Tishta smiled a thin smile. 'Perhaps.' Looking at the Woodenders, who were still curled in uneasy sleep against the Palisade wall, she said, 'Come along, now. Before the others here awake and complicate everything. Let me try to get you introduced to the Sub-Commander. Without his sanction, you can do nothing.'

Jonaquil paused, glancing back at the recumbent villagers. They seemed like helpless children there, shuffling in fatigued and un-comfortable sleep. If there was anything she could do to aid them . . .

'You *can* get me to see this Sub-Commander of yours?'

'Aye,' Tishta replied, an edge of irritation in her voice. 'I know the procedures. I've been here since the beginning. Gains us a kind of status.'

'All right. Take me to see him.'

'Good,' Tishta responded. 'This way.' Beckoning Jonaquil after her, she led off, picking a way through the mud. 'The Sub-Commander's tent is pitched outside the walls. He does not seem to relish our company overmuch.'

Jonaquil slowed for a moment, and looked Tishta straight in the eye. 'What would have happened if I had failed that little "test" of yours?'

Tishta returned her look, deadly serious. 'I would have made sure you never got to see Sub-Commander Gerrid. Ever. As I told you, I've a certain status here.'

With that, the older woman led on through the muck and mess and confusion till they drew near the gateway. The gates were open. People plodded in and out. 'This time of the morning,' Tishta explained, 'the guards are easy at the gate. Latrines are outside. We can walk right through and across to the Sub-Commander's tent. Unless we're unlucky, nobody will bother us. Sub-Commander Gerrid does his pre-dawn rounds, then returns to his tent for breakfast. Best chance to see him is early morning like this. He's human, then.'

'Human?' Jonaquil said.

'Wears that sorcerous helm of his all day. Only in his tent does he remove it. Told you we live close to *them* here. You get to know such things. Sub-Commander Gerrid is approachable, if you do it right. But watch him, girl. He's a hard man.'

Jonaquil nodded.

'He is not like the usual man-demon,' Tishta went on. 'The men-at-arms – if that's what one calls them – are as alike as peas in a pod. Officers are different, though. Instead of the demon faces, they have the look of beasts. Something to do with status, it seems. The Commander is like some great bird of prey. Sub-Commander Gerrid is a hunting cat . . .'

'Cat?' Jonaquil said.

Tishta nodded.

Jonaquil shivered, remembering. 'He commanded the group of riders that brought us here. A snarling-faced cat-creature. With no more caring in him than a rock.'

'So . . .' Tishta said. ''Tis him. Gives me the collywobbles, I don't mind admitting, when he is wearing that sorcerous helm. But he *is* approachable when it is off, if you do it right.'

Tishta led the way now through the Palisade gateway. Outside, the air was more chill, but cleaner, and a morning breeze blew in from across the river, carrying the murmur of running water and the scent of green growing things. Jonaquil sighed and took a deep, thankful breath. The dismal sounds of the Palisade behind her were all too clear and close. Her very bones still ached sickly with reflected misery. But for all that, the river air was like a bracing tonic.

The sun had just topped the crest of the Easterling Peaks on the Paudit's far shore, resolving the dreariness of the pre-dawn grey into pale, golden-green morning radiance. The Palisade, she saw, sat like a great, oozing sore on the river's bank. Near the shore, an ugly mass of ill-smelling waste and debris had piled up, the detritus of the camp fouling the river, webbed by trampled grass and churned-up mud. And on the river's far side lay scars left by the logging, like scabs upon the forest. Beyond these, though, was wild land, rising sharply away from the river banks, golden-green in the new morning light, the trees on the distant slopes looking thick and virgin as new wool. And above it all stood the naked stone of the Peaks, white-capped with snow. It lifted Jonaquil's heart to look upon such, clean as it was and unspoiled yet by *their* presence.

And then, as she took in the sight before her, Jonaquil suddenly gasped. There! By the bole of a felled tree near the Paudit's far shore, stood a tall, silent figure, a man and yet not a man, impossibly fine of limb and pale, the eyes in that pale face huge and dark and unblinking. There, clear as could be, staring straight at her.

Then gone.

Jonaquil blinked, shook her head.

'Jonaquil?' Tishta said at her side. 'Are you . . . ?'

'I am all right,' Jonaquil assured her. 'I just thought . . . I . . . I am fine, really.' Nothing at all now. She was not sure what it was she might have seen, if indeed it had been more than morning light playing tricks with her vision. Mountain Fey, some might call it. Others would simply laugh. She did not know.

Tishta pulled on her arm. 'Come.'

Jonaquil nodded, turning reluctantly from the wild land back to the Palisade's corruption. Her stomach churned again, and she had to swallow hard. Stuggling, she followed after Tishta as best she could along the Palisade wall.

'This woman is a Healer,' Tishta said to the two demon guards who stood duty, intricately bladed war-pikes at the ready, before the big field-tent set up just outside the Palisade. 'Came with the new bunch that arrived yesterday evening.'

One of the guards came forward a little, looked Tishta over with his inhumanly large eyes, hawked his throat loudly, then spat a large blob of yellowed phlegm on to the ground between Tishta's feet. 'So?'

'So, she should see the Sub-Commander. You know he has left standing orders that all Healers are to be brought to him.'

'So?' the guard repeated.

Tishta took a breath. 'So I am bringing her here to see the Sub-Commander.'

'Make it worth our while, woman,' the other guard put in, leering.

Jonaquil found it hard to believe that these creatures were really men. The illusion was perfect. The blinking eyes, the lips moving over yellow tusks, the mobile faces. She shivered, thinking on what dark knowledge might be required to produce sorcery such as this.

'I'll make it worth your while, all right,' Tishta snapped at the demon guard. 'I'll take her to the Commander and explain to *him* how you prevented us from seeing Sub-Commander Gerrid.'

The guard took a menacing step forwards, the pike raised. Jonaquil faltered backwards involuntarily. The guard glared at Tishta, but Tishta stood her ground, glaring right back.

This stand-off lasted for a long, long moment, then, without a word, the demon-guard turned and stalked off into the tent.

Jonaquil heard Tishta take a ragged breath. The older woman held her hands clutched across her belly, and Jonaquil could see that they were shaking. Small beads of sweat showed on Tishta's forehead and upper lip. Jonaquil put a hand on her arm, soothing. Tishta looked at her and smiled wearily, beginning to relax a little again.

'It's always like this,' she said, her voice quiet so that what she said did not carry to the remaining demon guard. 'Stupid, silly bastards are petty as spoiled children, pushing for every little thing they can. They will make your life miserable, given the chance. And take delight in it. Let them get away with it once, just once, and you're lost.'

The guard came back out from the tent. Without a word, with a sullen gesture of his arm, he ushered them in.

The interior was dim in the early light, and comfortably warm. A charcoal brazier gave heat and a kind of soft, glowing radiance at one side. In the centre of the tent's back half was a large folding desk. Two squat candles had been lit at the desk's corners, and, by their flickering radiance, Jonaquil caught her first glimpse of the man that was Sub-Commander Gerrid.

He was dressed in a plain sleeveless jerkin that left his long, sinewy arms bare. He had pale hair, cut so short as to almost be shaved, and prominent bony brows, under which dark eyes glinted in the candle-light. In front of him on the desk was a small roll of script-covered parchment, which he had been reading through, and a quill pen and inkpot.

'So,' he said, picking up a mug of some brew and sipping at it, 'we have a new Healer, do we?'

Jonaquil felt her stomach grumble painfully. It was mint tea he was drinking. She could smell its pleasant sharpness through the musty odour of tent canvas. It seemed utterly strange to see him thus as a man, to see him eating and drinking as any man might. Almost, she disbelieved all that Tishta had told her. How could this man be that same grim cat-creature that had marched them cruelly from their homes?

'And you . . .' Sub-Commander Gerrid continued, turning his attention to Tishta. 'I've seen *you* before. The woman who does man's work. You handle the horses for Gordin's work-gang, do you not?'

Tishta nodded, but remained silent.

Gerrid leaned forward across the desk. 'And just what do you hope to gain by playing escort to this supposed Healer of yours?'

'Nothing, Sub-Commander,' Tishta said. 'Your standing orders are that any Healers be brought to you.'

Gerrid laughed a dry, humourless laugh. 'And you take pains to obey my orders, do you?'

Tishta shrugged.

Gerrid turned his attention to Jonaquil. 'Perhaps,' he said, gazing at her, 'you have made private arrangements. Perhaps a woman who does man's work likes also to take a man's part in other things. Perhaps this young "friend" of yours would be willing to do you certain favours if you could successfully pass her off on me as a Healer.'

Tishta's face went pale and her lips compressed into a hard line. 'Is your land so befouled then, Sub-Commander, that you must see deceit everywhere?'

'Ahhh . . .' Gerrid breathed. 'Anger. Good. Maybe you *do* bring me a Healer after all.' Sitting back in his chair, he took a sip of tea and eyed Jonaquil in leisurely appraisal.

Jonaquil felt herself flush. She was dirty and she stank. She was tired and achy and still sick. She was angry at this man's insinuations, and angry at the manner in which he looked at her, as if she were some commodity.

'You are one of the villagers,' he said, before the sharp words that were building in her had a chance to come out. Which was probably all to the good, she thought, considering the situation.

'Aye,' she replied, taking a long, slow breath. 'From Woodend, along with the rest you drove here'.

'And you are a Healer?'

Jonaquil nodded.

'As you could have discovered yourself,' Tishta put in, 'if you had taken the time to ask her.'

The Sub-Commander looked at Tishta coldly. It was enough to silence her.

'The villager Healer, then?' he said to Jonaquil.

Again, Jonaquil nodded.

'Not particularly talkative for a woman, are you?'

Jonaquil said nothing. There was power in this man. She could sense it clearly; he wore it like a garment. It frightened her.

'Why should I believe you?' Gerrid demanded.

'She is a Healer, Sub-Commander,' put in Tishta. 'Why do you insist on doubting her word? We need Healers.'

Gerrid frowned. 'Who made *you* her champion?'

'It is not her I am championing.' Tishta's fists were clenched, and Jonaquil was surprised at the determined fury that showed plainly on her face now. 'It is the people you keep here, the people you work too hard and feed too little, the people who must live in this pigsty you call a camp and for whom you supply none but the most basic of necessities . . .' Tishta's first words had come in a rush. Now, she took a breath and continued more slowly. 'It is them I am championing, if I am championing anybody. We *need* Healers, need them badly. Without them, we will have . . . *you* will have a camp of the dead here. And then what will the Seer Tancred have to say?'

'Enough!' Sub-Commander Gerrid snapped irritably. 'I will *not* be lectured to by some rag-tag fool of a woman. Get out of here. Now!'

Tishta hesitated, seemed about to argue.

'Now,' said Gerrid, pointing to the tent's entranceway. 'Before you regret it.'

Without a word, Tishta turned and left.

'A woman of convictions,' the Sub-Commander said once Tishta had gone. 'And of no little courage, too.' To Jonaquil's surprise, he smiled suddenly, white teeth flashing. 'I prefer her type to the whey-faced, honourless grovellers most of you villagers become. Even if she *is* nuisance.'

Sub-Commander Gerrid leaned back once more in his seat, sipped at his tea, and gazed at Jonaquil in that infuriating appraising manner of his. 'What is your name?'

Jonaquil told him.

'You look young to be a Healer. The only Healers I have seen so far in this northern wasteland of yours are withered old crones.'

Jonaquil kept a grip on her irritation. He looked none too old himself. 'I am a Healer, nonetheless.'

Gerrid drank off the last of his tea, put the cup down, and leaned his elbows on the desk top. 'Why should I believe you, girl?' His face had gone hard and serious.

A pulse of quick fear surged through Jonaquil. This man had absolute power over her life, over all their lives, now that they had been brought to this place; she was only just coming to appreciate the full reality of that. He could do anything he wanted with her, anything at all, and she would have absolutely no recourse whatsoever.

But she refused to allow herself to be swept along by this fearful realization. She tried to stay calm, letting her fear waste itself into nothingness, and made herself look him squarely in the eyes. 'Why should you not believe me?'

He stayed there, silent, his eyes locked to hers for long moments. 'Very well. I shall give you the opportunity to show whether you are speaking truth or not. This Tishta was right. The camp does need Healers.' The Sub-Commander stood up and came round the desk until he was standing before her. He was a good head and shoulders taller than she. Taking her face in his hands, he tilted it up until she found herself locked there, staring eye to eye with him. 'A Healer must, perforce, have certain privileges. But do not make the mistake of using those privileges in such a way as to cause trouble. I will *not* brook that. Understand?'

She pulled away from him angrily. 'What do you take me for? I am a Healer. Are you so ignorant of what that means? It is a calling, not something to be used for one's own petty benefits or to cause trouble for others.'

'*Ignorant*, I am not.' He turned from her and went back to the desk. 'Do not misunderstand me.' Stooping, he blew out the candles. Daylight had come on enough so that the tent's interior was only marginally dimmed. 'A new order has come to this northern hinterland of yours, Healer. The Lords Veil are destined to rule here, as they are destined to rule in the south. This land is theirs now. You and all else here belong to them. And I am their steward . . . So, take warning. If you attempt to use the privileges of your position in any way to interfere with my tasks here, have no doubt about it but that punishment will follow, swift and certain. Healer or no Healer. Clear?'

'I have already seen one example of such punishment,' Jonaquil replied coldly, recalling the flogging she and the others had witnessed upon their arrival.

'Let that be a reminder, then, that I am in perfect seriousness. I make no idle promises, Healer. Accept things as they are. Accept the new order. You have no other choice.'

'You mistake me, Sub-Commander. You have nothing to fear from me. I have no wish to undermine your position.'

He laughed. 'That makes me feel *most* secure.'

Stung, Jonaquil glared at him. 'Your "new order" sickens me. It causes nothing but misery and suffering and brings human lives to nothing. But you need have no fear of my trying to undermine it. I am a Healer. I will heal everybody and anybody who needs me, villagers and demons alike. Including even you, Sub-Commander, should that be necessary. Unlike you, my calling is to nurture life, not twist and destroy it!'

Jonaquil stopped herself, self-conscious and breathless. It was a foolish thing, that outburst, foolish and self-righteous, and she regretted having let herself be goaded into it. But her visceral reactions to the sights of yesterday and this morning had suddenly fermented inside her to produce a burst of irrepressible outrage.

Gerrid smiled a slow smile. 'You have a sense of . . . honour, Healer.'

She only looked at him.

'I admire that. Honour is all too rare.' He went silent for a moment, gazing at her, then continued. 'You are right to call our different occupations "callings": callings they are. I am a Warrior, you a Healer. You may trust me to honour my calling, Healer. I only hope I may trust you to honour yours.'

With that, he gathered up the small roll of parchment on his desk, rose from his seat, and went to the far edge of the tent. When he returned, he held a cat-visaged helm in his hands, gleaming bronze and dark iron and white bone. Only then, seeing it in his grip, did Jonaquil truly believe.

Sub-Commander Gerrid gazed at her silently for long moments, then made a quick, peremptory gesture towards the tent's exit. 'Go now. Ask somebody where the Dispensary is. Present yourself there by mid-morning. I will make the necessary arrangements. If anybody tries to set you up in a work detail until then, refer them to me. Clear?'

She nodded.

'Then go.'

Jonaquil went.

# XIV

# The Miradore

Tai lay immersed in darkness. The end of all. He had come at last to the Shadowlands, to the realm of the dead. No more need he suffer at *their* hands.

He felt relief, but it was mixed with no little fear, for none knew truly beforehand what the Shadowlands might hold, save for those few wise souls who claimed to have risen above mortal frailty and to have made the journey, living, and returned.

Tai was no such wise soul, but he knew the Shadowland Parables well enough, and knew what any ordinary mortal man must expect: he would dwindle slowly now, wandering the sere Shadowland hills – his old self decomposing as surely as his old body – till he sank away from the Shadowland dark into the Beyond, from which his spirit would be swept up again into the endless swirl of new life.

But he would be Tai no longer, then.

He shivered, and remembered the old sad song, 'Ashlie's Lament', and the tale it told, of the girl Ashlie weeping over the still form of Levin, her dead lover:

> Bitter ash and leaf and thorn,
> The Darkling Hills lie sere and worn,
> Dark his sky, and my heart is torn,
> For he never no more shall see morning . . .

There would be no one to lament over his dead body, Tai thought, and none to recite the death litany for him. He would walk the Darkling Hills, fading, as all Shadowland spirits faded, sinking away from life into the great Beyond. The very thought made him tremble. He possessed neither the wisdom nor the simplicity to let go his life and fade peacefully, as the very wise and very young were said to be able to. He would struggle, as he had struggled, it seemed, all his life one way or another; but this would be the end for him, inevitably.

Only Colby might mourn. But Colby too would walk this same dark path soon . . .

Tai felt pain. He left hand pulsed with it, and his skull ached as of old. Body-memory, must be. The imprint on his newly loosened spirit of his boy's torments. He remembered the Shadowland verse:

> Long and long the body's hold,
> Body-memory deep and old.
> The ails of flesh and blood and bone
> Does spirit feel . . .

Tai felt his lungs expanding with breath, felt his heart beating. And about him only darkness. He did not know what to think. Such Shadowland beginnings seemed strange indeed. Where was the Shadowland landscape he ought to expect? Where the bitter ash and thorn? Where the humped, dry backs of the Darkling Hills?

He recalled the spider limbs and yellow fangs of the moving pack, the choking rush of blood as the fell-hound tore his throat away. His hand went convulsively to his throat. It was intact.

Hand. Throat. Breath . . .

It was more as though he were alive and whole again than dead and in the Shadowlands. He groped in the dark, winced as he felt the cauterized nub of the amputated finger scrape against some hard, chill surface under him.

Tai did not know what to think.

Before him, unexpected light glowed, startlingly bright. Tai levered himself stiffly up on his elbows, squinting. A figure stood over him, a mere blurred outline against the glare of light.

Hands lifted Tai to his feet. 'Drink this,' a voice ordered.

A porcelain cup of liquid was in Tai's good hand. He stared about, stunned, seeing a small room, a doorway through which pale light flowed . . .

For a long moment he could not grasp the truth of it, did not know how to feel. Dream . . . vision . . . fell-hounds and blood and dying . . . A fit of the shivers took him till his teeth chattered with it. He sagged against the wall for support, spilling some of the liquid from the cup in his hand.

He was alive. Part of him bemoaned the fact, for now would he once again be plunged into pain and struggle. But another part of him exalted. Alive! Still in the world. *Alive!*

'Drink,' he was commanded.

Before Tai stood a lone man, tall, cloak-shrouded. Glittering black eyes stared coldly from out of the shadow of the cloak's hood. Tai shuddered, recognizing that figure, and his pulse beat suddenly hard.

'I lose patience, boy. Drink!'

Tai felt the cup forced against his lips. The liquid in it was warm, surprisingly robust. He drank deeper.

'Good.' The other took the empty cup. 'Come.' He gripped Tai by the arm, pulling him through the doorway and into a larger room lit by several glowing orbs that hissed softly, not at all like the familiar sputter of candlelight. The room was full of stacked parchment scrolls, long feather quills, inkpots, a clutter of other, less recognizable things. Next a doorway at the far end, a squat wooden stool stood and a small board table, upon which lay bread and cheese and a flagon of drink.

Slipping back the hood of his dark cloak, the Seer settled into an upholstered chair next to a long, carved wooden desk. The hissing orbs cast an odd, pale light across his hairless face, making it seem bone-white as a naked skull. He pointed to the food. 'Sit. Eat. You will need nourishment after the Pit.'

Tai stayed where he was, on his feet, his belly clenched tight as a fist. He stared at the Seer apprehensively, not trusting such apparent solicitousness at all.

The Seer gazed back at him, silent, elbows on the chair-arms, fingers steepled. His cold eyes were unblinking.

Tai shivered, sick with confusion and fear. His limbs ached. His skull throbbed with the memory of the old hurt, and his injured left hand was a nagging torment. He felt unutterably weary and desperately wanted to sit, but dared not. That uncanny, hairless, naked-skull face, those black and staring eyes – the figure before him seemed to have no more humanity than a snake.

The Seer shifted position in the chair, and Tai skittered back instinctively.

'Stupid boy! Do you expect me to grow horns? To snap my fingers and turn you into a toad or such?'

Tai said nothing.

'I am Tancred, Seer to the Lords Veil. Do you know what manner of creature a Seer is?'

'Aye,' faintly. 'You are a . . . a sorcerer.'

Tancred smiled. 'And do you think me . . . *evil*?'

Tai did not know how to respond.

'Do you think me capable of doing anything I want? Of creating life through my dark magic? Trafficking with the dead? Casting all-powering spells that none can resist?' The Seer leaned forward in his seat, black eyes intent. 'Do you expect me to . . . *toy* with you now for my wicked pleasure?'

Tai swallowed, his head downcast, afraid to meet the Seer's dark, penetrating gaze.

'Stupid boy. The world is far more complex than you imagine. I am no evil creature from some child's story.' The Seer laughed softly. 'Good and evil are a child's concepts. There is only *power*, boy, and those who wield it. Those with power do what they do because they *can*. And those without the power must suffer accordingly. I am a Seer, a *see-er*, one who sees; a man like other men, save that I have greater power, and a greater destiny than most, for I was born with a gift, a great and rare gift . . . As were you.'

Tai darted a quick, confused glance towards him.

'You know what gift it is I refer to.'

Tai did not know what to say. Gift? He could not conceive of what the Seer might mean.

Tancred gazed at him in silent appraisal, black eyes agleam in the strange, pale glow of the luminous orbs that lit the room. 'We are of a kind, you and I, boy. I know what you possess.'

Tai only stared.

Tancred laughed then, suddenly and unexpectedly. 'Stupid boy. A gift such as yours, and you have no true idea.' He leaned back in the chair. 'Do you sometimes . . . *lose* the world? Do you have . . . fits?'

'Aye,' Tai conceded after a long moment's pause, his face flushed with shame. 'I drool. I have spasms. Men look at me and laugh.'

The Seer went abruptly, strangely silent then. His dark eyes stared unblinkingly at Tai. It made Tai uneasy, that stare, and he tried to pull away from it. But, to his dismay, he found he could not. He was held fast in some strange manner.

Without warning, Tai felt a sudden disorientating surge strike him. The world shattered into chaos. His senses dimmed to nothing. He seemed to twist in a swirl of movement. Then, for one timeless moment, he sensed . . . he was not sure what he sensed. It was surely not vision, for this was like a fit, and he had no awareness of eyes or ears, no familiar self. Yet he grew aware somehow of a pattern about him, straight planes of force forming an enclosing cube, a compact intricacy of something before him that pulsed with its own rhythm. And beyond, a huge, endless, impossible multiplexity of pattern, interwoven like a great, throbbing tapestry.

And then it was gone from him, as suddenly as it had come, and he lay crumpled on the floor, gasping.

The Seer laughed again. 'You know not what you are capable of, boy. It is a gift few possess. It makes you . . . *valuable.*'

Tai felt a strange, unpleasant pulse in his midriff. 'What . . . what did you *do* to me?'

'I released something within you that you have kept buried all your life.'

The world began to dissolve sickeningly about him once again. It was too much. Tai felt himself gag. He leaned suddenly forwards and vomited helplessly. The fits had always made him queasy. But this . . . this felt like having his insides torn open.

'Accept it, boy,' the Seer said, his voice hard. 'You have kept a portal closed all your life. Now it is time to open it. The world is far larger than you imagine, and holds things you *never* imagined. Accept it!'

But Tai could not. His belly heaved. He felt a painful roaring in his ears. His heart kicked in his chest and seemed to falter.

Then, as if something were twisted abruptly shut inside him, it abated. He looked up at the Seer, shaken to his very core.

Tancred glared. 'Stupid boy.' Rising from the chair, he went to a carved chest that rested against the other wall, bringing out a rag which he tossed over. 'Here. Clean up your mess!'

Haltingly, Tai did so, his belly heaving at the smell of it; though there was little enough, his stomach being so empty. When he was done, he took a long drink from the flagon on the table to freshen his mouth. The water was clear and sweet.

The Seer had returned to his seat, elbows resting on the chair's arms, fingers laced together under his bony chin. He frowned, his dark gaze focused unwaveringly on Tai. 'Broken, you would be of little use to me. And I have plans, boy . . . So we must do this the slow way . . .'

Tai shook his head confusedly. 'I don't—'

Tancred jabbed an accusing finger. 'You are a simpleton, boy. The world is larger than you imagine, in more ways than you can imagine, and ignorance and fear are a fool's companions . . . You think this northern hinterland of yours a big place. It is nothing! A collection of hovels amongst the hills. In the south dwell a hundred times, a thousand times more people, living lives you cannot imagine, wielding knowledge you cannot imagine.

'And that knowledge can be used to unlock certain . . . abilities. I am a member of an Order, ancient and powerful beyond your conception. We of that Order can accomplish many things.' Tancred smiled thinly. 'You experienced a portion of what we are capable of. In the Pit.'

'The Pit?'

'We can order flesh and bone and blood to our will.'

Tai sighed wearily. 'I don't understand.'

Tancred smiled again, a mere twist of the lips. 'I expect you do not.

Let me show you something then, boy. Come.' He rose from his chair, picked up a small lantern that hung from a wall-hook, and beckoned Tai to the door.

The Seer set off through a series of vacant corridors, one bony hand clutched around Tai's forearm, striding along at a pace that set Tai to panting. The lantern in Tancred's other hand hissed softly, shedding the same colourless radiance as the orbs in the room they had left. The black middle of the night it must be, Tai gauged, for everything was deserted, dark and silent. The only sounds were the muted slap of their feet upon the flagstone floors, the quiet hiss of the lantern, the swish and rustle of Tancred's cloak, and the panting of Tai's own breath.

And then they were through a doorway and into a large, open chamber. Tancred released him, and Tai slumped against the wall, gasping.

'Look,' the Seer commanded.

In the middle of the chamber stood a circular stone parapet. The curved wall of it reached as high as Tai's waist, perhaps, and the ring thus formed was at least twenty paces or more across. Tai could not imagine what purpose it might serve.

Tancred nodded towards it. 'The Lords Veil make certain demands upon me, as Seer. Among other things, I supply entertainment, a very special form of entertainment. It is a weakness the Veil has, this passion for the Pit.'

Silently, Tancred led Tai to the ring of the parapet. He held the lantern aloft, illuminating the enclosed area.

Perplexed, Tai turned. 'What—'

The Seer gestured downwards. 'Look!'

At first, strangely, Tai could make out nothing at all but a vague, shifting mist. Then details began to emerge. Stretched out below him, enclosed by the parapet, he saw what appeared to be a miniature landscape. Water, shoreline, an isle, rocky-shored and elongated. He could make out outcroppings of bare stone, and pockets of tangled greenery. He leaned closer. The isle filled almost all of the circular inner area of the parapet, but it was oddly difficult to judge the scale in any reliable manner; things sometimes appeared smaller, sometimes much, much larger.

Peering down, Tai saw a little stretch of cliff, a rocky spur running transversely out from that cliff, a small, dark pool of water abutting up against the face of the spur, tiny reeds and sedge lining its far side.

Tai backed away, not understanding, yet beginning to understand.

'Look closer,' Tancred ordered.

After a moment, Tai leaned over and stared down again. The little pool below him was oval, the water dark. It was as if he, Tai, were soaring high above. And, as he looked, he saw something move, saw several things move. Small, spidery-limbed, dark shapes loped along in a loose pack, quartering the reedy edge of the pond. Some small creature surfaced in the centre of the water, well away from the shoreline and the pack. Tai saw a tiny, sleek, brown-furred head, miniature furred arms moving through the water.

'No!' Tai breathed. 'No . . .'

'The Pit,' Tancred said. 'The Veil's entertainment. The *sport* the Veil enjoys so.'

Tai stood and stared.

'From a man's flesh,' Tancred said, 'a finger, say . . . From that, we can grow a miniature homunculus of that man. Through the use of certain arts and certain potions, we can have the man *be* that homunculus for a time, breathe and move and live . . . and even die as that homunculus.'

Tai blinked, still staring unbelievingly down at the small, dark pool below him.

The Seer gestured to the Pit. 'We watched you. The Veil found it . . . disappointing. You did not live up to his expectations.'

Tai shuddered, thinking of them leaning here at the parapet's edge, as he was now, watching as his throat was torn out by the fell-hound. He leaned over and pointed to the tiny figures in and about the pool below. 'And them? What of them?'

'They are Pit Folk.'

'But who . . .'

'Enough,' the Seer said. 'Come. We have been here long already. The Veil maintains only a small contingent in this Keep, trusting to the sea to be their guard but, even so, and late though it is, the night-guard still patrols these ways occasionally. And I do *not* wish to meet them hereabouts this night. It would make things unnecessarily complicated.'

With that, Tai found himself once more dragged quickly along through the dark, empty corridors.

Back in the same strangely lit room again, Tai lowered himself gratefully to the stool. He felt bone-weary, and shaken to his core. What manner of man could create such things as he had just seen?

Tancred was seated in his chair again. 'The world is not what most think it to be, boy. Most see only the illusionary surface shimmer of it, unaware of the depths over which they move. But some, a few, can perceive more. The shifting heart of the world lies open to them, the hidden patterns, the flow and ebb of underlying verity. I am such a one, boy. And so are you . . .

'Being a see-er means not only to sense the hidden patterns, but also to be able to change them. To reach, for instance, into the structures of flesh and bone and alter their growth to one's will.'

'I . . . I don't . . .' Tai stammered. 'I am not . . .' He licked his lips nervously. He wanted nothing to do with this craziness of 'see-ers' and powers and uncanny, will-ordered flesh. He could see no connection between such and his fits. And it had been far worse than any normal fit, what the Seer had provoked in him. He shuddered sickly, thinking on it. 'I have no gift,' he insisted. 'You are wrong. I lose the world. I go into spasms. I drool like an idiot. Sometimes I imagine things. That is all. I have no—'

'You have a special gift, boy. You will be *useful* to me.'

'No!' Tai blurted.

Tancred laughed. It was not a comforting sound. 'Become what I will make of you, boy, or return to your cell and live out your remaining days as a creature of the Pit, like the rest of those that came here with you. One or the other. Which will it be?'

'What of those others?' Tai asked quickly, thinking of poor Colby. 'If I do as you wish, will you spare them?'

'Those others are not part of what we discuss here. They are unimportant.'

Tai felt suddenly sick. 'But how can you expect—'

'Things are as they are. Your companions are destined to provide sport for the Veil. They will live out what remains to them of their lives in the Pit. Each Pit-life they lose will cost them – for a homunculus must be grown from living flesh – until nothing is left of them but limbless torsos. Then they will be put to death. A small thing this Pit is, compared to those the Veil has in the south, but it needs feeding nevertheless.'

Tai stared, stricken.

'That was to be your fate,' Tancred said. 'And will be still, if you refuse me.'

Tai opened his mouth but could find no words. Colby. Poor Colby. And the others. He thought of the limbless body he had seen the gulls squabbling over on the beach before the Miradore on the first day of his arrival here. The very horror of it held him speechless. Sagging backwards on to the stool, he felt at the painful nub of his amputated finger and trembled, thinking on what it would be like to go back into that dark cell and lie there waiting, helpless, being slowly butchered to provide *sport* for the Lords Veil.

'Do you refuse me?' Tancred asked.

Tai bowed his head. A great, hopeless anger swept him. His fists clenched into painful knots. His body quivered so he could hardly get breath. Always, *they* held the upper hand – demon or man, it made no difference. Always must he bleed and bruise, helpless, while they did what they wished to him and his. His own utter helplessness all but choked him. Almost, he flung himself upon the Seer, blindly, hysterically. But Tancred's black eyes – cold, utterly calm, unblinking as a serpent's – held him fast.

Tai shuddered. Give himself into the Seer's hands . . . and what terrible thing would happen to him? His insides still quivered sickly with after-sense of what Tancred had provoked in him. But to return to the Pit and the horror it entailed . . . He did not think he was strong enough to endure that.

'Decide, boy.' The Seer stared at him coldly. 'Decide!'

Tai shivered, helpless and hating. He was doomed and damned either way. He would find some way to kill himself, fling himself off a high wall to land a shattered heap on the rocks below. Better that than the Pit. Better that than become the Seer's creature.

But something in him would not accept the thought.

Despite everything, he was still not altogether alone in the world; he still had kin, and it was not his own life alone he was responsible for. Perhaps, Tai told himself, if he accepted this 'offer' – *appeared* to accept it – there might be some chance for him to . . . he knew not what. Escape? Come to Colby's aid somehow? Not likely. That was for the heroes in children's tales, not the likes of him. But he thought of the vow he had made to himself: to save his foster-uncle Colby, no matter what. His fate if he returned to the horrors of the Pit was sure. With the Seer there was, perhaps, some hope of *something*. He had already survived so much strangeness and terror.

'Well?' Tancred demanded. 'Is it to be the Pit? Do you refuse me?'

His heart thumping, Tai shook his head.

The Seer smiled. 'Good. And now there are arrangements that need to be made.'

Tai shivered. 'Wha . . . what will you . . . *do* with me?'

The Seer ignored the question. 'Wait here,' was all he said, and with that, abruptly, he strode out through the door.

Tai waited swaying on the stool, shattered and weary.

At the sound of footsteps, he looked up and froze. In the doorway stood two of *them*, demon faces all too clear in the light from the room's hissing glow-globes. Tai scrambled to his feet, tipping the stool over with a clatter and fetching up with the small of his back hard against the board table upon which the food sat.

Tancred appeared between the two demons. He smiled a thin smile. 'These two will do you no harm, boy. They are mine.'

Tai stared. 'Tell them to begone, then, if such *creatures* are yours to command.'

'Creatures?' Tancred shook his head. 'These are not creatures. They are men, boy, like you and me.'

'*Men?*' Tai said, unbelieving.

The Seer shrugged. 'Later, all will be made clear. Now, you will leave here.'

'With . . . with *them?*'

'With them, yes. They are yours to direct.'

'*What?*'

'They are yours to direct.' Tancred gestured to the two demons behind him. 'These are part of *my* guard, and will do as you tell them. Within reason.'

'Mine to . . . command?'

The Seer scowled. 'Yes. But do not try anything stupid, boy. These two will escort you to quarters I have arranged for you and will ensure your safety.'

Tai only stared uncomprehendingly.

The Seer gestured in irritation, and the two demon guards withdrew from the room, leaving Tai and the Seer alone. 'Listen, boy,' Tancred said, 'and listen well. There is illusion within illusion. The Veil is mine in ways they cannot begin to comprehend. Yet they think me their creature. It suits me that they think so. Appearances must be kept up. I have plans, but for all my power I must play games . . . The Lords Veil will not like it when it is discovered you are gone from your holding cell. I want you safe.'

The Seer turned, strode to the room's door, flung it open. 'There. All is explained. Now go! You try my patience. I have other matters to attend to.'

Tai felt a crawly feeling along his spine. Walk out of here alone in the company of two of *them*? But the look of the Seer's skull-like face gave him no choice in the matter. Slowly, he edged away from the table towards the door. The two demons stood waiting across the theshold, their great yellow eyes fixed on him. He hesitated, but the Seer only waved him off impatiently with a bony hand.

The door to the room closed behind, and Tai found himself out in the corridor, his heart pounding. 'Whi . . . which. . . ?' He had to swallow and begin again. 'Which way do we . . . go?'

One of the creatures held a hissing lantern, and this one pointed silently to Tai's left.

So off they trooped.

It was the eeriest feeling, moving in company with these two demon-faced creatures. Though Tancred had insisted they were men and not the fell things they seemed, Tai could hardly bring himself to credit it. Some dread enspellment indeed must it be to transform a man so. The two said not a word, padding along the empty corridors, and Tai found it hard to ignore the sickening conviction that he was once more being taken back down to his cell, a prisoner as before. But they neither pushed at him nor threatened him in any way, these two, and even adjusted their pace to his when he flagged. And it was upwards they moved, always up.

At the top of a long, curving flight of stone steps that left Tai gasping, they encountered a large wooden door through which Tancred's man-demons ushered him.

A rush of cool, sea-odoured air hit Tai, like a wash of bracing cold water, making him blink and stretch aching limbs and look about with sudden interest. The man-demons continued on, and Tai realized he was out in the open air, on an uncovered walkway skirting the low-slanting, slated roof of the Keep. A cool, fresh wind ruffled his hair. A few last stars still sparkled in the sky overhead, but the eastern horizon shone like pewter with the light of new dawn. The huge shape of the stone hound's head loomed nearby, and he heard the crying of gulls in the distance. Tai stopped, leaned against the chill stone of the chest-high, crenellated parapet that lined the walkway, and breathed long lungfuls of the bracing air.

The men-demons gestured him onwards impatiently towards another door at the end of the walkway, some fifteen paces along, that led to a round, windowed tower. Tai hung back. The air, the openness, the fresh light of the dawn, all were too exhilarating for him to relish going back inside so quickly. 'Yours to command,' Tancred had said of these man-demons. Now, perhaps, was the occasion for him to test that promise. He turned to them, swallowed, said, 'I would stay here a little while yet. The air is . . . pleasant.'

They stood staring at him, silent, their huge yellow eyes disconcertingly devoid of any recognizably human response. Tai felt his heart begin to beat harder. Now, surely, would he feel the thud of a pike-butt across his shoulders once again.

But no. One of them nodded. 'As you wish,' it said. The first words, these, that Tai had heard from either of them.

He could not quite believe he had done it so easily. Give commands to *them?* But these two stood there stolidly, waiting on him. He felt a sudden rush of elation.

Elbows on the chill stone of the parapet, Tai gazed off into the airy distance. He did not understand what Tancred was about, or why the Seer permitted him to give these demon guards orders. He did not know what was to be offered, or what taken from him. His insides churned painfully. The very memory of his 'interview' made him tremble.

But the fresh morning air was like a tonic, drawing him inexorably out of fear and memory back into the world. He tasted the bite of the salt air on his tongue, felt the dawn wind's fingers riffle his hair. In the distance, the improbable shape of the stone hound's head reared its bulk, strong and enduring as the world itself.

About the rocky upthrust of that head, gulls roared. Tai heard their cries and shivered momentarily, remembering the poor corpse on the beach. Near to the Miradore walls, a cluster of them fluttered and dived, as if in chase of something. Tai looked closer. Sure enough, some smaller bird skittered desperately away from them. One after another the gulls plummeted upon it, but the littler bird veered and darted so that they missed time and again, flapping back up in cackling frustration. It was only a matter of time, though, for soon more gulls came flocking, drawn by the cries of their fellows.

Tai's heart went out to the poor thing they hunted, beset so.

Along the Keep the chase came and, as the birds drew closer, Tai was able to make out more detail. The little one whirred desperately through the air, shifting this way and that. Blue it was, the plumage glowing brightly in the growing light. Blue, like the human-faced birds in the Lord Veil's chamber.

The hunted bird made a sudden sideways loop and dived straight towards the parapet where Tai and the demon guards stood. The gulls veered off, squalling. The blue bird came plunging on with such speed that it skittered across the top of the parapet and hurtled beyond to smack up against the stone wall on the inner side of the walkway. It tumbled down and lay on the flagstones at the wall's base, a ruffled heap, its small breast heaving.

Tai stepped towards it and saw small, terrified human eyes staring up at him.

But he was not the only one to move. Beside him, one of the man-demons came up and raised its foot ready to stamp out the poor bird's life. The little face puckered with terror.

'No!' Tai cried, elbowing the man-demon away in a clumsy rush. The foot came down wide, missing the bird. A hard hand thumped Tai in the chest, making him gasp.

'These,' the man-demon said, 'are not permitted outside the Keep alive.'

Tai reached down quickly, before either of the two guards could react further, and gathered the bird into his hands, ignoring the pain of his mutilated finger. He could feel it struggle in his hold, its little heart beating hysterically. 'I will take it inside with me, then.'

For a moment, it looked as though they would rip the bird from him, and Tai cringed back involuntarily. Then one of them said, 'As you value your life, see you do not let it escape. Understood?'

Tai swallowed. 'Understood.'

The man-demon stared at him appraisingly with its huge yellow eyes, then waved him along. 'Come.'

Clutching the twitching bird, Tai followed after.

They brought him to the tower at the end of the walkway, through a door and up a short set of circular steps, then into a small, round room. 'Here you will stay,' one of them told him. 'We will ensure your safety. One of us will be outside at all times.' With that, the two strode out, shutting the door behind them with a solid *thwump*.

The room had a bed, a chest, and a small table upon which sat a pitcher of water and some bread and cheese. Pale morning light washed in through a narrow, closely barred window above the table.

Tai let himself down wearily on the bed and opened his hands. His mutilated finger blazed with pain and he gasped.

In a sudden flurry of wings, the bird hurled itself across the room and against the window. The bars there were too narrow for it to be able to squeeze through, and it flapped helplessly, thumping again and again against the unyielding iron bar-rods.

An uncanny creature indeed it was, with that beakless, human-shaped head and diminutive human eyes . . .

When the throb in his hand had settled a little, Tai levered himself stiffly up off the bed and tried the room's door. It was locked, and the window solidly barred. Which made him a prisoner.

Yet it was a wash of relief he felt rather than dismay. Unexpected tears filled his eyes. Let the future bring what it might, Tancred, the Pit, whatever . . . For now, he was warm and dry, and there was food and drink, a bed in which to lie, and nobody to torment him.

To such had he been reduced.

The sight of the food suddenly made Tai's mouth water. Bringing the bread and cheese and the pitcher of water over to the bed, he settled back wearily. He ached to his very bones, and chewing was an effort. The food was good, though, the cheese rich and tasty, and, despite his first misgivings, it seemed to sit in his stomach comfortably.

In a little time he was looking around him with more interest.

By now, the bird had settled on the table near the window, little bright eyes fixed on him. Tai took a swig of the water and gazed at it. It was indeed the same startling kind of bird-creature he had seen in the Lord Veil's chamber. And a strange small creature it was, but not uncomely. The wings and back were blue and shimmered like finest satin, while the breast and face were a pale, russet-orange. The two colours made a striking contrast. A tuft of blue feathers capped the head, and the feathered face was dominated by the dark human eyes, fringed by what seemed absurdly long lashes.

A fetching little creature, in fact.

Tai put the water-flagon down, slowly, and reached for more of the bread. How had the little thing managed to escape from the Lord Veil's chamber? Holding a piece of bread in his fingers, Tai offered it.

The bird only flittered away nervously.

'Here,' Tai urged.

'Do your worst, man, and have done!'

The voice was high-pitched and tremulous, like a terrified child's, and it took Tai totally unawares. The bread fell from his fingers. He stared, open-mouthed.

The little creature stared back. He could see its orange breast pulsing with the rapid beat of its heart. Tai ran a shivering hand over his eyes. Bird's body, human head, human voice. 'Who . . . what are you?' he stammered.

But he got no answer.

'You are his creature,' the bird cried accusingly, hopping up and down. '*His!*'

Tai knew not at all what to make of this.

'His. The *Seer's.*' The small mouth almost spat the word. 'You are the Seer's creature!'

Tai swallowed. 'No . . . I am not . . . *No!*'

The bird laughed, a shrill peal of mirthless sound. 'I *saw!* You commanded his guards. Deny it. But I *saw.*'

'I don't—'

'You are his!' the bird all but screamed. 'His creature. *His!* Do your worst and have done!'

Struggling up off the bed, Tai lunged for it, stung by what it had said. 'Listen to me . . . I am not . . . Listen to me! *Listen!*' But it dived away, veering in desperate circles about the room, screeching unintelligible accusations. He leaped clumsily, trying to snag it from the air, but it was hopeless. Skittering beyond his grasp, it began to shriek wordlessly, a shrill, hysterical, little-child sound that made Tai wince.

He fell back from it on to the bed and lay there, breathless and shaking.

After a little, the creature went quiet.

At a stealthy flutter of sound, Tai lurched quickly up, squinting, his vision gone blurry with fatigue. The bird had dived for the piece of bread, still lying on the floor where he had dropped it, and now, with a quick dart, returned triumphantly to the table. He saw the creature had little hands – no more than skeletal fingers, really – at the leading edge of each of its wings. It held the piece of bread in these fingers and nibbled daintily at it, all the while eyeing him with black suspicion.

Tai slumped backwards on the bed. He blinked, trying to keep an eye on the bird, for he did not trust the queer, ungrateful little creature. But a wash of exhaustion went through him, numbing him. He yawned a great, jaw-cracking yawn. His thoughts began dissolving into foggy nothings.

He struggled against it, but to no effect. All the past days seemed to have descended upon him with a weight of exhaustion not to be denied. He had time to wrap himself clumsily in the blanket that lay across the bed, cast one last, uneasy glance at the bird, and then sleep swept over him, irresistible as a tide.

# XV

# The Palisade

'He is gone,' Jonaquil said sadly, turning aside. She stood in the disordered canvas tent that Sub-Commander Gerrid casually called the Dispensary, her head hung in weariness and grief. Before her, stretched flat on his belly on a makeshift cot, lay the remains of Hozias, the man Jonaquil had seen flogged the evening she and the Woodenders had first entered the Palisade.

This was the second day, now, the poor soul had lain here, half-delirious, his back a puffy mess of criss-crossed, weeping scabs. The flogging itself, while agonizing, might not have proved fatal. The reason for his death, though, Jonaquil knew to be all too simple; Hozias had lacked the will to live on. Even in the brief time she had been here so far, this initial dying of the spirit that presaged the final death of the person was something she was beginning to become familiar with. Far too familiar.

Jonaquil traced a blessing sign in the air above what remained of Hozias. 'A scathless journey in the darkness, friend,' she recited softly. 'A scathless journey and a fruitful end. Gone from the world of living ken. Into the Shadowlands . . . to begin again.'

The two men working as day-helps began winding Hozias in a tattered shroud, in preparation for hauling him off to the growing burial plot on the slope outside the Palisade.

'When you've finished wrapping him, leave him to rest here until his brother returns,' Jonaquil said to them.

Jonaquil sighed. Tym, dead Hozias's young brother, would be devastated. Morning and evening, before and after his day's work logging in the woods, the boy had come here to sit at Hozias's side, silent, often in tears, his thin hands clutched around one of his brother's as if, by holding on tightly enough, he could prevent Hozias from slipping away.

Jonaquil had learned Hozias and Tym's story, at least in part. It was all too typical in these terrible days. Their family was scattered or dead, even they did not know which, and here they had only each other left to cling to. And now poor Tym had no one. She did not know what she could tell the boy to ease this for him when he returned this evening.

Turning from the sad sight of Hozias's corpse, Jonaquil walked back into the dim interior of the Dispensary. She felt a hatred for this place, a growing, bitter hatred that etched its way into her like acid. And she was never free from the creeping, sickly feeling in her belly and bones. Healer's Sickness, that was, the soul-sickness of the flesh that had plagued her ever since the demon guards had first come to Woodend with fire and iron. It was the gift of all true Healers, this sensitivity to others' suffering. But it could be curse too, and here, in this terrible place, it was as debilitating as a rotten tooth.

About Jonaquil in the Dispensary lay a crowded array of rickety cots, pallets, and makeshift seats, each holding a sick and suffering human being. And those around her told the story of life in this camp.

Here was a small boy who had come in the day before, sobbing pitifully, the fingers of his left hand broken and swollen up like sausages. He had been injured in a hysterical struggle with other hungry children over grubs – grubs they stuffed hungrily into their little mouths! – which they had prised out from under a rotted log outside the stockade. There lay a young woman, her jaw bloodied and swollen, face and body a mass of purpling bruises, beaten half to death by other women because she had given her body to one of the demon guards in hopes of making her life here a little less insupportable. And here was an old man, rocking back and forth convulsively, his joints twisted up with the agony of arthritis and his own helpless misery. Weeping silently, he had told Jonaquil how his quilted blanket, the only thing that kept him warm at nights, had been stolen by a group of boys, hard-eyed and fearless, who terrorized the scattered old folk, stealing food and essentials from them, threatening gruesome reprisals if they reported anything.

And poor Hozias was not the only victim of the lash. The hawk-visaged Commander of this camp ruled with a cruel hand.

They were here to have their hurts tended, these wounded ones. But more than anything else, they came here in hopes of finding a little comfort, a little peace, some small relief from the daily misery of their lives.

As best she could, through the misery of her own flesh, Jonaquil gave them that.

She was not the only Healer here. There were two others, older women, as the Sub-Commander had told her. They could set limbs well enough, these two, administer salves and ointments and healing herbs. But they had none of the true Healing art. And they were too bitter, too full of hopeless hatred themselves to be able to minister to the misery about them. It was the bruises of the spirit that required healing more than anything else. Simple bodily injuries could be mended, but the deeper hurts could not be healed by the mere mindless employment of herbs or ointments.

It was the spirit, oftentimes, that broke before the body. In full Healing trance, Jonaquil could see plainly the nimbus of life-glow pulsing about all live beings, and from the intensity, colour, size, or shape of that ethereal, dancing nimbus could understand much about the living person. Early in the morning, she had looked in on poor Hozias, easing herself into trance, and seen the life-light about him dim and fading. And now, by mid-afternoon, he was indeed dead, his spirit fled to the Shadowlands from a life he could no longer endure.

Turning, Jonaquil looked back through the tent's dimness. The two men had all but finished wrapping the tattered shroud about Hozias. Their movements were rough and disinterested, as if the poor soul were naught but a lump of meat being wrapped for market.

Jonaquil shivered, clutching herself, and turned away. Men fought each other for the privilege of working here in the Dispensary because it brought an extra ration of food. These men before her cared nothing for the sufferers here. They were just filling their bellies.

The thought made Jonaquil queasy. All that grey-haired Tishta had first told her about life here was proving to be simple truth.

This terrible, hateful place . . .

Jonaquil pined for her home, yearned after familiar, dear Woodend, and for her ordered life there, and all the familiar faces. She was a virtual prisoner in this dismal tent of a Dispensary, and had seen not a single Woodender in the days she had spent here. It was like a stitch in her side, that yearning after her old life.

What had she and hers ever done to deserve a fate such as this?

Jonaquil took a long, sobbing breath, sore in heart and mind and flesh. Her hand moved for comfort to the amber nugget which still hung hidden against her skin under her shirt, the cobble Idris had bequeathed her. Feeling the amber's smooth warmth, Jonaquil saw in her mind's eye the twinkling eyes and solid, broad-cheeked, beloved face of her old teacher. In memory, she heard Idris speak: 'Everything contains a lesson, girl. Everything . . .'

Jonaquill shivered, the memory was so strong: a warm spring morning, she and Idris walking a hillside shining with new flowers, she hardly more than a girl, learning the gifts and banes of the true Healing. And then, before them in a little hollow, the pitiful form of a rabbit, caught in some boy's badly made snare, crippled but alive still and thumping in agony. Girl-Jonaquil had felt the poor creature's pain as her own, shrieked with every jerk of the little furred limbs.

And Idris, with all Jonaquil's Healer-sensitivity and more, had leaned over calmly, stroking the silky ears until the poor thing settled a little, then quickly broke its neck.

'The world is not ours to order, girl,' Idris had said to Girl-Jonaquil's tears. 'But no situation, however terrible, is empty. Learn from this small one's going. Death is sometimes a gift, girl. Nothing is so terrible that you cannot learn something . . .'

Yes, but how could she make dead Hozias's young brother Tym understand?

'Healer,' a voice said roughly from behind her.

Jonaquil whirled, stuffing the cobble quickly back inside her shirt. One of the demon guards stood there before her. Even knowing the sorcerous secret behind such a shape, Jonaquil could not repress a shudder, for the illusion of his inhuman-eyed, tusk-visaged, wet-tongued face was perfect. He had a metal flash on his shoulder, this one, marking him as one who ordered the armed squads that oversaw the logging operations.

'You are needed at the garrison,' he told her. 'Now.'

He put a gauntleted hand roughly on Jonaquil's shoulder and began to force her towards the door. 'I said *now*. One of my guards was injured in the forest and needs ministering to.'

Jonaquil blinked. An injured guard? She had never heard of such a thing. The sorcery that gave them their fell visage also seemed to give them an uncanny, indomitable resilience and strength.

The demon pulled her roughly towards the Dispensary doorway.

She shook his hand from her. 'All right. I am coming.' Remembering well Tishta's confrontation with the guards outside Sub-Commander Gerrid's tent, Jonaquil glared at this one. 'Do not presume too much, Squad Chief. One day *your* life may lie in my hands.' She paused and made herself look steadily at him. 'And I have a long memory.'

It was a terrible thing for her to do, using her gift as a threat like this, but it produced the desired result. He backed away from her and became immediately more respectful.

'My guard is injured and in pain,' he said. 'And he needs tending quickly.'

'And what of these others here? They do not need tending?' Jonaquil almost said. But she stopped herself. There was nothing to be gained by such accusations. Instead, without a word, she walked to the Dispensary's back corner and brought out her bag. 'What type of injury has this guard of yours taken?' she called back over her shoulder.

'Broken leg,' the Squad Chief replied. 'Got caught under a tree. One of the labourers felled it wrong. Said it was an accident.' He laughed humourlessly. 'That one won't be causing any more accidents.'

Jonaquil held her tongue. It was always unnerving talking with one of *them*, hearing petty man-sentiments voiced by such demon-faced, grim creatures. It was still so hard for her to think of them as ordinary mortal men.

As Jonaquil checked the contents of the bag before her, she noticed Beryl, one of the two older, resident Healers, standing in the dim back of the Dispensary tent. 'Could you bring me a set of splints, please?' Jonaquil asked.

Beryl said nothing, merely stood there sullenly.

Jonaquil sighed. As if she did not have enough to cope with! Those two – Beryl and Tillie – schemed together and did all they could, in petty ways, to frustrate her. To them, she was simply competition, another threat.

Jonaquil fetched the splints and bindings herself, dawdling as much as she dared, one eye on the demon-faced Squad Chief. Though he glared at her impatiently, he uttered no word of reproach.

Before leaving, she paused over the body of Hozias, wrapped now and ready to be taken away for burial. 'Remember,' she reminded the day-help, 'leave him to rest here till his brother returns.' At least young Tym would be able to make a last farewell. Precious little though it was, she had arranged that much for him.

Only then, feeling she had moved slowly enough to make her point sufficiently to the Squad Chief, did she follow him out.

The garrison was a solid log structure abutting the north-west corner of the Palisade, second only in size to the squat building of Tancred the Seer. Though quarters here were somewhat cramped inside, it was dry and clean and altogether far superior to the squalid canvas tents in which the camp labourers lived.

'What took you, woman?' demanded a burly demon as Jonaquil and the Squad Chief entered. 'Did you dally on the way with our "Chief"?' The man moved closer to her. 'Perhaps you'd like to dally here with me afterwards?'

Jonaquil swallowed her outrage and tried to ignore him.

'Be quiet,' the Squad Chief snapped.

'Just trying to make her feel at home.'

The Squad Chief turned, his inhuman yellow eyes lighting with anger, and the other sidled away.

Jonaquil was led along a corridor and into a back bunkroom where the injured man lay. He was indeed a man, not a demon; white-faced, shaking with pain. His eyes were clenched shut, but his mouth hung slack, and he seemed barely conscious. The odour of liquor was strong about him.

'He's been swigging grog,' the Squad Chief explained. 'For the pain.'

Bending close, Jonaquil saw it was indeed a bad break, with splinters of bone showing through the torn flesh of the man's lower thigh, the bedclothes soggy and dark from where he had bled.

She sensed the agony that throbbed in him, and felt bitterly pleased that this man was suffering so. It seemed only right that he and his should be made to suffer too. Looking down at him, feeling this way, Jonaquil felt a sudden, terrible temptation. It was a bad break, yes. A man could die from such a break. Infection could set in. Internal bleeding could drain the life from him.

She thought of remembered Idris, reaching down to the rabbit and breaking its little neck. It was no such simple option that lay before her here, but she *could* contrive this man's death. And none would be the wiser.

It was tempting. So terribly, terribly tempting . . . She could feel this man's pain echoed in her own flesh, could harden her heart with it, willing herself to . . .

But she could not.

Jonaquil knelt before the man-demon, panting. She heard again the voice of Idris: 'Everything contains a lesson, girl. Everything . . .'

Jonaquil saw clearly, then, how giving in to this dire temptation would be the first step towards disaster, dragging her into the mire of reprisal and revenge which would grow in her like a fungus until it had rotted her through and through.

It would be the very end of her as a Healer.

Jonaquil took a long, slow, shuddering breath, another, trying to clear her mind, letting the disturbing thoughts sink away through her. 'You must be clear as running water,' Idris had been wont to say. 'Empty as the morning sky.'

For this was the secret, the great secret of the true Healing art Jonaquil had learned from Idris: the true Healing did not lie in the use of herbs and ointments and the like. Jonaquil must become a channel through which something else, some Power could move, and it was only by keeping herself open and clean that she could have that Power move through her.

It was difficult at first, but the habit of long years took over. Her thoughts and emotions began to still, and Jonaquil eased slowly into the clear and welcome openness of the true Healing Trance.

Leaning forwards, she ran her hands gently across the area of the man's thigh, where the splinters of bone protruded, her palms hovering above his skin. She could feel uneasy heat generated there from the injury. The nimbus of light about him danced darkly, twisting and writhing into attenuated coils, and she could just make out a dark vermilion stain in the nimbus's moving intricacy over his thigh. With long, slow, deliberate motions, moving her hands in a coalescing pattern that repeated over and over, she gradually drew the energy about him into something more approaching its normal configuration.

The man eased a trifle.

And then the Power, eternally thrilling and mysterious, moved through her, and she felt her hands reach down into his thigh, pull and twist and push at the shattered bone there, realigning, gently palpating, setting bone and flesh and more-than-flesh, energy tingling through her fingers like water through a chute.

And then it was done.

She came out of the trance slowly, blinking, gulping air. The man's thigh was bruised and swollen and ugly looking, but the bone protruded no longer and the rupture it had caused in his flesh no longer bled. The man himself lay quiet now, asleep, stretched out on the bunk.

Gently, she began the process of binding his leg in the splints.

When it was over, she sat back and sighed. As usual, she felt light-headed: not tired exactly, but disoriented, as if she had been on a long journey and had only just now returned to look at old, familiar things.

'You do good work, Healer,' a familiar voice said from behind her.

Somehow, perhaps in some way as a residue from the trance, she was not in the least surprised to hear this particular voice. 'Thank you, Sub-Commander,' she replied without looking around.

She bundled up what remained of the splint-binding, and then sorted through her bag. Finding what she wanted, she turned and looked about her. Sub-Commander Gerrid stood leaned against the far wall, arms crossed, watching her. The Squad Chief was perched on the edge of a nearby bunk.

The Sub-Commander wore the inhuman visage of a feral cat now, golden-eyed and snarling. Jonaquil shivered as those eerie cat-eyes stared unblinkingly at her. 'He should sleep for a while,' she told the Squad Chief. 'When he wakes, give him a tea made from this.' She passed him the little package she had taken from her bag.

He hefted it suspiciously in his palm.

'For the pain. A tincture of arnica and poppy and other things. *Much* better than grog.'

'He won't be . . . crippled?'

Jonaquil shook her head. 'Not as far as I can tell. A bad break, and it will hurt him for some time to come. But, given time and rest, he should heal.'

'Good work indeed, Healer,' Sub-Commander Gerrid said from where he still leaned against the wall. He gazed at her with those eerie eyes of his, arms crossed. It was impossible to read anything human in that cat face.

'I commend you. I had thought perhaps that you might be . . . tempted into doing something foolish.'

She turned on him. For no clear reason she could put name to, she decided to tell him the truth. 'I *was* tempted. But giving in to such temptation would be the death of me.'

He blinked a slow cat-blink. 'You misjudge me, Healer. I do not mete out death as easily as all that.'

'It is *you* who misunderstand *me*, Sub-Commander. It is not your retribution I fear. Such an act would be the death of me as a Healer. That was my meaning.'

Gerrid smiled, at least she thought it might be a smile, a stretching of lips over ivory fangs. 'Honourable dedication to a worthy profession is commendable indeed.'

Jonaquil shrugged. 'I would have been killing a part of myself if had given into that temptation. You can do me no harm, Sub-Commander, worse than the harm I can do myself.'

As soon as the words were out, Jonaquil realized the complete truth in them. *They* held the power to do her harm. But what she could do to herself, to her own spirit, in response to that power was potentially far, far worse. She could hear once again the voice of Idris in her mind: 'Everything holds a lesson. All you have to do is see it.'

Jonaquil found herself smiling. A lesson indeed. She felt freed suddenly, seeing now how the hatred inspired by *them* in fact helped forge the links of the chain that bound her and the others here.

Sub-Commander Gerrid was looking at her appraisingly.

'I am finished here,' she said, gesturing to the exit. 'By your leave, Sub-Commander?'

He hesitated, still staring silently at her, then nodded.

Lifting her bag on to her shoulder, Jonaquil strode out.

Evening was well on by now, and the Palisade compound was crowded with men returned from the day's logging works. Jonaquil moved along through the press of people, feeling a thrill of satisfaction, more whole and content than she had been at any time since her forced departure from Woodend.

But the feeling was short lived.

As she neared the Dispensary, she heard shouting. A crowd had clustered at the Dispensary door. Feeling her heart sink, wondering what might have gone wrong now, she pushed her way through the crowd and inside.

The old Healers, Beryl and Tillie, were both there, standing impassively against one wall. In the Dispensary's centre, the two day-helpers wrestled with a screaming, kicking boy. Even before she could see him properly, Jonaquil knew who the boy was: Tym, dead Hozias's young brother, come on his evening visit.

'You took him away!' Tym was screaming. 'He's dead, and I never even got the chance to see him! He's dead. *Dead*! And you took him away ...!' Suddenly, Tym seemed to collapse. He went limp in the day-helpers' grasp and began to sob.

Jonaquil strode in through the doorway and looked to where Hozias had lain. The cot was empty.

Seeing her come in, Tym lifted his pale face to her. 'Why? *Why?*' His voice was plaintive and shaky. 'Why did you do it?'

'I told you to leave him here till the boy returned,' Jonaquil snapped at the day-helpers.

They only looked away.

Jonaquil turned to Beryl and Tillie. The older women kept their faces deliberately blank, but she saw a kind of sullen triumph in their eyes. 'How could you be so . . . so *petty*?' Jonaquil demanded.

Neither of them said a word, but the faintest of smiles curled Beryl's lip, a smile so thin it was a sneer. And that smile said everything. 'Think you can come in here and just take over, do you?' it said. 'Think you can order things to your own liking without so much as a "by your leave"? Well, we'll teach you, girl!'

Jonaquil felt like shrieking, like taking Beryl by the ears and thumping her against the wall.

Instead, the recent lesson still clear inside her, Jonaquil took a series of long, cleansing breaths, turned from Beryl and Tillie, dismissing them as best was possible, and knelt before Tym. 'I'm truly sorry, Tym. I tried to arrange things so that you could make your farewell, but it looks as if there has been some sort of mix-up. Please, forgive us.'

Tym looked up, his face twisted in grief. 'I'll never see him again,' he sobbed. 'He was all I had. Now they've taken *everything* from me!'

'Do not hate them, Tym,' Jonaquil said, softly. She paused, trying to think of some way to express what she herself was only just coming to realize. It sounded hopelessly pious and foolish, put thus, but she could think of no other way to express it: 'If you hate them, you give them power over you.'

But Tym was not listening. He had buried his head in her shoulder and was shaking, his whole body quivering with it. 'I'll kill them. I'll kill them!'

'No, Tym,' Jonaquil implored.

'Let me take the lad,' somebody said.

Jonaquil turned and saw it was Tishta.

'He needs to be away from this place now,' Tishta said softly.

Jonaquil nodded.

Tishta put an arm about the boy's thin shoulders and gently urged him through the Dispensary doorway, between the parted ranks of the crowd still gathered outside, and away.

Jonaquil stood, watching them go, feeling suddenly very tired and very sad and very, very old.

# XVI

# The Miradore

It was the black middle of the night, and Tai lay dead asleep, when the demon guards came for him.

The door thumped open and a sudden splash of pale radiance lit the room. The queer bird shrieked, fluttering hysterically. Hard hands rousted Tai from the warm blankets. 'Come,' a voice said. 'My Lord Seer calls for you.'

Tai struggled to his feet, shivering, heart beating hard.

The bird swooped about, still shrieking. 'Silence!' one of the guards hissed. He swatted at it with uncanny accuracy, knocking it out of the air so that it landed in a small, shivering heap on the bed. Then he whirled, a dark shape outlined by the pale light of a hissing lamp, and hauled Tai out of the room.

Barring the door behind him, the two guards took Tai along the walkway by the slanted, grey-slate roof, through into the main halls of the Keep and down, down. Tai could make out little of the way they travelled, for the hissing lantern was dimmed, casting only a faint and uncertain radiance. The man-demons, though, seemed to see in the dark like cats. He stumbled after them as best he could, still thick with sleep, trying to gather his shattered wits. He had slept most of the day through, the dead sleep of exhaustion, rousing only in the evening to lie dazedly in the bed, too groggy even to feel much of hunger. He had only a hazy recollection of night's deepening darkness, the bird hunched, a silent shadow in the far corner of the room. He remembered sleep coming over him again.

And then *this* . . .

Down and down they continued, until the stone walls about them began to be slicked with slimy moisture. Tai dragged his heels, shaking with apprehension. 'Where . . . where are you taking me?'

He got no answer.

'I *said*, where are . . . ?'

'Silence,' one of the two hissed. That was all. It was enough.

Tai swallowed, a sick feeling in the pit of his belly. He wished to be anywhere but where he was going. For one wild moment he thought of escape, of dashing off down the next unlit corridor they passed. But it was a hopeless notion.

The demon guards took him downwards through the maze of chill, dim corridors until they stopped at a closed wooden door. One knocked. They waited silently until the door creaked open. Remaining outside, the guards thrust Tai in, pushing the door to behind him.

Tai found himself in a large rectangular chamber. Hissing glow-globes cast a familiar, colourless light, illuminating several long trestle tables upon which was an array of queer objects. At the room's far end, the Seer stood leaning over one of the tables. Straightening, he gestured to Tai. 'Come.'

Tai edged nervously over, walking along the side of one of the tables. From the corner of his eye he saw a rack of glass vials filled with cloudy liquid. Next to them lay a heap of curved bone. Beyond, there was the gleam of bronze, twisted wires, and polished wood. Next to these stood a large, liquid-filled glass jar, in which floated things that seemed like so many severed, pale hands, but strangely boneless, and with too many fingers. They moved, squirming over each other.

Tai looked away, shuddering, not wishing to watch such things too closely.

The Seer smiled. 'Welcome to my laboratory.' He gestured about the room. 'Spacious, is it not? And so nicely located, set off as it is from the main section of the Keep. One cannot help but wonder what function the original builders intended this room to serve. The Veil likes this building because it provides a haven to keep certain. . . valuables out of harm's way. And I? I like it for its complexity. The original designers of this Keep seem to have had a liking for complexity. I trust you had no difficulty making the journey down here?'

Tai blinked, not knowing what to say.

'You are rested?' the Seer asked. 'You have eaten and slept?'

Silently, Tai nodded.

'Is there anything you need?'

Tai shrugged uncomfortably. This flood of casual small talk and apparent solicitousness was not at all what he had expected. It confused him.

The Seer stood looking at him, silent now, dark eyes unblinking as a snake's. The casualness had fallen abruptly from him, and the cold intensity of that gaze, the feel of power in the man, suddenly made Tai's skin creep. He felt as helpless as a mongrel dog before a cruel master. He tried to pull away from the Seer's intent gaze, but found to his dismay that he could not. He was held fast in some strange manner, like before.

156

Then Tai felt it happening to him again, the solid world dissolving away into sickening chaos . . .

'No!' he shrieked, every desperate instinct in him trying to fight it. But the chaos tore at him like a rip-tide, pulling him inexorably down and down into a seething confusion. He was stripped of his senses, yet he somehow sensed *things* near him, squirming and writhing like stricken serpents . . .

And then he was out of it, sagging weakly against the table, the hard wooden edge jammed painfully against his thigh. He heard the slosh of water from the big jar on the table at his back and shoved himself away. His vision blurred, and his belly was twisted into a painful, pulsing knot. His heart shuddered.

'Stupid boy,' Tancred said.

Tai only stared, sick to the marrow.

'You behave like a frightened, mindless child, resisting it so. It is a gift, boy.'

'I have no . . . no *gift*,' Tai returned through clenched teeth.

The Seer gestured impatiently. 'I will not argue. Come here.'

Tai hung back, his belly knotted in fear.

Tancred regarded him coldly. 'You try my patience, boy. You cling to your little world like a baby monkey to its mother's back. We must break you out of this rigid little world of yours or you will be of no use at all . . . Come *here*!'

Uneasily, Tai drew closer. The Seer might as well be talking in riddles for all the sense it made to him. In his very bones, Tai wanted nothing more than to be far away from the uncanny, confusing, frightening figure before him who offered the comfort of food and shelter with the one hand, and damned him to torment with the other. He felt Tancred's black eyes gazing at him appraisingly. The hairs on Tai's neck prickled in apprehension.

But no rush of chaos overwhelmed him this time. Instead, the Seer turned and reached for something that lay on the table. It was made of bone and iron and bronze, with blank, staring yellow eyes, each as large and round as the yolk of a good egg.

It looked like the dead remains of some strange, inhuman head.

Tancred pressed it into Tai's unwilling hands.

The yellow 'eyes', Tai saw, were cloudy membranes stretched across bronze sockets. Bone tusks protruded from an iron 'mouth', and bone and iron bands crossed the vaulted 'skull'. It felt heavy in his hands and strangely, unnervingly warm, almost like some live thing. He hefted it nervously, careful of his injured finger, not at all certain what the Seer might be intending.

157

'Come,' Tancred commanded, leading Tai through to the back of the room and out through another door there. A flight of steep stone steps led away from this into darkness. Tancred produced a small hissing lamp from somewhere. 'This way.'

Down they went until they came out into a large, low-ceilinged chamber lit by ordinary, sputtering torches set in iron brackets on the walls.

'Place it on your head,' Tancred directed, pointing to the thing still in Tai's hands.

Tai hesitated, uncertain.

'Put it on!'

Tai did, his hands shaking.

He felt a stunning rush of strength, like a solid, glowing core suddenly lit inside him. The room about him took on a brighter, sharper focus. He could make out colours where none had been before, could distinguish objects more closely. He stood there, staring, entranced by this new, brighter world. The chamber in which he stood seemed to glow, and he saw clearly now the shape of it – a large half-oval with a shoulder-high brick partition along one side, beyond which he could see more torchlit space, torchlight shadows dancing like fish in the sea . . .

And then, unexpectedly, Tai saw something come over the partition. It seemed at first, to be a man slinking along now with his back to the brick.

But this was no true man.

Tai stared, shaken. Darkly furred body, glinting eyes, the flash of sharp teeth. It was the same sort of creature he had met in the Pit. The fur-man of the dark pool. But that one had been as sleek as an otter, and this was scraggy, all bone and sinew, open sores and patches of pale skin showing through its tattered fur. It moved towards Tai, limping, its eyes fixed warily upon him. In its hand it held a long slat of wood, hefting the length of it like a club.

Tai did not understood this at all. This creature was no miniature creation. It was as real as he, as tall as he. He glanced hastily round at the Seer.

Tancred had vanished.

The ragged fur-man screeched, charging Tai. The furred face was a twisted mask of hate. It lifted the club aloft and brought it down in a double-handed blow aimed at Tai's head.

Tai leaped aside, his heart thumping, and was astonished to find he had cleared half the chamber.

The fur-man skidded to a halt and came after him anew, howling.

Tai felt impossibly light and strong, agile as a cat. As the fur-man lunged after him, Tai leaped to the top of the shoulder-high brick partition as if it were the easiest thing in the world.

He vaulted down on the other side, relishing the rush of air about him as he flew, and landed lightly on his feet. He spun round. The very stones of the wall scintillated. He felt . . . he was not sure what, exactly. An exuberance, a thrilling sense of being burningly alive. He could do anything, he felt. Anything.

Tai caught a flash of motion and whirled on the balls of his feet. A figure skulked in the shadows. So there was another of them here on this side. And another yet, by the sound of it, over against the far wall.

The fur-man clambered over the partition. The other two edged out of the shadows. They hefted long wooden clubs, but there any similarity between and the fur-man ended. The closer of them was hairless as an egg, with bony limbs and a greenish, warty hide. Huge eyes, bulbous as a toad's, dwarfed all else of its face. The other was furred right enough, but was squat and bulky and moved with a shambling gait, a long tail lashing about its legs. Its head was covered by a mane of matted black hair, out of which two mad, squinting little eyes glared.

The three circled nearer, and then, suddenly, they charged, clubs aloft, howling like crazed things so that the sound reverberated off the walls.

Tai skipped away, looking for some means of escape. But there was nothing.

The fur-man rushed him. Tai dodged the thrust of the club easily. The other two came for him in unison, though, and it was like trying to avoid a pair of crazed hounds. He ducked under the tailed one, smashed the other in the belly with a fist in passing.

The bony creatures crumpled.

Tai felt strong and fit, breathing easily. He loped across the chamber away from his attackers and vaulted atop the brick partition once again.

They came after him more slowly, silent now. The one he had hit lagged behind the other two, holdings its belly with one hand and gasping.

Tai felt the memory of that blow in his right hand. It had felt good, solid and powerful. He felt the strength flow through him like a vigorous current.

Without warning, something struck Tai painfully across the backs of his knees from behind.

Another of them!

Legs buckled, Tai tumbled from the partition and landed heavily on his side on the unyielding stone of the floor, the breath momentarily knocked out of him. A club struck him on the shoulder. Another blow smacked into the side of his helmeted head. He gasped, trying to suck in air. Blows rained upon him in an agonizing flurry. He lifted his arms to protect himself.

A sudden anger rose up in him then. Stupid creatures, these things arrayed about him, weak and skinny and stupid . . .

He rolled sideways and came up on his knees. Grasping the green-skinned one by one bony leg and its shoulder, he wrenched it off its feet. Using the creatures as a shield, Tai heaved himself upright. He backed away a few steps, then hurled the thing in his hands against the partition, feeling the strength power through him. It hit with a heavy *thwump* and slid unmoving to the floor, leaving a smear of glistening, dark blood against the brick.

Tai threw back his head and laughed.

The others hesitated, eyeing him with a desperate, hopeless hate. Three left now, with the newcomer who had struck him from behind come scrambling over the partition. Another fur-man.

Tai charged them. They howled, beating at him with the clubs, but he shrugged their blows off as nothing. He hammered them with his fists until he was able to wrench one of the clubs away and set upon them with that. He felt flesh and bone give way under his attack, the solid, satisfying thud of each blow reverberating all the way up to his shoulder joints.

Tai smashed them, blow upon blow, smashing furred flesh and bone, exalting, hearing them wail, smashing them until the club dribbled wetly at each stroke and the creatures became silent, unmoving, huddled tatters.

He stopped, then. He was hardly breathing hard. A rush of jubilation went through him, a pure joy of power and strength.

On the edge of his vision, Tai caught movement. Whirling, he saw Tancred lean over the brick partition, beckoning. Tai came over, feeling the Seer's presence douse the jubilant feeling in him like water would a burning flame.

'Remove it,' the Seer commanded.

Tai blinked. 'What?'

'Remove the helm.'

Tai found himself complying.

Strength washed out of him, leaving him gasping. He staggered to his knees. Before him lay the pitiful remains of the creatures he had killed. Poor, tattered, starveling things they were, hardly more than hide and bone. The skull of one was a shattered basket of bone, a dark ooze staining the floor under it. Tai looked at the helm in his hand and flung it from him in horror. He sagged weakly against the brick of the partition, putting a hand to it for support. His heart thumped painfully. The chamber dimmed.

The world begin to shatter about him into all-too-familiar chaos. He felt as if a hard, groping hand were twisting at something inside him, tugging, pulling, squeezing, tearing him apart.

He fought the terrible dissolution of it desperately, willing himself to feel the hard, gritty surface of the brick under his hand, holding on desperately to that sensation as a drowning man might clutch at a floating log.

*Fingers, gritty brick, cool and hard and solid . . .*

He came out of it still sagged up against the brick of the partition. His belly heaved and he was wretchedly sick.

'Stupid boy,' he heard from above.

'Leave me . . . alone,' Tai sobbed. 'Leave me *alone!*'

Seeing something leap over the partition, Tai cringed.

It was Tancred's two man-demons.

The Seer glided into view, his dark cloak swishing softly about him. 'Look.' Tancred gestured at the all-too-familiar demon face of the guard, then down to the helm still lying on the chamber's stone floor. 'It is called a spell-helm,' the Seer said.' It is not a true living creature, yet neither is it a mere object of iron and bronze and bone. Inside the casing lies a manner of living substance, drawing its life from the wearer. But the wearer also draws from the helm, the two joined each to each. There is life of sorts to a helm, and that life generates its own realness. That is what you see.'

Tai saw. And he thought of the terrible ease with which *they* had done the foul things they had. He understood now the dreadful exaltation of spirit that a spell-helm produced. He shuddered, looking at the poor dead creatures at his feet.

He had become one of *them*.

'The world is a larger place than you ever imagined, boy. And far more complex.' Tancred smiled his thin smile. 'I will open you, boy, one way or another.'

Tai shivered sickly.

'Return him,' Tancred ordered the attending demon guards. 'For the moment, I have other concerns.'

Silent, the two descended upon Tai. He cringed under their hard-handed grip. His arms and shoulders and back were one great, throbbing bruise where he had been beaten with the clubs. Wearing the helm, he had felt the blows hardly at all. Now, he could barely move, and the demon guards' hold upon him was torment.

Heaving him easily over the partition, the guards hauled Tai towards the steps leading back up into the room with the tables.

'Gently with him,' the Seer cautioned. 'I do not wish him harmed unnecessarily.'

The guards paused and loosened their grip. Tai groaned, trembling.

Stepping closer, the Seer placed a hand possessively on Tai's shoulder. 'He is valuable to me, this one.'

Still silent, the guards bowed. Then, at a gesture from the Seer, they ushered Tai up the steps.

At the top, Tai slowed, panting. His insides pulsed strangely, where Tancred had *molested* him. Looking back into the chamber below, he felt a sick horror at what he had done.

Tancred stood, arms folded across his chest, gazing at Tai where he stood at the stairs' head. The Seer's hard black eyes gleamed, and his lips were curved in a half-smile. 'Gently,' he repeated to the guards.

Tai shuddered and turned quickly away. The expression on the Seer's face was unnervingly familiar: an ordinary man might look upon a promising ram in just that manner.

The demon guards took him then, carefully, and pulled him through past the tables with their queer paraphernalia, and so out of the door and upwards through the maze of corridors towards his tower room. He stumbled, leaning upon their strong arms for support, an irony he liked not at all. But he was too exhausted to have overmuch choice in the matter. He went on as best he could, grateful simply to be alive and intact still, and took what help he could.

## XVII

# At the Verge of
# the North Wold

Old Crane squatted upon a rocky hillock. About her gathered those who had felt the calling and come southwards with her into the strange lands. All were silent, waiting.

Crane could see the far glint of the sea south-westwards. She had never been to the sea. From this height and distance, it looked like a great, moving blanket spread over the edge of the earth.

She watched the red orb of the sun dip low over the water.

A good place, this raised hillock. Here, she could sense more clearly the movement of the Powers through the world.

And she needed to sense things clearly, if she could.

The Dream seemed muddled beyond hope now, an interlacing of images that formed no pattern Crane could perceive: cold black eyes in a face like a skull; a young woman, a Healing-woman, with auburn hair and a weary face, pursued by a great hawk; the flicker of torchlight on hideous, tusked faces, contorted in fury; brown fur and blue feathers and bright, small eyes; a woman screaming, engulfed by flames; a bloody axe raised; a twisting, mutilated, limbless man; the pale, inscrutable face of the Fey.

Dreamwalker though she was, Crane could see no clear sense to it. Nothing like this had ever happened in her experience. Storm was loose in the world. Great changes were loose. She knew not how to move.

For days, she and hers had wandered the edge of the forest, gazing out into the grassy lands southwards. It was from that direction that the great change came and, indeed, they had glimpsed strange and frightening-looking creatures in the distance: man-shaped, yet tusked and frog-eyed, like the things she saw in the Dream.

Crane could feel something coming forth into the world, a niggling, nagging sensation that gave her no peace. It drew her. Her old bones ached with it. But she could glean nothing clear. Her Dreaming was utterly muddled and, stripped of that, she felt half blinded.

Hence did she sit up there watching brother-sun sink slowly into the distant waters, waiting.

On the ground at her side lay a lumpy bundle wrapped in worn leather. She looked at it and smiled. There was more than one way to seek direction.

The time was almost here. The world hovered, balanced between night and day. Powers moved more clearly in the twilight. Crane tucked back the white rope of her hair. Closing her eyes, she slowly blanked her mind of thought so as to hold herself in open readiness for whatever might come through.

Gently, she parted the corners of the leather wrapping and opened it out. Moving with a slow and ritual deliberation, she spat carefully three times into each palm, scooped the bones up from where they lay aligned on their leather bed, and cupped them in front of her. Eyes closed, she breathed life gently into them. Then, her old hands spreading suddenly like a bird's wings, she let the bones drop.

A sigh went up from the people gathered about her.

At first, her heart sinking, she could discern no pattern at all. It had been too many years, perhaps. She had relied too much on the Dreaming and let this simpler skill lapse.

Nothing.

She held herself clear and poised and unmoving, and waited.

Then the patterning snapped into clarity. Three interlocked designs. No. *Four.* In all her years, she had seen nothing like it.

The jagged thrust of Sunder lay there. Resting across it, large and strong, lay the oval shape of Flocking. Interlocked with that was the twisted spiral of Falling Away, the death tracery. And trailing off from Sunder, linking it with Flocking, was the Hand, but it was the Hand backwards.

Crane contemplated the linked intricacy of the patterns before her, trying to let the sense of it settle in her mind.

She looked at her people, gathered about her, waiting. 'I see death. And I see a sundering of things large and small. But also a returning, a coming round to the start. And . . . an unlooked-for helping hand.'

It was a strange and unsettling pattern. Sunder – breaking apart, injury, the thrust that shatters – but Sunder in conjunction with Flocking. She saw in her mind the white geese, flocking together for the autumn migration. Great rafts of them on the lakes. Coming together, an in-gathering in preparation for the journey to come. A *good* tracing, Flocking. But paired with Sunder . . . She did not know.

And the Hand, backwards. Help from an unexpected source? She was not sure.

And Falling Away, the death tracery . . .

Her companions stared at her, anxious, wanting to know in more detail what the bones had revealed.

'I do not know what to tell thee,' she said to them. 'Only the same as I have already told thee. I see a death, and a breaking of patterns large and small, but with the hope of renewal, perhaps.' She shrugged, her old joints creaking. 'Now thou knows as much as I. It is blind times in which we live.'

They stared at her, solemn-eyed as fowl.

'The thrust that shatters,' she murmured. 'The in-gathering. The unknown helper . . .'

But there was no help for her and her people now. No clarification. The call was still strongly upon them. There would be no returning to the mountains. Not yet. But how long? How many days more must they range hereabouts before some clear sign sent them onwards?

She did not know. Blind times indeed, in which to live.

# XVIII

# The Palisade

'What do you expect *me* to do?' Tishta said, shrugging. 'Such things happen.'

Jonaquil leaned forward, her hands fidgeting with her empty tea-cup. 'But I *cannot* just let this go on!'

Jonaquil and Tishta squatted on the ground outside the entranceway of the Dispensary tent. It was evening, and though the sun had not been long down, they kept their voices low. About them, the compound lay quiet in the night's early dark, and the big tent at their back was silent save for the snores and rustlings and moans of those invalided there.

'You *must* help me,' Jonaquil insisted.

The older woman looked down at her own tea, undrunk, and sighed. Tishta's face was strained and smudged with weariness. In the darkness, only her eyes showed any life, reflecting the dancing radiance of the distant lights of the night-watch at the Palisade gates like small, twin mirrors. She looked across at Jonaquil and shrugged again, but said nothing.

Jonaquil leaned towards her. 'They are selling medicaments privately, for some profit or other, those two. And the potions are needed, desperately needed, by the folk who come to the Dispensary for treatment. It is *unconscionable!*'

Trishta raised her hands, palms out. 'Such things happen. There is naught we can *do*, girl. Think! Who did you say you saw selling these simples?'

'Beryl.'

'And to whom did she sell them?'

Jonaquil shivered. 'Two men, hard-eyed as one of *them*.'

'Exactly!'

'But . . .'

'I know that sort. All too well. What would you do to stop men like that? Attack them physically? Do you expect me to?'

'No! I . . .'

'*Think*, girl! Interfere with men such as that, and you are asking for a blade in your back one dark evening.'

Jonaquil shook with outrage. 'People will *die* because of what Beryl and Tillie are doing. Innocent people!'

Tishta shook her head unhappily. 'You haven't been here as long as I, Healer. Such things *happen*. There is nothing to be done.' She glanced at Jonaquil over her cup. 'Unless you include yourself in what is happening.'

Jonaquil glared at her. 'How could you even *think* such a thing?'

Tishta shrugged. 'It is called looking out for oneself.'

'Is it not bad enough,' Jonaquil demanded, glaring at the older woman, 'that we have to contend with the guards and the work and the terrible conditions here? Do we have to contend with each other as well?'

'Yes,' Tishta replied, her voice flat.

'And you? You just ignore it?'

'I do not just *ignore* it!' Tishta snapped, a shiver of sudden anger in her voice.

'Then *do* something! Help me stop these men.'

'What would you have me do? Walk up to them and tell them that what they are doing isn't *nice*?' Tistha turned away. 'You ask too much of me, girl. Who do you think me to be? I have my own safety to look after.'

'You helped young Tym when we needed it,' Jonaquil said. 'I hear you have managed to get him assigned to your work-gang, to help you with the horses. How can you just sit back now and let something like this happen, knowing that it is the old people, the children, the innocents who will suffer?'

Tishta sighed. 'I *hate* this place, Healer. Hate it like I've never hated anything before in my life; it and *them* both. I . . . I do what little I can, aye. But it is a question of *survival*.' Tishta stabbed an accusing finger at Jonaquil. 'It is easy enough for you. What you do here is what you'd do anywhere. You follow your vocation. But for the rest of us, there is nothing here but hunger, back-breaking work, and that damned spooky building of the Seer's waiting for us eventually. That, and the knowing that everything, *everything* we've ever held dear is taken from us.'

Jonaquil stared. She had never seen Tishta like this, so weary, so hopeless-sounding. She started to say something, but the other cut her off.

'No. Not another word.' Levering herself tiredly up off the ground, Tishta emptied her cup and passed it across to Jonaquil. 'You ask too much of me, girl. I am sorry, truly. But you ask too *much* . . .' With that, she turned and stumbled off into the darkness of the open compound.

Jonaquil rose and watched her dwindle into the night, a tired, sad figure, stoop-shouldered and shuffling. A demon guard challenged her, and Tishta muttered some kind of response, the words lost in the dark. Then she was gone.

Blinking back tears, Jonaquil stood there staring blindly into the dark. Never had she felt so utterly alone and helpless.

Oh, how she *hated* this cursed place! It corrupted and destroyed. And she was powerless to prevent it. It seemed she was powerless to prevent anything: despite all her efforts, the Woodenders had been split up, scattered to different parts of the compound; despite her, the selling of pilfered medicaments went on; and despite her Healer's skills, people died regularly under her care, their bodies too brutalized, their spirits too worn and weary to hold further on to life. She might as well not be here for all the difference her presence made.

Instinctively, she reached for the cobble, the nugget of amber that still hung hidden and safe under her shirt, hoping for comfort, for advice. Jonaquil had never understood for certain just how much of a charm the cobble held: sometimes it seemed it was only her own recollections and feelings that evoked the memory of Idris within her when she held the amber in her hands; other times it felt as though the cobble spoke directly through her. It did not matter. So long as the comforting voice returned, she was never totally alone.

The amber felt warm and smooth and familiar in her hand as she held it, waiting. But the remembered wise old voice of old Idris spoke to her not at all.

Shivering, Jonaquil tucked the nugget back into hiding. Tears filled her eyes. She did not understand what had gone wrong, that the cobble should be mute like this. Yet another treasured thing was stripped from her. She did not think she could endure much more. Her belly and bones ached with the constant torment of Healer's Sickness. And her spirit ached no less.

This terrible, terrible place . . .

From inside the dark Dispensary tent, somebody moaned and called her name in a hoarse, weak voice. Wearily, Jonaquil lifted the entrance flap and went in. There was no sign of either of the two other Healers. Both Beryl and Tillie were, no doubt, soundly asleep somewhere well beyond earshot. Jonaquil put away the cups she and Tishta had used – a token gesture against the tent's disorder – and went to see who it was had called her. None slept but fitfully here; the calling of her name and her own movements, careful though she was, roused others, so that it was no little time before she had finished ministering to all who had need.

There was a kind of peace to be found in such service, but she was too bruised of spirit to feel any but a momentary respite. When she had finished, finally, she wrapped herself in a blanket and sat outside by the tent's entrance flap, sore and weary. The lights of the night-watch at the Palisade gates flickered in the distance, the guards' dark figures showing from time to time in silhouette. She felt wound up tight as a metal spring, brittle and strained almost to breaking. She took a long, measured breath, another, trying to clear her mind, calm her spirit. She must not let this place poison her, must *not*! For that, as she had come to realize, would be the end of all, and worse than death for her as Healer.

But she could smell her own unwashed stink all too clearly, and the ache in her bones and flesh gave her no reprieve. Despair dragged at her. And the black hate inside her grew like a tumour. She did not think she could endure much longer without breaking.

Alone in the dark, Jonaquil hugged herself and wept.

After a time, despite all, her head nodded and she dropped off into fitiful sleep.

And dreamed . . .

The Palisade shook, mud trampled crimson and black, bodies like so much rubbish underfoot. Blood and iron and shrieking. A demon-face shattered open in a gush of red. Man against demon, demon against demon, as if the very world itself had gone mad and only violence and hate were left.

She saw a great axe raised, shiny with gore, saw a man spitted like a pig by one of *them* and heaved aside.

Terrified and sickened, she tried to pull away. The mud gripped her as if with slimy hands. She struggled, heart thumping like a drum in her ears, fighting to make it through the Palisade gates and beyond.

The din of it dwindling behind her, she stood then, filthy and panting, outside the high log wall. Before her stretched the green of the wild lands, as it would in the waking world. And there . . . oh, there! Quiet under the elbow of an old oak, one of the Fey Folk stood. She – or he, Jonaquil could not tell – beckoned and, effortlessly, Jonaquil found herself next to the oak.

The pale face gazed at her, the great dark eyes wise and utterly strange. One long-fingered, impossibly slim hand brushed Jonaquil's face softly. Almost, she felt . . . she knew not what. Something. A promise.

And then the Fey was gone, and in her place stood an old woman, mortal woman true, face winkled as a dried apple, with moss-green eyes and a long rope of white hair. Behind this elder woman stood others, though Jonaquil could not make them out clearly. She heard a flutter of wings, saw an arm dark with fur, the bright flare of a life-glow so strong it dazed her dream-eyes . . .

With a start, rubbing at her eyes, Jonaquil came awake.

Her neck ached, for she had twisted it falling asleep. Her shoulder-joints crackled as she straightened.

The dream had left her shaken, frightened, elated.

A world gone mad, as if the Powers themselves had ceased to have influence. A world slid into hatred and violence unending.

*That* was what she had been dream-witness to. Or so it seemed.

But the Fey . . .

She felt a kind of residue of that one's presence still, as a sudden bright light might leave an after-image on the eye; like a soothing elixir.

And the elder woman and the others . . .

Jonaquil did not know what to make of it all. She felt her heart beating hard. Surely this was no ordinary dream? And some of it she seemed to have witnessed before, in the dream that had woken her on her first morning here: the violence of the fighting, the life-glow so bright . . .

Jonaquil rose, leaving the blanket she had been wrapped in, and shook herself. She could sleep no more this night. Not now. Her mind reeled. She felt six ways at once. What could such a dream mean?

Turning her back on the Dispensary, she walked off. She had no clear idea of where she might go, only that she needed to move.

Aimless, she wandered through the compound, her own inner turmoil making her blind to her surroundings, until, blinking, she found herself at the Palisade gates. Torchlight glimmered off polished iron and great demon eyes. The guards eyed her closely, but dared nothing to molest her. It was one of her Healer's privileges, being allowed to come and go through the camp as she wished, even outside the gates if needs be.

She walked on past the demon guards. For a moment it seemed they might stop her, but they let her pass, only admonishing her not to stray far. She said nothing to them, merely walked through the gateway in silence out into the clean night air beyond.

It had gone cold. Jonaquil hugged herself, shivering. She felt the swirl of emotions going through her still, volatile as white water. The dark bulk of the Palisade wall loomed over her, a solid, oppressive thing. She felt the eyes of the gate guards on her and turned her back on them.

Before her, the Paudit's valley was an impenetrable black hollow, the crested ridge of the distant peaks on the far side showing as mere black cut-outs against the star-dusted, glowing sky. Out here, there was not a sound to be heard from inside the Palisade. Only the rhythmic, background susurration of the Paudit's waters broke the night's total stillness.

In the great dark quiet, she could sense, almost, the Powers that moved the world, those great live forces that animated all. There were folk, she knew, who made images, putting shape to this or that Power. But Jonaquil, who felt a Power move through her when she healed, knew that such images were not the truth. The Powers were greater, or lesser, than human images of them. The Powers were themselves.

They were like strong currents under smooth water, save that the water was the world entire.

She shivered, half sensing them, and it seemed to her at that moment that the churning of feelings inside her was no more and no less than a reflection of the movement of the Powers through the world.

She in the world, the world in her . . .

Huge and silent, the world encompassed her, ancient beyond imagining, and utterly mysterious in the dark wrappings of the night. She felt her heart leap. The stars hung in silent glory over her.

The sheer, simple wonder of it made her breathless.

The dream had terrified her, disturbed and agitated her, yet somehow comforted as well. And now, beyond all expectation, blowing through her like a fresh wind, she felt herself a part of the world as she had not since that first terrible morning when *they* had descended upon Woodend.

Jonaquil blinked, blinked again, gazing up at the glittering, mysterious glory of the stars. She let out a long sigh.

'Beauty beyond price,' a voice said from behind her, uncanny echo to her own thoughts.

Startled, she spun about and saw the looming figure of Sub-Commander Gerrid standing next to her. He was man-shaped now; human eyes stared at her from a human face. Involuntarily, she took a step away from him.

'My apologies if I startled you, Healer,' he said. 'But you are not the only one in the camp to gaze up at the beauties of the night sky.'

Disoriented and uncertain, Jonaquil made no reply. She did not trust this seeming pleasantness on the Sub-Commander's part.

Gerrid stood at Jonaquil's side, silent, his gaze fixed on her. The starry sky thrilled her no longer. The air was chill, and she shivered, her arms dimpled with cold.

After a time, the Sub-Commander pointed away towards where a cluster of stars hung close to the horizon. 'See that constellation there? That is the Hunter, frozen forever in the chase. And there — see the scatter of stars before him? — there are his prey frozen in flight. Forever safe, but never free.'

Jonaquil looked at him uneasily. In the dim radiance of the starlight, his face seemed pale as sculpted marble. His eyes, shadowed under the brows of his forehead, were hidden from her.

'The spirits of the Old Ones,' he went on, 'that is what country folk call the stars in my land. Trapped up there, for ever.' He raised both hands out before him, palms out, in a gesture that encompassed half the sky. 'Un-dead, un-alive, forever beyond our reach. Sad and beautiful.' Dropping his arms, he turned to her. 'What else could they be, the stars?'

Staring at him, Jonaquil shook her head perplexedly.

He smiled a thin, humourless smile at her. 'Did you expect me to be some brutish lout, Healer, dead to the manifest beauties the world offers up to us?'

She did not know how to respond. Her growing hatred for this man, for his kind, for all *they* did, for all that Gerrid stood for, was like a solid lump in her belly. But she had expected nothing like this from him.

'Hate me if you wish, Healer,' he said softly. 'But do not under-estimate me.'

She could think of nothing to say in reply.

'Do you have trouble sleeping, Healer?' he went on, drawing close enough to her so that she could feel the heat of him, faintly, against her side. 'Is that why you are out here star-gazing in the dark? I hear nothing but good reports of you. If there is anything you lack, you have but to ask.'

She looked at him, and wondered for a moment if there were some way to approach the subject of the pilfering of medicaments from the Dispensary. But she brought herself up short. 'What would the price of that asking be, Sub-Commander?'

He smiled and reached a hand to her, quickly, so that the caress was there and gone again before she had a chance even to react. 'Everything has its price.'

'I want nothing from you, then.' She turned away from him, but too late. She felt his hands on her, drawing her back.

'We are adversaries, you and I.' Cupping her chin in one hand, he tipped her face up so that he could look her directly in the eyes. 'It is a special relationship.'

She pulled away from him, confused and angered, not at all liking this sudden, strange intimacy he was creating between them.

'The Victor and the Vanquished,' he said, 'locked together in their endless dance.' Then he laughed.

Jonaquil did not understand.

'An old belief,' he said. 'An old belief of country folk and simpletons.'

Jonaquil felt a long shiver go down her spine. There was something uncanny about this man. He was more complex – far more so – than she had imagined.

'The others . . .' Sub-Commander Gerrid shrugged. 'With but a few exceptions, the others here are nothing. They are no more than sheep to a herd dog. They will do anything they can to help themselves, to make themselves a little better off than their fellows. Half of them would turn on the others if I so wished it. But you, Healer, *you* are special. The others, by their actions, have forfeited respect. But not you. Not yet.'

Jonaquil turned from him.

He reached a hand to her again. 'Special. And with a certain winsome beauty, too.'

She shrugged his hand off. 'Leave me be! Go away.'

But it was she who moved off, away from him, back towards the Palisade.

'You disappoint me, Healer.'

To her surprise, there seemed to be genuine regret in his voice. She slowed, and turned to look back at him. 'What kind of a man *are* you?' she demanded. 'What do you want of me?'

He shrugged. 'Ask, rather, what you may want of me.'

An involuntary shudder ran through her. She stared at him for a long moment, then turned and retreated back towards the gate.

'Stop her,' he called to the guards there. 'Bring her to me.'

Two of the demon guards took her by the arms and hustled her back to him. She did not try to resist them. She refused to give him the pleasure of seeing her struggle fruitlessly.

The guards brought her to within a few paces of him. He dismissed them with a gesture. 'I can offer you protection, Healer.' He smiled and lifted his fist towards her. His knuckles brushed her cheek in a rough, soft caress. 'And my protection may prove more important than you realize.'

She slapped his fist down. 'Let me be! I want nothing from a . . . a *creature* such you.' She backed away from him, her heart thumping.

'So be it!' he snapped, stung. 'As you wish. But you are making a mistake.'

He turned to the demon guards, who had resumed their positions at the gate, and beckoned them. 'Take her to the Commander.'

Jonaquil faltered. 'What . . . ?'

'I told you,' Gerrid said curtly, 'that you were making a mistake.'

The demon guards took her then, hard hands tight about her shoulders and arms, and hustled her off. Sub-Commander Gerrid stood watching, silent, his expression impossible to read in the starlight.

And then she was dragged through the gate and back into the trampled Palisade compound, with no hope at all of resisting the spell-helm strength of the man-demons that took her. Despite the chill night air, Jonaquil felt suddenly hot and clammy with fear. What *mistake* had she made? What did the Commander want with her?

Through darkness and silence, the demon guards pulled her along towards the rear of the compound, where Commander Chayne kept his quarters. Their gauntleted fingers dug painfully into her upper arms, but she kept silent, having no wish to antagonize them. The other inmates were long abed in the crowded sheds and tents that served as housing, and there was no sign of a living soul. Jonaquil shivered. It might be a camp of the dead they moved through.

In the compound's far corner loomed the dark, solid bulk of the Seer's building. Along with the other inmates here, Jonaquil had always avoided looking at it, avoided even thinking of it. None so much as mentioned the building's existence under ordinary circumstances. Now, like it or no, she found herself close by it.

She could not help but remember Tishta's words: 'For you it is easy. But for the rest of us, there is nothing here but hunger, back-breaking work, and that damned spooky building of the Seer's waiting for us eventually . . .'

*That damned spooky building . . .*

Tishta had the right of it. As a Healer, she was safe; it was all too easy for her to overlook this building. There had been no sign at all for days now of the Seer's cloaked and hooded figure. And none had been dragged into that squat, dark building. She had almost forgotten its existence. Yet it was the real and terrible heart of this camp.

She did not wish to think on what foul things that building might hide. It epitomized life here: it squatted like some terrible, implacable creature, ready to devour them all, and they were entirely powerless to do anything about it.

She shuddered, glad when the guards dragged her past and up to the log structure that housed the Commander's quarters.

One of them stepped forward and thumped softly on a closed door with the butt-end of his pike. Jonaquil stood, waiting. Both the turmoil that had gripped her and the momentary elation she had felt were gone now, replaced by simple fear, like a cold lump in her belly. What did Commander Chayne want with her? She kept hearing Gerrid's voice in her mind: '*You are making a mistake.*'

The door opened. Her guard said something, received answer, and the door shut again. The whole exchange was too muted for her to make out.

Gripping her painfully by the arms, the guards began to drag her back the way they had come.

'Where . . . where are you . . . ?' she began, but then bit the words off short. Fruitless to ask such questions. Fruitless to resist while she was so totally in their power like this. It only offered the creatures an excuse to exercise the petty viciousness that seemed to give them such satisfaction. Thus far, all she had incurred were a few bruises on her arms.

But when she saw where they were taking her, and she had to force herself not to resist foolishly.

The squat bulk of the Seer's building.

They dragged her to a small doorway and knocked.

'Co-Commander?' one of them called softly.

She did not know whether to be pleased or frightened at the uncertain stammer in that one's voice.

The door opened. From within came a queer, colourless sort of light, not at all like familiar, wholesome torchlight. Commander Chayne stood there, a hissing lantern in his hand, his unhuman hawk face gleaming palely. 'What is it?' he demanded. But then, seeing who it was, paused. 'Ahh, the Healer.' After a moment, he gestured to the guards. 'Send her in. Then return to your posts.'

A hard hand at the small of her back propelled her stumbling through the doorway, and Jonaquil found herself inside. The door behind her closed firmly.

The Commander held the lantern aloft. He was dressed in black, with a long black cloak. About his waist an ornate belt glistened like silver fish-scales. His hands were sheathed in metal-studded, black leather gauntlets.

Black and silver human body with the head of a great, heartless bird of prey . . .

The non-human eyes stared at her unblinking. The feral beak opened and closed with a soft *clakk*. Jonaquil quivered, facing him.

He stepped close and placed one gauntleted hand under her chin to lift her face towards him, holding the hissing lantern over her. 'I have seen you in the compound. I am . . . interested in you, Healer.' The voice coming through that predatory beak was resonantly smooth, his movements possessed of a kind of studied grace. But it was like a veneer. Underneath, Jonaquil felt something feral and iron-hard and cold. It panicked her. He tilted her head to one side, leather-sheathed finger bruising her jaw, gazing at her. The sharp beak *clakked* softly. 'Yes . . . *interested.*'

Jonaquil shivered.

Seeing this, he laughed.

She felt her heart beat hard. She was afraid she knew all too clearly what he wanted with her.

The hand moved down from her jawline across her shoulder. She could hear his hissing breath. He stared at her hungrily.

She twisted away from him and fled desperately. Further into the building she went, blindly, intent only on escape.

Behind, she heard him curse, and then the thump of his strides as he came after her. She burst through into a low-ceilinged chamber where two long trestle tables filled the room. Hissing glow-globes set along the walls cast a pale, colourless light upon an array of strange objects: a rack of glass vials filled with cloudy liquid, a heap of curved bone, twists of gleaming bronze wire, liquid-filled glass jars in which floated things that seemed like so many severed, pale hands, except that they were strangely boneless and had too many fingers. They squirmed.

Jonaquil felt a sick dread at the sight of such things. But she was out of the chamber in an instant and beyond into a further room.

And then . . .

Almost, she screamed. Her Healer's sensitive flesh cringed. A human face was all she saw at first, a white oval in the queer, colourless light of another of the hissing glow-globes. Whether the face was a man's or a woman's, she could not tell. The eyes were wide with terror, the mouth open, though only a sort of pitiful mewling came forth.

Human head, yes, yet it was a pig's body that head was attached to, bound to a wooden pallet with leather straps. The poor soul's mouth open, the jaws working. The eyes rolled, showing whites. The pig's feet thrashed about.

Jonaquil thought she would be sick.

The Commander caught up with her. A blow across her shoulders sent her reeling into a wall, the breath knocked out of her. 'Stupid woman!' he snapped, and hit her again.

Jonaquil gasped, trying to shield herself with her arms.

'Get up!'

She staggered to her feet.

Across from her, the pig body rocked, and from the human mouth came a wailing cry.

Jonaquil stared, shaken.

Commander Chayne laughed, held high the lantern he carried still. 'I come here,' he said casually, gazing down upon the pig-creature, 'to look at the Seer's creations. It is . . . amusing.' He walked closer to the poor thing, which continued to wail. 'Shut up!' he commanded, and slapped the human head, hard, with a metal-studded, gauntleted hand. Blood welled up from the blow, but the wailing ceased.

He turned to Jonaquil then. 'Out.' Walking along behind, he pushed her roughly into the chamber with the trestle tables and through a side door she had not noticed before. This led into a small room, empty save for a wooden chest against one wall. The Commander hung the lantern he still held on a wall-peg.

'The Seer fashions many interesting things. You would be surprised at his ingenuity.' As he talked, Chayne lifted the lid of the wooden chest. 'I had originally given word to my Sub-Commander that you were to be sent to me at my quarters.' From the chest, he lifted out a length of blanket. 'But perhaps it is better this way.'

He spread the blanket on the rough-planked floor, and then reached to his head and removed the spell-helm. Carefully, he placed it in the chest, shutting the lid securely after. His human face was pale as a mushroom. His head shone in the hissing light, for most of his skull was shaved bare, with only a complicated top-knot of dark hair left.

'Remove your clothes,' he said.

Jonaquil only stared. Too much had happend this night: Tishta and the pilfering, the dream, the glowing wonder of the stars, Sub-Commander Gerrid, the poor pig-creature . . . She felt battered, as if a strong wind had been blowing through her. Or as if she were not large enough for all that this night had thrust upon her. She blinked. It was difficult for her to credit this thing was actually happening.

Commander Chayne gestured to her, impatient. 'Take them off. *Now.*'

Jonaquil felt her heart thump painfully. She thought of running again: the spell-helm was removed now; he would be . . .

But he was tall, and looked to have a hunting-bird's sinewy strength. Even without the helm, he would outmatch her easily enough if she tried to resist him. And she knew him for a violent, cruel man.

'Do it,' he commanded.

With shaking fingers, she began to comply.

He watched her. 'I wondered,' he said with impossible casualness, as if discussing some piece of daily trivia, 'if perhaps my Sub-Commander did not wish you for himself. He seemed less than eager to comply with my orders concerning you. It appears, however, that I was mistaken.'

Half undressed, Jonaquil froze.

'Or that he has more sense than . . . Why have you stopped?'

Shivering, she went on, eventually stepping out of the loose-legged trousers she had been wearing to stand there before him, naked in the colourless light. She felt herself flush, shaking with anger, fear, and shame.

The Commander grinned, looking.

He took a step near her, another, reached out a hand. She felt his leather knuckles brush across her breast, the metal studs like ice against her skin. With a snap, he flung the gauntlets to the floor and reached for her again, bare-skinned. Over her breasts his hand moved, down her belly.

It felt like a spider crawling across her flesh, and she shuddered.

He stepped back from her a little, grinning still. Then his hand came up and he thumped her with the heel of it, against her sternum, a quick, bullying thrust.

She stumbled backwards.

He moved towards her, thrust at her again, knocking her down on to her back on the blanket he had spread on the floor.

He stood over her then, triumphant, clearly expectant, waiting for her to cry out, to plead or curse, to strike him or attempt to flee. Something.

She did nothing. She would not give him the satisfaction. A cold anger had settled in her. Let him have his way. She would submit. But she would have her way, too, afterwards. She was not without power of a sort. Sometime, somehow, when he was not looking, she would get her revenge. She would . . .

*No!* That was *not* the way.

He might master her, yes. Ride her as he might ride his horse. But she must *not* let her own fear, her anger, her revenge-hunger overpower her. To do that was to become his creature entirely, dominated by him body and soul. She was a Healer. She must let this pass through her, as if she were a living, porous membrane, a breathing sieve through which so much pouring liquid could run.

*You can do me no harm worse than the harm I can do myself,* she had told Sub-Commander Gerrid.

Such a simple truth.

Standing over her, Chayne stripped off his clothing. He was thin as a rangy hound, eerily pale-skinned. A long, glowing shaft of light uncoiled from him towards her.

Jonaquil blinked. Almost like being in Healing trance, it was. She saw the nimbus of dancing soul-light flare into clarity about him. Never had she experienced anything like this. Only in the proper Healing trance did she normally see a person's glowing life-light so clearly.

He padded towards her, a pale figure enveloped in pulsing light. His life-glow was utterly unlike any she had seen: cold, shimmering, and dark — if light itself could be dark.

He reached to her, and it seemed to Jonaquil that she felt the aura of him as an icy exhalation that chilled her flesh. His hands gripped her hard. He turned her on to her belly, pressing her face into the mustiness of the blanket. He thrust into her, sudden as a blow. It was not her woman's hole he entered.

It *hurt*. She gasped, eyes watering.

Over her, he grunted.

She bit her lips to keep from crying out. She would not give him the satisfaction. She tried to feel herself a living membrane, porous, unaffected by that which went through her.

But, oh, it *hurt!*

And then something happened in her. Like something . . . breaking open. In her mind Jonaquil saw the very earth herself riven by storm and lightning, rent by great quakes. Yet the earth endured and healed, too great and fertile to be destroyed so easily.

And she . . . It was as if a Power moved through her, and she, Jonaquil, were the very earth herself. The earth suffered and endured, and in the end was ever and eternally alive.

She was Jonaquil, yet she was more. She was the earth, and the Powers that moved the world moved her. She, too, would endure.

Above her, Chayne finished, grunting, and went still.

Jonaquil took a long breath, afraid to move lest, by doing so, she should lose this thing that was happening to her. She felt herself a different creature, like a vessel much larger on the inside than out.

Chayne pulled out of her, and she felt his weight lift. He slapped her on the buttocks. 'Go,' he commanded abruptly.

She craned her neck and saw him stepping back into his black clothing. The light about him darkly shuddered. He looked at her, his face blank. 'Leave.'

Jonaquil got to her feet, delicately. She hurt. Looking at him as he stood there calmly, fully clothed again now, she felt her old self reassert itself — anger and hopeless hate, weariness, the black pull of despair. But the new self, the larger self, was there too, hurting and angered, but more, much more, than simply that.

His life-light shrunk about him, like a candle guttering, until it was only the faintest of glows she could discern. It seemed a drooping radiance. Suddenly, he seemed pitiful to her, like a small boy dressed up in an elaborate costume. His silly dreams of power and control and his silly, dangling piece of meat . . .

She laughed.

He struck her, hard, across the face. She staggered back, and though he had not yet put his gauntlets back on, blood filled her mouth.

Raising his hand again, he glared at her. 'Go, I said. Go!' He pushed her through the door, flung her bundled clothes after her. He reached then into the chest and donned the spell-helm. A great gout of spinning radiance whirling about his head with unnatural vigour. He laughed. Barely had she time to catch up her clothing before he hustled her roughly through the next chamber and out of the Seer's building.

And then Jonaquil found herself outside. The sudden coolness of the night air hit her naked skin like the slap of a fist, making her gasp. She fumbled quickly into her clothes and stood there, sagged against the rough log wall of the Seer's building for support, shivering. Her bruised flesh ached. She felt sick with outrage. Tears filled her eyes. She did not wish to think on what he had just done to her. It was obscene.

But shocked and sickened and violated though she was, she felt . . . *greater* somehow than what had happened to her.

Overhead, the great jewellery of the stars glinted above the enduring earth. And from each star she saw a radiating, glistening halo, blues and reds and greens. The very heavens danced with light.

She staggered back towards the Dispensary tent, weary and hurting, as if in a half-dream. The oppressiveness of the Palisade compound closed over her like a heavy blanket. Yet a part of her felt it not at all, and walked with the stars overhead.

Arrived at the Dispensary, Jonaquil stood, uncertain what to do next. A long shudder went through her. She felt dizzy, as if her insides were being whirled crazily about, and faltered to her knees. The image of him came back to her and she pushed it away, trying not to think on what he had done.

She hurt. She could taste blood still in her mouth. She felt unutterably weary.

Wrapping herself in the blanket – still on the ground where she had dropped it after the dream – she curled in upon herself, shivering till her body heat warmed the cold cloth.

Behind her, in the Dispensary tent, one of her patients grunted in sleep. She heard the snuffles and snorts of other sleepers. She smiled tiredly, feeling oddly at home.

In the dancing sky, a sliver of moon hung. She stared at the delicate, rainbow halo she saw about it, pulsing, as if to the rhythm of some great, immmortal heartbeat.

Slowly, gazing above, she gave herself over to sleep.

# XIX

# Hound's Head Isle

'Listen to me,' Tai said. '*Listen to me!*'

The bird only stared at him, its queer little face rigid with fright.

Tai took a cautious step nearer, but it shot away into the room's far corner, hunching itself on a torch-sconce set in the wall so that all Tai could see of it was the little dark eyes staring over the curve of one blue wing.

Tai hissed in frustration. He was beginning to wonder if the wretched creature had ever indeed talked, or if it had all been simply his imagination.

'Listen,' he tried again.

The little eyes blinked once, then looked aside.

'Can you *understand* me?'

Tai turned away and leaned wearily against the edge of the table under the window of his tower room, his back to the maddening little creature, and gazed out through the lattice of iron bars at the distant, tossing sea below. Brown clouds scudded along the horizon, their bellies reddening in the sunset. Gulls cried, free on the wind. Heartsick with envy, he watched them soar and wheel in the distance until with a sigh, he pushed away from the table.

It would be night soon, and sometime during the dark, Seer Tancred's demon guards would pull him down into the Miradore's dank underchambers once again, so the Seer could *do* things to him.

Tai shuddered. He did not think he could bear it. All day he had tossed on the bed, his mind filled with stark, disturbing images of the poor starveling creatures he had killed . . . a shattered basket of white bone filled with red-grey ooze; staring, blank eyes gone dusty in death; ribs sticking through grimy skin. He remembered the driving *thrump* of the club in his hand as it hammered furred flesh.

He had become one of *them*.

And more. His innards ached and throbbed. And he felt the world pulse about him at times, as if it were somehow sliding subtly in and out of focus. Never the true chaos of a fit, yet not the comfort of the familiar, solid world-as-it-ought-to-be either.

*I will open you, boy*, the Seer had said. Tai shuddered. Too many uncanny things had been happening. Tai did not know how to make sense of events. And something was changing in him. He could feel it. Perhaps many things were changing in him. He did not know.

It made his belly curdle.

So he had turned to the queer, human-faced bird in a last, desperate hope, focused on the only certainty left him now – Colby, his remaining kin. Better to die in some mad attempt at escape and rescue than to face the Seer's ministrations again.

Neither the demon guards nor the Seer himself had so much as mentioned the small orange-and-blue plumed bird, as if were beneath consideration. Yet, whatever it was, it had manifestly escaped from *somewhere* in the Keep – from the Lord Veil's chamber itself, perhaps – and it had talked, and seemed far from mindless.

Tai had thought that, perhaps, there might have been some hope of communicating with it, improbable creature though it was; that it might have knowledge of the Miradore that he had not. He had hoped for an ally of sorts, and that, with the creature's aid, there might be a chance – however slim and unlikely – of escape.

Vain hopes.

He stared at the bird where it still perched on the sconce, shook his head. 'Mindless creature . . .'

The dark little human eyes flashed at him.

'Mindless as a brick,' Tai repeated bitterly.

'Mindless!' the bird piped suddenly. 'I am not *mindless!*' It launched itself from the sconce and fluttered to the bed. 'You, you . . . you ugly *creature!*' Its voice was high-pitched and clear, like a young girl's, and perfectly understandable. It glared at him, orange breast pulsing with the quick beat of its little heart, the little human eyes dark with fury.

Tai stared at it, hardly believing. He took a step forwards, but it danced back nervously along the bed, away from him. 'I . . . I will not harm you,' he said. 'I only—'

'Liar!'

He reached a hand towards it impulsively. 'I will *not.*'

It proved a silly thing to do. The bird flipped into the air, shrieking, and returned to its perch on the sconce.

Tai took a breath, returned to the table. 'I will not harm you,' he repeated to it.

'Liar!' it repeated back.

Tai sighed. This was getting him nowhere at all.

'*His* creature!' the bird all but spat. 'You stink of *him.*'

'*Him?*'

The strange, diminutive human eyes stayed fixed with unwavering suspicion upon Tai. The little heart never ceased its rapid, anxious beating. 'You are the Seer's creature, and not to be trusted.'

'I am *not* . . .'

'Liar!'

Tai clenched his fists in frustration. 'Listen to me,' he said. '*Listen to me!* Would the Seer keep me locked away like this if I were willingly his? Do you think I would talk to you as I do if I were his? Surely you must see that? Surely you are not so mindless as to—'

'Mindless!' The bird swooped down once more from the sconce and skittered on to the bed, where it hopped up and down, little talons tearing at the blanket. 'I am *not* mindless! The rest, yes. They can do little more than chatter back the words spoken to them. They are only pretty playthings, silly playthings.' The little eyes blinked, and the face wrinkled in an angry intensity. 'But I am different. *They* think me like the rest. *He* thinks me like the rest. But I am *not!* You insult me, man! I have a mind and a will of my own.'

'Then help me,' Tai said impulsively.

The little head went back and the creature took a sharp breath. 'Help you . . . how?'

'Help me escape. You escaped from *somewhere*. You must know this Keep. Help me.'

The bird stared at him in silence, then fluttered its wings and hop-flapped over to the next table next to which Tai still stood. 'I have escaped many times, man, from the Lord's chamber, and returned. And none were the wiser.' A little laugh accompanied this, a high, peeling sound like a tiny, chiming bell, and it puffed itself up proudly. 'I am very good at it. I have been many places in this Keep, seen many things, all unseen myself . . .'

'Then help *me* to escape!' Tai shivered. He could not keep the desperation out of his voice. 'I *must* get away from him before it is too late. Else I *will* become his creature.'

The bird tilted its head to one side and studied Tai solemnly out of one little eye. Then it shook itself, hopped to the stone windowsill, and peered out at the darkening twilight. It chirruped nervously. Hopping back again, it did a little skittering dance of agitation along the table top. 'To feel the wind lift me like a strong hand, man, that is joy. To have the world under me and the sky all about. Not to have closing-in walls and tight air and stupid chattering in my ear all day long . . .

'But where would I go? There is *danger*, man. The great sea-birds . . . the world so big it could swallow you whole . . .' The bird's little body shuddered.

Tai sighed. What could he say? That the world was not really so very dangerous? Such naive assurance was laughable. As he had learned all too well in recent times.

There was only one thing to say that he could think of. One simple thing: 'Help me. And I will help you.'

The bird looked up at him. 'Why should I trust you, man?'

Tai ran his good hand over his face. The world seemed to pulse sickeningly about him for a moment. The utter incredibility of the situation – trying to persuade this suspicious, impossibly human-faced, volatile little creature into an alliance – overwhelmed him momentarily. But he took hold of himself, sighed, leaned forwards, feeling the reassuring solidity of the table top under his fingers. 'We have a common foe, you and I. We might be allies. We could help one another. Together, we could accomplish what neither of us could do alone.'

The bird hesitated. 'Fine words . . . But you have been with *him*. *His* guards protect you. How then should I trust you after that?'

Tai thumped the table top with his fist. 'I tell you, I am *not* the Seer's creature!'

The bird skittered nervously away.

Tai stood, nursing the sore nub of his finger – he had thoughtlessly used his damaged hand to bang the table with – and stared at it. 'I am *not* the Seer's creature,' he repeated sullenly. 'Believe or not as you will. But 'tis the truth!' He sighed, shaking his head. 'I must needs escape from here for my very soul's safety. And I need your help to do so.'

The bird hopped along the table top uneasily, its little talons making clicking noises on the wood.

'Can you guide me through the Keep?' Tai asked.

The little head nodded. 'I can.'

'There is somebody I must go to. My uncle . . . He is held in a cell. Underground. Off the big courtyard near the entrance gates. Do you know it?'

The bird frowned. 'It is bad to go there, man.'

'But you know the place? You could find it?'

It nodded, uncomfortable.

Eagerly, Tai leaned forward. 'Then you will help me?'

'Do you swear to help *me*, man, if I help you? Do you *swear* it?' The bird eyed him. 'And will you swear also to help my friend?'

Tai thought of two such strange little creatures fluttering about. 'Aye,' he assured the bird. 'You *and* your friend. But you must help me help my kin, too.'

'Swear to it, man!'

'I do so swear,' Tai responded. He did not know if the bird would properly recognize the significance of it, but he crossed his arms over his breast in the formal way and recited the proper phrase: 'On my own blood and bone, I do swear. I will help you and yours.'

The bird stared up at him for a long, silent moment, small orange face creased in anxious thought. 'I will help you, then, man. And you me. We shall be allies, as you said.'

'Aye,' Tai agreed. 'Allies.' Carefully, he reached forwards to where the bird perched on the table top, slipped his good hand under its feet, and lifted. The bird balanced nervously, perched on his knuckles, small enough for Tai to support comfortably. 'What are you called?' he asked it.

'Ree. I am Ree. And you, man?'

'I am called Tai.'

In the dying light, the blue and orange of Ree's plumage glowed softly, and the little dark human eyes with their long lashes were bright as tiny lanterns in that downy, startling human face. As unlikely a creature as could be imagined. Yet Tai, smiled. 'Ree . . . 'Tis good to have an ally in this forsaken place. Perhaps, between the two of us, we can find our freedom.'

'Freedom,' Ree echoed. 'Yes . . . *freedom!*' The bird leaped suddenly from Tai's hand, startling him, and did an aerial flip in mid-room. The little mouth opened in a shriek of exuberance.

Volatile little creature . . .

Tai felt his pulse begin to race. Against all probability, the chance he hoped for had indeed come, mad though it might be. He looked at the hand on which Ree had perched. It was shaking. But he had thought this through enough times already. He had only one slim chance of getting out of this tower room, and that only if he acted swiftly.

Heart thumping, Tai flung himself against the room's wooden door, pounding at it. From outside, Tai heard the ever-present demon guard mutter irritably. There was only the one guard this early in the evening.

Tai began screaming. He threw back his head and howled so loudly his throat burned. Ree shrieked in sudden, startled fright, adding to the noise.

Tai felt the door's outside locking bar go. He flung himself backwards into the room, still howling, landing on his back on the floor near the bed. Through half-closed lids, he watched the guard stride in.

'Silence!' the guard shouted, brandishing a war-pike.

But Tai continued to howl. And Ree, veering in hysterical swoops about the room, shrieked and squealed.

'*Silence!*'

Tai threw himself forwards, thrashed his limbs about, drooled spittle in great gobs, jerked his head back and forth.

The guard came nearer, staring suspiciously.

Tai rolled, flopping like a spastic fish, and came to rest on his belly against one of the guard's legs. He went silent then, still as a corpse, trying to control his panting breath.

The guard kicked at him, but gently. 'Get up. Get up!'

Tai moved not at all. Ree had gone silent too, now. Tai could hear the guard's breathing, so close was he, but dared not turn over and look.

Not yet.

He felt a gauntleted hand pull him over, and found himself staring suddenly into yellow demon-eyes.

Tai leaped then, reaching upwards, putting every shred of will and energy he possessed into the movement, and tore the spell-helm from the guard's head.

The man stared, white-faced and stricken, and Tai smashed the helm over his unprotected skull, driving him to his knees. The war-pike clattered to the floor.

Dropping the spell-helm, Tai dived for the pike.

The guard scrambled for the helm.

On his knees, the pike in his grasp, Tai turned and saw the guard standing, trying to fit the helm back on his head. Desperately, Tai lunged forwards, driving the slim, razor-edged point of the pike-blade into the man's throat and up under the chin, lifting him half off the floor, heaving desperately until he felt the blade's tip scour across the inside of the man's skullcap.

The man shrieked, once, and went over like a felled tree. The spell-helm clattered to the floor.

Panting, Tai dropped the pike-haft and ran to the door.

There was no sign that any had heard the sudden commotion: the walkway outside was empty. It all but dark now. Tai gave thanks that he had been sequestered up here so far from the inhabited part of the Keep.

He stumbled back into the room, panting like a hound, sick and shaky with delayed reaction to what he had done. The guard lay still, limbs splayed out like a rag doll's, a dark pool spreading on to the stone floor from his throat. Tai swallowed, wiped sweaty palms along his sides, staring. He reached down, yanked the pike free, and wiped the blade clean. Then he collected the dead man's spell-helm. It sat heavy in his hand, warm and strange.

'Come,' he said to Ree between gasping breaths. 'We must leave quickly!'

The little bird shivered, staring wide-eyed.

'Come *on*!' Tai urged.

With a sudden rush, Ree swept past him and whirred out through the door, free. Tai hurried after, pulse thudding like a hammer.

But when he stood outside, there was no immediate sign of Ree. Staring into the darkening night, he felt his heart sink. Without the little bird's knowledge of the Keep he would never find Colby.

A quick surge of anger went through him, followed by cold despair. What could he do now? He looked down at the spell-helm in his hand. Its golden eye-membranes seemed to stare back at him mockingly. He shivered.

He would *not* willingly let himself fall into the Seer's hands again. Come what may.

Leaning the pike against the wall behind him, Tai lifted the spell-helm and gingerly fitted it over his head. He felt the same, stunning rush of strength he had the first time. But now there was something different. A shudder of memory went through him, and a staggering burst of pain ripped up his throat and into the skull. Almost, he tore the helm off and flung it from him. But he had run out of such easy choices.

Clenching his jaw, Tai fought to master it, driving the memories away, dismissing the pain. The uncanny vigour of the helm seemed to flicker and dim, as if the strange life-force that animated it were dwindling, now that its original wearer was gone. But Tai was desperate, and he refused to allow any such thing. He knew what a spell-helm ought to confer upon the wearer, and he willed now for that to happen.

Slowly, painfully, it did.

Taking a long, shuddering breath, Tai looked about him. The night-time world was semi-illuminated by faint red-orange radiance and, in that glowing dark, he made out the small shape of Ree, huddled on the parapet at the far side of the walkway, close to the door leading back into the Keep proper. Tai breathed a sigh of relief. He reached behind and barred shut the door to his room, then lifted the pike from the wall. Moving soft as a cat, he padded across the walkway.

Ree chirruped nervously and skittered away from him as he drew up, dancing sideways across the stone. To Tai's spell-helm-enhanced vision, the bird's little human eyes seemed to glow with apprehension.

'It is still me,' he said in reassurance. 'Only me.'

The anxious eyes merely looked at him.

Tai suppressed a momentary flicker of irritation. There was no time to stand here making reassuring explanations. The Seer might decide at any moment to send the other guard up. They had to get away, down to poor Colby as quick as could be. Tai felt the spell-helm vigour surge through him, falter, then surge again. He willed it to steadiness, feeling confidence fill him along with the spell-helm strength, like a light going on inside him. Mad though this scheme might be, he felt fully capable of accomplishing it. He thought of his poor foster-uncle moaning in the darkness of his dank cell. Enough of delay. Onwards now to Colby, and then away.

Tai opened the door that led back down into the main Keep and waved the bird through. Ree hesitated, but then, with a soft flutter of wings, dived into the open black wedge between the half-open door and the stone jamb. Softly, Tai followed after, closing the door behind. Ahead, Ree chittered and squeaked nervously. Peering into the thick dark with his helm-enhanced sight, Tai could just make out the bird a dim little figure, standing flat footed and awkward on the floor of the hallway before him. He reached a hand down so that Ree could hop on to it. 'Shush,' he whispered. '*They* might hear you.' And then, 'Which way?'

'Down . . . down here and to the . . . the right after the stairs,' came the breathless reply. Ree skipped along his arm and up to grip his shoulder and perch there. He could hear the little creature still chirruping anxiously, but more softly now.

Tai slipped along dark and silent corridors, Ree piping directions from his shoulder. As he continued on, spell-helm vigour thrumming his bones, Tai began to feel lighter, stronger, his limbs moving with the spring-steel ease of a cat's. He felt like some predatory beast on the prowl, like some hero from a child's tale. He grinned in the darkness and strode along more rapidly.

The ways seemed utterly deserted. Recalling the remark Seer Tancred had made about the Veils maintaining only a small force in the Miradore, Tai wondered fleetingly just how few of *them* there were in this huge stone warren of a Keep. The fewer the better. If Tai's experience were any indication, the Miradore was mostly abandoned and empty. Perhaps there were very few of *them* here indeed . . .

Downwards Tai and Ree went, never encountering another living soul, until the stone walls began to feel damp.

At a junction of two corridors, they paused momentarily. With his spell-helm hearing, Tai thought he could detect a strange, faint shimmer of sound in the distance ahead, like the susurration of leaves in a wind. He suspected that Ree might have got them lost, and felt a momentary suspicion about the bird's abilities. 'Are you certain this is the right way?'

'Yes!' Ree replied. The little feathered body shivered. 'This is it. To the right, and down.'

Tai went as directed. The corridor led them along steadily downwards, turning and twisting as if it were a long spiral boring into the Miradore's foundations. The walls about them became damper, and the air thick with mildew. Water pooled at their feet. The temperature dropped. Soon they were splashing along through scummy puddles. The sound Tai had heard, though still faint, was grown louder now.

Nothing about these surroundings seemed familiar to Tai. He recalled clearly enough where his original cell had been, the corridor lined with cell doors . . . But nothing like this. Ahead, a faint light began to show. He slowed, uncertain what such a light down here might mean.

'It is all right,' Ree assured him in his ear. 'We are almost there now. Almost there!'

The noise Tai had heard was loud enough now to be clearly audible, a kind of soft, strange, humming babble.

This was not the corridor where he and Colby had been kept prisoner. 'Where are we?' Tai hissed at Ree. 'Where have you brought me?'

The corridor along which they were travelling emptied abruptly into an underground chamber, the ceiling dim overhead, the whole lit by some hidden, subdued light source Tai could not identify. A pungent odour permeated the chamber. He paused in the shadow of the corridor, his spell-helm-sensitive nostrils stung with the stink of this place. Before him, water slicked the walls in gleaming runnels. Both sides of the chamber were lined with a series of small, iron-reinforced wooden doors. Cell doors. The babble came from behind them.

'Where *are* we?' Tai demanded.

'A bad place,' Ree replied. 'A very bad place. Can you not scent its badness?'

At the sound of their voices, soft though it was, the babble of sound Tai had been hearing increased momentarily, and then went silent.

Tai shuddered. Spell-helm vigour or no, there was something about this chamber that made him feel sickly uncomfortable. 'Why have you brought me here?' he demanded. Time was passing. He wanted only to get to his foster-uncle. 'What manner of place *is* this?'

For answer, Ree launched abruptly into the air from Tai's shoulder and flew ahead towards one of the row of wooden doors on their right, hovering there. 'Here! This one.'

'Colby!' Tai hissed. Unthinking, he hurried forwards. Inset into the top portion of the cell door was a sliding wooden panel. Bending down – the door was very low – Tai slid the panel aside. 'Colby,' he called softly. 'Uncle, are you there?'

It was not Colby.

The opened door panel revealed a rectangular space spanned by iron bars. A furred arm reached out. A dark, furred face, all eyes and teeth it seemed, thrust itself against the bars, hissing.

Tai skipped back and away from the snarling, wild-eyed creature framed in the door's opening. A sharp-toothed fur-man it was, like that he had encountered in the Pit and after.

But Ree fluttered wildly now around the fur-man's cell door, calling, 'Skeefer, Skeefer!'

Tai understood none of this. 'What are you *doing?*' he demanded angrily.

Ree veered across to him. 'This is my friend. You promised to help my friend. You *swore* to it, man!'

Tai stared. This was not the sort of 'friend' he had expected.

'Quickly,' Ree urged. 'Quickly! We must set him free.'

'Ree?' the fur-man called out, his voice hardly more than a hoarse whisper. 'Ree? Iss it truly you?'

'Quickly!' Ree insisted. 'Set him *free!*'

Tai hung back, not liking this at all. This was not what he had ventured to do. And he had had experience enough with creatures such as this already. The bird had tricked him . . .

'You swore you would help, man!' Ree cried accusingly. 'You *swore* to it!'

Tai shook his head irritably. Damn the little creature! Why should he be called upon to keep his word if it resorted to trickery? Especially when he could make it do what he wished. It only required the use of a little force . . .

Tai caught himself. It was the spell-helm speaking in him; he felt that clearly. Like one of *them*, to think thus.

Tai moved forward, though uneasily, and lifted the heavy wooden bar that latched the cell door shut.

The fur-man tumbled out with a hoarse moan.

Tai stared, feeling sick. The creatures he fought at Tancred's conniving had been ragged and thin, not at all like the clean-limbed, sleek being he had encountered in the Pit. But what he saw now was far beyond that – a stinking and emaciated thing, ribs showing clearly through his fur, with patches of the fur itself missing in areas and raw sores spotting the exposed skin.

Ree buzzed about the starveling fur-man ecstatically, calling, 'Skeefer. Skeefer! My poor Skeefer. My *poor* Skeefer.' On his knees, the fur-man lifted a thin, shaking hand and Ree clung to it. He hugged the bird gently to him, murmuring, 'Ree, my Ree . . .'

Tai looked on in uncertain silence. It had the feel of a lovers' reunion, this improbable meeting.

The fur-man – Skeefer, as Ree had named him – looked up, seeing Tai clearly for perhaps the first time. His battered face set abruptly into a mask of bleak horror. 'It iss one of *them*!'

'No!' Ree told him. 'He is . . .'

'What have you *done*, Ree?'

The fur-man staggered to his feet, snarling. He pushed himself along the wall, his eyes never leaving Tai. 'Flee, my Ree,' he hissed. He shook her loose from his hand, sending her tumbling into the air. '*Flee*!'

'No!' Ree piped, fluttering back to him. 'He is not one of *them*. He will help us to escape!'

The furred head shook bitterly. 'For *uss*, there iss no esscape, my Ree.' He looked at Tai with bleak eyes. 'And why sshould one of *them* turn upon hiss fellowss and help uss?'

Tai felt irritation rise in him. Ungrateful creature! He had his own kin to free and better things to do than abide such nonsense. He took a step forwards, the war-pike in his hand. He had learned already how to deal with creatures such as this. The fur-man faltered back, lips exposed in a desperate snarl. Tai felt of a mind to—

But he stopped himself, shuddering. The spell-helm once more, it was. Tai remembered clearly how he had once felt, confronting the terrible, unhuman demon-faces of *them*. And now this fur-man confronted just such an unhuman antagonist, and he, Tai, was that demon, readying himself to act as *they* acted. He reached abruptly to the helm to rip it off. But part of him resisted. It took real effort to remove it, and his hands, holding the thing, shook weakly.

Strength leaked out of him. The lighting in the chamber shrank to dimness. He felt a thrust of sudden nausea knife through him.

Skeefer stared at Tai. 'Hisst . . .' he breathed after a long moment. 'It iss *you*!'

Tai blinked.

'The one the houndss took from me. In the Pit.'

Tai shuddered, confused, the nausea still working through him. It took effort to summon enough breath to speak. The chamber about him began to pulse sickeningly. He ran a shaking hand over his face. 'Who . . . what *are* you? What is this place?'

For answer, the fur-man launched himself at Tai in a sudden rush, slamming into him like a hunting hound, all teeth and snarling fury. Pike and spell-helm flew tumbling from Tai's grasp, and he went down, trying desperately to fend the fur-man's fangs from his throat.

Ree, hovering near them, made no move to interfere.

The wild force of the fur-man's attack drove Tai bruisingly against the damp stone of the wall. He felt hot breath on his face. The ivory fangs drew inexorably closer. 'Ree!' Tai cried, outraged. 'Ree . . . What of your promise?'

Ree hesitated, wings a dark blur as she hovered, then swooped upon the two of them. '*No!*' Ree darted at Skeefer's face, buffeting him with her wings. He loosed his hold on Tai momentarily and tried to fend her off with one hand.

It was enough.

Tai heaved the fur-man over, slamming him on to his back on the hard stone floor. Skeefer was wiry and quick, and filled with the strength of a desperate fury, but he was smaller than Tai, and had been starved and abused for too long. Tai pinned him to the floor, both knees on the fur-man's bony chest. He held him there, gasping, furious and confused and altogether unsure of what to do next.

'Kill me then, man,' Skeefer hissed up into his face, labouring for breath. 'I ssay kill me and have done!'

Ree's first words to him, that, almost exactly.

Tai let go his hold, stood up, panting, and backed away. He shook his head, confused, feeling anger and pity well up in him like twin springs. Ree shot past his shoulder towards the fur-man who crouched against the wall, a weary, gasping, bedraggled figure. The bird hovered over him anxiously until he took her in his hand.

Tai stared at the two creatures before him. Skeefer was half-otter and half-human it seemed, and strange indeed, nor any less so for his queer, hissing speech. But he was man-shaped and male clearly enough. And the manner in which he held Ree to him, a hold that seemed almost a caress . . .

Realization dawned, and Tai shook his head. 'I was not expecting *this*, Ree. Not that we should sneak down here to liberate your . . .' He paused lamely, not knowing what term to use. Lover? The two of them could not be lovers in any sane sense of that word.

Skeefer held Ree protectively, glaring at Tai. 'Sshe came down here once. Long ago it sseems now. An impossible ssmall creature.' He ran a dark furred finger gently across Ree's orange breast. 'Beautiful, and brave hearted ass any hawk.'

Ree chirruped wordlessly at the caress. 'As I have told you, man, I learned how to escape the Lord Veil's chamber. Many times I did so, always at night, flying about the Keep. One night, I found myself here, lost and afraid, and a voice called me, and there was Skeefer . . .'

Tai sighed. Lovers most strange, it seemed. And Ree had used him for her own ends. But Tai could not find it in himself to blame her overmuch. He felt overwhelmed with sudden, sharp pity for the two of them. What manner of life must they have led, the poor things? Nothing but chattel they were, used and abused . . .

But enough. The night was passing as they stood here. Tai strode over to the corner of the room where the pike lay, gathered it up, turned for the spell-helm. He lifted that, feeling the weight of it in his hands. 'We must away from this place,' he said. Tai felt the tug of the helm at him, an insistent, nagging little urge to put it back on.

'Yes!' Ree cried. She flipped out of Skeefer's hold into the air and whirred in circles about him. 'Out of here and away to freedom! *Freeeedom!*'

But Skeefer shook his head sadly. 'There iss no esscape, little Ree. Not for uss.'

She darted down about him. 'Yes, yes. There is. There *is!* With the man here to help us we can—'

Skeefer only shook his head the more. 'There iss no esscape. Not from *him.*'

Ree dived at him. 'We must try. We must!' In and out she flitted, beating at him with her little wings until he cowered under her. 'We *must try!*'

'All right!' he said then, making a sound midway between a laugh and a sob. 'Let uss try for freedom, then, brave heart.'

Ree ceased her darting about and came into Skeefer's hold. 'Yes. Yes! And with the man's help . . .'

Skeefer looked over sharply, his gaze fixed on Tai and the spell-helm in Tai's hand. 'Why sshould you make pact with the likess of uss, man?'

Tai saw the bitterness plain in Skeefer's eyes. He put the helm and the pike on the floor at his feet and stepped carefully towards the fur-man. 'I know *them.* I know *him.* I have seen too much of horror in this place. We are not enemies, you and I.' He reached both hands out to Skeefer, palm out. 'We are not enemies . . .'

The fur-man edged away. He looked Tai straight, his liquid-dark, animal eyes unblinking. Tai stayed where he was, hands extended in mute invitation.

'He might be our *friend*, Skeefer,' Ree suggested.

The fur-man snorted. 'He putss on the form of *them*. He iss one of *them.*'

'No!' Ree insisted. 'He is enemy to *them.*'

Skeefer's glance flicked to Ree, then Tai, then back to Ree. He shook his head. 'Ssuch ass he are not to be trussted.'

'We are not enemies,' Tai repeated, but he dropped his hands and the invitation they had offered.

194

'He is *not* our enemy, Skeefer,' Ree said.

The fur-man stared at Tai, silent, then reluctantly nodded. 'Between uss no enmity, then. But ssee that you honour your wordss, man . . .'

'And you yours,' Tai returned.

In the silence that fell between them then, they grew aware of the babble that came once again now from the rows of locked cell doors.

'What . . . what is it?' Tai asked, though he had a sad suspicion that he knew already what that sound had to be.

Skeefer said not a word, but turned instead and hobbled over to the cell door nearest him. Lifting the bar, he hauled the door open, then moved over to the next. In his wake, the occupants of the cells came tumbling or crawling, stumbling or squirming out.

Tai stared, unbelieving.

He saw a great bird, like a hawk, but man-sized and with man's legs and a man's head. He saw what seemed to be a small bear, but with hands and round, human eyes, blinking dazedly. There was a serpent, fork-tongued but human-headed, twice the length of a tall man and thick around as a barrel. And there were others, part-fowl or furred beast or lizard, and part-human, all part-human in some terrible way or other.

The chamber was charged with confusion. None of the creatures seemed in any better condition than poor Skeefer, and they crawled or hobbled or stumbled about, calling, mumbling, making odd, grunting sounds.

Tai was appalled at the insane mixing of human and beast, at the pitiful condition of them all. This was worse than anything he had imagined.

'You should not have freed them!' Ree said as the fur-man came limping back to where Tai and she stood. 'They will scatter. The guards will find them.'

Skeefer looked at her a little shamefacedly. 'What would you have me do? When will a chance like thiss ever come to any of us again?'

'You should have left them,' Ree only repeated.

Skeefer shook his head. 'How could I . . . ?'

'It is you, I came for, Skeefer. *You!*'

Skeefer smiled, showing his sharp, ivory teeth. 'Ass you alwayss ssaid you would, little Ree.' He let out a long breath. 'Though I did not believe it.'

Ree made a small chirping noise of derision. Leaving Skeefer, she coasted over to Tai, who was still staring at the uncanny, milling creatures. Alighting on his shoulder, she said, 'Pit Folk. These are the Pit Folk.' Ree's little body shook with a sudden anger. '*His* creations. For the amusement of the Lord Veil.'

Tai shook his head. 'I . . . I don't understand. Were you . . . ?' He was not sure how to ask the question. 'Were you *created?*'

'Ree wass born, man,' Skeefer said stiffly. 'And I too wass born. Jusst ass you. My mother wass born.' He bowed his head. 'But her mother wass not. And ssome of thesse here, they too were not born . . .'

Skeefer's face clenched tight as a fist. 'We were brought here from the big pens in the ssouth. In cagess and iron-bounded chessts, a long, dark journey. The little bodiess we inhabit in the Pit, thosse *he* can create many times for uss. We live thosse many little livess and die thosse little deathss. But we live here. *Thiss* iss the true life that bindss all our other livess together!'

With a shudder, Tai thought of what the poor soul had endured, imprisoned for all the years of his life, and though it was hard to guess, the fur-man seemed at least Tai's own age, perhaps considerably more. Tai recalled his own experience in the Pit. A whole life of such experiences. A whole life lived here. What must it be like?

And then, thinking thus, he suddenly noticed something. He had lost a finger to the Pit. Yet Skeefer appeared completely intact. 'How many times have you endured the Pit?' he demanded.

Skeefer shrugged his thin, furred shoulders. 'Many. Too many.'

'Then how is it . . . Why have you lost none of your limbs?'

Skeefer looked at him in puzzlement. 'Losst my limbss? Why sshould I losse my limbss?'

Tai held his hand out, the stump of the missing finger clear enough in the thin lighting about them. '*That* was taken from me. The Seer claimed it was needed to grow the . . . "homunculus", he called it, the small Pit body. Yet you . . . you are intact!'

'Of coursse!'

'And you have been in the Pit? Many times?'

'Yess! Have I not told you?'

Tai felt sick. 'Then it is *not* necessary to . . . to take a man's limbs from him in order to grow a homunculus?'

Skeefer's furred face took on a puzzled frown. 'A ssmall piece of flessh iss all *he* needss. Look . . .' He turned and showed Tai the sores along his flanks. '*He* cutss small slicess from me. That iss all.'

For a long moment, Tai could hardly breathe. It was too terrible to be true. Surely too terrible.

'Why do you assk?' Skeefer said.

'Colby . . .' Tai recalled Tancred's dismissal of Colby and the other captives: 'Each Pit-life they lose will cost them,' the Seer had said, 'until nothing is left of them but limbless torsos.'

Ree fluttered over to Tai. 'What is wrong, man?'

Tai felt sick, telling them of his foster-uncle's suspected fate. And all, it seemed, for no real need. All part of some dark, heartless design of the Seer's and nothing more.

'Come!' Tai said when all was told. 'We must *find* Colby!'

At the far end of the chamber, a commotion was breaking out. The man-headed serpent had coiled itself about some smaller creature – an impossible combination of rabbit and bird and human – and the poor thing was squealing terribly. Some of the other Pit Folk were beating upon the serpent. Others still attacked those. Pandemonium grew.

'Beware,' Skeefer said. 'The Pit Folk are not all mindful, and thosse that are, are half mad at besst. No telling what they may do now.'

Tai nodded. He did not like at all the eerie mob that was seething now about the serpent and its victim. The scene had an aspect of nightmare about it: the twisting, strange limbs, the shrieks and calls, the surge and movement of them all like some huge insectile mass. He shuddered. 'Let us away, and quickly.'

A sudden, desperate urgency gripped Tai. Too much time had passed while they dallied here. And they were mired now in the Miradore's dark underchambers with the unnatural pack of the Pit Folk scattering about them. And the Seer might already have discovered his escape from the tower . . .

Tai reached up the pike and replaced the spell-helm on his head. Strength flowed through him once. 'Let us *away!*'

They went out along the same corridor they had come in by, Ree guiding, but from Skeefer's shoulder now. Their pace was exasperatingly slow, for the fur-man could move only at a halting limp, and even then must pause frequently to rest, leaning gasping against the wall. Tai chafed at the delay. He wished to leap onwards.

Hefting the war-pike in his hands, he stared at the labouring fur-man. A thrust of the blade would solve the problem. One quick, simple thrust and Skeefer could be left behind, no longer an impediment . . .

Tai shook himself, shuddering. It was the creeping influence of the spell-helm once more. He ignored it as best he could and kept pace with his slower companions, urging them to what speed was possible.

'An ill death and long on *him*,' Skeefer panted during one of their forced pauses. 'On all of *them!*'

'Aye,' Tai agreed. The bitterness in Skeefer's voice was infectious. He, Tai, had learned to hate *them* well enough, and with reason. He could understand another's hate.

'Come,' Tai said, but more gently than before. 'Already we have spent too much time here. We must move on.' He reached a helping hand to Skeefer. The fur-man brushed it aside, but Tai insisted. He

197

helped Skeefer to rise and kept an arm about his shoulders for support. Skeefer pushed him away, stumbled, and nearly went down. 'Leave me, man!' he hissed. 'I can walk.'

Tai bit back on the irritation that rose in him and let the fur-man be.

Onwards they continued. Every corridor looked alike, dark and winding and empty. There was still no sign of the man-demons anywhere. The way led up now, though. At least so Tai thought. He did not understand how Ree could navigate, but she seemed to know well enough where they were headed. He thought of poor Colby, of himself opening the door to his foster-uncle's cell, of the look on Colby's face when he, Tai, came striding in.

'Come,' Tai urged, trying to help Skeefer along at a faster pace. 'We must hurry!'

But hardly had they taken a few steps before the fur-man said, 'Hisst! Lissten.'

Tai heard it then, a commotion in the distance. He had been too caught up in his own urgency to notice it before, even with his spell-helm-enhanced hearing.

'The Pit Folk,' Ree whispered fiercely, whirring about the fur-man's head. 'I *told* you, Skeefer.'

'Come,' Tai urged. 'Quickly!'

But the Keep was astir now. They could feel it in the air. Tai felt his heart sink. They had wasted too much time down in the place of the Pit Folk.

Rounding a corner, Tai suddenly saw a lone demon guard, war-pike aglimmer in torchlight. This was the first light that they had seen since leaving the place of the Pit Folk, and it seemed very bright. The guard's back was to them.

Tai felt a great surge go through him. He leaped forward, silent and strong, spell-helm strength thrilling his limbs.

The demon guard heard him, but too late. As he was trying to turn round, Tai's war-pike took him in the lower back, pinning him against the wall. But the guard's armour protected him, and the pike-blade could not penetrate. Tai dropped his pike and leaped in while the guard was still gasping from the force of the pike blow, and took him by the throat. Flinging him face down upon the stone floor, Tai put a knee against the guard's spine and hauled back on his throat until something broke with a soft snapping sound, like a stick of wet wood.

The guard went as limp as a rag.

Simple as that.

Tai felt exhilaration fill him. He snatched up his own and the guard's pike. 'Come,' he hissed to his companions. 'Come!'

Skeefer and Ree emerged from the corridor. 'Come *on*,' Tai urged, motioning them to hurry. He handed a pike to the fur-man, who took it eagerly. 'Let us . . .' Tai began, but then stopped, cocking his helmed head, listening.

The tramp of booted feet in the distance.

Skeefer heard it, too, then. 'It iss the end,' he hissed. 'There iss no escape for the likess of uss. Did I not ssay sso?'

A little distance off along the corridor, a troop of demon guards came suddenly into view. They carried torches, the dancing torchlight flashing off armour and gleaming yellow eyes and pike-blades. Ree shrieked and whirled hysterically into the air. A shout went up from amongst the guards.

Tai's first impulse was to charge, to cut through them like so much wheat. But there were too many for that, and his common sense overpowered the spell-helm's urging. Surprise had been on his side here, this first time. These newcomers could see him clearly.

Tai shoved Skeefer along, out of there and away, but he inadvertently pushed too hard and Skeefer stumbled, nearly went down. The pike Tai had given him fell clattering to the floor. Tai hissed in frustration, hesitated a moment, then lifted the fur-man bodily, flinging him over one shoulder like so much baggage, his pike in his other hand, and sprinted off and away. The strength still flowed through him and he ran as lightly as a deer, Ree darting along overhead.

The little bird plunged onwards, then doubled back for her slower companions, whistling and piping, her entire being vibrant with fear. 'Hurry, hurry hurry hurry,' she cried.

'Quiet!' Tai hissed up at her. '*Quiet*! You will lead them right to us.'

'Oh Hurreeeeee,' Ree whistled one last time, and then went silent.

Tai lengthened his stride, putting all he had into it. Through dark corridors and winding stairwells they fled, blindly, Tai's limbs still thrilling with strength even now, till the calls of their pursuers grew faint behind them.

They had headed downwards, into the dark and emptiness of the Miradore's lower reaches. The ploy had worked, at least for the moment. But, 'Where are we?' Tai asked when, eventually, he let Skeefer down and they took time to rest. The corridors about them seemed no different than any others: dark, quiet, deserted. The Keep was like a maze.

'I do not know,' Ree replied after a long moment's pause.

'Losst,' Skeefer groaned.

They stood unmoving for a dark time, not knowing which way to turn or how to begin. But the spell-helm would not long allow Tai to be inactive. He felt its vigour filling him. 'Come,' he said to the others. 'Let us go this way.'

'Do you know where thiss way leadss?' demanded Skeefer.

'No,' Tai said. 'But when all ways are unknown, one is as good as the next, no?'

Tai heard Skeefer laugh, a soft hissing in the dark. 'You are not eassily dissmayed, man.'

'Come,' was all Tai said in return. He was eager to be on the move.

With Tai in the lead, they made a way through the silent dark of those corridors, waiting for something, anything, to give them a hint of where they might be.

They came to a junction, took the left-hand fork, and found themselves in a low-ceilinged, curving corridor. On their left was a flight of stone steps. They almost passed it by unknowing, for the entrance was only a darker shadow in the darkness of the corridor. It was Tai's spell-helm vision that caught it. The stairs led upwards, and upwards was the direction they desired.

The stairway wound like a corkscrew; it was so narrow that Tai and Skeefer had to ascend with their shoulders twisted sideways.

'Do you know where we are, Ree?' Tai asked.

'No,' Ree responded, fluttering above. 'I do not know these stairs. The way is too tight to be one of the tower wells. I . . . I do not know where this may lead us . . .'

'Upwards, at least,' Tai said.

The steps went up and up in their tight spiral. Skeefer lagged behind, gasping. Tai would have helped him, but there was not sufficient room in the stairwell.

Upwards they continued, until, after a time, a faint radiance appeared above them. Ree flashed off ahead to see what it might be. Tai and Skeefer continued on their slower way.

Then they heard Ree shriek suddenly, and the deeper sound of demon-voices.

'Ree!' Skeefer called out, '*Ree!*'

'Quiet!' Tai hissed to him, and sprinted up the stairs, three at a time.

He emerged through a small doorway, bending to a half crouch to do so, and found himself upon a railed landing next to a large staircase. Before him were two demon-guards leaping and swatting at a desperate, screaming Ree. So totally absorbed were they that they did not notice Tai's arrival.

Having learned from experience, Tai took the first of the guards with a pike-thrust through the throat, between helm and armour. Using the pike's butt, he slammed the man against the wall, then skewered him with the blade. Simple.

The second was not so easy.

This one drove Tai back with thrust and stroke, the pike-blades ringing off each other harshly. Tai stumbled, went down on one knee. *Tlangg* went the blades. Tai thrust out, but his own blade only skidded off the other's body armour. Blow after blow he parried, clumsily, feeling the shock of each right up to his shoulder joints.

But then, from the stairs, Skeefer came leaping up. He flung himself upon the demon guard's back, legs about the armoured midriff, and yanked desperately at the spell-helm. The fur-man had not the strength to pull the helm off entirely, but he did manage to jerk it part-way. The demon guard dropped his pike and clutched with both hands at the helm, ramming it back into place. Hunching his shoulders, he ripped Skeefer away and flung him to the floor, then turned back to Tai.

But Tai thrust his pike-blade with desperate force up into that vulnerable area between armour and helm, and the demon guard died before he knew properly how it had happened.

Tai stood, panting, eyes on the dead guards. Even with spell-helm strength, he felt his heart pound. Yet he could not help but grin. So much for the vaunted invulnerability of *them!* He had killed four so far, and it seemed easy enough, once one knew how. Lifting his gaze, Tai turned and surveyed the landing. Skeefer lay sprawled against the wall, alive and unhurt it seemed, but utterly spent.

Of Ree, there was no sign.

'Ree,' Tai called. 'Ree!' He cast about, afraid he would find her small body heaped in a corner. But no. The landing was empty save for Skeefer and himself and the dead man-demons.

To one side, Tai now saw, stood a portal leading off from the large staircase: oddly carved stone formed an elaborate, though narrow entranceway. 'Ree?' Tai called, but softly.

No response.

Moving slowly, war-pike before him, Tai edged through the entranceway.

Beyond lay a large, high-ceilinged, circular room, dimly lit from small skylights set into the vaulting high above. This room was entirely empty but for a kind of wooden dais in the middle. Tai spotted Ree, unhurt, perched at the edge of that dais, staring down wide-eyed.

On the dais . . .

On the dais lay a queer, thrashing shape. It was a man's shape, yet it was entirely limbless, only stumps remaining of the arms and legs. The head was a ghastly, featureless oval, with empty pits where the eyes had once been and twisted folds of scar tissue marking ears and nose.

Tai shuddered. What foul things had been done to this poor creature to leave him like this? He felt an impulse to put the poor soul out of his misery. One quick thrust of the pike would do it. Easy enough . . .

But a sound from behind made Tai turn. Skeefer staggered in through the entranceway, his dark eyes glinting in the light. 'We are purssued!' he hissed. '*They* are below!'

'Quickly, then,' Tai said. 'We must away!' Turning his back on the poor, flopping thing on the dais, he hastened out.

The larger staircase here passed upwards from below. Sounds of movement came clearly from its lower reaches. Tai looked at Skeefer, exhausted and limping. This staircase was considerably more spacious than the little corkscrew steps they had followed here, and he would have no difficulty carrying the fur-man.

Twice he had to call to Ree before she appeared. It seemed most strange, and foolish, given their circumstances. 'Come *on*!' he hissed at her.

Holding Skeefer over his shoulder as he had before, Tai took the steps upwards as quickly as he might and still be silent. Sounds of movement came clearly from below. The stairs went up and up, past two more landings, and then, unexpectedly, they found themselves through a doorway and out beyond into the sudden, cold air of the open night. The sea-wind blew chill and wet, and stars lit the sky above. A half-crescent of moon hung low in the sky, washing all in faint radiance.

It was a flagstone portico of some sort they stood in, bounded on one side by the rearing bulk of the Keep, and on the other by a low wall. On the far side of this lower wall, the deep sea beat against rocks beneath.

Tai let Skeefer down against the wall. The fur-man slumped exhaustedly, feet splayed, head lolling. Tai, however, prowled about, back and forth from the wall overlooking the sea below to the doorway. There was no way out save by the stairs they had come up.

It was not a good place in which to be found out.

Tai came back to where Skeefer lay propped against the wall. He squatted next to the fur-man.

'We wait,' Skeefer panted.

'Aye,' Tai agreed, his eye on the doorway through which they had come. 'We wait. And we hope. There is naught else to do.'

The air was chill here. Tai felt spell-helm warmth fill him, but Skeefer shivered, hugging himself. The poor soul looked all but done in.

'It is huge and old, this Keep,' Tai said. 'Built long ago. Perhaps, if we are lucky . . . It looks as if *their* forces are only a fraction of the number the Miradore was built to house. It seems an out of the way place, this. Perhaps no one will come up here in the search.'

'Perhapss,' Skeefer returned, but his eyes, like Tai's, remained fixed upon the doorway through which they had come.

Ree fluttered down tiredly on to the wall by Skeefer's shoulder. She had been utterly silent since finding the room below with its eerie occupant.

'Why so quiet, Ree?' Tai asked softly, puzzled.

But there was no time for Ree to respond. From out of the doorway before them, suddenly, stepped a demon-faced guard, and another, and more after. And in the rear of these came Tancred himself.

'Behind me,' Tai called urgently to his companions. He stood there then, pike upheld, ready to sell himself as dear as might be. The sight of the Seer brought a shiver to his spine, but there was little real fear in him even now. Only a dark anger that his escape should be brought to nothing, and a kind of desperate thrill. It was the spell-helm, of course. And he was glad. Let them come. He knew what to do. Now could he properly give them back what they deserved.

The demon guards approached him cautiously enough. When the first made a feint at him, Tai met it with a clanging ring of iron blade on blade and a little splash of bright sparks.

The Seer watched, arms crossed, his black eyes cold and unblinking. 'Do not kill him. He is valuable. I wish him alive and unharmed!'

The demon guards ringed Tai, first one coming at him, then another, leaping in and out again too quickly for him to make any sort of hit.

'Enough of this play,' the Seer called. 'The Veil's guard will be upon us soon. Finish it before they arrive. Quickly!'

Tai readied himself for one last, desperate, exalted leap amongst them, a leap that would carry him, and as many of them as possible, into the Shadowlands.

But at the very moment he was about to move, a pike-blade came out of nowhere and smashed against the side of his head. The spell-helm took most of the force of that blow, but the intricate, hooked blade of the pike snagged some part of the helm and tore it from his head. Tai felt his own flesh tear as well, in a ragged gash across his forehead and through the hair on the left side of his head.

All the strength and exhilaration left him in an instant, and he collapsed to his knees, shivering, the pike falling weakly from his grasp. A cascade of blood from the wound on his scalp flooded his vision, blinding him.

The guards laughed, the same terrible laughter he remembered from his march with Colby and the others.

Hands reached for him. He tried despairingly to shake them off. But the hands came from behind, and he felt the furred warmth of them.

'The wall, man,' Skeefer hissed in his ear. 'The wall. The ssea.'

'What?' Tai said, not understanding.

But Skeefer said no word more. Clutching Tai by the arms, he dragged him over to the low wall behind and flung himself and Tai over it, over and down to tumble through the empty air.

Tai yelped in terror, feeling the plummeting speed of their fall. Above, he heard Tancred shouting in angry surprise. And then the sea hit him like a stone wall.

He plunged into darkness and cold and the terrifying surge and toss of the sea's great grip, and he had only Skeefer's hold on him to cling to. Water filled his lungs and he gagged, coughing, breathing in great, ragged gasps, only realizing belately that he had risen to the surface somehow, that Skeefer still held fast to him somehow. He saw a little dark whir of wings and heard Ree call out. But his head rang with the wound he had taken, and with the great smash of the sea. He had one long moment of despair, thinking: everything gone, all failed, Colby left behind, and then he felt himself whirled away into the surging dark of the sea and he had no thought for anything save the struggle for life and breath.

# XX

# On the Slopes of
# the Easterling Peaks

Sub-Commander Gerrid knelt in the bow of the small, flat-bottomed boat. The quiet splash of the oars and the murmur of water against the hull were the only sounds that broke the great, dark stillness of the night until, with a soft *scruunch* the boat hit the far bank. Gerrid leaped ashore.

Those awaiting him were dim figures in the blackness under the trees, mere moving blots even to his spell-helm-sharpened sight. Only the occasional low-voiced mutter, or a bitten-back curse as somebody stumbled, betrayed their actuality as living, breathing men-at-arms. Gerrid ordered the boat away. It coasted quietly off downstream, back to the Palisade.

The Sub-Commander smiled in the dark. He felt a fierce kind of pleasurable anticipation being out in the night like this, like some nocturnal predator on the hunt.

Three dozen men, most of a troop, slipped across the Paudit in the dark. A hunting party indeed.

Gerrid felt an exultant sense of freedom surge through him. It was *good* to be out of the Palisade. He had been cooped up too long in the wretched place, bound like a captive to a desk. It was not healthy. All he had done there amounted to little more than mere accounting. So many inmates, so much food needed, so much available, so many sick, so many floggings, so many new arrivals, so many deaths, so many of this and that and these and those.

It demeaned him. He despised it. No warrior should have to do such. And Commander Chayne, curse him, lorded it over all, keeping totally aloof of the daily drudgery required to run the camp, strutting like a bantam cook, never dirtying his own hands to even the slightest of degrees.

Gerrid had sent secret message after secret message to the Lords Veil, keeping them abreast of events here, as they had instructed he should. But he had received no acknowledgement whatsoever.

And the Seer had been nowhere to be seen for days now.

And meanwhile, the world went on without him, and all Gerrid had were tantalizing rumours.

Events were moving on, now that the conquest was all but finished here in the north. More than half the original expeditionary force had already returned southwards by now, with more doing so every day. Events in the south were picking up. Minmi city itself had fallen, or so it was said, and Sofala was next. If true, that spelled the end of the Lord Braxton's power. Lord Stauntery would be next and the rich lands of the Selva River delta. The Lords Veil moved from triumph to triumph. There would be deaths and promotions down there, careers to be made. All this, while he rotted away up here in this cursed northern hinterland.

It made one want to puke.

And, to add to it all, there was the matter of the Healer. A small matter, but it rankled out of all proportion. Another slight at the hand of Commander Chayne that Gerrid must endure. And the man would break that woman, sure – Chayne was not one to appreciate what he had.

What a waste. A comely woman . . . Gerrid remembered her leaning over the guard with the broken leg, auburn hair twisted up at the nape of her neck, her hands hovering with a peculiar slow grace, as if they had a life of their own, gliding over the ruptured bone and bleeding flesh like strange, ethereally graceful birds.

The image of her stuck in his mind like a burr.

Gerrid shook himself. Enough! Life in the camp was making him crazy. It was time to focus on what lay ahead this night.

He made a quick check to see that all were assembled and ready. Then, once satisfied, he started to lead them away from the river's verge. He wanted to be well away from the shore by dawn.

Glancing back from the edge of the trees, he saw the stars glinting coldly above the river. Near the horizon, he could make out the constellation of the Hunter. He gave the figure a quick salute of acknowledgement, fist against his helmed forehead. 'Wish me luck, Old One,' he whispered.

Gerrid laughed softly to himself, breath steaming in the chill air. Foolishness, old foolishness, asking benediction from the stars. As if they cared.

But perhaps it was a good omen, catching sight of the Hunter like this. Here, on this enterprise, he was under the Hunter's auspices. He laughed to himself again and turned and led the way into the thick dark under the trees.

Keeping the party together and properly organized, while moving upslope through the black, crowded jumble of trees, proved to be a demanding and delicate task. But Gerrid welcomed it. He took them slowly, passing back queries and commands to the three Squad Leaders, making sure nobody straggled haphazardly into the looming dark to become lost. The blood-deep exhilaration of the spell-helm, and the red-glimmer darkness of spell-helm sight, melded with the tense concentration to create a kind of dreamlike clarity of movement, like a long, slow, intricate and silent dance.

After a time, feeling that they had indeed come far enough, Gerrid called a halt. The men hunkered down, positioned loosely in their squads, silent, waiting. 'Scouts,' Gerrid whispered. 'One from each squad.' There was quiet movement in the dark, and he found himself facing the half-seen shapes of three man. The organization in all of this, the quickness of the men's response, pleased him. He felt the power of the helm course through him, felt the smooth orderliness of all about him; him at the centre, co-ordinating, controlling. This was life. Not the sticky confusion behind the Palisade walls. This was clean and clear and strong.

'Upslope,' he said softly. 'Spread out. Work your way up a few hundred paces and then settle in.' The men murmured a response and then melted into the dark. Gerrid learned against a tree bole, listening to the faint sounds they made as they fanned out and away from his own position. He did not really need to place scouts like this, but he had long ago learned not to give in to helm-induced overconfidence. One made one's balance with the helm, neither giving nor taking too much, for it could be a fell and dangerous thing. It was a question of will.

But spell-helm or no, he had a good feeling about this enterprise, had from the moment he conceived the idea; a gut-deep certainty that he was doing the right thing, slipping across the Paudit like this in the dark. It was a gamble. Commander Chayne knew nothing of it. At this very moment, Chayne was no doubt having his way with the Healer. He would be furious when he discovered what Gerrid had accomplished.

Just let the expedition be successful, though, and the Commander's fury would not matter at all.

Rebels. There were still rebels about. Some rag-tag group had started up here in the mountains, stealing down through the trees to make stealthy sallies during the past few nights, wreaking small acts of sabotage.

He had come out here to deal with them, thoroughly and completely.

Let word of *that* get back to the Lords Veil – and he would make sure it did – and Chayne would have to swallow his own bile. And perhaps the Lords would be reminded of his, Gerrid's, real skills; that he was wasted here and had suffered enough punishment.

Gerrid slid himself down to the base of the tree and squatted there.

There was nothing to be done now but wait. He was not unduly worried about making definite arrangements. He knew the sort of enemy he faced: untrained, impatient, angry, apt to rash acts and ill-conceived sallies. Such men made mistakes. There were always hotheads amongst such groups, and unless there was good leadership, the hotheads always prevailed. Gerrid had seen no signs of such leadership so far.

These rebels would make mistakes. Something would happen. He had only to hold himself and his men in readiness to take immediate advantage of whatever that something should be.

It was like this, sometimes. Sometimes you fought and planned a campaign down to the tiniest detail, an exercise in foresight, organization, planning and execution, as if you were the venerable Lord of Hosts himself and could see all and know all. Sometimes you used raw courage and brute strength and simply battered your enemy into submission.

But there came a moment, sometimes, when you had to play the Hunter, put yourself in what you felt to be the right place at the right time. And be ready, waiting with the Hunter's canniness. The difference between a good commander and a bad one, Gerrid knew, was being right about which approach to adopt and when. He smiled. Yes. Something *would* happen here in these wooded depths. He felt it in his guts. And he would be ready for whatever came.

After a time, the blackness of the eastern sky grew silvery with the beginnings of the new day. The gnarled boles of the trees stood silhouetted against the far, high light of the mountain dawn. Mist from the river curled about their trunks in feathery wreaths. Gerrid stood and stretched, feeling his joints crackle satisfyingly after the time spent crouched in waiting.

Hearing the soft sound of movement upslope, he turned and slipped a few paces up and around the tree where he had been crouched. Out of the mists, one of the scouts came slipping in. 'Men, Sub-Commander! A thousand paces above us perhaps. A dozen or more, moving down towards the river.' The scout shook his head and grinned humourlessly. 'And a noisy, clumsy, ragged-looking bunch they are.'

It took only a little time to get the necessary details from the scout and to deploy his men as seemed best. Gerrid felt a surge of elation. It was happening, just as he had felt it would.

He knelt behind an ancient, fallen tree now, his men fanned out in a loose arc. He waited with every sense brightly alert, but with a quiet mind, his concentration totally on the moment. He relished this. It was the Hunter's gift: singleness of mind, without disturbing thoughts or questions or uncertainties. It made him feel clean and whole and strong. The forest about him seemed to glow with promise.

One of the other scouts came coasting in with new information about the movement of the rebels upslope. Gerrid adjusted the positioning of his men accordingly. It was almost too good, this, too easy . . .

The sound of human voices cut through the forest stillness above them. A stick, stomped on by somebody's foot, cracked loudly. 'Moron!' Gerrid heard. It was only the barest of rasping whispers, but it carried clearly to his helm-sensitive hearing in the still, cold dawn air. 'Can't you walk more quietly? How can we ever expect to sneak up on . . . ?'

Gerrid shook his head. The scout had been right. This was indeed a clumsy, inexperienced lot. He could see them now, dim figures in the pearly dawn mist, working their way inexpertly down through the cover of the trees. From his vantage point below, he could clearly make out their upright, dark silhouettes against the lit morning sky behind and above them. Gerrid held up his hand in readiness to give the signal. He could see the pale smudges of these rebels' faces now, see the men slipping gracelessly down from tree to tree. Instead of being spread out as they ought to be for this sort of thing, they moved in a ridiculously tight wedge. They were only fifty paces upslope now. Easy prey, grouped up like that. Thirty paces. He tried to count, to get as exact an idea as he could of how many of them there were, but the intervening foliage and the very bunchiness of the group they formed made that impossible.

Twenty paces.

Now!

Gerrid's arm came down. The men behind him let out a great howl and leaped forward.

With astonished wails, the rebels scattered and tried to flee. Gerrid saw five or six of them go down, skewered. The rest, however, managed to flee away through the tangle of trees into temporary safety. He could hear them scrabbling desperately upwards, grunting and squealing like so many terrorized pigs.

It was to be a running game, then. 'After them!' he ordered. 'And remember, I want at least one of them alive and well enough to talk!'

His men bolted away like a pack of hounds. Gerrid, with a handful of men he had previously arranged would stay with him, watched, satisfied, as his hunters churned up the slope in pursuit. 'And now,' he said, 'we wait.'

Turning to the Squad Leader who had remained, he said, 'Let me know if any of those cut down at the beginning are still alive and able to talk.' Dismissing the man, he folded his cloak across the fallen tree behind which he had crouched, and settled himself. He stretched, grinned, relaxed. Things had gone better than he had any right to hope. All he needed now was a captive to question.

'Sub-Commander?' The Squad Leader he had detailed to check on the downed rebels stood before him. 'One of them is still alive. But I don't think you'll be able to get anything much out of him. He's mostly gone, by now.'

'Keep a watch on him,' Gerrid replied. 'Let me know if there's a chance.'

The man left and Gerrid went back to waiting.

In a little, the first of his hunters began to trickle in.

'Well?' he demanded.

Four of his men stood before him. They were dishevelled from the chase, twigs and bits of bark and leaves caught up in their armour and accoutrements. They had no captives. 'Had to kill them, Sub-Commander,' one of them explained. 'Scattered like rabbits. But when we caught up with them they turned and flung themselves at us. Couldn't help it.' The man shrugged, uncomfortable. 'Sorry, Sir.'

Gerrid nodded. 'Go on back and sit down.'

'Are any of the others back yet, Sir?' one of them asked.

Gerrid shook his head. 'Not yet. We'll just have to wait. Somebody is bound to bring at least *one* back.' With that, he dismissed the four of them.

Over the next while, his men straggled back singly or in small groups. They had one injury, a man with a painfully fractured arm. He had cornered a couple of rebels against the face of a small cliff but in the struggle to take them, had missed his footing on the slippery, moss-carpeted face of the rock and tumbled down to smash his forearm on a boulder below.

As of yet, however, not a single rebel had been taken alive.

Gerrid felt impatience begin to rise in him. The success of this impromptu ambush was something, but he depended on being able to get information concerning the rebel strength and the location of their main camp. He needed more than this little skirmish if he were going to outface Commander Chayne successfully.

Gerrid waited it out. The wounded rebel had died, without ever having been lucid enough to be questioned. Slowly, his men returned, one after another, empty-handed.

And then, upslope, he saw two fingers, one armoured and helmed, the other . . .

Gerrid smiled. Finally.

'I'd almost given up,' his man said, skidding down the last few feet of slope and flinging his captive on to the ground before him. 'Was on my way back when I spotted this one. Crouched down under the roots of a big tree, frozen stock-still like a frightened rabbit. Didn't put up any fight either, once he knew he was had.'

Gerrid gazed down at the captured rebel. He was a lanky man with a long scar marring the left side of his face. And that face was pasty white. The eyes, though, had a certain bleak wildness to them. One of the hotheads, Gerrid reckoned.

The man crouched on the ground, shivering, frightened, yet defiant. Gerrid took a step towards him. The man flinched, raised his head for one instant in a hate-filled, frightened stare, his eyes showing whites all around, then folded in upon himself, head tucked down. Gerrid almost laughed. These northerners were terrified by the spell-helm visages, ignorant rabble that they were. This fool looked as if he were about to wet himself at any moment.

And that, of course, was very convenient. It would simplify what was to come.

Turning on his heel, without having said a word to his captive, Gerrid walked off. 'Build a fire,' he ordered two of his men nearby. 'A hot fire.'

While waiting for the fire to be prepared, Gerrid made sure that nobody talked to the rebel. He was properly watched, of course, but otherwise left entirely alone. The Sub-Commander was well aware what fear could do to a man's mind, and he had every intention of allowing this man the time to conjure up whatever private horrors he was capable of.

Once the fire grew hot enough, Gerrid took a long-bladed knife from one of his men and positioned it in the glowing heart of the flames.

The rebel's eyes grew wide and he began to shake in little, uncontrollable spasms.

After a time, Gerrid pulled the knife from the fire. Its end glowed a sullen, smouldering red. Knife in hand, he walked back to his captive. 'Strip,' he ordered.

The man stared at him, trying to be defiant.

'Take your clothes off.'

The man shook his head.

Gerrid gestured a command. One of his man dealt the rebel a sharp smack across the side of his head. The man tried to resist and received another, then a third. It was enough.

A few moments later the rebel stood there, naked, pale and shivering, his arms clutched about himself self-consciously. Bluish bruises showed along the side of his head and cheek and shoulders where he had been beaten.

'The only thing I am uncertain about,' Gerrid said, 'is where to begin.'
He hefted the knife and spat on the glowing, still red-hot end. His spittle
sizzled off in a little puff of vapour. 'I could start with your eyes – or,
perhaps, your balls.'

The man shivered violently. His eyes darted about, looking
desperately for some sort of escape or refuge, but seeing none.

'Yes,' Gerrid continued, 'your balls, I think.' He took a step forward.

'Do – do – don't,' the man stammered. 'Please . . . *don't!*'

Gerrid smiled, a cat-snarl he knew the man would find terrifying.
'And why should I not?'

'I . . . I will tell you anything you want to know. *Anything*! But please,
please, *please* do not do that to me.'

Gerrid hefted the knife again. He moved forward. With a deft, light
jab, almost as if he were using a fencing foil, he scratched the glowing
end of the iron across the man's belly. There was a small sizzle. The man
screamed and stumbled back. Gerrid did it again, and a third time. The
man crumpled, sobbing.

'Remember,' Gerrid said. 'I *will* use this on you further if you do not
give me what I wish. Is that clear?'

Whimpering, the man nodded.

'Good,' Gerrid replied. He went back to the fire and made an
elaborate job of repositioning the knife there; he had no intention of
allowing such a useful threat to simply just disappear.

He walked back to the captive and sat down, making himself
comfortable against one of the trees. 'First,' he said, 'your name.'

'Joff. Joff the Miller,' the man said in a small voice.

'Well then, Joff the Miller, you may get dressed again now, and we
shall talk.'

It took only a little time to get what he wanted from the Miller. The man
babbled like a child, giving Gerrid names and background details, and
what amounted to plain old-fashioned gossip. He was pitifully eager to
supply information. It was the way with most such hotheads. Once
they broke, they broke completely.

After the interrogation, Gerrid sat musing. This Miller had told him
nothing terribly surprising. Gerrid had had enough experience with
this sort of fight to be well aware of the tenacity with which the
remnants of a group beaten in open battle were capable of resisting any
final defeat. As long as there were hills in which to hide, there would be
rebels. But, by the inevitable process of attrition that lack of supplies
and men brought about, such groups were doomed to be nothing but
mere nuisances in the long run. Only if some man, some special leader

emerged, could they prove to be a serious threat. Gerrid knew the almost magical effect a real leader could have. But there was obviously no such leader amongst this particular group. And they were far too vulnerable and weak to pose any real danger, for they lacked a crucial advantage: they had no spell-helms.

The taking captive of a man like Joff, a simple, single stroke such as that, spelled the end for them. That was how precarious their position was.

It was all Gerrid could have hoped for. Using this man as a guide, he could sweep upon this rebel camp and destroy it utterly.

The Sub-Commander set about organizing his men. Time, now, was the critical thing. They moved out quickly, travelling at a leg-stretching trot uphill, using spell-helm strength. Joff the Miller's directions proved easy enough to follow, though the man himself, panting and sweaty and clutching his branded belly, slowed their pace.

But it did not matter overmuch. Gerrid felt good. He was a hunter on the trail.

Once they were within a few thousands paces of where Joff claimed the rebel camp was located, Gerrid sent scouts out to gauge the best way to make the attack. The intervening time he spent making sure that his lines of communication and command were properly organized. He did not intend anything to go wrong here.

The scouts returned. The camp appeared quiet, and the watchmen on the camp's periphery were where Joff said they would be. All was well.

They were downslope of the camp, and Gerrid split his force in two, moving them in a long arc up and around the camp so as to be able to sweep down upon the unsuspecting rebels from the higher ground.

The group he went with worked their way as slowly and carefully as possible through the thick ranks of the trees. Though not as large as those downslope near the river, they were twisted and tangled together in a web of branch and trunk. It took a good long while and careful, slow work to make the circuit.

Finally, Gerrid crouched against a gnarly bole and was able to spy out the camp. There seemed to be about six or seven dozen men there in all. Perhaps more. A larger camp than he had anticipated. But he could imagine no difficulties here. Such men, armourless, ill-weaponed and without spell-helms stood no chance at all. A quick, howling charge and they would be cut to pieces.

Simple as that.

Gerrid waited until he received reports that all were in position.

The rebels remained quiet, unaware of what stalked them. Gerrid took a long, slow breath. Once more, he felt a liberating singleness of mind and purpose, but lit now with the belly-tightening anticipation of battle; it was the master game, this, the game of all games, where a single moment's lapse in concentration could spell death. There was no finer way than this to hone a man's spirit.

Easing his officer's double-handed sword from its sheath, Gerrid raised it and gave the signal. His force burst from cover behind him, shrieking like wild things.

The first wave cut through the startled rebels like a scythe through wheat. The camp was a moving, shouting confusion of men and blades and the splattering wetness of spilled blood. Gerrid fended off a clumsy stab at his belly, and dispatched the man easily enough with a single thrust of his sword.

Leaping over the downed man, the Sub-Commander led his band onwards, sword sweeping in great, deadly arcs about him. An arrow *plunked* harmlessly off his armour. Forewarned, he struck the next one out of the very air with his blade, laughing. His limbs thrilled with the exaltation of spell-helm vigour, and he threw back his head and roared. He cut through one rebel from shoulder to groin, tore his blade out and spun about, ready to take the next one through the belly.

And then, as happened sometimes, Gerrid found himself in a sudden, momentary eddy of calm in the midst of the fighting, his senses quivering and acutely alive to that which went on about him.

He saw one of the rebels go down, sprawled like a flopping puppet. The man had a long, shallow cut across the side of his forehead, and his left ear was half gone, the remainder a mass of old scar tissue. Above him, one of Gerrid's men raised his war-pike, two-handed.

The downed rebel tried desperately to scrabble away. The pike came down. But then something jolted the pike-man. A thrown rock crashed into the side of his helm, knocking it askew from his head. The man fumbled his pike, and fell across the rebel on the ground before him. Quickly, he scrambled back up to his knees, but now he was helmless. A hissing arrow caught him through the throat and he fell, choking, to the ground.

Gerrid howled. He flung himself forwards, slashing about him with vicious, two-handed swings. It was time to *finish* this.

And then, from the camp's far verge, a great shout suddenly went up, an animal-like bellow.

Into the fighting moved the biggest man Gerrid had ever seen. Red-haired, scar-faced, in his hand he held a huge, double-bladed axe. A comic figure, almost, swinging his silly woodsman's tool, clumsy and ill-clothed and foolish seeming.

But there was nothing comic about what happened next.

The huge figure swung the axe in deadly, whistling arcs. He moved like some wild demon, leaping and dodging and hurtling about with impossible great bounds. Nothing could stand against that axe. It was a carnage. Armour and helm were as nothing, and Gerrid's men were butchered like so many helpless animals.

It was not possible! One lone man, unhelmed, could not wreak such awful damage.

But it *was* possible. Sickeningly, undeniably possible. Certain victory had been in his grasp. And now . . .

Gerrid saw one of his men manage to cut a great slash along the axe-man's arm. But his man still went down, skull cloven, helm and all. Gerrid felt sick. All his planning, all his luck, gone. Everything gone. Hewed apart.

He plunged forward, sword up, to face this axe-wielding, red-haired demon who had come from nowhere.

The axe swung at his head and Gerrid ducked, stabbing at the man's unprotected legs. But the axe-man leaped high, as agile as any spell-helmed fighter, and only Gerrid's own helm-vigour enabled him to dodge back away from the great, whistling backstroke in time. The man's scarred face was a mask of insane fury, lips drawn back in a howling snarl. He came on, the axe leaping in great arcs, and Gerrid was forced to retreat, all his skill taken with simply fending off the great, flying axe-blade.

And then that notched blade and his own sword met, metal shrieking against metal, and the sword-blade shattered.

Gerrid scrambled away, his arms throbbing from the force of that shattering blow.

About him, all was chaos. The rebels, inspired by this terrible, unlooked-for leader of theirs, were striking back, going for the helms, always the helms, with rocks or swords or spears or bare hands. It was craziness, the sheerest craziness . . .

But it was the craziness that carried the day and won battles.

Shouting commands, Gerrid attempted to recall what was left of his men. It was hardly needed. They were already fleeing, those who could, fleeing the impossible destruction caused by that great axe.

Reeling, still not quite able to credit what had just occurred, Gerrid stumbled downhill with the shattered remnants of his force, skittering down as best they all could, racing for what safety they might find by the river, totally overwhelmed by this sudden, ignominious, utterly impossible defeat.

# XXI

# On the Slopes of
# the Easterling Peaks

Egil sprawled, his back against the rough bark of a tree, while his left forearm was tended to. It had been opened from elbow to wrist by the sword-cut. He was white and nauseous from loss of blood, and his head still echoed with the terrible cries.

It had happened again. The berserk fit had taken him, his dead wife wailing. He remembered it all imperfectly, but what he did recall sickened him. Blood and torn flesh and bone . . .

He shivered as the man tending his arm placed another stitch. The pull and tug of the needle seemed to pull his mind from him. He did not try to resist it. He wanted no recollections, no thoughts. He wanted only to sink away into darkness.

'Egil?' a voice said.

Egil could not bring himself to make any reply.

'He's going to be all right, Quince, isn't he?' the voice went on.

Quince, the man working on Egil, nodded. He finished binding the arm in a clean bandage and then stood up. 'Far as I can tell, yes. It'll hurt, but he'll be all right. As long as no rot sets in. And as long as he does not start using that arm again soon. If he does, he'll pull all the stitches. But he should be all right, yes.'

'Thank the Powers for that!' A man came round and squatted down beside Egil. Grey-haired Jordie, it was. He had a long, mottled bruise across the side of his face, and was sagging visibly with exhaustion and the delayed reaction of the fighting, but otherwise seemed not seriously harmed. And behind hovered the familiar, tatter-eared face of Hawl. And others behind him.

'Right,' Quince said with a weary sigh, packing up the rest of his paraphernalia. 'I'm off.' He ran a hand tiredly through his thinning hair, shook his head. 'There's others to see to. Don't use that arm. I'm off . . .' With that he lumbered away. Egil heard him muttering to himself. 'I hate this. Damnable slaughter. I *hate* this . . .' And then he was gone, lost in the chaos of the camp.

'How does it feel?' Hawl inquired, leaning solicitously over Jordie and gesturing to Egil's arm.

Egil did not know what to say. It was hard for him to think. His head rang sickeningly. His thoughts seemed to skitter about, like clumsy birds trapped in the darkness of a closed-up barn. He blinked, tried to focus, tried not to remember what he had done.

He was propped against the tree in such a way as to face the camp. It was a carnage-heap of the dead. Faintly, he could still hear echoes of the ghost-wails of his dead wife. She had come to him again, his Shawna, or he had imagined her, or something . . . He did not understand. It had been just like the time in the Blue Hills: he remembered only dimly the madness of slaughter and fury, his own rage and Shawna's hysterical fury bound inextricably together in some terrible fashion.

Now, but for the ghostly echoes only he seemed to be able to hear, a silence hung over everything. The eerie radiance of twilight illuminated the camp, the wooded edge of it darkly shadowed. The world seemed to be hanging, poised, ready to fall.

'You,' somebody said, 'you . . . I've never seen anything like that, Egil. What you did. It was . . .' the voice trailed off into silence.

Egil looked away uneasily. In the darkening light, he could make out the shapes of men moving about amongst the dead, moving with the slow, awkward movements of those shaken to the core by what they had just endured.

Egil felt memory rush through him. The swirling heave of bodies, screams, the wet smell of blood and fear. It sickened him. A dark tide seemed to engulf him. He shivered fearfully. His fists clenched up. Pain shot through his wounded arm.

'Egil?' somebody inquired concernedly. 'Egil, are you . . . are you all right?'

He did not know how to reply.

'You saved us, Egil,' somebody else was saying breathlessly. 'Just *you*.'

Looking up from where he still sat sprawled against the tree, Egil saw a young face, beardless, pale and shaken. The youngster stared at him as if he expected Egil at any moment to sprout wings and launch himself suddenly into the air and away. Clustered behind him were others, all wide-eyed, all staring with that same fixed, adoring attention.

The wailing of his dead wife rasped at the edges of Egil's mind. It was all too much, overwhelmingly too much. He just wanted to be alone, to be left alone.

Hawl, standing close to Egil, motioned the others away. 'Move back, Petry,' he told the youngster. 'All of you, move back. Give him room to breathe.' Turning to Egil then, he opened his mouth as if he wanted to say something, but the words died away into silence. He fingered a long, shallow cut across the side of his head on the same side as his mutilated ear. He looked at Egil, looked away, then stood there, shuffling his feet, staring now like the rest.

That staring silence was too much. Egil pushed himself away from the tree, stood shakily on his feet. He felt woozy and sick. His arm throbbed with pain. Every movement he made brought a protesting stab of pain from strained limbs.

Limping, he started across the camp.

'Where is he going?' someone demanded uneasily.

Nobody answered.

His back to them all, Egil limped onwards through the carnage he had made. Unseeing, he passed two men struggling to lift a third, whose legs were wrapped in soggy, blood-stained bandages. As he drew near, they turned to him, faces pale, bruised and weary. 'He's alive,' one of them whispered. 'He's *alive* . . .'

Egil paused. The two men stood there, their wounded comrade on the ground between them, and stared. Egil saw the same look in their eyes that he had earlier seen in the others'. A kind of current ran through the men about him as, one by one, they noticed him standing there.

Then a ragged cheer went up. 'Aie-ee-*haa! Aie-ee-*haa!' Those who still had weapons held them aloft. Those who did not, raised their clenched, empty fists. 'Aie-ee-*haa!' The cheer rose to a wild, wavering crescendo. 'Aie-ee-*haaaaa!' Men were thumping each other on the back, dancing impromptu, limping little jigs.

Egil felt his face flush. The hairs of his scalp lifted in a shiver. Something moved through him, something composed of all the strands of his recent life: of dead Shawna's wailings, of the dread faces of these southern men-demons, of his own despair and his own smouldering rage, of the shouted cheers of the men about him.

Standing in the midst of the dead, he raised his good arm. Unknowingly, he had brought the axe with him, clutched in an instinctual grip. It looked a fell thing indeed now. Hardly knowing what he did, Egil hefted the blood-crusted, gory blade above his head, shook it at the trees, the world, the sky.

A great shout went up from the men. 'Bloodaxe! Bloodaxe! Egil Bloodaxe!!'

Egil threw his head back and cried a great, animal howl. It seemed to come out of him of its own accord, in a great rush, all the misery and pain and terror and rage and anguish melded into a single, terrible, wailing cry.

The men wailed aloud with him, like wild pack-creatures gone mad.

Something coalesced, then. Egil moved as if in a dream. He heard his wife's wails, felt a sudden, unaccountable current of strength flow through him. Striding amongst the shattered corpses, wounded arm forgotten, he reached down to one of the killed man-demons and tore the demon-helm from his head.

The helm seemed a dead object, as dead as the man who had once worn it. But Egil felt the slightest of flutters vibrate through the thing, like a little, failing heartbeat. He felt the current of strength in him pulse painfully. Ghost-wails filled him. The helm in his hand shuddered as the strength coursed through. Egil's fingers tingled uncomfortably.

In his hands, the helm thrummed into life. The blind eyes of the helm seemed to glow. He held it aloft.

Unthinking, Egil strode to the man nearest him and handed the now-alive helm to him. The man reached a hesitant hand out, took the thing, but let it drop with a cry.

Egil reached for the helm again. He gripped the man in one hand, the helm in the other, and joined them.

The cheering died away.

Nobody moved, save the man in the demon-helm. But he seemed man no longer. Now, he wore the terrible, mobile demon features of one of *them*. He staggered spastically, tumbled over a corpse's limb, dropped to his knees.

But in a moment he bounded lightly to his feet once more, laughing. The laughter sounded chilling in that place of the dead. The man leaped a tangle of the fallen, moving with the lithe speed *they* had always shown. He plucked a pike from the sodden ground, lifted his demon head and laughed, the great tusks gleaming eerily in the last of the dying light. 'Bloodaxe! Bloodaxe!' he roared. 'Egil Bloodaxe!'

The men about shivered, hardly believing. But the cry rang with too much power. They took it up. 'Bloodaxe! Bloodaxe! Aie-ee-*haa!* Egil Bloodaxe! Aie-ee-*haa!*'

Egil strode through the dead, harvesting the demon-helms. He moved still as if in some dream, feeling no pain from his injured arm, not thinking of what he did, merely doing, doing blindly, reaching blindly, filled with power and the triumphant ghost-wails of his dead wife. For each helm he held aloft, the power surged through him, sparking the strange life failing there.

The camp came alive. Men vied with each other to receive the reanimated demon-helms. Those already helmed leaped and pranced and roared amongst each other. Soon they began stripping the dead men-demons of their armour and donning that themselves.

It was pandemonium.

And still Egil felt the strength in him undiminished. He had passed some hidden threshold, unknowing, and there was no way back now, even if he wished. And he did *not* wish it now. Shawna's wailings shuddered through his mind, but they brought him only a kind of fierce joy now. He felt his pulse beat to the soundless sound of them. A terrible exaltation filled him.

'Bloodaxe! Bloodaxe!' the men still fiercely cried.

He had reanimated all the remaining helms. The camp surged around him, ringing with the cries of the men in their new garb, demon faces alive with the same fierce joy that enlivened Egil himself. Egil raised the axe, soundlessly, waiting.

Silence settled slowly on the encampment.

Egil saw the leaping flames of his farmer's cottage, heard again the wails of his dying wife, his dead wife, and felt a terrible rage fill him. 'Now,' he cried. 'Now will we destroy *them*. With their own power we will destroy them. Rush down upon them and kill them all! Destroy them. *Kill* them! *Kill* them!' He cried it again and again, mindlessly, until the men about were crying it with him in unison, a terrible rolling chant of death that emptied their minds of all but hot fury.

'No!' a voice shouted, breaking the encompassing, mindless rhythm of the cry. '*No!*'

Egil blinked, looking round dazedly.

Jordie stood, his hands raised, palms out, shouting, 'No! No! *No!*' until somehow his lone, dissenting voice silenced all the rest.

'Have you all gone *insane?*' Jordie demanded of them. 'Rush down there to that Palisade and you'll accomplish nothing but your own deaths. Magic helms or no.'

'He has no helm,' somebody called. 'No helm . . .'

'Just jealous 'cause he can't share the strength.'

'Don't listen to him . . .'

'Just jealous . . .'

A few took up the cheer again. 'Aie-ee-*haa!* Aie-ee-*haa!* Bloodaxe! Bloodaxe!'

'Listen to me!' Jordie shouted. '*Listen* to me!'

The shouting drowned him out.

But then, by Jordie's side, Hawl suddenly stood, demon-helm off and held at his side. The sight of the helm, removed and un-alive, quieted the shouting men.

'Jordie's got the right of it,' Hawl cried. 'Magic helms or no, Egil Bloodaxe or no, we cannot just rush down there mindlessly. Think, damn you all. *Think!* How do you think *they* managed to find us up here in this hidden camp? What happened to Joff the Miller and the party of men that went missing last night? I'll tell you! Joff led them off on an ill-conceived foray against the Palisade, and walked straight into *their* arms! That's how *they* found out where we were. And now you want to charge mindlessly down there again.

'These helms give us a chance, a real chance to strike back, but we mustn't let them carry us away. There're too many of *them* down there. We may be able to meet them fair for fair now, but what does that matter if they outnumber us three or four to one? And they do. At least that. And the ones that got away from here will warn the rest.'

Egil felt the rage still coursing through him. He did not want to think. He did not want to listen to this man's talk. He wanted only to swing the great axe in his hands and to feel it bite flesh and bone. He turned towards Jordie and Hawl, the axe raised. He wanted no words, only death, the swinging of the axe and death . . .

Egil shook himself, shivering. What was *happening* to him?

The power surged back again, and he felt again the terrible rage sweep through him. But the pattern-building had been broken by Jordie and now Hawl. The momentum was lost. The rage in him burned lower, like a banked fire.

'*Think!*' Jordie was saying. 'If we rush down there mindlessly now, we're throwing it all away. We need to think, to plan things through . . .'

The men muttered, sullen and confused.

Hawl turned to Egil where he stood, still amongst the dead. Hawl ran a hand over his eyes, uneasy, clearly not sure who or what he was dealing with now that Egil the nobody had become, suddenly, Egil Bloodaxe. 'Egil, it's *madness* to rush down there like this. Surely you see that? Don't you? *Don't* you?'

Egil felt the men turn to him. He felt in his gut the sudden certainty that he could still take them out of here in a screaming horde. His heart leaped at the thought.

But . . . But . . .

But Jordie had the right of it, as Hawl had said. It was madness. Death madness. Better to wait, to plan, to use this new and unlooked-for advantage that had suddenly become theirs so as to utterly destroy *them* for good and all. Yes, better to wait, then . . .

A part of him screamed against such delay, and the ghost-wails raged in him. But he fought it down, just, took a long breath, nodded to Hawl and Jordie and said, 'Aye, better to wait. Better indeed to wait . . .'

Jordie breathed a great sigh of relief. 'Good!' he said. 'Now what we must needs do is . . .'

'We'll destroy them now!' someone cut in. 'Egil Bloodaxe will cut them to tatters.'

'Aie-ee-*haa!* Aie-ee-*haa!*' the cheer started again. 'Bloodaxe! Bloodaxe!'

'Enough!' Hawl roared. '*Enough!*'

Silence slowly settled.

'Helms off,' he called. 'We need to plan, to hold council, not strut about like so many gamecocks.'

The men complied, but there was a strange reluctance about it all. And each kept his helm close to hand, loath to be parted with it even for an instant.

Egil felt the strength that had been filling him falter away. His arm began to pain him, and he felt suddenly sick in his guts. Staggering, he made a way out from amongst the dead where he had been standing. Seeing his stagger, men rushed to his aid. A dozen pair of hands helped him across to a seat against a tree bole.

There was a stir in the camp now that had never been there before. Men grinned, moving with a will about whatever tasks they had to hand. Laughter floated on the air. A changed camp indeed.

Egil sighed, weary to his bones. He could still hear the echoes of dead Shawna's cries, but he was content with them now, aligned to them. He did not understand what had happened here, or what, exactly, he had done to enliven those fell helms. But some portal had been opened here today, a door into a future that held promise for them all, a future into which he could pour the rage that haunted him; a chance to destroy *them*, utterly and for ever.

Egil yearned for it as a moth for a flame.

# XXII

# Long Harbour

Shaking with cold, Tai staring dazedly about him. The sky was greying towards dawn, the moon set, the stars dying away. He blinked, trying to make sense of his surroundings, groaned as a throb of pain stabbed through his forehead. A confusing tapestry of shadows lay about him, and he could not, for the moment, understand where he might be. The dawn wind off the Bay cut him like a blade. He was soaking wet, wracked with shivers, his teeth chattering painfully.

'Drink this, lad,' a voice said.

An arm about his shoulders, supporting. Burning liquor in his throat. Tai gagged, twisting on his side and spewing water.

'Stewpid country lout,' the voice muttered.

'Whaaa . . . ?' Tai gasped. He was lying on his back, he realized, on hard stone. A figure knelt over him. It was difficult to make anything out clearly in the wan light, but it seemed to be a man's and not a demon's face he saw: a length of pale hair, a beard like a spade, glistening dark eyes.

The figure glared at Tai. 'All pecker an' feet an' no brains. What did ye think ye was doin' out here all by yerself on the quays? No wonder ye got yerself hurt so!'

'What . . . ?'

'Don't play the fool, wi' me, boy! Seen too many of yer sort since *they* razed the wold. Come in to Long 'Arbour an' get nothin' but trouble for themselves, 'angin' about the quays at night. Just askin' to get done by the local 'ead-thumpers. Stewpid country louts. And ye're just . . .'

Tai doubled over, coughing, spewing more water.

'Drink,' the voice said, softer now. 'Just the teeniest o' sips, mind ye. 'Tis what ye needs now to warm ye.'

Tai sipped from the flask the stranger offered, feeling the liquor's warmth burn through him. Who was this man hanging over him? Where was he? His last coherent memory was of the fight at the Miradore – the blow to his head that ripped the spell-helm off, blood filling his vision, the terrible plunge into the sea, the clutch of Skeefer's hands, the waters rolling over him, darkness.

And now . . .

Long Harbour, the man had said. Somehow, Skeefer must have towed him across Harbour Bay to the city. But there was no sign of the fur-man now. And what of Ree? Tai blinked, staring about, shivering. He felt hesitantly at the left side of his forehead with his good hand, winced as pain flared under his touch.

'Best we get ye away from 'ere,' the man leaning over him said. 'Can ye stand, lad?'

'Aye,' Tai responded after a moment. 'I think so.'

'Good. Upsadaisy then . . .'

With the man's help, Tai struggled to his feet. So woozy and weak did he feel, and so stiff and bruised, that it was a struggle for him to stay upright. He hugged himself, soaked and shivering. 'Where . . . where am I? How did I . . . ?'

'Come along,' the other said brusquely, ignoring Tai's questions. 'We've got to get away from 'ere to some warmth before ye catch yer death.'

Tai could see him more clearly now. He was a short man, barely coming to Tai's shoulder, dressed in raggedy, baggy clothing, and skinny as a rail. His beard and hair were a long, unruly cascasde in the dawnlight. He seemed to be carrying a staff of some kind, and something hung dangling over his shoulder. A string of somethings.

Leaning towards Tai, he reached out an arm supportingly. This close, there was a strong cheesy smell about him. 'Come *along*, ye great young lout,' he urged. 'We've got to—'

But the man's words were lost.

Without warning, and to Tai's dismay, the world about him suddenly fell away into confusion. An all-too-familiar, gut-wrenching plunge it was, into disintegration and stuttering chaos. He felt his heart pound shudderingly, felt the beginning of the old terror start to grip him as the solid world dissolved into dark, roiling nothingness.

But somehow, someway, there was a difference. Perhaps it was because of what the Seer had done, or tried to do to him. Perhaps it was just that he was changing. Or the world was changing. Or something. Tai knew not what. But though the chaos twisted and churned as ever, it did not call up in him the old soul-paralysing incapacity of terror it had once been able to. He felt sick and frightened. The chaotic whirl pulled him confusedly about. But he had been sick and frightened and confused too much of late to be altogether overwhelmed as he once might have been.

Almost, he rode it. But it was like riding the churning crest of a great wave. Nothing was there for him to grip. He was inundated, then rose out of it, overwhelmed, then out again.

And then he began to *sense* something.

It was like a great shuddering roar, but it was not sound. Like an explosion of light, but it was not light. Complex, intricate, pulsing like a great heart. It took him and shook him, bowling him over like a strong wind tumbling an autumn leaf, skimming him across nothingness . . .

But as he tumbled helplessly, he became aware of something else. Like a strand woven through that utterly overwhelming, tumultuous whole, pulled tight and thrumming as an individual voice. Voice? No. This too was not sound, nor sight either. And yet, somehow he sensed a *something*.

'*Taitaitaitaitaitai* . . .' Like a long, eerie melody, but a melody of motion rather than sound, or of shape without body, or . . .

Or he knew not what.

It called, soft but insistent.

And then he knew it for what it was:

Tai . . .

*Tai!*

Not his name, really. Not a calling in words or sound. But his name, somehow, in any case. Somebody searching, calling. And the caller . . .

Ree!

He could sense her clearly, sense the quiver of wings and the quick beat of her volatile little heart.

Where? *Where?*

He did not know. Could not find her.

He reached out, trying to beckon, to call her to him in turn, to draw her close, straining with some part of him he understood not at all, reaching, reaching . . .

And then he sensed something else entirely.

The tumult stilled.

This was no calling, but a feeling of moving along a path of some kind. And of other things moving too. Like a great whirlpool into which all other things were to be drawn.

A stutter of sensation that was not visual, yet echoed as visual images in his mind: an upturned face in sunlight, demon-tusks and yellow, unhuman eyes; an old woman's face, wrinkled as a dried apple, moss-green eyes staring at him; darkness, thorn and ash, cruelly taloned fingers splayed around a tree bole; a woman's face, tense with fear, auburn hair streaming in the wind; a wailing, a terrible endless wailing; a pale, not-quite-human face, dark eyed and patient and inscrutable . . .

And then, with a sudden flare of agony, something tore, or shattered, or simply collapsed – he did not know which – and the roil of the chaos took him down and down until he shattered into a sudden radiance and . . .

And found himself staring into the flickering flames of a smoky fire, panting, shaken, his limbs shivering uncontrollably.

'Shook like a dyin' 'addock on a wharf, 'e did,' a voice was saying somewhere over his head.

'With a blow to the head, there's no telling what might . . . Look! He's coming round.'

'Are ye all right, lad?' somebody asked, bending over Tai.

Tai looked up. He had to blink and rub his eyes hard to focus. It was the bearded man from before. 'Aye,' he replied weakly, nodding, but then regretted the movement as a spasm of pain lit the front of his head.

It was early morning. He lay wrapped in a dirty blanket, sprawled against a wooden crate of some sort, under an awning made of tattered canvas. His insides felt painfully knotted, as they always did after a fit, and he was shivering still, having tooth-rattling bouts of it. But he could feel the warmth of the day and of the nearby fire working their blessed way through him.

Squinting against the pain in his head, Tai stared about dazedly. He lay in a rubbish-littered, brick-walled courtyard, open to the sky. Dilapidated slate roofs showed beyond. Tai blinked, shifted position stiffly. The man leaning over him bent for a closer look. He was sharp-nosed and bony-faced, with dark eyes. His long, unruly hair and beard were thickly streaked with grey, but he moved vigorously for all that, and the dark eyes were as intent as a cat's.

'Are ye *sure* ye're all right, lad?' asked a second voice. 'Don't feel nauseous? Dizzy?' This second man leaned close and held out his hand. 'How many fingers do ye see?'

'Three,' Tai said automatically. 'I am all right. Truly.' He squirmed uneasily under all this attention.

Cursed fits.

But what had happened was like nothing he had ever experienced before. That great burst of *something*. And the other. As if, for a moment, he had brushed little Ree's very being and felt her searching for him. And brushed some other thing, too, that he did not undestand at all . . .

He did not want to think about it.

Cursed fits. Cursed everything! He was sick to death of mysteries and struggle. He put a hand to his throbbing head, flinched as he inadvertently scraped the nub of his amputated finger. Sick of *everything*, he was. And especially sick of pain . . .

'Just exhaustion, then, perhaps,' the bearded man said above him.

'Aye,' the second voice agreed. 'Most like.'

Tai craned his head to look up. A tall, bony man, this one, hairless as an egg, and as raggedly dressed as the other. He stood looking down at Tai through thick, wire-rimmed spectacles, the left-hand lens of which was a web of splintered glass, intact in the wire frame but useless. The man was old, Tai realized. His skin was papery, crinkled into a thousand complex folds around his eyes and mouth, and he moved with a brittle carefulness.

He squinted at Tai through the good lens, crouched down stiffly, cautiously on one knee, and probed with gentle fingers at the wound on Tai's forehead.

Tai winced and drew away.

'I'm a Curer, lad,' the man said.

'A Curer?'

'People come to me to have their ailments cured.'

'Like a Healer?'

'Something like, aye.'

Tai looked at him askance. This ragged man did not look like any Healer Tai had ever seen.

'And a damn fine Curer he is, too, ye ungrateful puppy!' the bearded one snapped. 'There's many a man who'd be honoured to be treated by—'

'Now, now,' the other said mildly.

'Stewpid country lout!'

'Don't mind his rough ways, lad,' the bespectacled Curer said. 'He carried ye here on his back from the quays. Ye're not the first body he's found down there of recent. It's bad times we're living in, right enough.'

He probed gently at Tai's forehead once more. The wound felt puckered and tight, and splinters of pain accompanied the man's exploration. The touch was light and smooth, though, the touch of somebody who knew very surely what he was about.

'How bad is it?' Tai asked tentatively.

'Ye need a few stitches across yer forehead here, lad. And the wound fever might set in, if ye're not careful. But it seems clean enough. Could've been lots worse. Hurts?'

'Aye,' Tai responded, flinching.

The man produced a small vial from somewhere, untwisted an intricately carved wooden plug that capped it. Holding the cap inverted in his left hand, he carefully shook out something like a tiny, whitish pea into the little bowl that the upended cap made. 'Here,' he said, holding cap and pill in front of Tai's mouth. 'Slide this under yer tongue and let it dissolve.'

Tai looked at it uncertainly. 'What is it, some kind of drug?'

The man shook his head. 'It's a remedy. Arnica. For the pain.'

Tai still hesitated, uncertain.

''Twon't poison ye, ye great daft puppy!' the bearded man snapped.

Tai dropped the pill from the cap under his tongue.

The Curer produced a sea-sponge and a package of some herbal mixture which he proceeded to dissolve into a bowl of water. Soaking the sponge in the fragrant, herbed water, he leaned across and began swabbing Tai's forehead with it. 'My name,' he said, 'is Willam. But most people call me Will. My friend here is called Ratter.'

Tai glanced across. 'Ratter?'

The Ratter grinned through his beard. Reaching behind him, he produced the long string that Tai had noticed slung across his shoulder back at the quays. It dangled heavily in his hand as he held it aloft for Tai to see what it carried. They were rats; limp, dead rats strung like so many fish on a cord.

Tai looked away quickly.

The Ratter laughed. 'Rats is me business. Dead or alive, as ye wish. Rats delivered as ye like.' He laughed again. 'Squeamish, are ye, lad?'

'Now, Ratter,' Willam said mildly. 'Be nice.' He dipped the sponge in the water once more and continued swabbing at Tai's forehead. 'And ye, lad? What're ye called?'

'My name is – aie! – Tai.' He could feel little clots of congealed blood lifting from around the wound as Willam sponged it. There was something astringent in the water that made the cut sting viciously for some moments. But after that it began to go numb. Or perhaps that was the effect of the pill the Curer had given him.

'What did you think you were doing out there, by yerself, down by the quays in the dark?' the Ratter suddenly demanded. 'Ye were just askin' fer trouble!'

Tai could think of no reply fit for this. He still had no clear idea himself of how exactly he had to come to be at the quays.

Willam began making the stitches, and Tai grunted, feeling the pull of the thread even through the numbness.

'Tha . . . thank you,' he said when it was finished. The wound throbbed, but it was bearable.

'The desensitization from the wash will wear off soon, but the remedy I gave you should keep the pain away for some while.'

Tai nodded gratefully, resisting the urge to poke at the new stitches. He shifted position where he lay propped against the crate, swallowed, and felt his mouth painfully dry. 'Is there any water?'

Willam produced a battered tin container and Tai sipped from it. The water tasted brackish. He wondered where it had come from. There was certainly no running water here in this dilapidated place. The courtyard was a litter-pit of dusty rubbish, except in the corner under the awning where the fire had been built. It was like a hill camp and, whilst Tai had little experience with the city, he did not think that such 'camping out' was normal for city folk.

'You . . . you live here?' he asked.

The Ratter looked grim. 'Aye, we do. And it's all 'cause of those rat-arsed, sheep-suckin', snot-nosed, shit-eatin' southern demons and their—'

'Hard times, lad,' Willam interjected in his mild way, 'since *they* took the city.'

'And an ill death and long may *they* die,' Rather muttered.

'Aye,' Tai agreed.

Willam wiped the good lens of his spectacles on a shirt-tail. 'Do ye have friends or companions ye'd like us to contact for ye?' he asked. 'Or are ye here in Long Harbour alone?'

Tai shrugged uneasily. 'I am alone.'

'More flotsam . . .' William shook his head. 'And yer kin?'

Tai swallowed. 'Dead. All dead or scattered.' He thought of Colby, poor Colby still trapped in the Miradore, victim to the Pit. 'Or nearly all.'

'An all-too-familiar tale, that,' Willam said soberly. 'There's too many in yer position these days.'

Suddenly, a small boy came skittering in through the entranceway of the tattered courtyard, crying, 'Ratter! Ratter!'

The Ratter got up quickly. 'What is it, Brassy?'

'It's . . .' the boy was panting. 'It's *them*!' He took a heaving breath, trying to get the words out. 'They're searchin' the quays. Everywhere! Door to door. Turnin' people out o' their digs. Ol' Taller got his arm broke 'cause 'e moved too slow when they told him. It's terrible, Ratter. They're madder'n a nest o' dawber wasps. It's *terrible!*'

The Ratter ran a hand through his beard, frowned worriedly. 'Why? What are they about? 'Ave ye' 'eard anythin', Brassy?'

The boy nodded. 'Lookin' for some deserter or prisoner or somethin', folks is sayin'. Somebody 'scaped from the Miradore on 'Ound's 'Ead Isle somehow. That's what 'tis bein' said.'

Willam whistled softly. 'I'd like to meet the man who could do *that*.'

Ratter snorted. 'Not likely it's true, Will.' He turned and patted the boy on the head. 'Thank ye, Brassy. Ye're a brave lad to come an' tell us.' The boy glowed. 'Now run along wi' ye to safety. Git!'

Tai stared about him blindly, his heart racing. He had no doubt at all who the demon guards were after.

'Come along, Will,' the Ratter was saying. 'You too, lad. Can ye walk all right? We've got to get away from 'ere.'

Tai staggered to his feet.

'Come on. Come *on*,' Ratter urged. 'We'll 'elp ye, lad, don't worry. Nobody's goin' to leave ye for *them* to find.' He bent down to assist Willam in stuffing some things into a bag, then helped the older man towards the courtyard's entrance. 'Hurry along, ye great lout!' he called back to Tai.

But Tai stood unmoving. He was sore and stiff, and his bones ached. Why not simply stand here and let *them* find him? He could thrust himself on to the end of a war-pike and end it, once and for all.

It was a small, nagging voice in him. Why not? He had undergone too much, was weary beyond measure of such chases. He was *tired*.

The Ratter eyed Tai. Reaching down, he produced a long staff with a wickedly barbed iron head. ''Ere,' he called, prodding Tai with the butt-end. 'It's me rat-skewer. Use it as a staff to help ye walk. Take it.'

Tai only stood there.

'I said, *take it!*' The Ratter thumped Tai in the belly with the staff's butt-end, hard enough to make him gasp. 'Now come *along!*'

Tai took the staff, blinking, and let himself be urged along. Despite himself, he felt a small smile curve his lip. There was something about the Ratter's abrasive energy that was not to be denied.

So out they went, the three of them, through the rubbish of the courtyard and into a narrow laneway beyond. Tai's head throbbed and his limbs were stiff as wood, but he found he could keep the pace well enough, for old Willam could not move very quickly. Tai handed the old Curer the Ratter's staff, finding that he could limp along well enough without it. But even then their pace was not much better than a brisk stroll, despite the Ratter's fussing and fuming.

Up one tattered alleyway they hurried, down another, across a refuse-choked square bordered by sagging wooden and brick buildings. There was no sign of other people, save for the occasional one or two fleeing like themselves, passing them by with quick, nervous strides. The whole city seemed eerily silent, except for a burr of commotion away behind them.

And then, up a narrow laneway ahead, Tai heard the unlikeliest sound he could imagine: birdsong.

They came out into a building-walled square. This was small, quartered by gravel walkways. Between these walkways, old tree-limbs, wooden posts, and bits and pieces of twisted scrap had been woven together to form an intricate, interconnecting jumble, through which a thick tangle of weeds and ragged flowers grew. Whirling about this jumble of things was a swarm of birds, loud and boisterous.

Tai stopped, staring.

Makeshift feeders were hung there, no two exactly alike, each surrounded by a shifting halo of beating wings, with birds dropping precipitously off and away, others hovering near or shimmying their way in towards the food, all whizzing about in what seemed an impromptu dance, whistling and warbling in a complex webbery of song.

'Bird Square,' Willam explained. 'Lovely sight, isn't it? We manage to keep it going, despite *them*. I love the little creatures, myself. They're so much purer than human people. So much more—'

'Will!' the Ratter snapped. 'Come *on!* There's no time fer ye to start off on that topic now! We've got to—'

A small, blue-winged form shot out of the whirring mass in the square. 'Tai,' a familiar voice piped. '*Tai!*'

Somehow, Tai did not feel altogether surprised. He remembered the fit, the strange sense of calling. 'Ree,' he called, holding his good hand out.

She landed on his wrist, small sharp claws pinching his skin. 'Tai! We did not know what had happened to you.'

Old Willam was staring, his eyes fixed in wonder upon Ree's glowing blue plumage, her orange breast and small human face.

The Ratter, however, paid Ree scant attention, save for one quick, narrow-eyed glance. He strode up to Tai and gripped him firmly by the shoulder. 'Ye've got to be out o' 'ere, lad. An' that right now!'

'Ratter!' Willam cried. 'What are you doing?'

'It's 'im, Will. It's 'im they're lookin' fer! It weren't no 'ead-thumpers gave 'im that wound. An' where else could such an . . . uncanny creature be from but *their* stronghold?'

Tai swallowed uneasily.

'*Is* it ye, lad?' the Ratter demanded. 'Truth, now.'

Quick panic knotted Tai's belly, but he nodded.

'Ye must be *out* o' 'ere, then!' the Ratter said. 'And right immediate, too!'

'Who . . . who *are* ye?' Willam asked.

Tai did not know quite how to answer that. 'I am—'

'What matters it?' the Ratter cut in. '*They* will be 'ere soon! We've got to get 'im away!'

Gazing raptly at Ree through the one good lens of his spectacles, Willam reached towards her, moving like a sleepwalker. He lifted a hand, stroked her blue-crested head gently, wonderingly.

'Will,' the Ratter snapped.

Willam looked at him, dazed.

'They've got to *go*, 'im and that . . . creature. *Will!*'

Willam swallowed, nodded assent. But he still stood gazing at Ree wonderingly. He took his spectacles off, polished them with the tail of his baggy shirt. 'Where did she come from?' he asked, squinting.

The Ratter, losing patience, yanked at Tai's arm, dragging him away. Spilled from her hold on Tai's wrist, Ree fluttered anxiously about their heads.

Tai wrenched himself out of the Ratter's grip, the sudden movement making his head throb. 'Ree,' he called, holding up his good hand. Ree fluttered over again. 'Ree, where is Skeefer?' Tai asked. 'What happened?'

'Skeefer is safe. By a river. We did not know what had happened to you after we were separated in the harbour. We thought—'

'Come *along*,' the Ratter urged. 'Every moment *they* draw closer.'

'Where are you taking me?' Tai demanded. Somehow, the knowledge that Ree and Skeefer were safe made all the difference. The apathy of exhaustion and despair had left him. He felt he had somewhere to go now. 'Can you get me out the city walls? I've a companion waiting, somewhere . . . Ree, where is he?'

From beyond the square, still in the distance but drawing nearer, came the sound of *their* commotion.

'Ye can sort that out later,' the Ratter said. 'I'll get ye out the city, lad, never ye mind. But ye've got to move now. An' *quick!*' He turned to Willam. 'Will, go through to The Anchor, do ye 'ear? Ye'll be safe enough there. I'll take Tai here away to—'

'No!' Willam interrupted. 'I'm coming with ye.'

'Will! Don't be stewpid now. Listen!'

The commotion was growing clearer and nearer by the instant. Two ragged young men came pelting suddenly through the square. 'Better move it, ye lot,' one of them panted in passing. 'They're right be'ind us.

'*Close* be'ind!' added the other, and then they were gone out of the square's far end.

The Ratter turned on Willam fiercely. 'Ye won't be able to keep up, Will, and ye know it!'

Willam looked forlornly at Ree, shook his head. 'All right,' he sighed. He held out the Ratter's iron-tipped staff to him, offering it. 'Ye'll be needin' this, I don't doubt.'

''Ang on to it fer me. I'll be usin' me feet, not that. Now get *on* with ye, ye ol' fool!'

'Right,' Willam replied. 'Best of luck to ye, lad, and to yer . . . friend,' he added, taking one last look at Ree.

Abruptly Willam disappeared into a narrow cut between two

buildings on the side of the square. Ratter led Tai, with Ree fluttering close, out of the square's far end, following the route of the two young men through into a maze of refuse-cluttered alleyways beyond.

From the square behind, there came a great rush of beating wings, and a cloud of birds ascended in a mass. Beyond came the rumble of voices and clank of iron.

"Urry along,' the Ratter urged.

Heart pounding, the stitches in his forehead throbbing painfully at each step he took, Tai hurried as best he could.

It was a stumbling, confusing journey, of which he had little clear recollection: one decrepit alleyway after another; the foetid dark of a cellar somewhere, his buttocks pressed against damp earth, his head thrumming with real pain as Willam's remedy wore off; the quays; the *lap lap lap* of seaweedy water near his chin as he lay scrunched up under a wharf, Ree huddled into his shoulder, while the tramp of iron-studded boots reverberated through the wood above him as a troop of demons marched by; darkness and stars; the rock and dip of a boat under him, muffled oars dipping smooth as bird wings; the *scrunch* of the keel against sandy shore; the whisper of trees in the dark as he stumbled up a wooded slope . . .

Then nothing at all, until sunlight shafting through a green tangle of tree-limbs roused him.

Blinking, Tai stared about. He lay alone in a small, hillside glade. It was early morning. A softly rustling wall of greenery enclosed him. Birds choired all about. Where was he? He struggled shakily to his feet, groaning at the stiffness in his limbs, and at the thrust of pain the movement sent through his head. His insides were twisted up uncertainly – they had not been quite right ever since Tancred's molesting – and he sensed a sometime faint pulsing in the world about him. He felt hot and flushed and very, very thirsty.

Through the trees, he heard the bubbling song of running water and struggled up a slope towards it.

A small pool met him, cupped by moss-coated rocks in a shadowed hollow beneath a pair of giant, age-twisted oaks. The air was cool and fresh and soothing. He plunged his arms in up to the elbow, moaning at the coldness and the pleasure of it, splashing his hot face and the stitches across his forehead, drinking, feeling the coolth of the water fill him like a cordial.

Sighing, he collapsed back next to the pool and stared up into the web of jointed branches above. No sign of human habitation was there hereabouts, no indication of *their* presence ever having blighted this spot, only the grey-brown oak-limbs, dancing greenery, the glowing blue of the sky beyond. Birdsong like a tapestry.

It was as if *they* existed not at all.

Tai could hardly believe it. He was out of it, away and safe. Or so it seemed, though indeed he had no true idea of where he might be, or how he had arrived here. He wished he had been able to thank the Ratter properly . . .

Safe.

The word rang in his mind. If his patchy recollection of the voyage here was at all reliable, he was north of Long Harbour proper, most like, somewhere up on the northern shore of the Whitewash Ferth.

Safe.

He luxuriated in the word. The cool forest air was like a balm. For the first time since that ill-fated morning in the High Hills, it seemed, he could breathe easy. He was out of it. And all he need do to stay out of it was walk north and into the wild lands. It was said there were folk living there. He could walk northwards, find them.

A new life. No more fighting. No more struggle.

*Safe.*

Tai sighed, thinking on it. He felt the world about him shiver uncertainly for a moment with incipient chaos, then coalesce. His heart thumped at the spasm, settled. He shuddered. The fits were become too strange . . . He did not wish to think on them. He had endured too much in the past weeks. His home gone, his old, familiar life. Too much of pain. His kin gone.

Colby . . .

Tai groaned. Poor Colby, prisoned in the Miradore. Tai closed his eyes, lying back against the cool, leaf-padded earth. He did not wish to think on Colby, either. The stitches in Tai's forehead throbbed, and he put a hand gingerly on them feeling at the little knots old Willam had tied. He listened to the whisperings of the oaks above him, the myriad voices of the hidden birds.

Poor Colby . . .

The sudden snap of wings overhead made him blink.

'Tai,' something called softly.

And there was Ree, perched on one of the pool's rocks, her little feet half buried in glistening emerald moss.

'Ree!' he said, levering himself up on his elbows.

A splash of water, and behind her came Skeefer, wading along knee-deep in the stream that fed the pool. The fur-man was no less thin and worn-looking than he had been in the Miradore, but he moved now with a feral, light-footed assurance he had lacked before. Stepping out of the water, he squatted next to Tai. For long moments he remained silent, his dark eyes intent. Water runnelled from his sleek fur. Then he grinned, an animal stretching of the lips, more a casual snarl than any simple human smile. 'I would have left you, man, once we were sseparated in the harbour. But sshe would not.' He gestured to Ree with one dark-furred, water-sleeked hand. 'Sshe inssissted on finding you. Remember that, man. Remember what you owe her!'

Tai blinked. He did not know what to say.

'We will leave you food,' the fur-man went on. 'Fish and berries. And *they* have losst your trail, so you will be ssafe enough now.'

Tai tried to lift himself to a sitting position. 'What are you—'

The fur-man shoved him back with the heel of his hand. It was no friendly gesture. 'Sstay ass you are, man. We will bring you food before we leave. But do not try to sstop uss!'

Squinting with pain, Tai struggled to his knees.

'Skeefer!' Ree cried, as the fur-man leaned forwards to push Tai down again.

'We musst *go*!' Skeefer hissed, turning to face Ree. 'We musst leave him!'

'No,' Ree said.

'We *musst*!'

Tai edged sideways away from the fur-man and propped his back against the gnarly bole of the nearest oak. He sat there, panting, eyeing the two before him uncertainly.

Ree fluttered about the fur-man. 'Skeefer, *please* . . .'

Skeefer looked away from her, sullenly. 'It iss craziness, my Ree. You sspeak of crazy thingss.'

'It is not . . .'

'Death! And worsse than death.'

Tai understood none of this. 'What do you—'

'Be quiet, man!' Skeefer hissed at him, showing teeth.

'Skeefer!' Ree cried.

'Enough. I will lissten no more to thiss craziness of yourss!' The fur-man turned to Tai, his face clenched angrily. 'You owe her your life, man. Sshe hass ssaved you, brought you out of thiss city. You helped her. Sshe helped you. The bargain between you iss finisshed. Releasse her!'

Tai looked at Ree in confusion. She fluttered over to a moss-topped rock near to him, her little mouth open to speak.

'No!' Skeefer hissed. 'Ssay nothing!'

'I will *not* be quiet!' Ree cried in her piping voice.

The fur-man hissed. 'I ssay you will! Or—'

'Or *what?* What will you do?'

Skeefer half rose, bristling like a dog, hackles raised across his shoulders and back. Ree's small orange breast quivered with the frightened beat of her heart, but she gave no ground.

For a long moment the two stared at each other, then Skeefer sagged, faltering back to hunker glumly on his heels. 'It will be our undoing, my Ree.'

'No need for you to be involved if you do not wish it,' Ree returned defiantly.

Skeefer flinched, as if she had given him a physical blow.

'Oh, Skeefer,' Ree piped then. 'I am sorry. Please! I did not mean . . .'

The fur-man reached to her, and Ree flitted across, leaning her little orange head into the caress he gave her.

Tai stared, utterly confused.

The two looked across at him, brown-furred and orange-feathered faces tight with feeling. 'Do it, then,' Skeefer said to Ree. 'If you musst.'

Ree hopped from Skeefer's hold and fluttered over to land on Tai's knee. She looked at him, very serious. 'Listen, man. There is something important I must tell you.'

Skeefer snorted, but said nothing.

Ree opened her small mouth, paused, looked at Tai, looked away. She skipped a little along his knee, nervously.

Tai leaned down towards her. 'What? What is it?'

'I have heard a thing, man. It is only rumour, but I have heard it. About the Lords Veil and . . . *him.*'

'Tancred?'

'Yes, the Seer.' Tai saw a flutter of agitation go through her. 'It is said about the Lord Veil that . . . that there is more than one.'

Tai rubbed at his eyes confusedly, shook his head, understanding none of this. 'What does—'

'Listen, man! Just listen.'

Tai listened.

'It is *his* work. As he created those like us, and others, so he has fashioned more than one Lord Veil.'

'You mean like in the Pit?' Tai suggested.

'No, man. This is different.' Ree paused for a moment, as if trying to think of the best way to say what she wished. 'The doubles the Seer fashions of the Lord Veil are no mere tiny folk. They are full, living, breathing men, the same in all ways as the original man. And they are all the same man at the same time. What each double experiences, what each double knows, so all the others know. One man who is many. Many men who are one. The Lord Veil has conquered your northern land while he conquers the south, being in both places.'

Tai took a breath. He still did not understand how this had any connection with what Ree and Skeefer had been arguing over. And besides, it all seemed too fantastical for belief.

But Ree went on quickly, before he might say anything. 'I have heard things said, man. In the south it was, before we were brought northwards to your land. From those such as the Lord Veil, the Seer takes a far higher price than from Pit Folk. I have heard, man, that the *born* Lord Veil has given arms, legs, ears, eyes, tongue. These are the prices the Seer has extracted. I have heard that the born Lord Veil is now no more than a legless, armless torso: blind, deaf, tongueless.'

Tai started, recollecting the poor, mutilated thing they had seen in the tower chamber in the Miradore. 'You mean—'

Ree nodded her small head, the little dark human eyes dead serious. 'It was the born Lord Veil we saw in that chamber. What remains of him . . . I am sure of it.'

'But . . .' Tai's mind struggled. 'But if the Seer need not take more than a sliver of flesh from Pit Folk like Skeefer here, why does he exact such a price from the Lord Veil?'

'Power, man.' It was Skeefer now who answered. 'We are merely underfolk, Pit Folk the likess of Ree and mysself, powerlesss againsst him. *He* need extract no price for what he doess to uss. But the Lord Veil hass *power*.' Skeefer shook his head. 'You know nothing of the ssouth. It iss an old land riven by old rivalriess . . .'

'There are others,' Ree put in. 'The Lord Veil has taken this northern land of yours by fire and blade. He seeks power through conquest, yes, but his real attention is focused southwards, and all his moves here are only part of a larger scheme that he hopes will bring him more power in the south. In the south, there are others like the Veil. Ambitious men. Lords and war-leaders.'

'Think on it, man!' said Skeefer. 'Thesse ssouthern Lordss control domainss vasster than your entire northern land here. Each thinkss himsself a great Lord. Each sstruggless againsst the resst for asscendency . . . War and sstruggle. Whole realmss gained and losst . . .'

'And behind each of these Lords stands a Seer such as – ' Ree swallowed uncomfortably, finally saying the name – 'Tancred.'

'They pay uss no heed,' Skeefer hissed. 'But we ssee more and know far more than they give uss credit for. There iss power and there iss power, man. The Sseer and hiss kind have their own aimss. The Lordss think themsselvess great and powerful. But in their sstruggless againsst each other they ssought aid. The Sseer and hiss kind gave them aid, oh yess. But at a price. He and hiss risse to power on the backss of men like the Lord Veil.'

'And poor Colby,' Tai said, beginning to understand, 'must lose his limbs lest the Veil learn that the price the Seer demands for his . . . *services* is needless.'

'Exactly so,' Skeeter replied.

Tai shivered. It all sounded so incredible. What terrible sort of place must this southern land be? Lords and wars. He had a quick vision of realms in struggle, like great, many-limbed beasts rending each other. Tai gazed at both Ree and Skeefer with new respect. It was too easy to undervalue their acumen, bird and beast as they seemed. It took no little courage, and no little intelligence to have survived as they had in such a place . . .

'And I have heard another thing, also,' Ree was saying now. 'The conquest of the north was pursued for the resources and power that the domination of such new land would bring the Lords Veil. But it was pursued also because here, far from the south, they could find a secure refuge for the helpless, born Lord Veil that would keep him safe from his southern enemies. For it is said that if the born Lord Veil were to be killed, then all the others, the created ones, would die also at that very same moment.'

'You mean—' Tai stared.

'Yes. Kill the born Veil, and all are finished. Sever the head from the body, and the limbs die.'

'And the Miradore was the refuge they found,' Tai said.

Ree nodded.

Tai leaned back against the oak for support. He thought of *them*, by one stroke bereft of their leader – their *leaders*. He thought of demon troops lacking direction or co-ordination, confused, disheartened. He knew them to have human weakness, despite all fell appearances. One single blow could be the deliverance of his homeland. And he had stumbled into this 'secure' refuge and stood over the helpless born Lord Veil, war-pike in his hand, all unknowing. One simple thrust of the blade was all it would have taken. He had almost done it out of simple pity.

Tai clenched his fists, his amputated finger burning. He felt sick. Too late. Too late . . .

But Ree was looking up at him, her gaze intent. Tai glanced at Skeefer, grim-faced and silent, then back to Ree. He had a sinking certainty as to what she would say next.

Say it she did.

'We must go back, man.'

Tai swallowed. 'To the Miradore?'

'Yes! Too late! I realized too late who it was we saw in that chamber.' Ree launched herself into the air, whirring about. 'Now we know. Now we must go back there! We *must!*'

Tai swallowed. He did not think he was able. It was a mad enterprise. 'But how can just the three of us . . . ? There will be guards . . .' A sudden thought struck him. 'If that was the *born* Veil we saw, why was he not guarded more strongly?'

'He was guarded, *is* guarded,' Ree said. 'We were inside that ring of guards.'

'They could not have expected to have the likess of *uss* running free insside the Miradore,' Skeefer put in.

'Aye,' Tai agreed. 'Aye . . . But then how ever would we break through into the Miradore again?'

'I know that Keep, man,' Ree answered. 'Many and many a time have I travelled it, escaped from the Lord Veil's chambers.'

Tai shook his head. 'And what of Seer Tancred? Will he merely sit idle while we do this thing?'

Ree snapped her wings nervously, but her head was up, her little face set firmly. 'He is powerful, man, but not *all* powerful. Did he not underestimate you and me? He can do things no ordinary man can do, but he cannot do *all* things.'

'But—' Tai began.

Skeefer snorted, a soft, hissing, derisive sound. 'I have tried talking, man. Sshe iss unbending.'

Tai stared at Ree. What she suggested was outrageous. Simply to walk in there and kill this all powerful southern Lord: it was something out of a child's story.

But, if they did attempt it, there was a chance for Colby, too. Perhaps, once back in the Miradore, he could manage a way to rescue his foster-uncle. Perhaps . . .

Tai shook his head. It was all craziness! Skeefer had named it true.

Hauling himself up to his feet, he leaned shakily against the oak. He did not know what to do or what to say. He ran a hand wearily over his eyes, winced as a finger accidentally brushed against a stitch.

Skeefer too had risen to his feet. But the fur-man was staring off downstream, snuffling softly like a hound. The breeze blew up from the Ferth, but Tai could scent nothing in particular.

'What is it?' Tai asked.

'Shussh!' Skeefer waved him to silence. Then, 'Wait here.' He padded away, moving softly off through the greenery at the stream's verge.

Tai looked at Ree but said nothing, only stood there waiting, his heart beginning to thump anxiously.

When Skeefer returned, his face was grim. '*Them,*' he said.

Ree whirled about the pool in dismay. Tai felt his heart sink. 'Where?'

The fur-man gestured uphill. 'Come. I will sshow you.' He led them upstream, threading a way through more of the huge, gnarly oaks, moving across the outcroppings of stone and springy hummocks of mossy turf with far more ease than Tai could manage. The going was upslope, more and more steep as they went on, and Tai was soon gasping.

Leaving the winding course of the stream, they scrambled up across a bare, rocky bluff, at the top of which was a stand of wind-twisted birch. Crouched there amongst the softly creaking, twisted boles, they could look out and see the country below. Tai let himself down on his elbows, panting, his head a throbbing torment. It was a moment before he was able to take in the vista presented before him.

Below lay a tumbled green expanse, tree and hill and glade leading unbroken along the northern shore of the Whitewash Ferth, along to the far shoreline westward, where the moving expanse of Harbour Bay glinted in the morning sun. Out in the watery distance stood the little stony knob of Hound's Head Isle. Tai shivered, gazing upon it.

Closer to hand lay the Ferth itself, separating them from Long Harbour. Across the water, the city covered all they could see of the Ferth's southern shore. Morning smoke blew up from chimneys. Boats plied the quays. People scurried about, busy at their tasks. Voices called, small but clear in the distance.

Their side of the Ferth showed no sign of habitation, and lay empty and quiet save for . . .

Save for movement near the shoreline some ways down from them. Tai squinted. Sunlight glinting coldly on polished iron blades, the quiet rumble of voices. A face looked up and he saw the unmistakable tusks and yellow demon-eyes. His heart kicked in his chest. It was one of the images he had seen during his last fit, though neither 'image' nor 'seen' was altogether the right word. An upturned face in sunlight, demon-tusks and yellow eyes.

What did it mean? How could it be?

And how could *they* have followed him here?

From below came a sudden, animal howl; hound-like, yet no true hound ever made sound like that. Tai caught a glimpse of a moving, spidery grey form. All too familiar.

'Fell-hound,' Skeefer hissed. 'We musst flee!'

Tai shook himself, struggled to his feet. Looking across at Skeefer, he saw a kind of grim satisfaction on that dark furred face. So much for Ree's mad heroics, then. They had only one chance now, if there were to be any hope of keeping their lives and their freedom: they would have to flee into the wild lands. Any thought of returning to the Miradore was the sheerest of madness.

Tai peered across the glinting expanse of Harbour Bay at the distant shape of Hound's Head isle. The Miradore, the *born* Veil, Tancred, poor Colby . . .

'Come,' Skeefer insisted. 'We musst away. Quickly!'

Ree snapped her wings in agitation, then launched herself airwards. Skeefer had already begun to slip over the hilltop on which they crouched and away beyond. Ree chirruped at Tai to hurry.

Tai hesitated, his mind flooded with conflicting thoughts, then struggled along after his companions as best he could.

# XXIII

# On the Wooded Verge of
# the North Wold

Old Crane squatted on her heels on a rocky outcrop at the high forest's verge, looking down into the distance. The rest of her people were a lengthy, safe distance back amongst the woods, and she had been here, alone, for long and long, gazing off into the grassy, flat, strange southern lands.

Her old joints ached from too much waiting.

Under her, Crane felt the earth's soft, ancient voice, talking of Sun and Sky and the dancing of Rain; of waiting, and of strength.

Nothing of aching joints for *her*.

Crane shook her head. She was becoming an old and peevish woman, irritable now as any silly girl-child made to wait too long. The Dreaming took shape in waking life in its own sweet time. She, of all people, knew *that*. Enough that the terrible muddling of things had ceased, at least for the moment, and that she had clear direction again.

For the Dream had been utterly clear: her squatting alone, as she squatted here now, on the rocks by the forest's high verge, looking out at a rolling, willow-spined little river vale that stretched downwards towards the far sea; and then the creature, winged, furred, man-shaped, making its way upslope towards her.

The Dream was utterly clear, yes. But utterly strange.

What could such a creature be? Spirit or Flesh? What terrible changes, what strange gifts, what unknown things might it bring?

Crane sighed. She tilted her head back and took a long lungful of air. It tasted of morning coolth, but also of the day-warmth of coming summer. The scent of green things, of growth was in it. And the scent of summers past, too; all the summers past, good and bad, all gone now. The world spun on. The great dance was danced.

The world changed.

Too old for this, she thought uneasily. Too old to live in a cusp time like this. She sighed again. Leaves chattered in the trees about her. A crow called in the distance. The world spun on.

Below her, something moved.

'Ahh . . .' she breathed.

The crow cawed again, stutteringly, and flapped her graceful way into the air. From the hedge of young willows that formed the spine of the vale below there came a faint, rasping crackle, a quick, half-guessed movement in the green tracery of willow-shadows.

A bird fluttered out and into the open. Blue wings, orange breast. It was not like any bird Crane had ever seen.

More movement, a dark hand outlined against a bough, bright eyes in a dark, furred face.

Crane shifted uneasily. What sort of creatures were these? They did not have the feel of spirit-people, yet never, never had she seen anything like what emerged below: man-shaped, yet otter-sleek with fur.

And then there was a third. A true man this, young, slender, travel-worn.

Crane swallowed. The Dreaming did indeed work in mysterious ways. Not a single creature, then, but three-in-one.

Crane was as silent and still as the rocks among which she squatted, and stayed so, watching. Those below moved warily, as if expecting trouble. Or looking for it.

The blue bird fluttered near. With a shock, Crane saw that it wore a human face. She had met spirit-people like this, but never flesh-people.

The three made a weary way uphill towards her, climbing with the stumbling, clumsy tiredness of those who had fled too far, with too little rest. Fugitives. And behind them she sensed the presence of the dark something that had come from southwards to trouble the world. For a moment, she saw the three before her as stricken victims of some gruesome plague, come here to infect her and hers.

They drew nearer. Crane knew how to turn prying eyes away from her, and almost she stayed still and unseen and let them pass her unknowing.

But the Dreaming said otherwise.

Her old heart skittering, Crane stood and gave them formal greeting. 'I see thee, strange people who walk towards me.'

It made her smile, inwardly, the way the man moved then, starting in six directions at once, spluttering surprise. Unwise, perhaps, to startle such creatures thus, but she wanted them unbalanced a little for this first meeting. She had, after all, no good idea of what she was dealing with, and any small advantage at the beginning might be to the good.

The man sketched a shaky sign at her with his fingers, a warding sign, it seemed. The fur-person merely crouched, shivering, and the person-faced bird flew to him.

She repeated her greeting. 'I see thee, people who come from the lowlands.' But they said nothing, only stared. She had not expected manners from such outland persons, but their blank, wordless stares left her uneasy. Could it be they did not understand human talk? Were they *that* strange?

'Who . . . who are you?' the man said finally. It was not manners, but at least it proved he could understand her. He stooped and picked up a fist-sized rock, hefting it threateningly. He stared at her as if she were some spirit creature.

Crane could feel her old heart begin to tremor. What might these creatures be capable of? But she kept her voice calm. 'If you hit me with that rock, man, you will never hear answer to your question.'

The man blinked, lowered the rock self-consciously.

Not a creature of violence, then, at least not by habit. Crane felt comforted in that. There was something special about this young man. He shimmered, almost, with it. There was the feel of a true-seeing man about him. And more.

Crane felt a shiver go through her belly. Whatever it was, it was too deep-buried-over in him for her to sense clearly. But he was gravid with it. Like a seed-pod ready to burst. And the Dreaming had brought him to her, or her to him.

He had a desperate look about him; he was thin to the bone, with a half-healed cut across his forehead, pink scar and stitches. And he stared at her still, eyes wide, as if in recognition.

It was far from clear to Crane what pattern was shaping here. Like a blind woman, she must feel her way along. She looked the young man clear in the eyes. 'I am called Dreamwalker,' she said.

'Dreamwalker?'

Crane nodded.

The man's eyes narrowed uncertainly. The orange-breasted bird fluttered about the fur-person, its strange person's-face wide with anxiety.

The man ran a hand over his eyes tiredly. 'You startled us. We looked not to see people here in the wild country. Are there villages nearby, then?' His face took on a sudden look of expectancy. 'Have folk escaped up here away from *them?*'

Crane shook her head. He spoke in a peculiar fashion. 'I am not sure what thou means, man.'

He blinked, uncertain, opened his mouth, closed it once more, looked around at the stony, empty slope about them.

'What are *you* doing here?' a high, piping voice demanded of her.

The person-faced bird's voice, Crane realized. So it was not only the young man who was capable of talk. 'I?' Crane said to the question. 'I am waiting for the three of thee.'

Crane took a sharp breath. Had she gone too far with them? All three were staring at her now. The man hefted the rock, unthinking.

'Peace,' she said, holding her hands palm up before her. 'I mean thee no harm. True.'

That helped, but only a little.

Silence grew between her and them.

'What brings thee here?' she asked.

The man ran a hand across his face, sighed. 'We are pursued,' he said, glancing uneasily back they way they had come.

The man's clothing – woven fabric it was, unlike the animal hide she wore – was ragged and worn, and they were thin to the bone, all of them. The fur-person's ribs showed clear through his fur. Crane felt suddenly the shadow of the thing from which they fled, and shuddered. But it was not near them now, that she could sense clear enough. 'We have time,' she told him. 'It is not close, that which follows thee.'

'How do you know?' he demanded. 'And how . . . how would you know to be *waiting* for us?'

Crane shrugged. 'It was in the Dream.'

He only stared at her.

'And thee?' she prompted. 'What is it, man, that drives thee and thine here, so ragged and weary?'

The fur-person hissed something quietly into the man's ear, too quiet for Crane to hear.

The man shrugged, shook his head.

The fur-person turned to Crane then, his hackles bristling like a dog's. 'What makess you sso hungry to know?'

So the furred one could speak as well: strange speech, but understandable. 'Fair question,' she responded, looking him straight in his dark eyes. She saw no willingness to trust her in those eyes, only suspicion. This furred one had the feel of deep hurt about him.

'And one that deservess fair answwer!' he hissed.

'Who *are* you?' the man put in. 'What are you doing out here on this empty slope. And what is this talk of dreams?'

Crane shrugged. 'There is danger behind thee.' The man made to interrupt, but she waved him to silence. 'I can aid thee. I think that may be what I am fated to do, I and mine.'

'Who *are* you?' the man repeated.

'And why would you help the likess of uss?' demanded the fur-person.

Crane smiled. 'Who I am would take long to tell. As for aiding thee . . . It is of the Dream.'

'Dreams again.'

'I am Dreamwalker to the people. I dream Dreams.' Crane sat back on her heels. 'I was drawn here by the Dream. Some dark thing is come from the south. Thou − ' she gestured to include the three of them − 'are come from this dark thing.'

'We are never one with *them!*' the man said hotly.

'*Them?*' Crane asked. She was still feeling her way through this. 'Though we be strangers, the Powers have linked us, for good or ill. But thy coming brings changes for me and mine . . . I must know more of thee before I let thee nearer to my people.' Crane leaned forward and looked at them directly. 'I *shall* deal with thee, one way or another, here and now, before I let thee near my folk.'

They stiffened. The man's fingers came up in a warding sign, and she noticed that the small finger on his left hand was gone. 'Is it threats, then?' he demanded.

Crane could feel the prickling of fear in them. Good, she thought. A little fear is good. For she herself was not entirely as confident as she made out. While she was not without certain resources, she reckoned them little enough against the creatures before her should they decide to use bodily violence against her.

She held up her hands, palms out. 'I mean no harm. True.'

The man stood, stiff and uneasy. 'This talk gives me the wobbles.'

Crane smiled. 'For giving thee the wobbles, man, I am most sincerely sorry.'

He smiled back then, grudgingly. 'What would you of us, then, if you mean us no harm?'

'I have never seen persons such as thee. Tell me who and what thou are, what has befallen thee, what brings thee here.'

'And if we do, will you aid us, you and yours?'

'Ah . . . I first must hear thee out. Tell me of events in the southwards lands.'

He sighed, glanced at his companions, shrugged. 'Worse things than you can imagine are coming to pass southwards.'

'Tell me.' She smiled again at him. 'And perhaps thou could begin by telling to me thy names.'

He looked back uneasily, scanning the vale up which he and his two companions had come.

'There is time,' she said quietly.

All lay quiet and undisturbed below. He hesitated, then sighed. 'Aye, all right.' He sat down across from her. 'My name is Tai, once of

Fallingbrook, in the South Wold. This – ' he gestured to the person-faced bird – 'is Ree. And with her is Skeefer.'

The little bird perched on the furred one's shoulder, her orange head close against his furred cheek. There was almost a lovers' closeness between these two. And then there was the buried *something* about the man. He had the feel of a true-seeing man, certain. Yet not quite like any true-seeing man she had ever felt. And in him she could sense things a-borning.

Crane shivered, feeling herself on the very cusp of the cusp now, waiting for them to begin their tale.

## XXIV

# In the Wooded Verge of
# the North Wold

It was wild country through which they moved, and Tai found it hard keeping up with the old woman. She was knobbly jointed, all sinew and bone, her arms and hands blue-veined where they showed through the loose sleeves of the ragged, animal-skin frock-shirt she wore, and she looked as though a stiff wind would send her tumbling over. But she moved with an uncanny ease, skipping along – with the aid of her stick – up slopes that left Tai and Skeefer gasping. Where they struggled through the thicker growth at a stream's side, she seemed to float through. Never a twig snagged in the long, white braided rope of her hair, and she never seemed out of breath in the slightest.

The last of the grassy Wold lay behind them. It was steep-sloped forest she led them through; oak and beech, blue-green and quiet and dim. In the distance, north and east, glimpsed occasionally through the trees, stood great, blue-toothed mountains, streaked with snow on their heights.

Tai watched the pale, flashing soles of the Dreamwalker's bare feet as she skipped on ahead. It was good to be putting pursuit in the distance behind them like this, undeniably so, but he and his companions were bone-weary, and it had been too long since last they had eaten properly. He had none of this Dreamwalker's grace, nor her uncanny, seemingly inexhaustible endurance.

'How much further?' he asked, stumbling to a halt. His head ached, the stitches throbbing hotly. He stood bent over, wheezing, hands on his thighs. Skeefer collapsed against a tree, tongue lolling, and panted like a hound. Little Ree's breath whistled tiredly.

'Soon,' the Dreamwalker said to them. 'My people are not so far, now. Soon thou will see them.'

Tai stared at the old woman. He did not know how he felt about this Dreamwalker, with her queer speech and queer ways.

A face wrinkled as a dried apple, moss green eyes gazing at him. It was another of the 'images' from the queer fit that had taken him in Long Harbour, like the uplifted demon-face he had glimpsed back by the Ferth. He did not know what to make of such things. Seeing her appear so suddenly on the slope by the forest's verge had made the short hairs on his neck prickle. He had *recognized* her, though he knew not at all who she was.

He wanted not to think on it.

The woman did not seem in herself to be any sort of threat, though, and the offer of aid she had made on behalf of herself and her people, once she had heard him out, could not be refused. Tai hardly dared let himself believe in such aid. Their need was too desperate – only Ree's high-overhead vantage had enabled them to avoid their demon-faced pursuers thus far – and this offer seemed too convenient to be true.

This Dreamwalker was unlike any other person he had ever met: old and wrinkled and frail-seeming, yet with some hidden quality to her, like a light that filled her, unseen most of the time, but there nonetheless. Perhaps she could aid them indeed. Tai wondered if her people were all as strange as she.

He straightened himself, breathing a bit more easily now. By his side, Skeefer's panting had all but ceased. The Dreamwalker looked at them and smiled and, smiling, skipped off again.

As best they could, Tai and the others struggled after.

The Dreamwalker brought them along the banks of a swift rushing rill. A campfire burned there. Tai saw a scattering of flimsy shelters of white birch-bark, amongst which were perhaps two dozen people: men and women: even youngsters almost children. Like the Dreamwalker, they dressed in animal skins, some of them hardly more than mere twists of leather about their loins, but there was a bizarre lack of commonality amongst them. Some had long hair, some short, some had close-shaved, naked skulls. Several had coloured paints smeared across their features.

Every eye was fixed on the newcomers.

'I see thee, my people,' the Dreamwalker called.

'We see thee, Dreamwalker,' came the reply. And then: 'We see thee, Fulfillers-of-the-Dream.'

After that, expectant silence.

It took Tai a long, uncomfortable moment to realize that this was a formal greeting of some sort, though he did not understand at all what that 'Fulfillers-of-the-Dream' might mean. 'We . . . we see you, you . . . people,' he stammered out, trying to feel his way through this.

By now, Tai and the others were encircled by a silent, staring group. This close, Tai could smell the pungent odour of the gathered people, a thick combination of smoke, leather, and ripe sweat. One of them reached a hand out to Skeefer, stroking his fur in amazement. One made a jumping grab at Ree where she perched on the fur-man's shoulder. Ree peeped shrilly and whirled aloft and away to circle overhead. Tai felt hands upon him; not aggressive, but insistent.

The Dreamwalker stood, leaned upon her stick one-legged, the sole of her left foot propped against her right knee.

Tai did not know what to do.

But hands took him, friendly enough, pulling him along to the fire, Skeefer next to him and Ree fluttering nearby. A woman with a green-painted face offered him a bark container of stew. Skeefer, he noticed, was receiving the same treatment. And even Ree, for all her flightiness, was accepting some.

It was, Tai had to admit, excellent stew.

'Tell the tale thou told me,' the Dreamwalker said when Tai and his companions were done eating. 'All must hear it before we can aid thee.'

Tai looked around him. What he saw seemed far from reassuring. The fire, the flimsy birch-bark shelters, a few raw animal hides stretched and drying, a brace of mountain birds hung from a limb near where he sat. No stock animals, no buildings, no tools or implements or weapons of metal, only rough stone blades, short-bodied bows and grey-fletched, stone-tipped arrows.

Tai felt his heart sink. Such people as these could offer nothing in the way of useful aid. One look at the terrible demon-faces of *them* and these folk would flee in terror.

He stood up, raised his hands. 'We thank you for your hospitality, but there is naught you can do to help us. I see that now.' He glanced across at Skeefer and read similar sentiments on the fur-man's face. Tai sighed inwardly, facing the truth. These people would be worse than helpless against *them*. The hope Dreamwalker had offered was come to naught. 'My companions and I must be on our way. The longer we stay here the more danger we expose you to.'

'We are not so helpless as thou seems to think, man,' Dreamwalker said.

Tai sighed. 'You do not understand. That which has—'

'Tell us thy tale!' a voice said.

'Tell us! Tell us!'

The people crowded close about the fire, perhaps not entirely menacing, but not entirely friendly either. Tai glanced at Skeefer. The fur-man shrugged glumly.

There was little choice, it seemed, but to do as was demanded.

So, as he had told the Dreamwalker, Tai told this odd gathering about *their* invasion of the Wold; told about spell-helms and man-demons; about his own and Skeefer's and Ree's experiences; about the Miradore and the Pit and Long Harbour and all the rest. Of the fits, though, and of Seer Tancred's special interest in him, Tai remained silent. He did not wish to think on such things.

The people listened in silence, big-eyed, till it was done.

'So,' said an older woman in a rasping, throaty voice. 'The Dream becomes waking truth at last.'

Dreamwalker nodded. 'Change comes amongst us. Storm is loosed.'

'It is war, then,' somebody said softly.

'Aye,' Tai agreed. 'War it is. Bloody war brought to us uncalled-for.' He ran a hand over his eyes, trying to think how to tell them what he must. 'That which follows us would mean only sure destruction to you and yours. You must let us—'

'We will aid thee,' a man said. 'We must stop these southern man-demons before they come northwards into our wild lands. Such is our task here. Such is the Dreaming that drew us.'

The sheer, innocent effrontery of it all but took Tai's breath away.

Skeefer, who had been silent ever since their arrival here, stood up, shaking his furred head. 'You underssstand *nothing* of *them!*'

'Thou knows us not, fur-brother,' Dreamwalker said.

'No wordss can ssay how terrible *they* are! You do not undersstand.'

Dreamwalker looked at him solemnly. 'It is thou who does not understand.'

The gathered people had gone silent and grim.

'Skeefer means no harm by what he says,' Tai ventured. 'You truly cannot know what manner of creatures these demons be unless you have first-hand experience. A strong man's belly cramps with terror at the mere sight of them. They have the strength of many and wear strong armour and are almost impossible to harm. What could you do against such as that? We must be gone from here, my companions and I, and that as soon as can be. Otherwise, we will bring certain disaster down upon you. And we wish not to repay your hospitality in that manner.'

The gathered people only looked at him in continued, grim silence.

'It is truth, this,' Tai said. 'You must believe me. You *must* understand.'

An old, one-eyed man stepped forward and looked straight at Tai with his good eye, the other naught but a wrinkled socket. 'As Dreamwalker says, it is *thee* who must understand. Does thou think us such empty-head people that we do not know there is more to the world than that which we ourselves have experienced? Does thou think us stupid?'

'No,' Tai replied quickly. 'No, of course not.'

'Does thou know all there is in the world?' demanded a young woman with jagged black lines along her cheeks.

Tai shook his head.

'We have,' said Dreamwalker, 'strengths thou knows nothing of.'

For a moment, Tai almost believed her, such pure conviction did her voice carry. He felt a surge of hope that, perhaps, she *did* have some secret strength that could be brought out to aid them. But then more sober judgement asserted itself. What could a people such as these – ragged and simple, without even so much as an iron knife between them – possibly do against *them?*

Absolutely not a thing.

Tai ran a hand over his eyes. He did not wish to offend these people. 'Your offer is a generous one, but there is nothing you can do. Please believe me.'

'Storm is upon us,' said the old, one-eyed man, 'and change rides the wind. Dreamwalker has Dreamed these things. The world moves as the Powers move.'

Tai shook his head in confusion.

Dreamwalker stepped close to him. 'We have lived long and long in the mountains, away from the rest of the world. But now times change. Storm is loosed. *They* must not be permitted into our lands.' She looked around at the people gathered around her. 'We must do what we are called upon to do.'

A murmur of solemn, communal agreement greeted this.

'And what are you called upon to do?' Tai asked uneasily.

Dreamwalker looked at him, utterly serious. 'We must destroy these man-demons that pursue thee.'

'No!' Tai said. 'You must not try. You have no idea of—'

'Is their death so painful for thou to think of?'

Tai shook his head. 'No. You do not understand. It is *you* who will be killed, not *them*. You do not even have iron weapons!'

The one-eyed man smiled. 'Do you value iron so much, then?'

Tai pulled at his hair in despair. 'What you plan here is *suicide!*'

The smile was gone from Dreamwalker's face now. Her moss green eyes glinted suddenly hard. 'These demons that pursue thee, they are such that no ordinary person can stand against them: has thou not said as much?'

Tai nodded.

'Then we will not send *ordinary* people against them.'

Tai looked at the ragged band, young and old, men, women, near children. It was all too pitiful.

Dreamwalker had turned to her people. 'It is the death-path we must walk.'

The people gave silent, solemn assent.

Dreamwalker took Tai by the arm and glared into his face. 'Does thou think I have my name for nothing? Does thou think I know *nothing*? I am Dreamwalker to the people. I walk far places. I have seen many things. I *know* things, Man-from-far-away.'

Tai tried one last time. 'You and your folk haven't the strength, Dreamwalker. You will only get yourselves killed!'

She led him to the fire then, along with Skeefer and Ree, and sat them down. The rest of her folk gathered close about. 'It is not simple body-strength we will use against *them*, man.' She paused. Then, 'Does thou know of the Shadowlands?' she asked suddenly.

'Of course.' Tai shuddered, remembering his own mistaken sense of having reached that dim realm himself after his experience in the Pit at the Miradore. 'Everybody knows of the Shadowlands. It is the threshold of the great Beyond, where the newly dead go, before being brought back into the great cycle of life.'

Dreamwalker nodded, 'But it is not only the dead that may go to the Shadowlands. The living, too, may visit there.'

Tai had heard tell of such, but never truly believed it. 'But only the dead . . .'

'There are ways to free the soul from the body. I have far-voyaged in this fashion. I have guided others. I can guide others now. To the Shadowlands we go, and back again.'

Tai stared at her. 'And do *what*?'

'Each who makes this Shadowland journey will die a little, and be reborn, bringing a little of death back into the world. And that shadow-death we can pass to others, killing them. Has thou never heard tell of such?'

Tai shook his head.

'Those who walk the death-path and return will be warriors the like of which these southern man-demons have never encountered. But walking the death-path in this way is a terrible act, man. It is a tearing of the very fabric of the world, and the death will have its way, in one manner or another. Those who return *must* shed it to another or die themselves.' Dreamwalker shook her head. 'A terrible act indeed, but it is terrible times in which we live.'

Skeefer spoke up then. 'Thosse that make thiss journey . . . they will be able to fight againsst *them*? Be able to sstrike and kill *them*?'

Dreamwalker nodded, solemn.

'I will make thiss journey, then.'

'It is no simple task, fur-brother. All will return, I hope, but sometimes the soul is trapped, undead, unliving, torn slowly between the worlds until it is left a tattered, gibbering thing.'

Ree piped in alarm and fluttered about Skeefer's head, but he waved her away and turned to face the Dreamwalker, his furred fists clenched determinedly. 'I *will* make thiss journey. I have an old vengeance to ssettle with *them!*'

Dreamwalker gazed at him for a long moment. 'Thou is certain sure of this, fur-brother? Thou is willing to make this journey and to bring death back into the world with thee?'

Skeefer nodded. 'Yess!'

'Very well.'

'And me!' Ree piped. 'I will not let Skeefer do this alone!'

Dreamwalker shook her head. 'Thou is not a warrior, little Ree. Thy strengths lie elsewhere.'

'Yess!' Skeefer agreed. 'You musst not go, my Ree.'

Tai swallowed. Looking at this strange woman, he found himself unaccountably believing everything she said. There was a sudden, solid authority to her, despite the fact that what she talked of sounded the sheerest lunacy. He had experienced too much already to be quite as willing as he might once have been to deny strange things. And also, having once experienced – while wearing the spell-helm – what it was like to be able to strike a blow at *them*, he was loath to pass up another opportunity. He felt sudden hope surge in him. 'And I,' he said. 'I too will make this journey.'

Dreamwalker's green eyes turned to him. 'No. Not thee.'

'Why?' Tai demanded. 'Ree, I understand. It is as you say: she is no warrior. But you allow Skeefer to!'

'Thou,' she said, 'is different. Thou is a true-seeing man, and more. Though it is a hidden thing in thee still. Thou is the hidden-inside-man. Such as thee need special preparation. There is no telling what might happen if thou makes such a journey unprepared.'

Tai shook his head. A true-seeing man? A hidden-inside-man? Such names made no sense to him. 'I will go,' he said.

Dreamwalker regarded him silently for a long moment. 'Be warned, man. I cannot predict what might happen. Not to thee.'

'I *will* go,' he repeated.

'Very well,' the Dreamwalker said. 'Be it as thou wishes. Perhaps there is a pattern forming here.' She turned from him and squatted by the fire, busy with something there.

Tai went to her, curious.

From a leather pouch, she sifted a pale yellow powder into a small, carved wooden bowl. Then, to this powder, she mixed several pinches of something she drew from another, different pouch. 'This,' she said to him over her shoulder, 'is wet-smoke. Used properly it looses the soul.'

Tai looked on uneasily as Dreamwalker beckoned to a young man seated next her. She took up a slender length of hollow cane. Carefully, she loaded several pinches of the mixed 'wet-smoke' into a hollow at one end. The cane's other end, Tai saw, was fitted with an odd, rounded wooden stopper with a small aperture through it.

The young man Dreamwalker had beckoned squatted down before her. She stared at him in silence, and then began to chant, keeping her green eyes fixed on his. Tai could hear nothing of the words she might be chanting, only a sort of continuous, keening mutter. The man began to dip and sway slightly where he squatted.

Dreamwalker then lifted the cane pipe, put one end to her lips and extended the other towards the man. He, in turn, took the offered end and placed the wooded stopper into one of his nostrils. His movements were slow and weirdly graceful. The two faced each other in silence, the man's nostril filled with the stoppered end of the cane, the cane's other end pressed against Dreamwalker's lips.

She took a long, slow breath, then blew, hard, through the hollow cane.

The man tumbled backwards, grunting, his nose streaming bloody ribbons of wet mucus. He hawked and spat and moaned. But then he recovered himself and returned, to have Dreamwalker refill the cane and place it into his other nostril, so that the whole procedure was repeated again.

And so it went, each in turn receiving the keening chant and double nostril full of what Dreamwalker called the wet-smoke. Those who had already received it began to moan and writhe about, then to lie silent, quivering a little, until they became deathly still.

Tai watched uneasily while Skeefer took his turn, rolling and writhing like the rest.

Then came Tai's turn.

He felt suddenly reticent. What had he committed himself to? He had no notion of what he was supposed to do. Dreamwalker had said they would bring death back with them from the Shadowlands. But what did that mean? Perhaps she was just a crazy old woman forcing some poisonous potion upon others.

The Dreamwalker beckoned to him. He was the last. Slowly, he went to her.

The chanting, even this close to her, still held no recognizable words for him. It was a ululation of sound, surrounding him. He blinked, blinked again. Dreamwalker's green eyes seemed to grow, becoming deep green pools. He felt the end of the cane in his fingers, guided it to his nostril.

The force of it, when she blew the breath into him, was like an explosion of burning cold through his skull. The half-healed scar across his forehead sang with sudden agony. But he levered himself off the ground – how he had come to be on the ground he was not certain –and returned to have Dreamwalker fill his skull again with that liquid, freezing pain.

His body felt very small, and very large.

He heard the Dreamwalker's chanting still, but faint, fainter, faintest. Darkness swirled round him.

Tai was chilled with a bone-deep, Shadowland chill. It was as if he had never been warm, could not even remember what warmth might have been like.

The darkness was strange: moving, shuddering. No true dark at all.

He was walking. He had, or seemed to have, a body, Shadowlands or no. His own solid, familiar, aching body. He felt breath go in and out his lungs coldly, felt the muscles pull along his legs as the slope on which he walked grew steeper, felt his heart beat with terror.

A dim landscape was slowly exposed about him. Grey slopes of distant, half-seen hills, a darkly glowing grey sky, cinders and the cracked spines of dead leaves underfoot.

He moved on, upslope, knowing not what he was doing here. He felt terrified, his heart racing in his breast like some small, hysterical thing.

What was he to do?

'We will bring death back with us,' Dreamwalker had said. But Tai saw no 'we' here. There was only himself, terribly alone. And how was he to bring anything back? How was he to bring even himself back? Lost and gone forever he was like to be in this terrible place.

He clambered along the slope before him, having no better thing to do. At the crest of it, he looked across into a kind of vale. On the far side, he saw moving figures. Dreamwalker's people he was certain. Between him and them, filling the vale, lay a dark wood. But it seemed not so very large. He started off down the slope intending to push through it quickly and join the others. But at the wood's border he stopped. The black shapes of the trees seemed to reach for him, limbs twisted into strange positions, bristling with long thorns like iron spikes. Skeletal leaves rustled in the still, cold air.

Tai shuddered. But he had no choice if he were to find the others. He pushed forwards, gingerly lifting the thorny limbs aside. Under his feet, fallen leaves crackled, as if he were walking on a layer of tiny, dried bones. It was too dark to see anything clearly. He struggled on, stumbling on the treacherously uneven ground, hoping that he would break out soon.

But the wood seemed to go on forever.

And then, before him, he saw a glimmering mere. The water lay still as dark glass. Leaning over it, Tai saw his reflection clear as clear.

But that reflection of his own familiar features began to change. His face seemed to be split open from within, bursting like a ripe fruit and, as he watched, horror-struck, a new face took shape. His eyes became large, oval, like glowing lamps, his mouth wide and gleaming with ivory fangs.

From out of the image before him, a bony hand reached up, water runnelling wetly back down along the arm. Tai felt a cold touch. Something hard as iron brushed his cheek. The thing began to rise up out of the mere at him.

For one long, terrible moment Tai could not move. Then, shrieking, he fled, slipping over the hard ground, stumbling, skidding through grey-spined leaves underfoot, skittering as desperately as any hunted hare until, finally, he fetched up with an agonizing thump against the rough bark of a tree bole and slid to the ground in an exhausted heap.

He crouched there, panting, his head and heart pounding. A dull, persistent ache began to grow in his middle, as if the whole of his insides were nothing but an empty hollow. He felt nauseous. He leaned against the tree, pressing his face into the cold, rough surface of the bark.

A sudden, penetratingly clear *crack* brought his head up with a snap.

In the dimness between the Shadowland trees, he saw something moving with the artful, slow steps of a predator; long, spindly legs, stick-thin arms, spiky fingers, oval lamps of eyes, yellowed ivory fangs in an opened mouth. Tai pressed himself back close against the tree. A long, chill shiver snaked its way up his spine.

The thing drew closer to him, and now he could hear it breathing in soft, hissing gaps. The pale ovals of its eyes glowed softly in the dark.

Tai saw the thing's fingers, momentarily splayed out against the bole of a tree, long bony fingers with talons hooked and sharp as a hunting owl's. Tai gasped. It was another 'image' from the Long Harbour fit.

They would rip through him as if he were naught but ripe cheese, those talons. He could feel how it would be: the talons sharp and cold, his own skin stretched, punctured, ripped and shredded until the wet red flesh underneath was exposed.

Tai shuddered.

The creature stalked closer to him now, closer still, until it was crouched not two paces away, hunkered down on its heels, knobbed knees up around its pale and fleshy ears. It thrust its face forwards, snuffling at him, the flat ovals of its eyes glimmering in the tree-muffled, Shadowland dimness.

Tai felt his belly cramp up with cold terror of this impossible creature. Its skin was wrinkled and folded and pebbly with orange fungus growth. It exuded a sickly, sticky odour that stung the back of Tai's nostrils. He felt like some hapless frog staring into the cold, deadly eyes of a serpent.

It grinned, showing the yellowed gleam of its fangs, and reached forward. With one taloned finger it traced a line from Tai's throbbing forehead to where his heart hammered under his ribs.

Tai shuddered. The thing's talon felt like cold iron, sharp and paining.

'I am you,' it said in a croaking voice. 'You are me. We are what we are.'

Tai understood this not at all.

It laughed an ugly laugh, and then held out a taloned hand, palm up, beckoningly. Tai felt his bowels loosen in panic, but he raised himself unsteadily to his feet, uncertain as to what he was doing, or what the thing before him might be suggesting. He felt hot now rather than chilled as he had been, feverish and weak and without hope, and yet incapable of resisting whatever strange momentum was building here.

'You have always feared me,' it said. The thing capered and hopped queerly, enticing him on, grinning and leering. It spoke no more, but the motions it now made were clear enough. *Run*, it was gesturing to him. *Flee!*

Tai fled, understanding nothing, terror-filled, crashing through the maze of the dark forest as he had before, his lungs and head on fire, his poor heart beating fit to break. Behind, he could hear the thing's ugly laughter.

But it dwindled, that laughter, until after a time the dark wood was silent. Tai fell against a twisty tree bole, his lungs heaving, utterly spent.

The sound of movement made him snap his head around. He saw a procession of people coming towards him, winding a serpentine way through the trees across the hummocky ground. For an instant, Tai's heart leaped. Dreamwalker's people!

But no. For as they drew close, Tai saw that they were riven through. Like animals after the autumn slaughter they seemed. The moving dead. Tai shuddered, pressed against his tree, staring.

They paid him no slightest heed, merely proceeded on their sad, limping journey. To the Darkling Hills they must be going, where all the dead must travel in their quest for ending and new beginning. Tai rose, desperate. Perhaps if he followed these shades, he might find a way out of this dark wood . . .

Behind him, Tai heard hissing breath. Whirling, he saw the fell thing that had been pursuing him. It laughed and, laughing, reached for him.

Tai felt a burning pain through his gut. The thing had ripped his belly open with its talons, still laughing.

Hard hands pushed him stumblingly away, and Tai fled once more, helpless to do aught else, holding his torn belly in with his hands, laughter pursuing him through the dark. He felt such terror that his mind almost died of it. The black maze of the trees all about him, cruel laughter at his heels, his belly on fire with pain. He was naught but helpless prey, at the mercy of this dread hunter. It could attack or not, strike or not, as it would.

When he could run no more, he stumbled onwards, moving through the eternal confusion of the black trees. He understood none of this. Why did this creature pursue him, only to push him away once more? It was like some terrible, incarnate enigma, striking with its own unfathomable rhythm.

Silent and sudden, as if his thinking about it had somehow conjured the thing up, it appeared again before him, sliding from behind the dark, tangled boles of the trees. Its eerie eyes glowed. With quick, certain movements, it came for him. Tai stared, unable to move, stricken by this so sudden appearance. Crouching down, it clutched Tai's hands in its own, then leaped suddenly to its feet, hands raised high above its head. With a yank that nearly dislocated Tai's shoulders, the thing dangled him in mid-air, held like some hapless infant, with his feet kicking helplessly. Tai felt something in his belly tear.

The thing laughed, a long, loud, ugly sound, and flung Tai to the hard ground.

Tai landed with a tumbling thud. Before he could so much as blink, the thing was upon him, straddling his heaving chest, taloned fingers boring agonizingly into his ribs. Its great, flat oval eyes blazed into his. 'You have always feared me,' it croaked, repeating what it had already said. 'Fear me more.' The talons tore him. He felt his ribs being cracked apart. The dark forest about him shimmered into a red, tangled haze.

Tai struggled, shrieking, but it was no use. There was naught he could do to resist.

The thing tore him apart like a wet, ragged doll.

But when it was over, when he had been ripped and devoured and destroyed, Tai still somehow remained, a bodiless, focusless soul, pulsing with the residual agony of what he had just endured.

Despite everything, he still *was*.

All his life Tai had feared just such a terrible, tearing destruction as this. Each time the fit took him, he had felt himself being torn apart.

And now it had happened. That thing had risen from his own self and destroyed him. Wet red destruction.

His worst nightmare come real.

But he had survived it.

And what he experienced now was queerly familiar. An empty, formless, dropping-away sensation took him. Only nothingness and dark about him. Moving chaos. It was like what occurred when the fits took him. That terrible overwhelming. But now, somehow, it seemed not so terrible. He had experienced too much of terror to be so simply overcome.

Though no bodily perception was left him, he somehow *sensed* the same foul creature stalking him still. Its cruel laughter suddenly filled the moving chaos all about.

Tai felt the terror fill him.

But for an instant only. There was, after all, naught more the thing could do to him. Tai laughed – though he had no mouth to laugh with – and felt the thing cringe. It was helpless before him now, for he found he had no fear of it left. It had risen up and destroyed him, yet he was not destroyed.

Under his laughter, the thing came apart like smoke.

It seemed to Tai then that he had been struggling with the foul thing all his days. But now that struggle was finished. He felt . . .

Tai did not know how he felt. Everything was too new.

He hovered, bodiless, for a timeless time.

The moving chaos about him began to still.

Blinking, he suddenly saw a green tracery of wholesome trees about him, the blue of the sky shimmering beyond. But the dancing leaves on the tree's limbs were translucent, mere glowing façades. Through them he sensed a deeper patterning. Like shadows, but shadows that were their own independent forms. An intricate tapestry.

He heard the wind whispering in the leaves. Under his back he felt solid earth. Lifting a hand, he traced the rough texture of bark, the coolness of damp moss. But underneath, he felt such *complexity*.

Tai allowed himself to glide through the misleading solidity of the trees to the under-patterns he glimpsed beyond. It was not sight he used, or hearing, or any of the familiar senses that had served him all his days. Yet he *sensed* clearly the hidden patternings. They were solid, and yet not so at all. Huge, yet small enough to perceive in their entireties. The elegant complexity of them overwhelmed him. Like a thirsty root absorbing the rain, he drank all in. He was amazed, filled, complete.

And then, through the intricate latticework of under-shapings, he *sensed* a moving cluster of radiance. No true light-radiance, this, for the under-patterns he perceived had nothing to do with the body's senses. Yet his mind had no other means of relating to what he perceived. And so he 'saw'.

He drew himself closer to that radiance.

Luminous forms, they were, moving in a shifting group, each glowing with a soft inner light.

Tai followed these strange, luminous creatures until they ceased to move. He waited, then, as they waited. How he knew they were waiting for something, Tai understood not. But wait they did, and he with them, admiring their radiance. They seemed softly glowing jewels, strung across a webbery of upthrusting, intertwined, delicate shadow-shapes.

And then another group of radiance appeared. The members of the original group were each a single, shining shape, glowing with a single, soft glow. The newcomers, though, appeared bulbous, with a queer, dual hump. And each was composed of a double light.

Before Tai could begin to come to terms with the strange differences that marked these newcomers, the original group abruptly flung itself forward so that the two groups became one in a sudden, seething, angry struggle of movement.

At first, Tai did not understand what was happening. But then, slowly, it revealed itself to him. Those of the single glow group, it seemed, were trying to extinguish the double glows.

For now he grew aware of a thing he had missed before. Each of the single glows had a sort of dark root, a grafted thing, attached to them. He could trace those grafted roots, down and down, through the intricacy of under-shapes towards—

Bodiless, Tai shuddered. It was death the single glows carried grafted to them. Death that would drag them inexorably down through all patterning into the dark formlessness that underlay all. He felt, suddenly and clearly, the terrible struggle each had to keep from being drawn away into the darkness. And they sought, he now realized, to transfer that grafted, dark root on to the double glows.

Perceiving all this, Tai had a sudden instant of revelation.

The Dreamwalker's people.

*Them.*

For an instant, he saw the fighting clearly with his world-eyes, the leaping, demon-faced shapes of *them*, Dreamwalker's people no less lithe, skipping like squirrels between the green trees. He heard howls, saw blood flow.

The strange dual perception lasted but a moment, but while it did he was aware of the two levels: the leaping, howling bodies superimposed over the glowing under-beings of light; the single glow of Dream-walker's people, the double glow of *them*.

Tai's world vision faded, the solidity of moving bodies dissolving into moving radiance. He *sensed* clearly the struggle before him intensify. The single-glows spilled forward, were driven back, some of them tumbling away and beyond, down death's dark root. But none of *them* followed.

The bitter hopelessness of it all suddenly overwhelmed Tai. The demons were triumphing once again. Was there nothing that could overcome them?

But the Dreamwalker's folk, he now realized, had indeed begun to bring some of the demons down, transferring, somehow, the black death-root that they carried grafted to their own souls, and sending some of *them* to the beyond.

But it was not enough.

Everything in Tai cried out that he must not remain a mute, helpless witness. But he knew not what he might do.

And then the strange, double glow of *them* caught his attention. Why was it *they* had a double radiance when Dreamwalker's people only a single?

The spell-helms. Of course. The strange life Tancred had said dwelt within the helms. The radiance he *sensed* was soul-radiance, then. The double glow was half human souls, half the part-alive creatures that animated those fell helms.

Tai reached, or stretched, or attenuated some part of himself, he knew not what it was. But somehow he came close to the glowing embers that marked the helms. It was, he found, as if his will were a palpable thing, like a set of hands he could *reach* with. Haltingly, he worked at one of helm-embers, trying to extinguish it. But he did not know what he was doing, or how such a thing might be done. Had he lips, he would have cried out in frustration.

And then, almost despite his efforts, the first spell-helm glow winked out of existence. He did not know what he had done and struggled with the next and the next.

In the end, it was a matter of smothering them, of willing himself to be water to their fire, ice to their heat, darkness to their dully glowing radiance.

They did not die, for they had been soulless and never truly alive. Instead, they simply dwindled.

But *they* died. Tai witnessed them dropping off into the long beyond, one by one, as the Dreamwalker's folk grafted the roots of death onto them.

And then it was over.

Tai felt himself coalescing, his bodiless self compacting. Shadow-shapes whirled and swirled, shuddered and shifted until . . .

Until he opened his eyes groggily and saw solid trees all about him and the green eyes of Dreamwalker gazing down at him concernedly.

Blinking, Tai made out the shapes of moving people behind her. He heard shouts, saw hands raised on high. Tai struggled to back away, but his limbs were stiff as wood.

'It is all right,' Dreamwalker said to him. 'It is over.'

Tai shook his head. He felt thick-witted and frail. The noise about him was confusing. 'What . . . what is happening?'

'It is over,' Dreamwalker repeated. 'My people dance.'

At this moment Skeefer came prancing up, Ree whirling in bright circles above his head. 'We desstroyed *them*!' Skeefer crowded. 'I never thought to ssee anything like it.' There was a long, bloody welt across his shoulder and chest, and his fur was matted in places with blood, but his eyes were afire. 'All of the helmed demonss that purssued uss are desstroyed!'

Tai opened his mouth, closed it. He knew not what to say.

The Dreamwalker looked down at Tai. Her face was lined with weariness and she leaned heavily on her stick, but she seemed to have taken no hurt. 'Tai knows of what happened,' she said to the fur-man.

'Have you told him already, then?' Ree asked, hovering close. 'Is Tai going to recover well and certain? Has the strange fit left him?'

Dreamwalker smiled. 'See for thyself, feathered-sister.'

Ree swarmed about Tai, chirruping and joyful, for Skeefer was returned to her and *they* were defeated.

Tai shook his head groggily. 'It is true, then? All of the man-demons that pursued us are killed?'

'Yess!' Skeefer hissed triumphantly. 'Dead and desstroyed.' A shudder passed through him, and he shook himself wearily. 'Death iss a terrible ally, man. I would not wissh to take part in ssuch a battle again ssoon. But that pack of demon-helmed villainss will never hunt again.' The fur-man grinned fiercely, showing his sharp teeth. 'Thiss markss a new beginning, man!'

Tai took a long, shuddering breath. He had witnessed the fighting, played his part, but he still could hardly believe it. Nobody had ever defeated *them*.

Tai shivered. He caught Dreamwalker eyeing him knowingly. '*They* nearly overcame us, man. Only when their helms died were we able to destroy them.' She was aware of what he had done; he *sensed* her knowing clearly.

Tai felt weary beyond belief, his limbs shivery and weak, but he managed to prop himself on one elbow to watch Dreamwalker's people at their dance. Their movements were both joyous and sad, celebrating triumph, mourning those who had not returned. He saw wounds on several, and each face was pale and weary; they were shaken by what they had done, it was clear. But now they concluded the doing of it with tears and laughter and the whirl of limbs. He *sensed* the underlying pattern they wove together, dancing life back into themselves.

For Tai could see and hear and smell and touch the familiar world, but underneath that, or beyond it, or inside it – he knew not what it was – he could also perceive clearly the hidden patterns that underlay all.

Hidden no longer.

'New beginningss!' Skeefer cried again.

The Dreamwalker looked at Tai.

'Aye,' Tai agreed. 'Aye. New beginnings indeed.' But he shivered. He did not know what, exactly, was beginning in him. It seemed very, very wonderful, but very terrible too. And he did not understand it at all. What manner of being was he become?

# PART THREE

# CONVERGENCES

# XXV

# The Palisade

'What news?' Gerrid demanded of the guard that brought the noonday meal.

The man said nothing, merely pushed the wooden dish of potato gruel through the slot at the bottom of the door and on to the dirt floor next to Gerrid's cot.

'What news, man?' Gerrid insisted, gripping the iron door-bars. 'Tell me!'

The guard stepped back quickly. 'Seven more gone.'

'Seven!' Gerrid shook his head. 'And what does the Commander do?'

'Commander Chayne continues to deny the truth of your claims.'

'Idiot!' Gerrid spat. 'So he keeps sending men out into the hills to be hewn down by this demon-spawned axe-man. Why doesn't—'

But the guard had withdrawn already, and Gerrid found he was talking to himself.

How *dare* the man! Gerrid would have happily ripped the helm from the guard's head and broken the fool's neck for such crass insubordination. The Sub-Commander kicked the wall, hard, venting his anger. Wretched fate, to be imprisoned here ignominiously like this, with his spell-helm taken – he ached in his very bones for his helm – and no hope of escape from this stupid captivity, short of a reprieve from the Commander himself. Precious little chance of that!

He had been ruined since that one, terrible instant when the axe-man had appeared in the midst of the fighting up in the Peaks, as if from nowhere. What manner of being was he, *could* he be? Gerrid had never seen the like.

Those amongst his men who had survived that ill-fated battle talked about the man as if he were some sort of demon. And now, though Commander Chayne apparently was making every attempt to quash it ruthlessly, there were widespread and spreading rumours, growing more outrageous with each telling no doubt, of the axe-wielding demon of the heights. They fed into all the men's latent anxieties, those rumours. It was all too easy, southerners that they were and unused to this northern wilderness, for them to believe that this wild land harboured all manner of weird and supernatural creatures. There were moments when Gerrid himself found it hard to entirely deny. He had seen the impossible, demonic carnage the man had wrought. What normal man could do such a thing, unaided, against spell-helm power?

Gerrid kicked aside the thin gruel the guard had brought. He felt no hunger. He was ruined. What matter that he had been privy to the inner councils of the Lords Veil? What matter that he knew the secret of the third Lord Veil? What matter that his career was unblemished till now? All his hopes were broken. All because of that cursed, impossible, axe-wielding hill ruffian!

Gerrid clenched his fists. It was all he could do not to howl his anger and frustration.

Ruined!

Commander Chayne had stripped Gerrid of his Sub-Commander's rank and imprisoned him in this makeshift gaol-house. Bad enough, that, though Gerrid had fully expected something of the sort. But worse was Chayne's complete, bare-faced denial of the substance of Gerrid's explanation. No axe-wielding hill-champion existed, according to Chayne. No terrible defeat had occurred. Instead, the Commander insisted that Gerrid had made some stupid blunder, lost men to some natural hazard – rushing mountain torrent, sudden cliff, something of the sort – and had made up an outrageous series of lies to cover his own mistakes.

So he stood accused officially of incompetence.

It made Gerrid want to puke. He had returned to the Palisade, knowing he would face the ignominy of his defeat, because he felt it important – more important than his own career – that Chayne and the Lords Veil know what was breeding in the Peaks.

And now . . .

The ridiculousness of his own accusations seemed to bother the Commander little. Gerrid understood well enough that the Commander himself did not necessarily disbelieve Gerrid's story. But Chayne had the nobility's easy habit of dismissing trouble – what noble ever believed himself incapable of getting out of trouble? – and this situation presented far too good an opportunity for Chayne to pass up. He could pull Gerrid down from Sub-Commander rank and break him, then instate somebody of his – Chayne's – own choosing. Somebody properly biddable. And since it was all too clear by now which way the wind was blowing, it did nobody any good to side with Gerrid.

Gerrid clenched his fists. He could get no message out to the Lords Veil. He could do nothing. The always and forever struggle for power. This time he was the loser.

He took a long breath, trying to calm himself. Perhaps, just perhaps, not all was lost.

The Commander, it seemed, had let himself be blinded by his own ambitions. For, try as he might, in however ruthless a manner, Chayne could not squelch the rumour-mill, and could not calm the hidden fears that grew daily when a squad he sent out failed to return. The Commander ought to send a large force, large enough to overwhelm entirely any single hill-champion, demon or no. Or he ought to stop sending out the regular patrol squads. But Chayne could not call off those patrols without acknowledging the truth of Gerrid's claims, and that Chayne would never do. So he kept sending those small squads to whatever sad fate awaited them out there in the wilds.

The force here in the Palisade was all that was left now to garrison this part of the north. That news had come the other day with a rider from the west. The conquest was complete. The war of the Lords Veil here in the north was won. Only the Long Harbour on the coast and the Palisade itself were to be left garrisoned now, west and east, with the wild land between lying emptied and pacified. All the rest of the original invasion force was returned down the long road southwards, for that was, and had always been, the centre of all.

But the conquest of this northern hinterland was *not* complete, not so long as there were men like this inexplicable axe-wielder at large. The worst thing imaginable: that was what Chayne's approach amounted to. In the arrogance of his own blind ambition, he was disastrously underestimating the seriousness of what confronted them.

It gave Gerrid hope, that. He was ruined for certain as long as Commander Chayne remained in charge. But Chayne was making mistakes. And there was still no sign of Seer Tancred returning, so Chayne was denied support from that quarter.

Gerrid had followers still, despite that they could not show themselves at the moment. Just let Chayne make that one fatal mistake too many, then things might indeed change.

Captive no longer.

Gerrid took a long, slow breath, let it out. He was a prisoner, powerless, de-helmed and in disgrace. But he still lived. He would wait. Something might happen. Something *had* to happen. He could not believe that this ignominy was the end of him.

He would be ready. When Chayne made that final, fatal mistake, he, Gerrid, would step into the breech. The Lords Veil would be informed. One of them at least must surely be here still in this northern hinterland. The situation would be handled.

Gerrid would be revenged.

XXVI

# The Palisade

Jonaquil stood in the open gateway and watched as the last of the logging gangs came straggling hastily back up the slope from the River Paudit towards the Palisade's sheltering walls.

The work-gangs had begun to go out as usual this morning, traipsing off in the cold grey light of the pre-dawn. But something had happened.

And now there were demon-faced guards everywhere, moving about like a swarm of angry bees in the wan, early morning light.

Jonaquil had been up since well before dawn, unable to sleep for the dreams. It had been long days since last she had slept soundly. The familiar dreaming had haunted her since arriving here: the green-eyed old woman and her strange companions, the fighting in the Palisade. But since Jonaquil's confrontation with Commander Chayne, it had grown overwhelmingly forceful, and more and more it was the violence, the blood and iron and shrieking, that filled her nights now, the compound awash with struggling bodies, a great axe raised, wet with gore. It grew starker and stronger each night, leaving her sitting bolt upright in her bed in the dark, soaked with sweat and shivering at the memory of it.

Now, as she stood here by the gate, her belly was tight with premonitory dread. She felt it clearly, even through the constant torment of the Healer's Sickness that ate at her. Not since the morning the demons first came to Woodend had she had such a strong gut sense of some dire event to be. On the ground at her side lay her remedy bag. She had brought it instinctively.

The work-gangs from the forest drew closer, work unstarted, herded back up towards the Palisade gateway by dour-faced demon guards. Jonaquil recognized Dara, who had been Mayor of Woodend.

'What is it?' she asked of him as he passed close by where she stood in the gateway. 'What has happened?'

She hardly knew Dara. He was thinner now, lean, the pudginess that had been so much a part of him worn away by the life here. He seemed more like a chance-met stranger with a vaguely familiar face than the village Mayor she had known for so long.

'Somebody's hurt,' Dara said. He stood before her, face and fists clenched. 'One of the guards, more than likely, or they wouldn't have *you* here, ready and waiting.'

Jonaquil flinched at the flare of his anger, seeing the nimbus of life-light about him leap. Since that strange and terrible night with Commander Chayne, she saw the life-lights of all – the flickering, wavery ones of the inmates, the unnaturally vigorous, twinned ones of *them* – with no need to be in trance. 'I received no command to come here, Dara,' she said. She lifted the small bag of remedies and slung it on her shoulder. 'I was drawn here. I am a Healer. It is not for me to decide who I should or should not heal, even in this terrible place.'

The anger drained from Dara and he seemed to slump. 'I know, Healer. It's not your fault. It's *them!*'

There was sudden noise and movement down on the Paudit's bank, and they both turned to look. A squad of demon guards had formed up, pikes at the ready.

They waited. There was a palpable tension in the very air about them. The whole of the Palisade was wound up as tightly as a coiled spring; had been for days now.

'Things are all wrong, Healer,' Dara said wearily. 'Somebody's *out* there.' He shook his head despondently. 'It ought to make things better for us. But it just makes them worse.'

Jonaquil did not know what to say. Dara was right. They had all heard the rumours that accompanied Sub-Commander Gerrid's sudden and unexpected fall from power. Demons in the Peaks. *Something* had happened, that was sure. Those of the Sub-Commander's force that returned at all had done so battered and bloody.

And since then, patrols had been disappearing entirely, simply never returning from the forest. All in the Palisade knew about it.

Small good, however, had come to the Palisade inmates. Recent events, as Dara said, had only made things worse. The demon guards were nervous and bad-tempered. Senseless beatings were becoming commonplace.

Jonaquil glanced back into the compound, where three pathetic figures dangled from a makeshift gallows. Commander Chayne seemed now possessed by a black, enduring rage. On his instructions there were floggings, detentions without food, all for the slightest offence, or no offence at all it seemed sometimes. And the hangings had begun.

Jonaquil shivered sickly, thinking on it.

The work-gangs being herded up the slope had by now all filed past Jonaquil and through the gate. Only Dara still remained. One of the demon guards shoved him on irritably. 'Take care, Healer,' Dara called back over his shoulder, and then he too was gone.

Jonaquil watched him and the others straggle into the compound and crouch there in silent, unmoving groups against the wall, tired men, slouch-shouldered and thin and draggled, worn to nothing but nubs of their former selves. So many bedraggled corpses they might have been, save for the weak flicker of life-light radiance about them.

From out the forest on the Paudit's far bank came several demon guards, Commander Chayne at their head. He splashed across the river, gave a curt command to the Squad Leader of the group arrayed on the near bank, swung on to a horse a guard held waiting for him, and cantered up towards the Palisade. Seeing Jonaquil at the gateway, he reined in abruptly before her, staring coldly at her with the unhuman eyes of that terrible pale hawk's face of his. About him, a dark, double luminance leaped and flared with unnatural spell-helm vigour.

Jonaquil shuddered. What with the confusion of the camp, she had not seen the Commander face to face since that night he had done what he had done to her.

That terrible, strange night . . .

Commander Chayne looked at the remedy bag slung over her shoulder. 'It is convenient that I find you here, Healer,' he said. 'There is an injured guard. Down there.' He gestured to the river with a black-gauntleted hand. 'Go to him. I want him alive long enough to talk.' The Commander's gleaming hawk-face was blank of any readable human expression, but the anger was clear in his voice.

Jonaquil let out a long breath. So it seemed only a hurt man after all. But her belly was clenched in a tight, premonitory knot still. She was left puzzled and uncomfortable. 'What . . . what has happened?'

Commander Chayne eyed her coldly. 'Do as I say, woman. The Squad Leader will tell you what you need to know. Do you have the Healer's supplies you need in that bag?'

Jonaquil nodded.

'Then do as I command.'

He leaned towards her. She heard the *klikk* of his hawk's beak. For one awful moment, she thought he was going to command her to return to his quarters once she had finished tending the hurt guard. But he did not. 'Go,' he ordered, motioning down to the river. 'Go!'

Jonaquil turned and stumbled down the slope.

The Squad Leader met her by the Paudit's shore. 'He said we were to escort you into the forest, Healer. For your safety.'

'Why?' Jonaquil demanded. 'What has been happening out here?' It was a measure of her time here that she could ask questions like this of one of *them*, as she would ask of any normal man, and expect answers. Her status as Healer gave her a certain privilege, and familiarity had eroded the fear of them she had first felt. Familiarity now also made her able to read the unease on the demon-face before her.

'Into the forest with you, Healer,' the Squad Leader said. It was not quite a command, but more than a mere request.

Jonaquil remained where she was, still wishing answers.

'Quickly,' the Squad Leader insisted. '*He* is still up there, watching.'

Jonaquil glanced back over her shoulder. The Commander sat astride his horse at the gateway glaring at them.

She let herself be led down to the river, where the waiting squad of guardsmen formed up as escort, and then she splashed across the icy water of the ford and up towards the forest on the wild further shore.

The trees stood high and dark and thick, looking impenetrable as a wall. Jonaquil remembered the Fey she had seen, or thought she had seen, on her first morning in the Palisade, as she stood outside with Tishta, gazing into the Paudit's wild shore. She shivered, thinking on it.

The Squad Leader urged her onwards. This was the first time Jonaquil had been into the forest. She expected it to be thick and dark as it seemed from beyond, choked with vegetation and oppressive. It was not.

The trees had a sort of massive presence, trunk after rearing trunk woven together into dim obscurity above and on either side of the winding path along which she and the guards picked their way. There was little or no vegetation on the ground, and this gave an odd kind of dim spaciousness. The air was cool, quiet. Blue-green shafts of light slanted softly down.

Jonaquil took a deep breath. She had expected nothing like this. Something opened in her in response.

She had been irrevocably changed by that strange, terrible night with the Commander, changed in ways she was still trying to come to terms with. Since that night, she had grown more sensitive, seeing life-lights always now, feeling the Healer's Sickness in her bones worse than ever, tormented by the memory of what had been done to her, and by the bloody and violent dreams. Yet it was as if her inside had grown, if such a thing could be, giving her a greater capacity to endure such painful things. And there were times when, as on that night, she felt a part of her walked with the stars.

Such a time was this, now. The Healer's Sickness was dwindled, and she stood where she was in the middle of the path, transfixed by the green-leaping spirits of the trees. A luminance filled the wood, and she sensed the great, slow, wise dance of the trees all about her.

'Move along, Healer,' the Squad Leader said.

'It is . . . *beautiful*,' Jonaquil murmured.

The squad leader barked a laugh. 'Beautiful! This wretched place? A man can't see a thing twenty paces in front of him here!' He put a hand on her arm and hurried her along. 'Enough tree-gazing, Healer.'

Jonaquil allowed herself to be hustled along, a little dazed as she was. As she walked onwards, though, she began to feel herself coming more and more alive. This far from the Palisade's human misery, the Healer's Sickness in her was lulled. The coolth of the forest air was like wine. The trees shimmered still, though soft now.

She slowed, drinking all in, and the Squad Leader yanked her along. She shook loose his gauntleted hand. 'What has happened?' she demanded. It was time to make this man-demon properly acknowledge her Healer status. 'I will move no further,' she told him, 'till I receive answers to my questions. What has happened? Why was the Commander so angered?'

The Squad Leader stared at her measuringly, his huge, unhuman eyes wrinkling in irritation. Then he nodded, once, acknowledging her. 'As you will, Healer. We do not know what happened. Men died up ahead here. We don't know how. One of them is still alive, just. The Commander wants you to heal him so he can talk.'

'But how was this man injured? What *happened?*'

'We don't *know!*' he snapped at her, the great, ivory tusks of his mouth showing ominously clearly. 'Now come. We have a distance to go.'

They had come to the edge of a work-clearing by now, where the logging gangs hacked into the forest. The ground along which they walked was carved into ruts where the great trunks had been dragged down to the slipway leading to the river, and masses of trimmed foliage and branches lay piled haphazardly about.

But though this must be familiar territory to the demon guards about her, Jonaquil saw that they moved tensely, eyes flitting from tree to tree, shadow to shadow, as if they expected some terrible creature to leap at them without warning. And her own belly remained tight-knotted still. It was as if there was something in the very air—

A sudden clanking noise made Jonaquil, the Squad Leader, and the entire squad whirl and start momentarily, but it was only the sound of the empty hauling chains as a pair of patient draught-horses was led from the side of the clearing and along the broad path to the slipway and back to the Palisade. It was Tishta leading the horses, Jonaquil saw.

Jonaquil raised a hand in greeting, but the older woman did not look up. Busying herself with the horses, she was quickly gone.

The Squad Leader gestured, and their little troop marched on, silent and tense, leaving the work clearing behind. The forest path dwindled away and they were left having to make their own straggling way through the trees. The Squad Leader consulted with one of the company, adjusting their course by that one's advice.

Onwards they walked.

And then, abruptly, Jonaquil made out two demon-faced guards kneeling next to a tree in the near distance before her. The unnatural double nimbus of their life-lights stuttered and flared. Upon the ground between them lay a third guard, curled in upon himself. In the forest silence, Jonaquil could hear this third one moan, an animal sound of pain.

'We managed to get him this far,' one of the kneeling guards told the Squad Leader as Jonaquil and company drew up, 'but we put him down to change position, and when we lifted him again all he did was scream.' The speaker wrung his hands uncomfortably, his demon-face screwed into an uncertain frown. 'I know Commander Chayne ordered that we should . . .'

'Enough,' the Squad Leader said. 'Let the Healer see to him.'

The two man-demons shifted aside.

The man on the ground moaned. Jonaquil saw the life-light about him flicker and dim. For the first time, she realized that he wore no spell-helm. He had on the scale-mail armour all the demon guards wore, but it was an altogether human face she looked at; a white face, twisted in pain. Blood drooled from the corner of his mouth.

Jonaquil knelt down. The man lay curled in upon himself, arms wrapped tightly about his belly, legs drawn up in a sort of foetal curl. Gently she tugged at one of his arms. The man moaned and resisted, pulling away from her touch and curling more tightly into himself. She had felt bone twisting loosely under flesh when she gripped him. Broken, that arm, badly broken. It must be giving the man agony to keep it pressed to him like that.

What had happened?

Still gentle as could be, she tried to roll him out of his foetal curl and on to his back. He screamed, a long, shrill screech.

Jonaquil perservered. She had witnessed too much pain in recent times to be overly daunted by this man's screams, and if there was any chance of saving him, she must see what the extent of his injuries were. But when, finally, she managed to roll him over, she stared, horrified.

Across his belly, the armour had ruptured, leaving a wet hollow filled with a tangled coil of purple intestines. Only the desperate clutch of the man's hands, fingers splayed out across the tumble of wet intestinal coils, prevented the whole mass from spilling out of his torn abdomen.

Jonaquil shuddered. What could have caused such an awful wound?

After a moment, she ran a questing hand delicately over the area, sensing in herself the hot wet pulse of the torn flesh, the cool, hard serrations of the scale armour that held it. He flinched from her and, flinching, moaned hoarsely. She looked at his face. His eyes were closed. His head rocked to and fro in a kind of spasmatic counterpoint to the moaning.

'Can you do anything for him?' one of the man's hovering companions demanded.

'I am not sure,' Jonaquil replied, though she felt little hope that there was anything she might be able to do.

'What if we carry him in relays back to the Palisade? Never put him down. It's putting him down that hurts him. What if we—'

Jonaquil shook her head. 'The journey would kill him. Certain.'

'But there must be *something* you can do!'

Gazing down at the wounded man, Jonaquil suddenly realized that, hard as she tried, she could see no nimbus of life-light about him now. The man was dying. It was already too late. She stood then and turned to the man-demons beside her. 'There is nothing I can do for him.'

The two stared at her. 'There must be *something!*' one of them insisted. 'You're a Healer!' He approached her, his demon-face twisted menacingly. 'Or are you planning to let him die because he's not one of your own?'

Jonaquil stood her ground. 'I let *no one* die if it is my power to save him.' She pointed to the man on the ground. 'This man lies beyond any help I, or anyone else, can give.'

The complete, open certainty with which Jonaquil said this had its effect. The man-demon before her backed away.

Long moments of stiff silence followed, punctuated only by the wounded man's dying moans.

Then the Squad Leader came forward. 'Can you get him so he can talk, Healer?'

Jonaquil shook her head. 'Look at him. His soul is already half in the Shadowlands. How can—'

'Answer my question!' he snapped. 'Can you get him to talk? Is there some drug or other you might give him?'

Again, Jonaquil shook her head. 'There is nothing. The man is all but dead. Look at him!'

The Squad Leader stared down at the wounded man for a long

moment, turned back to Jonaquil and gave her a hard, appraising look, then nodded. 'So be it, then.' He gestured to the man's two companions. 'You know what has to be done.'

They nodded grimly.

'We must return to the Palisade, and that quickly.'

Still silent, the two nodded once more.

'Do you wish me. . . ?' the Squad Leader said.

'I'll do it myself,' one of the two replied softly. 'He was my friend.'

The Squad Leader beckoned Jonaquil away.

From behind, she heard a voice say, softly, 'Forgive me, friend.' Then there came the tearing sound of iron across flesh, and the moaning was cut off in mid-note.

Jonaquil clenched her fists. With those hideous demon-faces and impossible strength, it was easy to think of *them* as true demons. She was not sure how she felt, witnessing this human aspect of them.

'Come,' the Squad Leader said to her. 'We must return to the Palisade.'

The squad of demon guards about her had formed into a loose double column. They moved off through the forest at a quick dog-trot, carrying the body. Jonaquil jogged along with them as best she might, but she still felt the uncomfortable knot of premonition in her belly. Something was yet to happen.

'Come along, Healer,' the Squad Leader said irritably. 'We must . . .' But he did not finish.

From ahead, came the hail of a voice.

'What is it?' Jonaquil heard somebody near her ask. She stared ahead through the trees, feeling her belly quiver.

But it turned out to be only more familiar man-demons.

'That's Tykso's bunch, isn't it?' a guard next to Jonaquil suggested.

'Don't know. Can't recognize them clear in this cursed tangle of a forest.'

'Looks like . . . Isn't that Sylke?'

'Can't be! His squad was the first to disappear.'

'Looks like Sylke to me.'

The Squad Leader raised his hand. 'What squad?' he called out to the newcomers.

But the only answer he received was a howl and a sudden surge of man-demons from out of the trees on all sides.

Somebody dragged Jonaquil heavily to the ground. She heard shouts, screams, the *ttlang* of iron on iron, the thud of running feet. The same hands that had dragged her to the ground now hauled her up again. 'Run!' somebody shouted at her, pulling her along bodily. 'Run!'

Jonaquil did not know what was happening, could make out nothing of events about her except confusion. She ran.

Skittering downhill, hauled along too fast, she tripped, rolled, thumped painfully against the trunk of a tree. She struggled to her feet and kept running, her heart hammering in her breast. But somehow, in her fall, she had become turned about and confused and found herself alone and utterly lost in amongst the trees, with the sounds of fighting dwindled into the distance.

And then there was silence.

Jonaquil stood leaned against a tree, panting, confused, her heart hammering still.

She heard a noise behind her and whirled. It was one of the demon guards. She waited for him to beckon, to say something. He did neither. Instead, seeing her, he bounded forwards, grabbed her up, flung her over his shoulder like a sack of flour, and cantered off back the way he had come.

Hanging head downwards, Jonaquil beat at his armoured back with her fists in outrage, her heart hammering. She had never been treated like this before. But it was pointless to struggle, she knew that. The demon-strength of *them* was well beyond anything she might be able to resist. There was nothing she might do.

He ran with her through the forest, running with the impossible strength and endurance that *they* possessed. In no long time, they were back to where it had begun. She was dumped to the ground, struggled back to her feet, furious.

Jonaquil stared, shocked.

The ground was littered with dead man-demons. And stripping the dead . . .

Human men!

But standing about were more man-demons. It made no sense.

One of the demons came towards her, a Squad Leader by his raiment. 'Good,' this one said to her captor. 'You found her. Bring her along. Quick.'

The demon reached to lift her again but she fended him away. 'I can walk!'

He would have ignored her, but the other gestured him back. 'Let her walk if she pleases.'

'What has *happened* here?' Jonaquil demanded.

'None of this concerns you, woman. Do as you are told and you will not be hurt.'

Jonaquil stared at him, shocked. 'Who *are* you?'

The strange Squad Leader smiled, lips peeling back from the great tusks set in his mouth. 'We are those who will rid this land of *them* forever. We are liberators, woman. And you are going to help us.'

Jonaquil did not understand. 'Why,' she demanded of him, 'would you want to free us from your own kind?'

'Not *my* kind, woman!' he snapped back. 'I may look like one of *them*, but I assure you appearances are deceptive. Aye, you may best believe *that* indeed. We are not *them*. Nothing like *them!*' The man-demon stopped, turned to her, and lifted off the spell-helm he wore.

Jonaquil saw a human face, thin, tired-looking. One ear was half missing and mangled. 'My name is Hawl,' the man said. 'I lost family, friends, village, everything to *them*. Now is the time of our revenge!' He put his helm back on, and once again it was the all-too-familiar demon features she faced, not the man. 'Come,' he said, gripping her by the arm. 'We must hurry.'

He strode onwards, moving at a pace Jonaquil found hard to match, ignoring entirely any questions she tried posing him.

A group of demon guards crouched at the forest's verge. Yet her guide did not hesitate to join this group. It must be the other-*them*. It was most confusing, this.

'I do not like it,' one of the other-*them* was saying. 'There is too much improvising in all of this. What if it all goes wrong? What then? We shall have no second chance.'

'And no better chance than this one now, Jordie,' another insisted. 'We *must* take it. Now!'

'Aye,' another agreed. 'Perhaps the Powers are working in our favour in all of this. Another opportunity like this is unlikely.'

They turned, hearing Jonaquil and her guide approach. 'Good!' somebody said. 'You have her.'

Jonaquil moved up the sloping rise leading from the Paudit river to the Palisade. About her strode a squad of demon guards. But it was the other-*them* surrounding her.

'Not too fast, woman,' one of them said. 'We must arouse no suspicion in the Palisade.'

Jonaquil was seething. These men behaved worse than *them*, if such a thing were possible, ordering her about with an infuriating arrogance and explaining nothing. But she swallowed her irritation, and slowed her walk a little, playing her part in the plan these self-styled 'liberators' refused to explain.

She was to be the key they would use to unlock the Palisade. She could see that much clearly enough. With her, a familiar and easily recognizable figure, the squad that accompanied her could walk right in through the gates. Outwardly, it must seem the same squad that had gone with her into the forest, the one apparent addition being the body they carried. Only Jonaquil knew that the demon-helms were worn now by other souls.

She walked onwards.

At the entrance, they were met by the gate-guards. 'Dead!' The word went round as all saw the body plain. Demon guards and inmates began to crowd the gateway, curious, shocked. Man-demons muttered angrily, seeing the state of their fallen comrade. In the chaotic press of the crowd, growing more confused by the moment, one of *them* was hard jostled by an inmate. He lashed out, left the man screaming, a long, bleeding gash across his face.

There was an angry surge, an ugly rumbling of voices. But a cry from the walls brought all to a halt, and turned every eye towards the river.

Marching up the sward leading to the Palisade came a troop of man-demons.

'Who is it?' Jonaquil heard a demon guard next to her ask.

'What can they be doing here?'

'Where are they from?'

The Squad Leader of the gate-guards ordered his men to close the gates. 'Things are too unsettled to take chances,' he told them. 'I don't like this. Strange companies coming out of the forest. We will wait for Commander Chayne's orders before admitting anybody.'

But when his men tried to carry out his order, they were stopped by the other-*them*. Scuffling broke out. A pike swung up, came down, somebody cried out.

'Stop!' the gate-guard Squad Leader cried. 'What do you think you're about? *Fools*! Stop it!' But before he could do anything further, a pike-blade took him under the chin, carrying off spell-helm, head, and all in a wet cascade.

Outside the Palisade, the troop came on at a dead run.

They hit the still-open gateway like a storm wave, smashing back all before them, demon guards and inmates alike, driving onwards with triumphant howls, leaping and lunging like true, irresistible demons. And among them, suddenly, Jonaquil saw—

At first she could not credit her eyes.

A man, no demon, a huge man, swinging a great, double-bladed axe, howling demonically and hewing down all before him.

Jonaquil fell back and away, as did the other inmates. Those that could not were smashed under the feet of the fighting demons.

It was shrieking bedlam all about, mud puddling red with blood. Iron blades *tlaanged*, spitting sparks. The hideous, demon-tusked faces grew contorted with fury.

'Bloodaxe!' voices howled. 'Bloodaxe! Bloodaxe!'

The great axe rose defiantly, bloody and grim.

It was the image Jonaquil had seen in the dreams. Demon against demon, the bloody axe raised on high.

A hard hand suddenly thumped Jonaquil as she stood staring, took her by the shoulder and shoved her backwards against the log wall. Looking about, she saw Commander Chayne astride his horse, silver hawk's face glinting coldly in the sun, shouting commands.

Nearer to hand, a Squad Leader called out, 'Clear the area! The Commander wants inmates rounded up and kept under guard at the far end of the compound. Clear the area!'

Jonaquil felt the rough shove of one of *them* once again. Other inmates were being herded about her. Demon guards hustled the people towards the back end of the enclosure, hastening them onwards brutally with the butts of their pikes at any sign of resistance.

The fighting at the gateway still raged.

Commander Chayne cantered close by where the inmates were herded. He leaned from the saddle to give further orders to an under-officer, then wheeled his horse and gazed towards the gateway. Most of the Palisade's demon guards were engaged at the gate now.

A rumble went up from the crowded inmates, an angry, sullen communal muttering, and they began to surge haphazardly against their guards.

The demons beat them back.

Commander Chayne called commands to the gateway, keeping his vantage point, ignoring totally the confusion at his back.

A lone inmate managed to slip free of the cordon of demon guards. He was quickly cut down. But others followed, scattering like rabbits. One of them, fleeing the guards, saw the Commander's back still turned. He made a great, desperate, running leap, and landed astride the Commander's horse, full against Chayne's back.

The Commander swung round and viciously backhanded the man away. But the impact had been so unexpected that he, too, was swept out of the saddle and fell sprawling to the ground.

Seeing him there, like that, on his back, momentarily helpless, the inmates let out a great, bestial cry. The hated Commander, the one responsible for the miseries in their lives, the one they hated above all others, was momentarily helpless.

They broke forwards in a chaotic, howling mass. The suddenness of it took the demon guards by surprise, and the inmates swept through them by main force of bodies.

Commander Chayne looked up, had one instant to realize what was happening, and was then overwhelmed.

He managed to half rise and fling away the first of those to attack. But more hands reached for him, hauling him down. His pale hawk's visage showed clear for one final moment, then it was ripped from his head, and Jonaquil saw his man's face, hard-featured as the hawk's, almost. He raised himself above the crawling mass about him, shouting for help, but no help came. Guards could not get through the furious press of people about him. They beat viciously at backs and heads and arms. But it was too late. Commander Chayne went down, torn apart in a storm of bitter hate.

And that storm enveloped the Palisade entirely.

'*Get* the bastards!' somebody in the crowd shrieked. Somebody else lunged foward and flung himself upon the nearest demon guard. Jonaquil saw the poor man spitted like a joint of meat by the guard's pike; but as he went down, wailing, the weapon was yanked from the guard's hand and three more inmates promptly leaped upon him and beat him to the ground.

The enclosure became an abrupt, boiling mass of bodies. The weeks of hardship and unending toil had left such a bitter residue that once it had begun, once the opportunity was offered to strike back at their oppressors, the inmates went quite berserk. They screamed and shrieked like crazed beasts, tearing the demon guards down and beating them, ripping the spell-helms from their heads, kicking them, stabbing them with their own weapons, striking out, striking back, venting the hatred that had been building in them all the days of their captivity here.

Feeling sick, Jonaquil backed clumsily from the fighting and stumbled off along the wooden pales towards the back side of the enclosure. Once far enough away, she stopped, panting. It was like the end of the world, screams and shrieks everywhere, blood and dying.

She felt the rush of bodies go past her then. Looking up, she saw Sub-Commander Gerrid come racing along, followed by a handful of man-demons. The Sub-Commander's feline visage was twisted in a snarl. Jonaquil expected him to fall upon the inmates, to lead a charge to the gateway, something of the sort. But no. Instead, he and those few he led made for the Palisade's back wall. Once there, they flung wooden ladders against it, preparing to swarm up and over the paling.

'Hurry!' she heard Gerrid call. 'Chayne has doomed himself with his own stupidity. This place is fallen! Hurry!'

A nearby demon guard attempted to bar their way, stepping in front of one of the ladders. The Sub-Commander cut him down.

'Hurry!' Gerrid exhorted once more. Then he and the rest were over the high wall and gone.

The fighting by now had spread out from the gateway, demons and other-demons hacking and hewing at each other. Inmates skittered about like stinging insects, howling their hate and taking whatever vengeance circumstances allowed.

Jonaquil shuddered, her sensitive Healer's flesh clenched in agony. Crouched against the rough wood of the wall, she rocked back and forth, moaning. She felt something press against her. Squinting to see, she made out a young boy, one of the camp's ragged youngsters, who scrunched himself against her, whimpering. She put an arm about him. Soon others joined them, children, women, men. All those not filled entire with hatred and the battle-madness gravitated to this eddy in the chaos.

About them, the fighting raged. There was no clear sense to it, no manner to tell friend from foe. It seemed an insanity of violence. *They* died, spitted on pikes, hacked by wet blades. But others died too, choking in their own blood, crawling on shattered limbs, howling.

Jonaquil saw not just men and man-demons hacking at each other, but saw also the queer double lights of *them*, the glowing life-lights of the men, man-light and demon-light intertwined, fizzling, shooting, flaring up in great gouts of terrible colour, shadowed by the lunging, dark iron of the pike-blades.

And then, witnessing this, she began to realize that some terrible thing was wrong here. The struggle for victory was over, the battle won. *They* had been reduced to nothing but a shattered remnant. But the fighting continued unabated. She witnessed the other-*them* begin to turn upon demon and human inmate alike, saw inmate attack inmate in senseless frenzy, like a pack of wild things gone insane with killing rage.

The people about Jonaquil cowered in terror. She tried to calm them, patting arms, hugging the children, reassuring them that all would be well.

But the fighting drew inexorably closer, blood and iron and shrieking.

The end, it seemed. Jonaquil drew a shuddering breath. Her dreams come horribly, horribly true.

And yet . . .

Yet there had been more to her dreams than only this madness of blood and violence. She remembered the old woman with a long, braided rope of white hair, and moss-green eyes in a face wrinkled as a dried apple; a man furred like an otter; a bird with a queerly human face; a young man, dark-haired, glowing like a torch in dark air . . .

And what of the Fey? She had almost forgot that one, for only the once had she dreamed of her, or him. What of the promise she had felt from the Fey?

Jonaquil knew herself to be no true-dreamer. Her gifts lay in other areas. But this recurring dream could be no ordinary one. And there was, somehow, a growing feeling in her of incompleteness in the events about her; a conviction that, despite all appearances, this was not, indeed, the end of things at all. In the midst of the human destruction all about, she began to feel hope.

A child at Jonquil's side wailed. Unthinking, Jonaquil reached out. Seeing the poor little thing's life-light madly swirling, she spread her own radiance about the child's, calmingly.

And then about the next child, and the next.

It was a new thing to Jonaquil, this gentle blanketing of another's life-light. But then she had never been so acutely aware of that living glow as she was now. Breathing fear in, Jonaquil breathed out calm. She tried to think herself of the stars, the trees, the enduring earth herself. The children's wildly jittering life-lights began to smooth themselves. Jonaquil expanded herself further, seeing the radiance flow slowly from her like glowing honey, and those about her, all unawares, began to settle. The terror in them dwindled. The group as a whole settled more comfortably against each other. They breathed a long, communal sigh.

Jonaquil's small band sat still, like an axle about which the wheel of the fighting revolved.

Then two demons tumbled towards them, grappled together, howling. They burst in upon Jonaquil's enveloping radiance in a leaping thrust of wild light. The demons' life-lights faltered, flared, calmed. The two of them fell apart, blinking their huge, unhuman eyes confusedly.

At the centre, Jonaquil sensed a growing focus of will amongst those about her as, all unknowing, the group willed an end to the conflict. Jonaquil urged the glowing radiance encompassing them to expand. It was her life-light, and yet not only just hers now. It was her will that made it expand, and yet not only hers. Like a slow spreading wave, the radiance soaked over the shouting chaos of the Palisade.

The terrible roil and bursting flare of the battling life-lights began to settle.

Men and man-demons lowered their weapons haltingly, gasped, blinked, stared about them like lost souls.

A strange, startled silence slowly settled in over everybody.

Long moments went by.

And then, 'We're . . . free,' a voice whispered.

The place was so silent that the words, whispered hoarsely though they were, carried clearly. 'Free,' somebody else repeated. *'Free!'* A great, communal, wordless shout went up from the inmates then. People hugged each other, swung each other around by the arms, wept, danced and leaped, and spun about hysterically.

Then the jubilant inmates noticed a swarm of demons coming from the gateway. Silence fell once more, a tense silence.

But, one by one, the demons removed their helms, flinging them high in the air in celebration and catching them again. 'Free!' they shouted. 'Free!'

The inmates shook their heads confusedly – only Jonaquil knew anything of the identity of these other-demons – but that 'free' rang through the Palisade like a cleansing spell.

Jonaquil felt the thrill of it move through her.

She gazed about, breathless with all that had occurred, searching the crowd. Perhaps the rest of her dream, too, might become true before her eyes – the green-eyed woman and her strange companions. But all Jonaquil saw was the axe-wielding man. A human man he was, certainly, but there was something not quite right with him. A queer double kind of life-light flickered crazily about him. It made Jonaquil shudder sickly to see it.

He was hugely tall and broad, red-haired, and familiar somehow. As he drew closer, she could see that his arms and face were scored by a ragged pattern of scars. She searched her memory. Surely, if she knew this man, she would remember seeing those scars before. But she could not.

'Jonaquil!' a voice called suddenly.

Turning, Jonaquil saw a young woman with an infant on her hip. For a long moment, the woman was naught but a stranger to her. Then, with a start, Jonaquil recognized her. 'Inda?' she said. 'Inda! It *is* you. And the child too!'

Indeed it was Inda, with the child she had carried from Woodend that very day of his birth. Twenty years ago, it seemed now. But the child looked well enough. Gaunt-faced, perhaps, but then so were they all.

'Healer!' Another voice called out.

Looking round, Jonaquil saw old grey-haired Tirry.

'Jonaquil!' she heard once again, before she could say anything to Tirry, and suddenly it was a Woodend reunion. Others came along, looking for family and friends. From out of the crowd, more villagers appeared, and Jonaquil found herself in the midst of a whirlpool of laugher and greetings.

Dara came up.

'Mayor?' old Tirry said. 'Dara, is that *you?*'

The once Mayor of Woodend shrugged. Lean and hollow-cheeked now, he little resembled the corpulent man Tirry had once known. 'Tirry,' he said, his voice wavering. 'Tirry. It's *good* to see you hale and whole.' The two men embraced.

Jonaquil saw Guthrie and Inda holding each other, and that simple tableaux of husband, wife and child brought tears to her eyes, such a precious thing it was in this place.

All across the Palisade's central enclosure, scenes of reunion similar to the Woodenders' had been happening. The compound was a sea of laughter, excitement, and tears. Now, as Jonaquil looked around her, she saw that a kind of order was being introduced. By the gateway the newcomers had gathered. 'Egil!' voices called. 'Egil!'

Jonaquil stared. The big red-headed man with the gory axe and scarred face . . . Could this be Big Egil, whose cabin on the village outskirts had been fired by *them?* For all his height and bulk, he was thin now almost to emaciation. And the scars: how had he got those terrible scars? A changed man, he was. Once again, Jonaquil had a sense of something not quite right about him.

Somebody next to Jonaquil had also heard Egil's name being called. 'It's Egil,' he cried, pointing. 'Look! It's Big Egil.'

The gathered Woodenders stared.

Somebody shouted loudly enough to carry across the compound. 'Egil! Egil. Over here!'

The man turned and stared at them. Jonaquil saw in his face none of the familiar features she remembered, only a strange, animal ferocity.

'What's *wrong* with him?' somebody demanded. 'Doesn't he see us?'

But Egil made no move to draw near them.

Jonaquil heard somebody else say, softly, 'The poor man. The *poor* man, losing his family like that. And look at those scars . . .' and she could not help but feel the same way.

It sobered them, this apparition of an old and familiar face, but one so changed that he no longer could, or no longer would acknowledge them.

As she stood there, a man came rushing up to her. 'Healer,' he panted, tugging on her arm. 'Come quickly.'

All around her were hurt and wounded. Her own flesh was

quivering now with reflected agony. She turned and hurried off towards the dispensary, stopping to examine this one or that, shaking her head, swinging between hope and sick worry as she examined wounds.

Freedom had come upon them this day. But at what price?

# XXVII

# In the North Wold

'There . . .'

Tai turned, blinking, and looked.

'There,' the Dreamwalker repeated softly.

Above the sloping meadow before them, a lone crow slow-winged its way gracefully through the air. The Dreamwalker's stick marked its flight. 'How does the crow fly?' she said. 'Where does she get the feathered grace to dance upon the wind? It is the Powers, those same Powers that move through thee and me and the world. Look at her flight! See how she rides the currents of the wind, balancing, balancing, letting the wind take her, taking the wind with her.'

Dreamwalker turned and looked at Tai. He returned her gaze for a moment, then looked away. The old woman put a hand gently on his arm. 'Just as the crow balances on the river of the wind, so our spirits balance on the river of our lives.'

The bird wheeled above them, her dark pinions spread like long fingers to stroke the wind. 'Feel the human echo of the crow within thee,' Dreamwalker said. 'Look at her! She and the wind are one, balanced, united, one singleness through which the Powers move. Feel the connection, the sameness, between thine own thoughts and the flight of the bird—'

Tai cut her off. 'It means nothing to me, Dreamwalker. Just words. Empty words.'

The old woman gazed at him, her moss-green eyes narrowed. 'Thou is an ordinary man no longer. Thou must *learn*.'

'I do not know what I must do.'

'Be like the crow . . .'

'Words!' Tai snapped exasperatedly. He stopped walking and stood there, eyes closed. All about him, he could *sense* the world. It was like sensing bones under flesh, and yet not like that at all. Nothing to do with his body senses, his world senses, yet he 'saw', his mind having no other manner of interpreting the hidden patterns all around him: the upwards-reaching of the grass underfoot; the pulse of Dreamwalker's people and the twined glow of Skeefer and Ree ahead; the arc of the crow in the sky; Dreamwalker herself, quiet at his side; and the great, intricate, pulsing sweep of the wide world, going away and towards them, within and without them, stretching beyond, deeper or higher or further than he could sense.

Tai opened his eyes, saw the ordinary familiar world as he always had. Yet under it, or in it, or shadowed by it – he did not know how to express what he sensed – was the other, the underskeleton, the deeper patterns.

He still experienced, sometimes, a remnant of the nauseating terror that had always marked the fits. Sometimes the transition came too suddenly: one instant he stood in the familiar solid world, the next a moving bulk of shadow-patterns, like some great beast, was upon him. But the fits were gone.

Or, rather, he was gone beyond such fits. That which he had denied all his life had risen up to overwhelm him. In the queer halfway realm of the Shadowlands, he had battled the beast and lost, and in losing had won.

For what had haunted him all his young life was not the utter dissolution he had feared, but something entirely other. The world was not as he had thought it to be, not solid and simple. Each fit had plunged him partially beyond the ordinary solidness of the world. But, terrified as he had been, he had always struggled back. Now, he had fallen entirely through the ordinary world, and instead of the terrible, formless chaos he had once feared so, he had found instead that the 'underside' was actually full of pulsing complexity. The once familiar and solid world was no more than a manner of façade.

He was changed for ever.

'True-seeing-man,' Dreamwalker called him. Because, she said, he could see now into the world's soul.

But it was more than merely 'seeing'. He found he could . . . *change* the world. This *sensing* of his could be a *doing* thing. He *reached* and altered the manner of the crow's flight, holding dual vision and watching with his world-eyes as the bird veered suddenly. Aye, he could do such things, but he found it wearied him. After the troop of man-demons that had trailed them from Long Harbour were destroyed, he had lain for days in the wild camp of Dreamwalker's people, weak as any new-born babe.

He did not know, yet, what he could do.

'Come,' Dreamwalker said gently, bringing him out of himself. 'We must keep walking.'

Tai blinked, shook himself. The wound across his forehead itched and he scratched it, gently. The stitches were gone now, snipped away by Dreamwalker's careful hands. He could feel the puckered scarring the stitches had left. Dreamwalker looked at him inquiringly, waiting. He nodded, and they walked onwards.

The green expanse of the North Wold lay spread round about them, leagues of rolling grassland. They were following the bank of a feeder-stream southwards towards the River Whitewash, which ran, a glittering ribbon they could just catch glimpses of now, in the far distance. Behind them, the blue teeth of the Bone Peaks reared themselves into the sky. A cool northerly breeze tousled the meadow-grass all about. The sun shone warm. Ahead, Dreamwalker's people moved lightly through the knee-high green.

Tai watched Skeefer plunge happily into the river, moving with the unconscious grace of an otter, sputtering with laughter as Ree darted about him. It was enough for those two, this simple freedom of the day; to be able to walk, to dive into the river's current and out again, to fly in freedom, to laugh.

Tai envied them their innocence.

Somehow, through the patternings he was now so sensitive to, he could *sense* the long pull drawing him and the others southwards towards the Whitewash. It was like being upon a steep slope, all movement tiring and difficult except that which took them downhill.

But where, and into what were they being drawn?

Dreamwalker felt that pull too, Tai knew. She led her people southwards by it. But all she would say by way of explanation was, 'It is of the Dream, man, and will reveal itself when it reveals itself.'

Which explanation Tai found no help at all.

As Dreamwalker said, he was no longer an ordinary man. He had to learn all over again how to live. But all her talk of crows and such-like meant nothing to him. He could find no 'echo' of the crow within himself.

And he was no happier for all this new 'gift' that was his. For all the change in him, the world remained the same. Colby lay in captivity still, *they* ruled unchecked, and in the Miradore a featureless, limbless Lord Veil still lay.

A sudden, twittering cry from Ree brought Tai back to his surroundings.

'What is it?' Dreamwalker called.

'Over there. Oh, come quickly. Come!' and then Ree was gone, darting off on the wind, along the river's bank, towards a low mound that lay ahead of them. Tai squinted ahead, staring, but could see nothing save vague, moving shapes.

He shivered uneasily, slipping into that other mode of perception, feeling the shift and flow of previously hidden patterns. Distance seemed to make less difference when he perceived the world in this manner. What his world-eyes had been able to see only as vague, far-off shapes, he could now *sense* clearly. Ahead, figures moved, braided each to each in some sort of mutual web. And they circled about something possessively, these beings; about something that had no life-sense left.

Drawing closer, Tai saw them with his world-eyes. On the crest of the low mound that lay ahead by the river's bank were the slinking shapes of several wolves, and two limp corpses. They were human, those dead. The sad shape of a stiff arm stuck up from the turf that covered the mound.

Unthinking, Tai *reached*, intent on destroying the beasts. He had a farm-lad's fear of wolves.

But a hand on his arm, and the will behind the hand, constrained him. 'They have not hurt thee,' a voice said softly at his side, Dreamwalker's voice. 'Why does thou wish them harm?'

Tai shook himself, came out of the 'otherness', and turned to the old woman. Without realizing it, he had drawn the knife he now wore, a blade he had taken from one of the dead man-demons they had left behind them when they quitted the forest.

'Those are *wolves* up there!' he said. 'We had to deal with their kind every winter in the south. Sheep-thieves and worse, they are.'

'Does killing mean so little to thee, man, that thou would do it so easy here?'

Tai shrugged, uneasy.

'I know these four-legged hunters, too,' Dreamwalker continued. 'And I tell thee there is no need for such violence.' With this, she started forwards, towards the wolves.

'Wait!' Tai said.

'I wish to find out what it is they have found, these eaters-of-anything.'

Tai stared. 'You are just going to walk up there?'

Dreamwalker nodded. 'They will do me no harm.'

Tai looked about him, hoping for support in stopping this craziness, expecting to see Dreamwalker's people tense and uneasy in the wolves' presence. But no. They evidenced no signs of nervousness, simply gazed up at the mound and the wolves as if such were an ordinary, everyday sight. Staring at the wolves, Tai hefted the knife in his hand. 'I shall come with you, then.'

Dreamwalker looked at him, her green eyes narrowed, then nodded. 'But if thou must bring *that* with thee – ' gesturing to the knife – 'then promise that thou will not use it unless I tell thee to.'

Tai shook his head. 'You don't know what you—'

'Promise me!'

Tai shook his head, sighed, sheathed the knife. 'As you wish.'

The old woman nodded, then headed up the long, grassy slope. There were five wolves: big, grey-furred animals with sharp ivory teeth and bright eyes. All five pairs of eyes turned unblinkingly.

Dreamwalker halted about twenty paces from them. They shifted about uneasily. The biggest of them padded a few steps towards her and stood glaring, his head hung low, fangs shown in a snarl, growling deep in his chest.

'Go away,' Dreamwalker said. She spoke as if she were addressing a group of wayward children. 'We only wish to look. Thou may come back for thy meat when we have finished.'

The creatures stared at her.

She strode right up to them, waving her stick, not pausing at all in her steady advance. 'We want none of thy meat. Thou may come back. But go now. *Go*!' As she drew close, they melted away from her, growling, but slinking aside like chastened puppies until eventually they came to rest in a circle about thirty paces from the bodies, seated on their haunches like a pack of huge dogs, tongues lolling.

Tai shook his head in amazement.

Dreamwalker gestured, and Tai and several of the others came up. He heard Ree skitter in the air above him, nervous at the wolves, yet curious, too. Skeefer sidled up, the frown on his face showing clearly how uneasy the situation made him.

Tai looked at the dead, an older man and a younger. They might have been father and son. Villagers from somewhere in the Wold, by their clothing, what there was of it left. They were not pretty.

'This morning,' Dreamwalker said. 'They cannot have been here any longer.' She pointed to the older man. 'This one had his skull split by something.'

'But what happened here?' Tai demanded. 'Who are these two? Who *did* this?'

One of Dreamwalker's people cast about, feeling the grass. 'These two camped here, overnight,' he said. 'They were surprised, at dawn probably. Look. See here the marks of the attackers in the grass?'

Tai looked, but could see nothing special, just grass.

'Heavy feet . . .' a young woman said softly.

'It hass the sstink of *them*, thiss place!' Skeefer spat. '*They* did thiss.'

Tai looked across at Dreamwalker. The old woman nodded. 'That is what it would seem.'

The sad dead lay before him, no more than meat now. The split skull was just the sort of wound one of *their* war pikes would leave. There was no sign of weapons of any sort, no sign that these two might have been armed. Tai could not read the grass as Dreamwalker's people might, but he could read enough so it seemed plain that these poor souls had been killed with little or no struggle. Two more, nameless and innocent, dead at *their* hands.

Tai clenched his fists. 'Death and destruction, blood and pain, that is all *they* ever brought to this land. A curse on them!'

Skeefer hissed in agreement.

Tai scratched at his chin, staring sadly down at the bedraggled figures of the dead. 'We must bury them.'

'No,' Dreamwalker said. She gestured at the hovering wolves. 'The meat is theirs.'

'What?'

'It is the way, man,' she said mildly.

Tai glared, outraged. He could *reach* the wolves, snuff out their hungry lives. He could make things happen here the way they ought to.

But Dreamwalker had turned from him and was already striding away, her people with her.

Tai, too, felt the long pulling southwards that drew them. He sighed and made the blessing sign over the two ragged corpses. 'A scathless journey in the darkness, friends,' he whispered. 'A scathless journey and a fruitful end. Gone from the world of living ken. Into the Shadowlands to begin again.' It relieved him, a little, being thus able to recite the death litany for them. No person deserved to have to make that last journey unblessed.

The wolves were beginning to edge closer now. Tai slipped away and down the mound, following Dreamwalker and the others. He felt the familiar, helpless anger light in him. *They* had done this, just as *they* had done so much else. If he could, Tai would destroy all of them, utterly, completely, for ever.

If he could—

Tai stopped suddenly.

Perhaps he could ... He thought of how he had snuffed out the spell-helms during that strange battle in which the man-demons trailing them from Long Harbour had been destroyed, of how he had begun to reach out, unthinking, to snuff out the wolves' lives.

Could he do it to *them*? Snuff them out like so many candles. Rid the land of them entirely?

He did not know.

He felt the heat of the anger in him, the strength of it. While that anger blazed in him like this he felt he *could* destroy all of them. By himself, with no help needed save for that anger.

All he asked was to be brought close to those who had done this killing here. That was all. And then he would see what he might do. And they would see what he might do. He yearned for such a meeting, burned for it . . .

A hand gripped his arm, bringing him out of himself. 'Be careful,' Dreamwalker said. 'Be careful how thou moves the world.'

Tai looked at her uncomprehendingly.

'Thou is no ordinary man now. When thou *reaches* like that, thou must be very careful. Thou must only change the world when the world blows change through thee.'

Tai shook his head.

'Thou must learn, man. Remember the crow.'

Tai shook off her hand, which had remained on his arm, and turned from her. 'You make no sense, old woman.'

'Beware what thou brings upon thyself.'

He ignored her, marching angrily through the grass. No more need he let such acts as this he had just witnessed go unavenged. No longer was he helpless. He felt as a torch, burning, and he ached to set loose the destruction of that fire within him.

They continued on towards the Whitewash, Tai out ahead. The anger burned unrelentingly in him. He did not know which way he was going, and yet, somehow, he knew.

After a time, Tai saw the smoke of the cookfires in the distance. He felt towards those fires with his other-awareness, and *sensed* clearly the strange, entwined, double pulse of *them*.

The anger flared in him.

He ploughed onwards towards the fires, caring not whether *they* saw him, leaving Dreamwalker, Skeefer and Ree, and the rest forgotten behind. He felt the ache of destruction within him.

It was a large force of man-demons, on the move across the Wold, it seemed, and halted for a rest break. Demon-faced guards stood watch beyond the makeshift camp. As Tai drew near, they gazed at him with their inhuman eyes, but made no move towards him.

For a fleeting moment, Tai wondered at this. It was not what he would expect from them. But he gave it little thought. Slipping into that other-awareness, he *reached* to the nearest demon guard and, with the full power of his anger, snuffed away the double pulse that marked helm and human life intertwined, crumpling it as a man might crumple a brittle leaf in his hand.

The guard fell bonelessly to the ground, dead in an instant.

Tai felt the triumph mount in him. He *reached* to another guard, another, another still, tearing the the life from helm and man, leaving only gutted corpses.

His awareness spread out. He could do it. He *would* do it! He would kill all of them. He began to fashion a kind of net from his anger, spreading it over the camp, drawing all into it so that he might destroy each and every one of them.

But then, with sudden unexpectedness, he sensed *men*.

Ordinary human men.

It shook him, for he had almost drawn these men into his death-net along with the man-demons.

The shock of it snapped Tai out of that other-awareness, and with his world-eyes, he could now see the confusion his killings had caused. Demon-faced guards ran here and there, shouting questions, staring at their dead fellows. But amongst them ran also men, ordinary men. They were dressed in tatters, these men, but they went armed with swords, axes, even with the men-demons' war-pikes. And they stared with equal confusion upon the dead guards, and shouted questions equally. And they seemed on equal terms with *them*.

Tai's anger sputtered. He stared about him, not understanding.

'Find who did this!' he heard a voice cry. It was a man who gave this command. Dressed in scale armour like one of *them* he was, but a man, nevertheless, grim-faced, only a gristled nub left of one ear.

Shaken as he was, it took Tai a long few moments to realize the strange thing that was happening. All about him, men-demons and men were searching. Yet he stood clear in their midst and they did not seem to see him at all.

What was wrong with them? How could such a thing be?

At his side, suddenly, he heard Dreamwalker's voice. 'I have turned their eyes from us, man.'

He started, having had no sense of her near him at all.

'They look, but not at thee or me.'

It was true. Those about looked everywhere but directly at him. If their gaze chanced to fall upon him, their eyes skittered aside. Heads turned away, men-demons slithered aside to pass them.

It was most, most strange.

'But how . . . *how* could it have happened?' he heard a man-demon demand.

''Twas a sorcerer, I tell you,' one of the men said. 'I *saw* him. Twice as tall as any normal man, he was. With eyes like great lanterns.'

'Sorcerer!' somebody else snorted scathingly.

'How else do you explain poor Mowdy's death?' asked a man-demon.

'Only the stupid would believe in a lantern-eyed killer sorcerer that disappears into the air!' said a man standing next to the demon.

'Are you calling me stupid?' demanded the demon.

'Piss off,' the man said and walked away.

'Come,' Dreamwalker hissed in Tai's ear. 'We must leave.'

Tai resisted. His anger was all but forgotten. 'What is happening here?' he demanded. 'How can it be that men keep equal company with *them*? What is *happening* here?'

An insistent pull on his arm was all the reply he got from Dreamwalker.

And then, across the far side of the camp, he saw something that shook him further. A woman walked into view there. She had a strong, big-eyed face framed by long auburn hair. She was staring directly at him.

Slipping momentarily into his other-awareness, he sensed the life of her glowing more strongly, more brightly than all those about her.

'What is she?' he whispered uneasily to Dreamwalker at his side. 'How is it she sees us when none of the others can?'

Dreamwalker, too, was staring. 'She is a . . . a Healing-woman.'

'How do you know? Do you know her?'

Dreamwalker shook her head. 'It is a thing of the Dream, man.' Then, before Tai could do or say anything further, she took him resolutely by the arm and steered him out and away from the camp.

The woman who had seen them followed at a tangent, her face pale, eyes fixed unwaveringly upon them.

Their paths intersected beyond the fringe of the fires, by a small hill that gave them shelter from the eyes in the camp itself.

Dreamwalker waited, standing one-legged, the insole of her left foot snug up against the inside of her right knee, balanced against her stick. 'We see thee, Healing-woman,' she said in the greeting of her folk.

The woman stared at them. 'Who . . . who are you?' She shuddered. '*What* are you to mask yourselves from other's eyes, and to bring death with you so easily?'

Tai looked at her, seeing the tousled auburn hair, the big eyes, the weary firmness of the face. And he *sensed* some special flare of life about her. 'Who are *you*?' he returned.

She stared at him, tense and uneasy. 'You glow with anger, stranger.'

Tai felt it leap suddenly in him once more. 'Anger at *them*! The cursed invaders from the south. The invaders *you* serve!'

The woman looked at him steadily. 'Those in this camp are not from the south. This is not one of *their* camps.'

'Don't lie to me, woman! Do you think me blind and stupid?'

'Not blind, anyway,' she said.

Tai took a step towards her, the anger in him rising once more. He began to *reach* for her, but Dreamwalker's grip pulled him to a halt.

'*Stop* it!' she hissed. For the first time ever, he heard something like true anger in her voice. It shook him.

'Forgive him,' Dreamwalker said to the woman. 'He does not yet know what he is.'

The woman nodded. She had not moved, but her eyes were slitted now, like a nervous cat's.

'I am Dreamwalker,' the old woman went on. 'At least, that is my use-name. My true-name is . . . Crane.' Dreamwalker smiled. 'A true-name is power, friend. Use me gently.'

The woman smiled tentatively back. 'My name is Jonaquil. And I would never . . . *use* you, Lady.'

Dreamwalker said, softly, 'We recognize each other, thou and I. The Powers' work it is. I have seen thee, as, I think, thou has seen me. In the Dream.'

Jonaquil nodded. 'Aye. You and . . . others.'

Tai interrupted, pointing an accusing finger at Jonaquil. 'You still have not explained why you consort with *them*.'

'This is not one of *their* camps,' Jonaquil said. 'Already have I told you that. It is men who make up this camp, men from villages and towns in the Wold, who have taken *their* weapons for themselves. It is demon faces you see, but ordinary northern men's souls behind those faces.'

Tai stared. 'Then those I destroyed were *not* of the southern demons?'

Jonaquil shook her head grimly. 'If you thought to kill some of *them*, you were mistaken. Those you killed were northerners, not demons from the south.'

Tai bit his lip in anguish. The anger went sodden in him.

But even so, he could not help but feel a little rush of excitement. Men had defeated *them*, had wrested away weapons and helms and were using them. Now northerners could face these southern demons on equal terms! 'Who are these men?' he demanded.

'They are from all across the Wold,' Jonaquil replied. 'Some are members of a rebel band who fought against the southern man-demons, many are former inmates of a grim camp beyond the Blue Hills, others are hangers on who have joined during the march.'

'And where do they march to?'

'To rid the land of *them*. Or so is the claim.'

Tai took a sharp breath. But before he could say anything further, Dreamwalker intervened.

'You say these men . . . "claim" to rid the land of the southern demons?' she asked. 'Why only "claim"?'

'They claim,' Jonaquil said, 'to be the enemies of *them*. They claim they fight to free the land. But they do terrible things, these men. It is as if putting on *their* form and power moulds the soul in *their* image.'

'What things do these men do?' asked Dreamwalker.

Jonaquil shrugged uneasily. 'Killings . . . sometimes. They wield too much power. Only this morning, northwards in the Wold, two camp hands who had tried to desert were caught and killed out of hand. Father and son. They wanted no more of fighting.' She sighed. 'Now . . . now they have their wish.'

Tai shook his head in guilty confusion, remembering the righteous anger he had felt over that killing. Not *them* at all then. Things had once been simple: *they* were to be defeated and the Wold freed; a hopeless ambition it might be, but simple and straightforward for all that. Now, suddenly, the world was simple no longer.

He turned to Jonaquil. 'What plans do these men have?'

'They march on Long Harbour now. For a final confrontation with these southern man-demons.'

Tai could not believe it. 'That is madness!'

Jonaquil shrugged. 'Madness or no, that is what they intend. There is a leader amongst them who is – unstoppable. And so they march through the Wold, collecting supplies and men as they travel.' Jonaquil closed her eyes, opened them again. 'They conscript men, demand food, take by force what they are not offered. Like a band of locusts, they are.'

'And what does thou do in such company?' Dreamwalker asked.

'I am a Healer. I have been with them since this march began, back in the camp I told you of, the Palisade. I am needed here. I do what I can. And I . . .'

'Yes?' Dreamwalker urged.

'And I . . . dreamed of you. And him,' pointing at Tai. 'And others. I felt . . . drawn.'

Dreamwalker nodded. 'The pattern is forming.'

Tai only stared.

A sudden commotion came from the camp on the other side of the hill behind which they talked, shouting and the clash of moving men in armour.

'They are breaking camp and moving on,' Jonaquil said. 'I must return.' But she hesitated, looking at Dreamwalker and Tai uncertainly.

Dreamwalker stepped forwards and put a wrinkled hand on Jonaquil's shoulder. 'Go, girl. But take care. We are well met here, and shall meet again yet. I feel it in my bones.' She pushed Jonaquil onwards, gently. 'Go, now.'

With Jonaquil returned to the camp, Dreamwalker pulled Tai away with her out into the wild grass.

Tai stumbled after. He felt torn and confused, uneasy about what he had done, and could do. Turning, he saw the crowd of men and man-demons come out from behind the hill and wend its way westwards and south, away from them. Tai pulled himself from Dreamwalker's hold and stopped. 'I have power, Dreamwalker,' he said. 'I do! I have proved that. But what do I use it for? If these others in the camp here are enemies of *them*, then I should—'

'No, no, and *no*!' Dreamwalker said.

Tai looked at her, surprised.

'Thou is a true-seeing man. See true, then!'

Tai shook his head. 'I don't—'

'Listen, man! Thou is special, and can see into the world's soul. *I* can do no such thing. For me, the world's soul shows itself to me only in the Dream. Sometimes, yes, I catch a glimpse of the hidden patterns, feeling them in my bones. But thou can sense direct and clear the shape of things.'

'But I do not—'

'Shush! It is new to thee. Thou has *much* to learn. And the first lesson is: thou hast no choices. *Feel* thy way.'

'But—'

'*Feel* it!'

Tai felt himself sliding over into his other-awareness. The moving complexity of hidden patterns shimmered all about him. He *sensed* the distancing pulse of the man-demon band, the light-footed glitterings of Dreamwalker's people nearby in the upwards-leaping green, spiralling Ree and Skeefer . . .

On a deeper level, or a further, or a higher – he knew not truly what it might be – he *sensed* a drawing together, a node. Like a huge, elegantly twined knot it seemed, tied from the skeins of many lives. Or like a slow, inexorable whirlpool, sucking all into itself. Or a great, funnelled slope down which all were skidding.

All these and yet none of these, really.

But he was one of those woven into this node. He and others: Dreamwalker, Jonaquil, a man with a great, gory axe, the skull-faced Seer, a screaming woman engulfed in flames, the Lords Veil, others, whom he could not yet sense clearly.

Tai could catch no clear glimpse of what sort of future this might be he *sensed*. No vision or dream was this, no clear sight of future events. Yet the force of it was undeniable. The world moved, people moved, the pattern drew itself together.

And he was a part, whether he willed or no.

Tai came out of it panting, his heart hammering in his breast. The world shimmered dizzyingly about him and his world-eyes watered.

He could feel the pull almost painfully clear upon him now, despite that he was no longer open to his other-sensing.

Colby. The Miradore.

It was time to turn about, to attempt what Ree had once suggested. Circumstances were ripe now, as they had not been before.

Tai looked at Dreamwalker. She had been right. This was no simple matter of choice. The pattern was there for any who were not blind. 'Hound's Head Isle,' he said to her. 'In Harbour Bay. That is where I must go.'

Dreamwalker nodded. 'And I with thee.'

'Aye,' Tai agreed after a moment, feeling the rightness of her suggestion.

Tai swallowed. He felt exhilarated, as if he were standing atop some enormous rise and was about to launch himself off and away.

Dreamwalker smiled. 'Thou is learning, man.'

Together, the two of them stepped along through the wild grass, towards Skeefer and Ree and the rest.

# XXVIII

# In the North Wold,
# Near the River Whitewash

'No!' Jonaquil cried. 'Stop it! *Stop it!*'

But she was too late.

Spell-helmed men leaped amongst the terrified, bleating flock of sheep, war-pikes swinging. Penned by a rock-walled enclosure as the sheep were, it was carnage, all blood and shredded wool and quivering red meat. The helmed men roared with laughter, hefting steaming chunks of the poor, butchered animals aloft.

The farmwife stood outside a crumbling stone hut, white faced and weeping, a small child clutching her skirts. On the ground before her lay her man, moaning, opened by a pike thrust as he had tried to protect his sheep.

A dog barked hysterically, and was cut dead.

It was only a small group of helmed men, this, moving on the fringes of the main company. Jonaquil had spotted them making for this outlying holding, while the main force smashed through the dilapidated village down the hill near the river. Sensing tragedy, she had hurried after. Little enough was there left hereabouts, after *their* destructive sweep through the land. What little remained had been cobbled together from disaster through sweat and heartbreak – a stone hut, a few sheep.

Jonaquil stood, panting, blinking back the tears, too late to do aught except witness the slaying of this family's last hope. She had seen the like of this far too often in the days since the rag-tag army she marched with had left the Palisade in its sweep across the Wold towards Long Harbour. For the surviving, hapless folk whose lands they marched through, this 'army of liberation' was become as dreadful as *they* ever had been.

Before her, Jonaquil saw the demon-helmed men begin to move in on the farmwife.

She ran towards them. 'No!' she cried. '*No!*' She elbowed her way through and stood protectively in front of the terrified woman. 'Leave her alone!'

The men laughed, wet lips peeling back from long tusks.

'And how will you stop us, woman?' one of them demanded.

'Now we have two instead of one!' said another, reaching a blood-spattered, gauntleted hand towards Jonaquil.

Jonaquil felt her heart turn in her chest. Their double helm-and-human life-glow flared menacingly. She batted the gory hand away. 'Do you not know me?' she said, making her voice steady. 'I am Jonaquil, the Healer. Your very lives may depend upon my services!'

'It's other services I'm interested in now, woman!' the reaching one snapped.

'Wait,' said one of the others uncertainly. 'Perhaps—'

'Piss off!' replied the reaching one. 'She's mine.'

'*Back away!*' a new voice called suddenly.

Jonaquil whirled, and there, standing next to her as if materialized out of the very air, was grey-haired Tishta. In her hand, Tishta held a long-bladed iron knife. She glared at the clustered men. 'First one of you who tries anything gets this blade up his throat.'

The helmed men laughed, scoffingly.

'*Try* me, arseholes,' Tishta returned. She stood unflinching, the knife loose and dangerous-looking in her hand, as if she knew *exactly* what to do with it.

Inhuman yellow eyes blinked. The men shuffled about uncertainly.

'Take your meat and go,' Tishta told them, gesturing with her chin to the butchered sheep.

For a long moment they stood their ground, stiff and threatening as hounds. Then, 'Come on,' one of them said. 'We'll get a good dinner out of this at any rate.'

And with that they were gone.

'Whew!' Tishta breathed. 'And may they choke on it good and proper, the bastards.'

'Tishta!' Jonaquil exclaimed. 'What are *you* doing here? I had no idea . . .'

Tishta smiled. 'I've been along with this mad rabble since it first left the Palisade. I've been sort of keeping an eye on you, girl. From a distance. Since that last talk we had about the pilfering in the Dispensary, well . . .' The older woman shrugged uncomfortably.

'You should have come to me.'

Tishta's smile widened. 'I did. And just in time, too, it seems.' She looked after the helmed men, striding off into the distance, laden with their butchered sheep, and shook her head. Then she slid the blade into the sheath at her belt. Her hands shook as she did so. 'Bastards,' she muttered.

Jonaquil reached a hand to Tishta's shoulder. 'Thank you.'

Tishta shrugged self-consciously. 'I owed you.'

'*Owed* me?'

'For letting you down.'

'But you—'

'*I* felt I owed you.'

Before Jonaquil could say anything further, a moan from the downed farmer brought them both back to the more immediate demands of the situation.

The farmwife stood frozen where she was, as if her very mind had been shaken from her. 'Comfort her if you can,' Jonaquil suggested to Tishta. 'And I will see to her man.'

Tishta nodded.

Jonaquil knelt beside the farmer. A quick scrutiny showed that the poor man had been gutted like one of his sheep. The life-light about him was already dimming into nothingness. There was nothing she could do for him, except, perhaps, mourn. Yet one more victim. She stood up, shaking her head at Tishta's look of inquiry.

'Bastards!' Tishta hissed.


'Like a rag-tag swarm of locusts,' Tishta said, shaking her head. 'Orderless but purposeful, sweeping all before them.'

'Aye,' Jonaquil agreed. 'Locusts indeed.'

The little stone cottage and its sad inhabitants lay behind them now, like so much else, only one of numerous such poor places the great liberating army had overrun. Jonaquil and Tishta traipsed tiredly along at the back of that army, the Whitewash on their left, the green expanse of the Wold all about.

Before them moved hundreds, garbed in raggedy farmers' clothing or hunters' leathers, scale armour taken from *them* or even ancient ring-mail, helmeted, bareheaded, armed in every conceivable fashion. And stitched through the surge of men, holding all together, loped those who had put on demon shape. Those were many now, since the fall of the Palisade. The same feral ferocity was on every face – human and demon like. It made Jonaquil shiver, so unhumanly, mindlessly fierce did it seem.

'This is madness,' Tishta was saying, gesturing at the mass of marching men stretched away before them. 'No plans have been made, no councils held. There is something in the air, in the blood.' She pointed suddenly. 'There. Look at that!'

On the fringe of the crowded column ahead of them, a group of ordinary men howled, dancing a queer, high-stepping dance while they brandished weapons.

'It is as if they are all mad with drink,' Tishta said. 'But it is not drink.'

'It is those fell, sorcerous helms,' Jonaquil returned. 'They work upon the spirit of those who wear them.' She sighed. 'I have tried, but they will listen to no warnings of mine. They will listen to nothing!'

The two women had been plodding up a long, gradual slope, and now they found themselves atop a rounded hill. Jonaquil stopped. They had been marching now for days. Her feet ached, her back ached. She leaned over wearily, panting.

Below, they could see the dark, communal mass of the army flowing like slow liquid across the greenness of the Wold. Jonaquil shivered. This march had developed a deadly momentum. It was as if they were caught in the current of some intangible, huge river and swept along. And that current flowed not just round about these men, but *through* them, filling them, moving them all forwards in a single, ragged surge, like a great wave rolling onwards to smash against its objective.

It was late afternoon, the sun warm in a clear sky, but Jonaquil felt a long shiver go through her. It was not just this army through which something moved. She could feel it in herself, too. Dreams and strange meetings: the elder woman with the moss-green eyes, the young man whose life-light glowed like a torch. Jonaquil's nights were still dream-wracked, blood and flickering torchlight, the elder woman and the young man . . .

It was as if she stood not just upon this grassy, solid hill under her feet, but upon some other, larger, intangible promontory. Every step she took funnelled her down, down. But towards what?

'Are you all right, girl?' Tishta asked at her side.

Jonaquil blinked, coming back. 'Just weary is all.' She looked at the other woman, wondering if she could confide in her. But how to explain? She did not understand it herself. Folk from her dreams appearing out of nowhere; invisible, it seemed, to all eyes but her own. This sense of *pulling*.

'You sure, girl?' Tishta pressed. And then, 'Look, why don't we desert?'

Jonaquil looked at her, puzzled.

'Isn't that what one does from armies? Why don't we run away? These madmen are just going to get themselves gutted. Why should we be part of that? I reckon that if we are canny, we should be able to—' The look on Jonaquil's face stopped her. 'What? What is it?'

'I . . . I cannot, Tishta.'

'Why? What do you owe this rabble? Nothing!'

Jonaquil shrugged unhappily. She could think of no sensible way to explain what was going through her. 'I must stay. I am drawn to it.'

The older woman snorted. 'Healer's dedication. Humpf!'

Jonaquil let it go. Good enough, that explanation. 'I cannot leave. But you . . . you go.'

Tishta shook her head. 'Not and leave you.'

'But—' Jonaquil began.

Tishta swallowed, looked at Jonaquil, looked away. 'I have nowhere and nobody to go to.'

Jonaquil nodded. She put a hand on the older woman's arm. 'Neither do I.'

The two of them began walking once more. The downwards slope of the hill pulled at them, quickening their steps. Jonaquil stumbled in the grass; only Tishta's quick grip saved her from a tumble.

'You sure you're all right, girl?' Tishta asked.

'I am just weary, truly. But less so, now that I have a . . . friend with me.'

Tishta smiled. 'A friend lightens any load, it is said.'

'In these mad times,' Jonaquil said, 'a friend is more precious than food and drink.'

'Aye,' Tishta returned. She shook her head, looking down on the moving army below them. She pointed. 'Madness indeed. And it's *him* that's at the heart of it!'

The army had got on ahead of them. From their vantage point on the hill's slope, it seemed shaped like a huge, moving tadpole. And at the centre of the tadpole's head strode Big Egil – or the being Egil had become, rather, for he was no longer the Woodend farmer Jonaquil had once known. To her sensitive eyes, he was like a torch furiously burning. Jonaquil avoided him. There was something about him that gave her the shakes. He was not . . . right.

Tishta spat. 'He's leading all into bloody disaster, that one.'

'Aye,' Jonaquil agreed soberly. She was very much afraid that this rag-tag army marching onwards to fling itself upon Long Harbour was moving towards its own utter destruction. It was a token of how queer all this was that none seemed to see that possibility save her, and now Tishta. All they saw was Long Harbour and blood and vengeance.

She looked across at Tishta. 'The whole world is mad,' she said, quoting an old, old verse, 'save for thee and me.'

Tishta laughed. 'Aye. Save for thee and me.'

They continued downwards after the army, drawn along inexorably, like so much else.

# XXIX

# Long Harbour

Moving through the crowded jumble of dirty buildings, Crane grimaced. The raggedy folk all about put her in mind of a flock of crippled birds, unable to fly, massing together with a manic fervour. There was a confusion of spirit here, a darkening of awareness she sensed in her belly. Squads of demon-faced guards cut through the crowds, stitching fear through the streets, binding all together with it. Crane could feel the enveloping oppression, like a dank, dark fog. It was a sickly place, Long Harbour, and it stank. She longed to be out of it and back once again in the cleanness of her mountain forests.

But that was not to be.

She had a feeling in her bones about this city. She had been drawn here, as a leaf whirled along by a river's current is drawn irresistibly to the sea. And just as there was no returning for the leaf, so would there be none for her. She remembered the death tracery the bones had shown when she threw them.

Crane shook herself out of such dark thoughts. This place ate at her like a chancre. 'Phawg!' she muttered in disgust. 'How can people live like this? Like maggots in a corpse!'

Ahead of her, Tai beckoned, ignoring her question. 'This must be the place,' he said.

Before them was a shabby little doorway set at the head of the narrow street along which they had been making their way. It was early evening, and the street entirely shadowed. In the dimness, a rusted metal anchor, suspended by an equally rusty chain, hung above the door from a blackened iron beam sticking out from the building's front wall.

'The Anchor,' Tai said, and walked through the doorway.

Inside, there was enough noise and stink and smoke to make Crane's head reel. It was one great, low-ceilinged, lantern-lit room. Across the back wall stretched a waist-high wooden bar behind which were arrayed bottles and flasks and large wooden barrels cradled in iron brackets. Folk jostled at the bar, shouting and laughing, and in the open middle of the room a mass of people pranced and jigged to a raucous tune blown by wheezing musicians.

Pulling at her arm, Tai led on through the jostle and press of the crowd towards a flight of steps. 'Old William said it would be this way,' he called back to her. 'Up the stairs.'

Crane sighed. They needed a boat, and somebody to sail it, in order to cross Harbour Bay to Hound's Head Isle. That was why – leaving her own people and Tai's companions safely in hiding well away from the city – she and Tai had slipped into Long Harbour. There was no telling how long it might be before the rabble army they had encountered in the Wold descended upon the city. They had to arrange the boat and be out of here before that.

Tai claimed he knew people in the city who could help. Indeed, near the waterside they had met a Healing-man with glass over his eyes, who directed them here. Crane, however, could not see how this loud and crowded place they had just entered would lead them to a boat. She knew nothing of cities, admittedly, and did not like this one at all, but they only seemed to be getting further and further away from the water.

But young Tai moved onwards, and she perforce clambered up the stairs behind him, using her stick, her old knees creaking.

The steps led to another room, even noisier than the one they had left, for added to the shouts of the people was the barking and baying of a number of dogs. A waist-high, circular wooden ring was set into the floor at the end of the room furthest from the stairs. Dogs leaped and barked, people leaned over the top of the ring, elbows or armpits on the wooden edge, gesticulating wildly and calling and pointing things out to each other.

There was a burst of shouting, accompanied by the wailing of a dog in sudden agony, and a strange, high-pitched squealing.

Tai forged a way into the crowd, tugging Crane after him. He moved confidently through all this human chaos. Too confidently, perhaps. He worried her, this true-seeing man who was little more than a boy, yet was possessed of such a gift. He worried her indeed.

They had reached a vantage point, now, where they could overlook the ring's wooden side. Inside the containing walls, Crane could see dozens of small, brown-grey bodies scurrying about shrieking and squealing.

Rats.

At the edge of the ring, furthest from where they stood, a number of these beasts were clustered about and upon some object, worrying and tearing at it hungrily. It took her a long moment to identify it as the shivering and bloodied remnants of a dog.

Crane turned away, sickened.

Long moments after, once the hubbub had died a bit, she chanced another look. The inside of the ring was empty now, except for the rats themselves and a short, wiry man with grey-flecked hair and beard. He was nonchalantly removing rats by the handful from a large wicker cage, and dumping them on to the sandy floor of the ring. The rats squealed and struggled, but not a single one of them bit or scratched him during this process.

'Good batch tonight, Ratter,' a voice called from the ringside.

'Did poor Login's mutt in right proper!' someone else offered.

''Urry up about it, Ratter,' a third voice urged. 'we 'aven't got all night!'

'Keep yer mouth shut, Toory,' the man called the Ratter said, not bothering to look up, 'or I'll stuff one o' these beasties down yer gullet.'

The crowd hooted at this, and a comment was made about another part of the unfortunate Toory's anatomy where the Ratter could stuff a rat with better effect.

There were no more calls for the Ratter to hurry up, and he finished his task with leisurely efficiency. Then, swinging the empty cage up ahead of him, he vaulted nimbly over the wooden side of the ring.

Tai detached himself from the ring and called out, 'Ratter. Ratter!'

The grey bearded man turned and, seeing Tai, blinked. 'Ye!' he exclaimed. 'What are *ye* doin' back 'ere! Did I not tell ye to—'

'Ratter,' Tai interrupted. 'William sent me. I have to talk with you. It is *important!*'

The Ratter looked unconvinced.

Crane felt Tai begin to exert some of his other-sense towards the Ratter; a nudging, nagging compulsion to draw this man into the momentum of the pattern she and Tai were part of. She put a hand on his arm. 'Do not. He is a part, or he is not. Nothing thou can do will make him so.'

Tai's face darkened momentarily, but he relented. 'Ratter, please. I *must* talk with you.'

The Ratter stared at the two of them. 'A'right, then. If ye must.'

He led them away from the ring to a relatively quiet corner of the room. Tai quickly told why they were come, dwelling on his foster-uncle's captivity and omitting mention of the limbless, born Lord Veil, as he and Crane had agreed was the more sensible course.

But when the Ratter realized what they were about, he shook his head in disbelief. 'Going to the Miradore! Ye must be crazy, or stewpid, or both. And ye must think me crazy too, if ye expect me to 'elp ye find a boat!'

Tai held out his hands. 'Ratter, you don't understand. It is part of something . . . larger.'

The Ratter only shook his head. 'Ye're talkin' crazy, lad.'

'It is in the Dream,' Crane put in.

Ratter snorted. 'Dreams! Ye *are* crazy!'

'Crazy or not,' Tai said, 'we are *going*.'

Ratter reached a hand to Tai. 'Look, lad, all ye can 'ope to accomplish is to get yerself killed. And why ye want to be goin' around with strange ol' witchy women like this 'un I don't know. Why don't ye—'

'Come along,' Crane said to Tai. 'This man is of no use.'

Tai hesitated for a moment, then shook the Ratter's hand from his arm and turned to follow.

'Wait!' the Ratter called.

Tai turned. 'Will you help us?'

The Ratter drew breath, sighed, nodded glumly. 'Aye, I'll 'elp ye. But *much* against me better judgement . . .' He paused, then looked at Tai. 'It's Costa ye needs to see, I reckon. 'E's a smuggler, Costa is. Knows boats well. And 'as the connections.'

'How do we meet this Costa?'

''E's 'ere tonight. Always 'ere on nights like this. That's why Ol' Will sent ye round.' The Ratter gestured to the crowd about the ring ''E must be around somewheres . . .'

The Ratter led them, eventually, before a man wearing loose trousers and a long, open jacket of blue cloth, cross-stitched with gold thread that glittered brightly in the flicker of the lamplight. A small, gold lamé cap perched on the back of his head and several large gold earrings dangled from his earlobes. In his left hand he carried a slim black cane with an intricate golden pommel. 'Ratter,' he said, smiling.

But before Ratter could make any reply, Costa turned from him and gestured peremptorily with the cane to a nervous, pinched-faced little man who was trying to mooch past. 'Login,' he said, 'I am *very* disappointed.'

The little man shuffled embarrassedly.

Costa hefted the cane in his hands, as if he might be intending to clout the man with it.

'Please, Master Costa,' the nervous Login pleaded. 'Me dog did 'is best. 'E really did. It was them rats what . . .'

Costa brandished the cane and the man before him all but grovelled. 'Never mind,' Costa said then, smiling. 'It is all part of the sport, I suppose. Here – ' he produced a coin from the side pocket of his jacket – 'step downstairs like a good fellow and bring up another bottle of that fine southern wine they try to keep hidden from us. Losing money is thirsty work.'

The little man smiled eagerly, and, bobbing his head, trotted off downstairs.

'Well,' said Costa, turning back to the Ratter once more, 'have you any inside tips for me? Perhaps you can change my luck. I've just lost five gen on Login's pitiful little runt of a beast.' He laughed. 'I should have known better than to take old Login at his word!'

The Ratter shrugged. 'No tips for ye, friend Costa, but I do 'ave somethin'.'

Costa cocked an eyebrow quizzically.

'I've brought along some people who'd like to meet with ye.' Ratter gestured behind him to where Crane and Tai stood.

'Business?' Costa queried.

'Of a sort,' Ratter replied.

'Business . . . of a sort,' Costa repeated. He took a long, appraising look at Tai and Crane, slowly twirling the black cane into his hands so that the golden pommel glittered in the light. 'You intrigue me,' he said.

Looking beyond them, he made a beckoning gesture. 'Here comes Login with my wine. There is a room in the back we might use.' He took the bottle from out Login's hands, and they followed him through the noisy crowd to a door set in the back wall. Costa led them through this into a small room, in the centre of which stood a trestle table with benches down either side. Costa sat himself at one of these benches and uncorked the wine with a deft twist of a little knife he produced from somewhere.

'Let *me* do the talkin',' Crane heard Ratter hiss in Tai's ear. Then he closed the door and quiet descended upon the room.

'So,' Costa said, pouring the wine into a goblet that had sat on the table. 'What is this business "of a sort" that you wish to discuss with me?'

'The lad 'ere,' Ratter said, 'is Tai. 'E's from out in the Wold. I knew 'im before, from Ol' Will's. Will looked after 'im.' He pointed to the line of the healing scar on Tai's forehead.

'So?' Costa said, sipping the wine.

'Tai's uncle was taken by *them*.'

'My sympathies, I'm sure,' Costa said, sipping more wine. 'Though I must say that I'm having difficulty imagining what any of this has got to do with *me*.'

Tai stepped forward. 'I intend to go to Hound's Head Isle to free my uncle.'

Silence settled on the table for a moment.

'And how am I involved with this?' Costa asked.

'I need a boat to get me there.'

'You alone?'

'Myself,' he gestured to Crane, 'and Dreamwalker here, and some of her people. Two dozen all told, perhaps.'

Costa laughed, shaking his head. 'Was it your brains they removed, friend?' he said to Tai. 'Is that how you got that scar across your forehead?' He turned to Ratter. 'You must think me mental. Ratter, what *can* you have been thinking of? These two are mad, pure mad. Get them out of my sight.'

Tai took a step towards Costa. 'I *need* that boat!'

The smuggler skipped nimbly back off the bench and away from the table. The cane came up in his hand and, with a deft twist, he unsheathed a long, slim metal blade from it. 'Come no closer. I assure you I'm quite willing to skewer you if I must.'

Crane felt Tai *reach*. It was an instinctive action on his part, compounded of anger and frustration.

Instinctive it was, but ill-aimed and iller-conceived, for Tai did not yet know the full extent of his strength. Crane had none of the raw power young Tai possessed, and the true-seeing gift was not her gift. But she was a woman sensitive to the hidden shifts and currents of the world. Quick as an eye-blink, she *reached* in her own manner and deflected what Tai had sent, so that, instead of crumpling the smuggler, all it did was rip the sword from out his hand and spin it end over end to slam point first into the wall.

Backing a few stumbling steps away, Costa stared at where the blade had stuck, quivering.

Tai stood pale and silent. Crane said no word of reproach to him. There was no need. She could see that he understood what he had done, and nearly done, and was shaken by it.

Crane felt her old heart thumping; it was a long moment before she could get her breath properly. 'We need a boat, man,' she said into the silence that held the room.

Costa shifted his gaze from the quivering blade. 'What have you brought here?' he demanded of the Ratter.

'I . . . I don't know,' the Ratter said, his voice hardly more than a whisper. 'I don't understand.' He stared at Tai. 'What did ye do, lad? What's 'appened to ye?'

Tai seemed to have recovered himself again now. He stepped forward and sat on one of the benches at the table. 'We mean you no harm,' he said. 'Truly. All we wish is a boat.'

Costa only stared.

'Come,' Tai gestured. 'Sit down.'

Hesitantly, Costa did so. His eyes were still big. 'What . . . what are you to be able to commit such fell sorcery?'

'What I am would be long to explain,' Tai replied. He sighed. 'And I am not certain myself, truth to tell.'

Looking on from her vantage, Crane saw Costa's hand creep up his sleeve. To where the little knife he had used to uncork the wine was concealed? He was a cunning man, this one, like a raven: sharp-eyed, quick, alive to any opportunity.

Crane leaned forwards to the table, prodding the smuggler with her stick. 'I would not try him too far, man,' she warned Costa. 'Thy little blade may prove more dangerous to thee than to him.'

She saw Tai's surprise, for he had missed entirely Costa's surreptitious movements. He stood quickly and *reached*. The little blade came skittering out of Costa's sleeve and embedded itself in the wall next to the other blade.

He was learning fast, young Tai.

Costa sat frozen, his face gone white.

'We want a boat,' Tai repeated.

Costa took a shaky breath, another. He put a hand out for the goblet of wine that still stood on the table and took a long swallow. His hands, holding the goblet, quivered. 'To . . . to take you to the Miradore,' he said.

Tai nodded.

Another long swallow of the wine, and Costa recovered some of his poise. 'A boat I can get you, yes. But it will be expensive. How would you be planning to pay me for this boat?'

'We have no money,' Tai began, 'but . . .'

Costa poured himself more wine, laughing softly. He seemed altogether in possession of himself now. 'You expect me to *give* you this boat. For charity's sake?'

Crane saw the irritation rise in Tai and motioned him back. 'Have a care, man,' she said to the smuggler.

Costa froze, the wine goblet part-way to his lips.

'We have no money,' Crane said. 'But Tai here, and I myself, are able to *do* things. As thou has no doubt noticed.'

Costa swallowed and nodded.

'What if,' Crane went on, offering the bargain she and Tai had previously agreed upon, 'we were to grant thee a . . . request?'

Costa shook his head. 'A *request*?'

'Find us a boat and somebody to sail it for us, and we will grant thee any one thing thou may request, providing it is within our abilities to do so.'

'*Anything?*'

'So long as it is within Tai's abilities, or my own. We have our limits, man, like all things.'

'And how would we seal this bargain?' Costa demanded.

'You have our word,' Tai told him.

'And am I to trust you on your word alone?'

'Are we to trust *thy* word, man?' Crane returned.

Costa laughed. 'All right, then, old woman. We will trust in each other's word.' He reached for the wine goblet and took another swallow. 'As for my price . . .' He looked around the room, his eyes alight. 'It is gold I want. Fill this room with gold for me and you shall have your boat this very evening.'

It was Crane's turn to laugh. 'I told thee we have our limits, man. What thou asks is impossible.'

Costa frowned. 'Why then, I shall . . . I wish that . . .' He scratched his ear irritatedly. 'What *can* you do?' he demanded.

'Many things.'

'That is no answer!'

'Ask, then.

Cost's face puckered with thought. 'I want . . . I wish . . .' He ran a hand over his eyes, shook himself. 'I begin to think this is a bad bargain I have made for myself. What wish ought one to demand from sorcerers?' He turned to the Ratter, who had stayed silent all this time, wide-eyed. 'What would you ask, Ratter, if you were in my position?'

The Ratter shook his head, shrugged.

'Much help *you* are,' Costa said accusingly.

The Ratter merely shrugged again.

'The boat,' Tai said. 'Do we get the boat?'

'Aye,' Costa sighed. 'I shall get you your boat.'

'And somebody to sail it?

Costa sighed. 'Aye. But I cannot guarantee anything big enough to take – how many was it you said? – upwards of two dozen. I will get a boat. You have my word on that. But I cannot promise you it will be as big as you wish.'

Tai leaned forward, about to speak, but Crane put her hand on his shoulder. 'Let the pattern build of itself,' she reminded him softly.

'We need the boat tonight,' Tai said. 'We wish to leave as soon as possible.'

'Very well,' Costa said after a pause. 'Tonight it shall be. But you owe me, right?'

'Aye,' Tai agreed. 'We owe you. As Dreamwalker says, anything you ask for is yours, if it be within our abilities.'

'And when you return, you will grant me my request.'

'Our word on it.'

'And if you do *not* return?'

Tai shrugged.

'Only the Powers know the answer to that, man,' Crane said.

Costa looked at the goblet in his hands and shook his head. 'That may be, Lady, but I begin to think that I have made a bad bargain. A good boat on nothing but the word of a pair of crazy sorcerers.'

'We are in your debt,' Tai said.

Costa nodded, 'Let us away, then.'

With that, the four of them trooped out of the room, through the noise of the crowd about the ring, and down a set of rickety back steps into the chill, dark air of the night.

Crane shivered. It was the air, yes, but also more than that. She felt in her bones again that inexorable pull, a sense of the leaf being drawn by the current to the sea.

And for the leaf, there was no return.

# XXX

# Approaching Long Harbour

Jonaquil stood, hugging herself for warmth. It was the dark beginning of the night, cloudy and starless, and cold near the river. She watched men down at the shore trying to beach the last of the ungainly cargo barges the army had used as transport across the Whitewash. The men heaved and grunted and cursed, even those with demon-strength. Finally, the last barge was manhandled into place and the ragged horde aboard it spilled ashore.

Jonaquil stood where she was, staring into the night. She felt numbed. They were so close to Long Harbour now that lookouts on the hill nearby might see clearly the glitter of the city's night-lights.

At her side, Tishta breathed a long, sighing breath. 'So we are arrived.'

'Aye,' Jonaquil said uneasily. From where the two women stood, they could glimpse only the flickering edge of the city's radiance, lighting the sky like a faraway torch. Jonaquil shivered. Her belly was tight with something being born in the world, and dream images still filled her mind. She felt the *pull* that had drawn her here along with all the rest.

'What will we be doing this time tomorrow, I wonder?' said Tishta softly. 'Like leaping into a dark pit, this. You don't know *what* might be down there to meet you.'

Jonaquil nodded, silent, feeling the same.

'Don't reckon it will be anything *pleasant*, though,' the older woman added.

Jonaquil kept her silence, not knowing what to say. Reaching into her linen shirt, she clasped the amber nugget that was her legacy from Idris, still kept safe and secret between her breasts. The amber felt warm in her hand; but no comforting, remembered voice spoke to her. It had been long and long since that had last happened. She remembered first slipping the cobble on, the day *they* came to Woodend. It had seemed a thing of power then. It held no power now. Perhaps this was due to some hidden influence of *theirs*, or perhaps she had changed, or the cobble had simply faded with age. Or perhaps it had never been much more than her own desire and imagination at work. Whatever the case, one more thing had been taken from her, and any hopes she might have had concerning it were dead. In children's stories, such talismans always come miraculously to the heroine's aid at the last moment. But this was no child's story she lived, and she no heroine. The cobble was only a piece of amber, warmed by her own body heat; she was alone.

'You *sure* of this, girl?' Tishta asked. 'I reckon we might still be able to make a run for it, you know.'

Jonaquil hugged herself in distress. 'I *can't*, Tishta. But you—'

'We've *been* through that already.'

'Aye,' Jonaquil said. 'Aye . . .'

The two women stood silently together in the darkness.

All about them lay the ragged bulk of the army, hundreds of dark shapes. There was a continuous scuttling, as of so many enormous insects. Most of the men, though, particularly those without helms, simply sprawled in a daze of exhaustion, shivering in the chill night air.

A surge of movement made Jonaquil look up. She saw the big form of Egil come striding past. There were no fires and precious little food. But where Egil walked, it was as if a wind moved through the weary men.

'I heard it took twenty of them to give him those scars,' Jonaquil heard somebody nearby say of him in a whisper. 'But he killed them all!'

Another added, 'It takes two ordinary men just to *lift* that great axe of his, never mind wield it in a fight . . .'

'Look at him!' somebody else muttered. 'The Powers move through him. You can sense it. The evil ones will be destroyed. With him at our head we are blessed by the Powers themselves!'

'We *cannot* fail! Long Harbour is ours . . .'

Tishta snorted. 'Fools!'

'He is no ordinary man, that one,' Jonaquil said, watching the figure of Egil moving away in the dark. To her eyes, he glowed like a torch, a glowing rage that bled into those about him. It was as if his whole being was centred on destruction. Jonaquil could almost indeed believe what the men said about him, that some Power *did* move through him. Those gathered here felt it and fed on it and thought themselves privileged to be a part of such a thing.

And at dawn . . .

Jonaquil felt a shiver go through her belly. She looked around at the rag-tag force gathered here. How many of them would be left this time tomorrow? How many of them would be crowding the Shadowlands?

'Healer!' a voice called abruptly.

Jonaquil turned and looked. It was the man Jordie: grey-haired, sombrely thoughtful, one of the leaders – if this rag-tag army could properly be said to have leaders.

He stood now, his face haggard with exhaustion, beckoning. 'Healer! Come along. And bring that assistant of yours with you. The time draws nigh. We have to make preparations.'

'Blood and tears,' Tishta said, shaking her head. 'That is what we are preparing for.'

'Come *along!*' Jordie called impatiently. 'I've been looking for you everywhere.'

'Coming,' Jonaquil called, and she and Tishta walked over towards him.

# XXXI

# Long Harbour and
# the Miradore

Tai crouched behind the corner edge of a dilapidated building, along with Dreamwalker and the Ratter, peering ahead. No street-lighting shone here. The night was cloudy and starless, the dark thick as treacle. It was difficult to make out more than dim, half-guessed shapes. Tai could *sense* clearly the double glow of demon guards about on the streets, though.

'This way,' the Ratter whispered. 'Costa's 'ad more than enough time to make 'is arrangements. If 'e isn't ready an' waiting with yer boat down at the quays by now, well . . .' Ratter shrugged. 'We'll find out soon enough, I reckon.' With that, he led off through a maze of darksome, winding alleys, heading towards the quays.

They came to the waterfront easily enough, and, once there, slipped quietly through an area of stacked merchandise. The air was chill, and thick with the wet, seaweedy odour of the Ferth. To their left, less than a hundred paces away, the lamplight of a guard-post flickered. Nearer at hand, two silhouetted figures, demon guards, paced their rounds, the murmur of their voices carrying soft but clear through the still night air.

'Keep down an' move quiet,' the Ratter hissed. 'Luck alone'll get us through 'ere,' he added to himself, shaking his head. 'Don't understand where all these guards is from. What's 'appening down 'ere on the quays tonight?'

The two guards turned in their rounds and retraced their steps. 'Now,' the Ratter said. 'We'll try an' cross 'ere before they come back.' He led off, quick and silent, but before he could bring Tai and Dreamwalker more than halfway to the next bit of concealing cover, a new set of demon guards appeared.

'That's torn it,' Ratter grumbled. 'We're for it now.' A long knife hung from his belt. He crouched there, hand on the knife's hilt, lips drawn back, for all the world like one of the rats he was named for.

'Shush, man,' Dreamwalker told him. 'And stay still.'

Ratter shook his head. 'They'll see us, certain sure, even in this dark. Only chance is to make a run for it . . .' He drew the knife, rose to a crouch, ready to bolt.

Tai put a hand on the Ratter's arm, holding him still. He could *sense* Dreamwalker turning the demon guards' attentions.

The two guards walked within several of paces of them, noticing nothing at all, and continued onwards.

The Ratter stared after them unbelievingly. 'How . . . ? How did ye . . . ?'

'Come,' Dreamwalker said. 'We must find the boat.'

The Ratter stood, a little shaky on his feet at first, returned his knife to its sheath, ran a hand over his face, shook himself. 'This way, then.'

He took them along through the merchandise stacks, under the dark arch of a bridgeway. They had to avoid another set of guards here, and yet another again further on. They ran and crouched and hid and ran again until, eventually, Ratter led them through to a set of cold, slimy stone steps at the harbour's edge. The sound of the water as it *lap-lapped* against the stone below came clearly to them. 'The boat should be down 'ere,' Ratter said. He turned, squinting back into the darkness the way they had come. 'Seems clear.'

Down the steps he led them, to where they could make out the dim shape of a boat bobbing gently in the water.

'Who comes?' a soft voice demanded from below them.

'It's *us*.'

Down the last few steps, and they came to where the boat was moored, Costa standing nearby. He was still dressed in the gold-trimmed blue jacket, with the black cane in his hand. He bowed mockingly. 'Hail comrades well met. I was beginning to think you might not make it. What kept you?'

'Guards,' the Ratter replied. 'Feckin' guards everywhere.' He flicked a quick glance back at Dreamwalker and Tai. 'Don't know 'ow we made it through without any of 'em seein' us.'

'Well, you're here now, and that's what counts,' Costa said. 'Here is the boat I promised you; a trim enough craft, too. And large enough to take all your friends, if you're willing to sit squashed up a bit.' He handed the boat's painter to Tai. 'May it bring you to your destination safely.'

Tai nodded his thanks. 'And the man to sail it?'

'Should be along any moment.' Costa turned to Ratter. 'And now, friend Ratter, it's time for you and I to leave.'

Tai reach a hand to Costa's arm. 'Perhaps you should wait till the man who will sail the boat arrives.'

Costa shrugged free. 'I said he will be here. Do you not *trust* me?'

Tai stared at the man, suspicious. But he could *sense* no lie in the pattern of things here. 'All right,' he said. 'Go, then.'

Costa nodded to Ratter. 'Let's be off.'

'Might be better if we just stayed 'ere fer a bit. Somethin's goin' on tonight.'

'Nonsense!' Costa replied. 'I know these quays blindfolded.'

The Ratter looked unconvinced. 'I've 'unted these quays most o' me life. I know 'em too. If there's too many—'

'It'll be an easy enough job to slip by the guards,' Costa interrupted. 'I've done it before. Many's the time. Come on!' He took the Ratter by the arm and urged him back up the stairs. 'Remember,' he whispered back over his shoulder to Tai and Dreamwalker, 'you owe me!'

'We remember, man,' Dreamwalker replied.

With that, Costa and the Ratter were gone.

Tai reached a hand to the boat's gunwale. The craft bobbed under his touch like an animal. He had no boat-craft, but he could *sense* the manner in which the sail, once the mast was properly stepped, would cup the wind, how the craft could spring forward if given its head rightly . . .

Tai smiled. He could *sense* many things now. More and more as the days went by. He *sensed* the pattern moving through this moment as he stood here breathing the night's velvet dark. It was as if they rode a current, Dreamwalker and he, a current that took them where they needed to go.

He looked across at Dreamwalker, nodded to the boat, began to let himself into the bobbing craft to wait there for the sailor Costa had assured them would be by.

Dreamwalker shook her head, motioning with her hand for him to wait. She stood one-legged, leaning upon her stick, listening.

In the distance, they heard a sudden commotion. The quick patter of footsteps followed from above and two figures came slipping down the stairs.

'Good! Ye're still 'ere.' It was the Ratter's voice, breathless.

The commotion in the distance grew closer.

'Quick!' Costa hissed. 'Into the boat before they catch us up.'

The four of them scrambled aboard, Tai and Dreamwalker astern, the other two amidships. The craft bounced and rocked under them, sending water splashing against the quay walls. Costa unshipped a pair of oars that lay in the boat's bottom and gave one to the Ratter. 'Hurry!' he hissed. He and the Ratter brought the boat about, pushing against the stone walls of the quay with the oars, then nosed it out into the blackness of the water.

Fitting their oars into the locks, the two rowed off softly until Long Harbour began to dwindle behind them in the darkness, and the sounds of the commotion with it.

A stiff breeze was blowing now from the east. In the sky above, the clouds started to break up, rushing along in tatters. Starshine shone on the water. Costa and the Ratter stopped their rowing and took a breather. 'Rat's arse!' Ratter cursed. '*That* was feckin' bad luck.'

'What happened?' Tai asked. He was beginning to learn limits to his other-sensing: he could perceive under-patterns and shapings, but the detail of faraway events, no.

'The whole o' the quays was alive with guards,' Ratter said. ''Aven't seen the like in weeks.'

'Sorcerers!' Costa spat. 'Great lot of use *you* were.' He shook his head, spat again, stared off morosely at the lights of the quays glimmering in the distance.

There was a sudden flutter of wings and the small, darting shape of Ree came skipping out of the darkness. Unlike Dreamwalker's folk, who lay hidden on the Ferth's wild north shore, Ree and Skeefer had been waiting for the boat out in the water. Tai heard the soft sounds of Skeefer's movement nearby.

The Ratter, seeing the flitting shape of Ree outlined against a momentary glow of starshine, dodged sideways, dropped his oar, and nearly tipped the boat with the frantic grab he made to catch the oar again before it disappeared over the side. But disappear it did anyway, with a splash. 'Rat's *arse*!' he hissed, staring at the water to try and locate the missing oar. 'What was that, a bat?'

But Costa was staring at Ree, who had come to perch on Tai's knee. 'It's . . . it's got a *human* face!'

'Who,' demanded Ree in her piping voice, 'is *this*?'

'And it *talks*!' Costa said, eyes big as apples.

At that moment, from over the side, Skeefer's furred arm appeared with the Ratter's missing oar.

'Aieek!' the Ratter yelped, and tumbled backwards over the thwart on which he had been sitting, ending up on his back, legs in the air, struggling to right himself.

'What are you *doing*?' Costa demanded, his voice tight. He stared at Dreamwalker and Tai with big, frightened eyes. 'Why have you summoned up these . . . these . . .' The words dwindled on his lips.

'Who are thesse two?' Skeefer asked, his elbows hooked over the gunwale, water streaming from his furred face. In the starshine, his small, sharp white teeth gleamed like pearls.

The Ratter was up on his feet in an instant, Costa grabbing for his cane, the boat canting over, Ree whirling in agitated circles.

'Enough!' Dreamwalker cried. '*Enough*!' But she was laughing, and that laughter defused the tensions that had so suddenly threatened the boat's equilibrium.

It took a little time, but eventually Skeefer was brought aboard and positions were sorted, introductions made, order re-established.

'They are . . . *your* creatures?' Costa asked respectfully of Dreamwalker, once he had been introduced to Skeefer and Ree.

Dreamwalker shook her head. 'They are nobody's creatures but their own.'

'Yet they do your bidding.'

'Of their own free will.'

Costa shook his head in amazement, staring.

The Ratter's attention, however, was for Long Harbour and the quays. 'Look!' he hissed, pointing.

There were figures moving about the waterfront, and the flicker of torchlight. With a snap, more torchlight came to life, bobbing on the water.

'Boats,' Costa muttered.

More lights flared into life out in the waters of the Ferth. None too near, yet menacing for all that.

'No chance of slipping through *that* to put us ashore,' Costa observed soberly.

A shifting mosaic of torchlight separated them from the city now. And from the Ferth's wild north shore as well, where Dreamwalker's people waited in hiding. Only behind them, westwards into Harbour Bay itself, was the way clear.

'I don't *like* this,' Costa muttered.

They waited, coasting silent on the dark water. The scatter of torchlit boats came no nearer to them, but neither did it disperse.

After a time, Dreamwalker looked about her and sighed. 'It seems we have been left little choice.'

'Aye,' Tai agreed. He *sensed* the closing off that was happening here, and a pulling like a soft tide towards the Miradore. It made him uneasy. To have to leave Dreamwalker's people behind like this . . . It did not augur well.

'We have only the one way to go,' Dreamwalker said, looking out along the Ferth towards the dark heave of Harbour Bay.

'What are you talking about?' demanded Costa.

'Hound's Head Isle,' Tai answered him.

'Oh no!' Costa said. 'Not with the Ratter and me aboard you're not.'

Dreamwalker pointed to the hedge of bobbing torchlight. 'Would thou prefer travelling in *their* company?'

*

With the mast stepped and the easterly wind filling the sail, the little boat sizzled through the waves, water at the prow glimmering in quicksilver splashes. Harbour Bay was a dark, moving expanse over which the boat leaped. Tai huddled miserably before the mast, his belly heaving with each leap. He was out of balance with the sea's rhythm. Dreamwalker too had seemed, at first, to be discomforted by the boat's motion. But she was fine now. Using his other-sense, Tai tried to quell his stomach by main force of will, to rebalance himself, sure that was what Dreamwalker had somehow done. But he could not find the knack of it. The sea's balance was a constantly changing rhythm of shifting equilibriums. All he succeeded in doing was making himself feel worse.

So he hung on miserably, while Costa chuckled and made snide remarks about sorcerers being weak in the belly.

After what seemed an endless time, the Ratter eventually called out, 'There she lies,' and in the distance ahead Tai sighted the dark bulk of the isle looming before them.

'Far as I can make out,' Costa said from his place at the tiller, 'we're about halfway along it. The Miradore should be to our left, southwards.'

Costa turned the boat and they coasted along the shore of the isle. It looked a rugged, unwelcoming place. Then, rounding a rocky spit of land, they caught their first glimpse of the Miradore itself in the distance. Tai clutched at his aching belly as a surge of nausea went through him. He remembered all too well his last approach to this place.

Sliding into his other-awareness, Tai *sensed* the Miradore. To his world-eyes it was merely a dark and distant shape. To his other-sense, however, it pulsed like a great, luminous heart. Tai felt a skittering of terror, fierce ambition and hate, pain and quick joy and fear, reflected in the communal under-pattern of the place. But there was more. Radiating from it were waves of . . . Tai was not sure, but it was like a rhythmic pattern beaten out on some great, intangible drum.

Tancred!

Tai *knew*.

The beating pattern pulsed out from the Miradore's heart, moving irresistibly through the world, seducing it, shaping it, guiding and lifting and moving, trying to force events into rhythm with Tancred's desires. Tai had *reached* his will to move things in the world, but nothing like this! Tancred's will extended out like an enormous, living web, tangling past and future and present.

Suddenly, Tai misgave everything that had occurred over past days. Tancred's will tainted all.

Only an instant, did it take Tai to perceive all of this, and then, behind the beat of that tangling will, he *sensed* a cold *awareness*.

Quick as an eyeblink, Tai drew concealment about his little band, drawing the pattern of them-in-the-boat into a sharply tapering, tight little dart that could pass through the Seer's beating web undetected. He held the illusion intact, learning as he went, one small part of him wondering at the ease with which he did such unreal things.

He waited then, breathless, for the *awareness* in the Miradore to notice.

There was no change.

It had worked!

A rush of pride went through him. His misgivings evaporated. The sickness in his belly dropped away. He felt a quiet exaltation, balancing his strength, utterly a part of the moment, like a dolphin riding a wave.

Tancred could not stop him. He and his companions would reach Colby and set him free. *Free!* He felt this in his bones, felt it in the evanescent patterns he *sensed*. And after Colby, the Veil . . .

Tai grinned a fierce grin. No longer was he helpless.

It felt *good*.

Holding the dart-pattern of illusion firm, he slipped into dual vision, seeing the ordinary world as well as the other.

'I can keep us free from the Seer's attention,' he said softly to Dreamwalker. 'Can you turn the eyes of any guards from us?'

Dreamwalker nodded in the dark, a mere half-guessed motion. It was enough.

They made landfall in a small, sandy cove surrounded by jaws of dark rock that hid the rise of the Miradore from sight. The Ratter skipped ashore from the bow and hauled the boat up along the sand until it caught. The others came after, until only Costa was left onboard.

The isle seemed dark and forbidding at this cold moment of the night.

'I,' said Costa, 'will stay with the boat.' He shivered, peering into the dark. 'I'm a simple smuggler. No hero to go striding out to take on the likes of *them*. Are you with me, Ratter?'

Ratter shrugged uneasily. 'I don't—'

'Don't be *crazy*!' Costa snapped. 'This is *their* isle.'

Tai cut in. 'I am maintaining an "illusion" that keeps us all safe from . . .' He was not sure what to say, for Costa, like most, was unaware of the Seer's existence. He began again. 'If we leave you behind, I cannot guarantee that you will be safe.'

Costa swallowed. 'Oh,' he said. 'A sorcerous thing, is it?'

'Aye,' Tai answered, not knowing what else to say.

'Oh,' Costa repeated. He hesitated, then stepped unhappily out of the boat, clutching his cane.

Silently, they made a cautious way inland, Tai first, along with Skeefer, Ree perched on the fur-man's shoulder, then Dreamwalker and Ratter and Costa. Little grew hereabouts but tough sea-grass and sedge. Sharp rocks underfoot made the going treacherous. They had to climb a rocky promontory, helping each other over the uneven and hummocky surface. From the top of this, they could see the Miradore once again. To Tai's world-eyes, its bulk was huge and featureless, with no lights showing. To his other-sense, though, it pulsed mesmerically. He could feel the seductive pull of it and resisted. He kept the illusionary dart-pattern intact about his little band, screening them from the cold awareness he felt so clearly behind the beating pulse.

'Do ye know where ye are?' Ratter asked of him in a whisper.

Tai looked with his world-eyes. There was the dock at which he had first arrived with Colby. There the roadway leading up to the gateway. 'Yes,' he said softly.

''Ow do we get in, then? Place looks a right fortress.'

'And what about watchers?' Costa demanded. 'I suppose you've thought of that?'

Tai looked at Dreamwalker.

'It will work or it will not,' she said. She stood up, leaned on her stick, and gazed at the Keep. 'Let us try it.'

'Right,' Tai said, standing up with her. He turned to the others. 'Dreamwalker will keep the guards' eyes from us. Let us go.'

He set off downslope towards the Miradore, Dreamwalker with him. Skeefer came padding along, Ree on his shoulder. From behind, he heard Ratter and Costa arguing together in fierce, subdued voices.

'Well *I'm* goin',' said the Ratter, and scurried along.

After a moment, Costa followed. 'You're all *mad!*' he hissed.

It was, indeed, a strange feeling, walking thus boldly towards the Miradore's dark bulk. It seemed to take an age to cross the intervening distance. The area about the Keep was open, empty of any cover. A part of Tai expected to hear shouts of alarm at any second, and the skin on the back of his neck prickled coldly. But another part of him felt confident in the momentum of what they did here.

Finally, under the shadow of the great wall, they stopped.

'Further along,' Ree said softly, 'is a little door.'

They moved further along the wall until they came to it. ''Ere it is,' Ratter whispered. Tai moved his hand over a small, thick wooden door, studded with iron nails. He *sensed* the pattern of the door's locking mechanism, feeling the small iron teeth clench each other like a jaw. He *reached* and unclenched them.

There was a faint, soft *tlickk*. Turning the door's chill iron handle, he pushed it inwards, slowly.

They slipped in, finding themselves in a courtyard. At the far end stood several guards, demon faces glimmering in the light of a lantern. They did not look round.

Tai tried to orient himself. They stood now at the edge of the Keep's main courtyard. Despite the night-darkness, he recognized the entrance to the cells where he had been first put. And where Colby ought now to be. There was much to do this night, but Colby came first, before all.

'That way,' he whispered, gesturing towards the entrance to the cells.

They moved off, stepping boldly across the courtyard in plain sight of the demon guards, plainly unseen.

Tai pushed at the door leading to the cells. It moved, but stiffly, with a little screech of complaint from the hinges. One by one, they ducked inside.

Before them lay the dark, stone-walled corridor leading to the cells. Ahead, faintly, came the red glimmer of low-burning torches. The place was dead quiet. A damp cold seeped from the stone walls about them.

Dreamwalker collapsed against the wall, gasping.

The Ratter reached to her concernedly. 'Are ye all right, Lady?'

She smiled wanly. 'It is tiring to do such.'

'I never would've believed it!' Costa exclaimed, staring at Dreamwalker. 'Walked right in, we did, plain as could be . . .'

But Tai had attention only for the corridor ahead, where his foster-uncle lay. 'Come!' he urged. 'Along this way.'

Colby . . .'

How long had it been since last he had seen his foster uncle? Tai did not know. Too much had happened. He had lost count of days. He only hoped, with a fierce hope, that the time had not been too long, and that the Veil's Pit had not been too . . . hungry.

Tai cast ahead with his other-sense, trying to locate his foster-uncle's cell. He could *sense* the pulse of life that came from within each cell. Tai shuddered. Each pulsed with pain.

And then, ahead, he grew aware of Colby.

'Here,' he called softly, and led the others to his foster-uncle's cell door. 'In here.'

But now that he was arrived, he could not, suddenly, force himself to go in. This was what he had lived for since first being brought to the

Miradore – to free his foster-uncle. All had gone impossibly well so far this night, everything falling into place to get him here. This was the moment he had anticipated. But not a sound could he hear from behind the door, and though Tai could *sense* Colby within, the pulse of him was faint and wavery.

Tai shivered. He lifted the cell door's locking bar with shaking fingers, and pulled the door open.

The cell stank of damp and rotting flesh and excrement. Tai gagged. He lifted one of the low-flickering torches from its sconce on the outer wall and held it into the cell. In the far corner, he saw feet protruding from a blanket, and under the blanket, Colby, huddled in a dark mass.

At the sound of Tai's entrance, Colby moaned and tried to scrunch himself further into the corner.

Remembering his own experiences of what it was like in these cells, Tai said quickly, 'Colby . . . Colby! It is me, Tai. I have come for you.'

But poor Colby only moaned the more.

The Ratter peered in from behind Tai. 'What sort o' terrible place . . . ?'

Tai handed him the torch, silently, and turned to his foster-uncle. Kneeling, he put a hand gently on Colby's shoulder and tried to turn him. The blanket that covered Colby was filthy and encrusted under Tai's hand. Tai tugged harder. 'It is me, Colby. *Me*, Tai. I have come for you.' But Colby only moaned and struggled, trying weakly to resist.

Tai took hold of the blanket and peeled it off.

What he saw then brought him to his feet, staring.

Both of poor Colby's arms were gone entire. He shuddered and moaned incoherently, rocking back and forth, scrabbling with the oozing stumps of his arms to press himself further into the corner.

Tai felt his stomach heave and he stumbled backwards, gagging. But then, overcome with the pity of it, he knelt again at his foster-uncle's side and wrapped his arms about him. 'Colby, poor Colby,' he moaned, holding the man and rocking.

Colby struggled at this hold on him, terrified.

'Colby,' Tai said. 'Colby!' But his foster-uncle showed no signs of recognizing him. 'Poor soul,' Tai murmured. 'Poor, poor soul . . .'

Tai wept. Too late. He was come too late.

There was a soft sound of movement, and Dreamwalker squatted at Tai's side. She reached a hand gently down to Colby and stroked his forehead. 'Thou must set him free,' she said to Tai.

It took a long moment for her meaning to sink in, and when it did, Tai experienced a shuddering, terrible moment of revelation. He was indeed going to set his foster-uncle free, as he had *sensed*. But not, *not* in the way he had anticipated.

'It is thine to do,' Dreamwalker said.

'He does not even *know* me!'

'All the more reason. It is his time, man, past his time. He aches for the Shadowlands. Does thou not *feel* it?'

Yes, he felt it. Poor Colby's spirit was filled with a yearning for an end. Like a fish out of water it was, burning in air, aching desperately for the cool of its proper home.

Weeping still, Tai *reached* . . .

It was not a difficult thing to do. Colby yearned so, all Tai had to do was give his poor spirit the smallest of nudges and it was away, freed, dwindling over the dark threshold of the Shadowlands.

Tai came back to the cell, the tears hot on his cheeks, his own spirit shaken to its core.

Dead Colby hung in his arms, limp and pathetic.

Tai took a long, shuddering breath. What agonies must the poor soul have endured here?

At that thought, the old, familiar anger roused in him. *They* had made poor Colby suffer like this. Tancred and the Lord Veil. For *sport*!

Tai lowered his foster-uncle's still form to the cold stone floor and stood up. It was time to make *them* pay. He felt the anger like a living force within him, himself blazing like a torch with it.

Whirling, he strode out of the cell.

'Hey!' Costa called, but Tai was gone already, oblivious, down the corridor. He half heard the patter of their feet behind him. He did not care. Up a winding flight of steps he flew, taking them three and four at a time, round and round dizzyingly, feeling a kind of ecstatic rage flow through him like a current.

At an intersection at the top of the stairs, he encountered a pair of demon guards. They stared at him, the yellow eyes shocked. But Tai merely *reached* and tore the creatures' lives from them with a single terrible, unseen blow. The guards collapsed, clattering to the floor, and Tai charged onwards. He felt the rage growing invincibly in him now. Like spell-helm vitality it was, but more, much more . . .

Tai reached out, trying to *sense* the whereabouts of Tancred. But beyond the generalized feeling of *awareness* that pulsed through the Miradore, he could locate nothing. The Seer seemed everywhere, and nowhere. Tai slowed his rushing advance and stood confused, uncertain which way to go. The corridors were many and complex. His whole being was now one great ache to come at his enemies, to punish them. But he stood balked.

Some distance off, he *sensed* beings moving, a Demon-helmed squad.

He laughed, softly. Little did the foul creatures know how easily he could destroy them.

But he *sensed* now a second moving configuration – his companions!

He heard a shout echo from the distance along the dark corridors, *sensed* the pulsing motes of his companions, and all about . . . *them*. Tai felt the cold touch of fear, realizing suddenly what he had done.

In deserting his companions as he had, all unthinking, he had taken from them their protection. He was still invisible to the Seer's attentions, having instinctively protected himself. But they had no such cover. Only he was now hidden in the dart-pattern he had originally fashioned to conceal them all.

Furious, Tai ran, and running, *reached* ahead of himself desperately, tearing into the men-demons near his companions, ripping them out of life and into the Shadowlands.

He arrived panting, dizzy and nauseous from what he had done. About lay the demon-bodies, sprawled like so many rag-dolls. Only his five companions remained. Tai leaned against a wall, trying to catch his breath.

'Man,' said Dreamwalker, 'there was no need for all this death.'

'What?' Tai gasped.

'There was no need. *They* had not seen us.'

'I heard a . . . cry.'

'*Them* calling to each other.'

'Not *you*, then?'

Dreamwalker shook her head. 'Not us. I had hidden us from *their* sight. Could you not feel it?'

Tai clenched his fists. He felt the anger flare up in him, like a great burst of fire.

'Man!' Dreamwalker said. 'Look at thyself. Thou is becoming as *them*. Thou kills without thought in thy fury. Violence is a Power that moves in the world. Allow it too much sway and more begets more, and still more. Violence *breeds*, man. Does thou not see that? Has thou not seen too much of that already?'

But Tai only shook his head angrily. He had no time here for pious, silly lectures from ungrateful old women.

'Why did you follow me?' he demanded in irritation.

'What else were we to do?' Costa replied.

Tai stared at his erstwhile companions. He did not want these five with him now. They would be nothing but an impediment. He wished only to be alone and free to wreak his vengeance.

'Come,' he said, angry at being saddled with the responsibility of them. 'We must away before more of *them* find you.' He turned and beckoned. 'This way.'

But Dreamwalker shook her head. 'No. That is not the way, man.'

Tai glared at her. 'This way is clear. I *know*.'

'It is not the way that needs to be cleared,' Dreamwalker said. 'Thy mind is clouded with power and with anger.'

Tai could see them all looking at him uneasily now, like so many anxious fowl. He felt sick, almost, with the fury that gripped him. He was so close to attaining the vengeance which for so long he had been powerless to achieve. He *reached*, encompassing the Ratter, Costa, Skeefer, Ree, and Dreamwalker with his will, netting them into a single joint pattern that would follow his bidding. It was for their own good, this. They would see that in the end. He would find some safe place to leave them. No further delay or interference would he brook, from them or any person.

Obedient to his will, Ratter, Costa, Skeefer, and Ree turned to follow as he directed. But not Dreamwalker. The willing he tried to force upon her went through her, or she through it, as if he were trying to fashion liquid water into some solid, unchanging shape.

Dreamwalker stared at him, her green eyes hard as stone, but she said nothing.

Tai was completely furious now. Balked at every turn! He felt the moment slipping. All too soon their presence would be discovered, and demon guards would be upon them in greater and greater numbers. Even his new-found strengths could not cope with too many of *them* at one time. He had to get away from here, had to accomplish the act of vengeance before—

'Welcome back, boy,' a cold voice said suddenly from behind him.

Tai whirled. There in the corridor stood Seer Tancred. Tai *reached* out furiously.

Nothing happened.

He tried to move, but found his muscles frozen.

Tancred laughed. 'You made too many mistakes, boy. And now you are mine once more.'

# XXXII

# The Miradore

Crane stared at the Seer, seeing for the first time the tall, cloak-shrouded figure, the skull-like, pale face. The eyes in that face glittered like black stones. She *felt* the man's inner form and shuddered: he was such a bent creature. All will and power and desire. All self, only self.

Crane had not the true-sight like Tai, but she half sensed a painful shifting about her. Tai stiffened, his limbs shuddering, hands clawing at the empty air about him. Then he went rigid as a stone statue. Only his eyes stayed alive, flitting desperately in their sockets.

The Seer smiled, and the smile gave him a ghastly look. 'Concealing yourself as you did was clever, boy. But you should never have come back for these others once you dropped the concealment from them. A silly mistake. You have grown, boy. But not enough. I am glad I brought you back to me before you could do yourself any serious damage. You do, after all, still have your uses . . .'

At the startled look in Tai's eyes, the Seer nodded. 'Oh yes. It *was* my doing that brought you back here to the Miradore after your unfortunate escape. I underestimated you there, boy. But then, you had help, did you not?' Tancred turned his cold gaze upon Skeefer and Ree. 'How kind of you to keep them ready for me like this. You hold them. I hold you. Simple and elegant.'

Crane saw the desperate effort Skeefer and Ree made to break free from what gripped them. But to no avail. They were utterly helpless.

Tancred laughed. 'I shall look forward to properly punishing these two. As for the rest here . . .' he shrugged. 'They are of no importance, merely flotsam trapped in the net I wove to return you to me.' The Seer walked over to Tai and stood before him. 'The world is a complicated place, boy, and under the illusionary surface shimmer, the underlying, hidden patterns of it are more so. One *wills* a certain pattern to come about – in small ways in flesh and bone, for instance, or in larger ways in the greater world – and the result is ofttimes surprising.

'You have a true gift, boy. Greater, perhaps, than I first realized. You have surprised me. It has been long since anybody surprised me so. You will make a *valuable* tool.'

Crane listened to all this uneasily. Not having been under Tai's control when the Seer took him, she was not now under the Seer's control either. Something which Tancred had, so far, appeared to overlook.

She found herself shaken by the sheer brazen power of the man.

But something had to be done.

She stepped away from the corridor wall where she had been standing, her old heart thudding in her breast. 'The world,' she said softly, leaning on her stick for support, 'is full of surprises.'

The Seer turned. 'It is indeed,' he said, regarding her with cold, narrowed eyes.

'Thou is a meddler,' she told him.

He smiled at this. 'You *disapprove* of me, old woman?'

'Thou moves against the Powers of the world. Thou is a bent man.'

Tancred laughed. 'How quaint you are.'

Without warning, Crane felt a sudden unleashing of power. It was like a pouring of searing heat into a cool place, painful and debilitating, unlike anything she had ever experienced.

And then, it was as if a great hard hand were wrenching at her soul, ripping it out and away and towards the Shadowlands, tearing, tearing . . .

Thorn and ash, the dim humps of the darkling hills looming before her . . .

But Crane was no ordinary woman. The Shadowlands held no terror for her. She had walked their periphery before this and returned.

And return she did now, feeling her body quiver as her spirit poured into it.

Tancred stared at her in disbelief. Then he smiled. 'Perhaps you, also, may have your uses, old woman.'

A great rush of fear and weakness swept over Crane then, as though she were naught but a small child faced suddenly with things far too overwhelming for her to cope with. The room seemed to twist and heave about her. She felt her heart begin to race.

But she was not a child, nor had been for many a year. She had never experienced this thing Tancred was producing in her, had never imagined it possible to do such. But she had herself experienced much.

She blanked her mind, calling upon the long years of experience that had made her Dreamwalker. The debilitating fear was growing now, growing into a stark, all-encompassing terror. Her heart stammered with it. But she had faced fear before. One of the first lessons of any Dreamwalker was to face fear, to let the fear pass through her and not to lose the Dream. Crane brought all her considerable powers of concentration to bear and focused on allowing the fear, and the sense of debilitating weakness, to pass through her, leaving her unaffected. It did not entirely work: the Seer was far too strong, and too subtle. But it worked well enough.

Tancred stared at her. 'You . . . surprise me . . . old woman,' he hissed, the words coming out slow and harsh, his face stiff with the intensity of his concentration.

'You are not the . . . only one . . . with . . . skill,' she replied. Each word took an agony of effort. She moved forward, one step, another, straining with each movement.

The Seer reached an arm to her, finger out, stabbing.

Her heart began clamouring wildly. As best she could, she stilled it. The fear in her redoubled. But it had little effect now. Fear was fear, great or small, and once one knew how to cope with it, one coped.

Tancred's eyes widened.

Crane managed another few steps, and then a thick blackness began to engulf her, like a choking cloud. She squinted uneasily into the clinging dark. Not a sound could she catch save the thumping of her own heart in her ears. And then, glowing palely before her, she saw a face, a great-jawed toad-face, mottled and warty. The foul creature loomed out of the dark, big as any mountain bear. The mouth was all fangs, gleaming with ribbons of sticky saliva. She smelled the rottenness of its breath and recoiled, gasping.

The thing moaned. The eyes in that warty face bulged hideously. But they were human eyes for all that, human in their knowing look. It stalked towards her on four taloned feet, moving like a powerful, clumsy dog.

She started to back fearfully away and then stopped. There was a certain *feel* to this creature.

It moved upon her, mouth agape.

She stood her ground.

With a moaning cry, it leaped, the great yellowed fangs coming together to . . .

It passed through her like a cloud, dampness and coolth, and was gone into nothingness.

Illusion.

Crane willed her sight to come clear. The darkness slowly dissolved. There stood Tancred, stiff-faced and glaring.

In her right hand, Crane still clutched her old, familiar walking stick. With slow, deliberate, painful movements, she moved closer to the Seer. He backed away from her, the two moving in a kind of deliberate, slow-motion dance. Crane approached. Tancred withdrew. Crane stepped to the left. Tancred to the right.

Crane could shift him, she had that satisfaction. But he was stronger than she.

Tancred laughed, a brittle staccato sound. 'You are tiring, old woman. You are already mine.'

The end came soon and suddenly.

Crane stumbled. Feigning a weakness that was only a little more exaggerated than what she actually felt, she let herself sprawl to the stone floor. But she sprawled towards him.

Tancred stood over her and laughed.

In the middle of his laugh, she lunged forward on her knees and thrust the end of her stick into his abdomen, hard as could be.

The Seer was a powerful, subtle, supremely confident man. Crane's move was all too simple, and all too quick. Tancred crumpled, retched, and the force and the fear that had gripped Crane evaporated.

Before the Seer could properly recover, Crane raised her stick, two-handed, and brought it down with a *craakk* across the side of his hairless skull. Tancred crumpled.

Crane stood, gasping, her heart thumping painfully. The Seer lay still, his skull bleeding from the gash her stick had made. She saw the rise and fall of his ribs as he breathed. He moaned. His arm twitched.

Shivering, Crane raised her stick. He was a bent creature. There was no other way. No other.

He moaned again, moving, and she struck him. Tancred howled. He managed to drag himself up on hands and knees. She felt him try to work his will upon her once more. But she beat at him again and again until her stick became sticky and dark with his blood.

Standing over the still, dead thing he had become, Crane felt herself sway, weary beyond belief. She collapsed to the floor, her mind in a dark fog. Cheek pressed against the cold stone, she squinted upwards to see young Tai and the others staring at her, staring at the Seer's smashed, dead form, their mouths open in shock.

'Are you all right?' a voice asked. Tai's voice. The scar across his forehead was livid, his face pale and shaken, features pinched with concern. 'How did you . . . ?'

'Beat him to death with her stick,' Costa said in awe.

Crane could hardly believe it herself. She stared at the still form of the Seer. The world *was* full of surprises.

'Dreamwalker! Are you hurt?' Tai once more. 'Speak to me!'

'I am alive. That is something, yes?' But Crane felt utterly, utterly weary. She was too old. This last confrontation had broken her.

She thought of the death tracery the bones had shown when she threw them. A part of her had known, ever since that evening on far Mount Stroud in the Bone Peaks, that she had been fated never to return from this. Her part was finished. Long and long had she lived. Long enough. She had done her part. She felt her old heart falter. Now it was time to leave.

But no . . .

Storm was still loose in the world. The cusp-time was not yet over. She felt that true. Perhaps because she hovered so near the Shadowlands now, she could sense the looming shape of it more clearly. There was some pattern still to be completed. She could feel it as a great, amorphous yearning all about her.

'Help me up,' she said, panting. 'There is that which must yet be accomplished.'

They stared at her.

'Help me up!'

Hands reached, and she was pulled gently to her feet.

'The Veil,' Ree piped.

'Yess . . .' hissed Skeefer in agreement.

'The Veil,' Tai echoed.

Crane nodded.

# XXXIII

# Long Harbour

In the chill, quicksilver moment before dawn, they stood massed before the city, man-demon faces and men's alike tense and fixed. Looking ahead, Jonaquil could make out a long, dark shape, like the body of some huge, supine beast. But it was men, many, many men, sweating and frightened and furious. Curling vapour hung in the air about them from their breath.

Long Harbour loomed before them, a massive, dark, jagged outline against the fading stars on the western horizon.

Jonaquil shivered with nerves. She felt helpless and foolish standing here behind this rag-tag army, her bag of remedies over her shoulder, Tishta and others with her, trained or half-trained, ready to try and help those who would be injured. What good were she and her little group amidst such numbers? What was she *doing* here?

But her belly was knotted with dread certainty. Dreams and portents had led her to this moment. She looked across at Tishta, shivering.

'Luck, girl,' Tishta said softly, reaching to her.

'Luck,' Jonaquil returned.

At the fore, Egil raised his great axe aloft, the metal blade shimmering strangely. He let out a single, echoing roar, like some great hunting beast's, and then brought the axe down again, aiming it towards the city.

In a rush, as one single entity, they charged.

It was uncanny. The steady *thump thump thump* of running feet, the panting breaths of men, the clink of metal, the creaking of leather. There was no shouting, no battle yells, just the strange, communal sound of hundreds of moving bodies. Everything seemed to blend together somehow, and it seemed suddenly to Jonaquil that Egil, far ahead of her now, moved on the crest of a strange, living wave.

At any moment, Jonaquil expected to see a rain of spears come down on the running men. She felt ill at the thought. But there was nothing. Shouts went up from the Long Harbour watchtowers. She could see the dark shapes of men-demons moving about.

Once, Long Harbour had been a walled city, but the walls were of

336

little account now. Too many gateways and entrances, small and large, had been punched through them. The human wave broke against the city walls and shattered into a dozen groups, bottle-necking up into various gates and entranceways. Squads of demon guards tried to hold the entrances, but were swept aside in the flood that poured in.

And then, somehow, they were through and the city lay open before them.

The moment was strangely anticlimactic. The streets were dark and empty and silent. Apart from the brief commotions on the watch-towers, it almost seemed as if their entrance had gone unnoticed. The men hesitated, puzzled. They had been prepared for fighting and death and iron, not empty, dark streets and silence. Into an open square they poured, milling about skitterishly.

A troop of demon guards appeared, dog-trotting along in orderly fashion down one of the streets leading into the square. The rabble of men and men-demons swarmed over them in a brief, screaming, confused mass.

When it was done, Egil strode through, ripping spell-helms from the dead. To Jonaquil's eyes, a great, searing light roared about him. The helms he held glowed with it when he passed them on to others.

Wounded were carried back to Jonaquil and the others waiting for them. She moved in a kind of daze, her sensitive Healer's flesh agonized by the suffering all about, feeling a pulse here, holding together a pumping artery, giving instructions and advice.

And it had only just barely begun.

The army began to move off through the streets, a vast, boisterous fury taking hold. There seemed no further resistance to be found anywhere, and the men began to cheer, anticipating victory.

The city was coming alive now. Windows opened around the square. Faces peered out of doorways. Slowly, a great cheer went up from the people as they realized what was happening. Egil's men whooped and threw their caps in the air. 'Free!' half a hundred voices shouted. 'Free now!' And, 'Death to the southern man-demons!'

It got taken up as a general chant: 'Death to the man-demons! Death to the Southerners!'

People began to spill out into the square from their houses. Everywhere was shouting and struggling crowds. Some of the citizenry launched mistaken attacks upon those amongst the liberating army wearing demon guise. Some of the army fell to looting, squabbling amongst themselves over their stolen gains.

It was noisy, disordered chaos.

And then, through the roar of the gathered crowds, Jonaquil heard screams.

A mass of men came streaming wildly down one of the streets feeding into the square. Behind them coursed a howling pack of demons. And in the demons' midst rode a lone horseman, dressed in soot-black plate-armour, his head showing as a mere silver, faceless orb. In his hand he wielded a long, coldly glimmering broadsword. 'Onwards!' he cried. 'Drive them on. We have them now!'

'What is *that*?' Jonaquil heard a man near her ask in horror, pointing to the faceless one.

But then more men came pouring out of a street on the square's other side, pursued by more howling demons. And at the head of this demon group was another faceless, black-armoured, sword-wielding horseman, impossibly identical to the first.

'It's a trap!' somebody wailed.

'They were expecting us all the time!'

From their different directions, the two demon groups charged forwards. The square became a howling mass of struggling bodies. Wherever any of the two faceless figures rode, men fell back in terror. They seemed invulnerable, those two. No thrown blade could harm them, no sword-thrust strike true through the black armour they wore. The few brave souls who attacked them direct met quick death on the broadswords' glimmering blades.

It rapidly became a rout. Only moments before, it seemed, the square had been filled with victorious revellers. Now men were fleeing in every direction, leaping wildly over the fallen bodies of comrades or enemies, intent only on saving themselves.

Then Egil sprang forward, shouting. Men rallied about him. Jonaquil saw Egil swing his great axe with terrible, bloody effect. The uncanny, berserk rage had taken him, and he spread terror in the ranks of the demons. His own forces surged forwards, inspired, screaming, 'Blood-axe! Egil Bloodaxe! *Bloodaxe!*'

The sheer brutality of it made Jonaquil shudder sickly.

Egil and the men with him hewed a way through the demon soldiers, scattering them, leaping and howling, iron blades bannered with whipping blood.

And then Egil drew close enough to confront the nearer of those faceless horsemen.

For a moment, a weird calm seemed to settle on everything. Fighting stopped, as if by some unspoken command.

Waving his own forces back, the faceless one dismounted. Egil stood glowering, ragged and torn and furious, more grim-seeming and deadly than any demon, his axe raised. He stood a full head and shoulders above the figure before him. But the faceless being looked at Egil and laughed. He held the broadsword balanced in one hand and beckoned with the other. 'Come, Raggedy Man. Come and meet your death at our hands.'

From amongst the crowded demons, the other faceless one appeared, vaulting easily over the heads of those in the front ranks.

Jonaquil shivered. The glowing nimbus of light about these two eerily identical creatures was far huger than any normal human man's, huger than any spell-helm-enhanced man's. Radiance snapped and sparkled and flared about them like a bonfire. And more than this. There seemed to be some sort of strange ribbon of light that wavered out from each to disappear far off into the distance.

It was like nothing Jonaquil had ever seen.

In the square before her now, a cleared area had opened up around these terrible, faceless creatures and Egil. The square was dead silent. All eyes were fixed upon the combatants.

One of the faceless ones stepped forward. 'Come,' he called, the voice coming from the mouthless head unnaturally strong and clear. He beckoned. 'Come. Death awaits you . . .'

With a roar like a bear, Egil charged, the axe high.

But while Egil's force watched, stunned, the faceless one leaped clear over Egil – fully twice the height of a grown man into the air – and landed light as a cat behind him. Again, he laughed. 'You will have to do better than that, Raggedy Man.'

Egil skidded to a halt and whirled back about. This time he came more slowly. He swung the axe in sweeping, deadly arcs, but the black-armoured, faceless figure skipped lightly away at each swing, laughing still.

Watching this from a distance, Jonaquil felt her belly clench. This faceless being, whatever he might be, was playing, merely *playing* with poor Egil. What sort of fell creature was this that could leap twice a man's height into the air and showed no concern at all over furious Egil and his deadly axe?

And there was the second one, too, standing there calmly watching.

Egil's opponent had changed tactics now. When Egil swung the axe, it was met by the broadsword. The *tling* of metal striking metal marked each stroke and counter-stroke, and bright cascades of sparks.

Egil was panting like a hound, his face an inhuman mask of mindless fury.

The faceless one backed away easily, apparently still as fresh as when he had begun. 'It is time,' he said. 'You begin to bore us.' With that, he leaped forward with a sudden, impossible agility. At that same precise instant, his double leaped as well. The first one struck out, the glimmering broadsword a mere blur of motion, catching the head of Egil's axe on the sword-blade, wrenching the axe from Egil's grasp, and sending it flying end over end to land crashing on the flagstones. From behind the second one kicked Egil's legs out from under him, not even bothering to raise his sword.

A gasp went up from those crowded around.

'And now,' a faceless one said, taking a two-handed grip on the glimmering broadsword. 'Now will we send you into Death's lands . . .'

Egil struggled up to his knees, but halted there. Two swords were raised against him now. He stared blankly from one to the other.

Jonaquil too stared. With Egil dead, they had not the slightest chance here. All knew that.

And there seemed not a thing she or anybody else could do about it.

# XXXIV

# The Miradore

Through the maze of dim-lit corridors, Tai and the others raced, Ree fluttering in the lead, guiding. Only so quick could they travel, though, for Costa and the Ratter had Dreamwalker slung between them. The old woman was too weak to walk unaided.

The Keep was alive now, Tai *sensed* it clearly. The alarm had been raised. No longer need he conceal them from the Seer's attentions – the beating pulse and cold *awareness* that he had previously *sensed* animating the Miradore was no more – but there were still demon guards to worry about. He did not have Dreamwalker's subtlety of ability, and was far from certain he could keep prying eyes from seeing this little group in the manner she had.

Half dead, she seemed now. A wrinkled, frail old woman. It was still with difficulty that Tai brought himself to believe that she had done what she had. Helpless, he had witnessed her shrug off all that the Seer had willed upon her; he had seen her walk through all the patterns Tancred had woven, and strike him down.

Tai shivered as he ran, remembering.

Ahead, he *sensed* demon guards. 'Ree!' he hissed, calling her back. He slowed, gesturing to the others, casting about for a way around what came at them.

But the demons were coming too quickly, drawing closer with each breath he took.

'They're ahead,' he told the others. 'Follow me and hold together.'

With that, he set off at a run, the others following. Down a curving corridor they went, emerging at an intersection. A flickering torch in a wall sconce cast its radiance upon the gleaming blades and unhuman faces of a squad of demon-guards suddenly ahead. A shout went up. 'Keep close behind,' Tai called to his companions, his heart thumping, running still. He *reached* his will out, ramming through the squad of demon guards like an iron bolt through a stack of eggs, leaving them smashed and littered in his wake, feeling the old exaltation of rage burn through him as he did so.

Past the crumpled demons he led his companions and beyond.

'Which way, Ree? Quick! We must away from here before the commotion draws more of them down upon us.'

'Here,' Ree piped. 'Downwards now.'

So downwards they went, relying on the small bird's knowledge of the Miradore, following the only way they knew to their goal. They ran when they could, walked when their wind ran out, ran once more. Costa and the Ratter, Dreamwalker still between them, huffed along at the rear. The section of the Keep they moved through remained quiet, but they could hear the echoes of commotion in the distance.

Tai had taken a torch from above and held it aloft now to light their way. Soon the walls about them became damper. Water pooled at their feet.

'Yes,' Ree breathed. 'This way.'

Onwards they continued, splashing through the dank, empty corridors until, some time later, Ree slowed. 'Somewhere here . . .

A flight of stone steps showed in the flickering light of Tai's torch. They almost passed it by all unknowing, for the stair's entrance was only a patch of dark shadow. But Ree pounced upon it, crying, 'Here!' triumphantly.

The stairway corkscrewed narrowly upwards, making it an awkward, slow business, carrying the exhausted Dreamwalker. They arrived at the top panting and shaken.

But they were given no time to recover.

Half a dozen demon guards stood alert and ready upon the railed landing the corkscrew staircase emerged on to. Tai *reached* again, tearing *their* lives away.

He stood there, panting, his heart hammering.

Before them was the carved stone portal, the entranceway.

The little group straggled past the dead demons and through into the high-ceilinged, circular room beyond. There, in the dim light from the skylights above, lay the dais with its grotesque, thrashing, mutilated occupant.

Feeling his heart clutch in his breast, Tai *reached* to that thrashing shape. He had torn the life from so many of *them*. A simple matter now to wrench it from this pitiful thing.

But what he *sensed* was no ordinary man's presence. Power pulsed about the thing before him, radiating outwards in huge, pulsing ribbons, flowing through the Keep, through the world, through to the distant pulsings of other men. Some felt very far off, southwards, some not so far. Nine in all, those others. Nine pulsing beings that were one, or one that was nine.

Tai struggled to tear the glowing spark of life from it as he had from so many men-demons. But he could not, somehow, manage to grasp hold properly, as if the thing on the dais were some manner of many-limbed, slippery beast that slid from his grasp nine ways at once as soon as he gripped it.

He tried harder, panting at the effort, but to no avail.

Tai blinked, coming back, his world-eyes showing him the thrashing, mewling shape. It was limbless, eyeless, hideous. He had not harmed it at all.

The others stood staring. 'Is this *it?*' Costa said in a hoarse voice. He and the Ratter were only just coming to an understanding of what they did here.

Nobody answered.

And then, abruptly, Tai became aware of more demons coming upon them. A large force, storming up the big staircase. And amongst them was something the like of which Tai had never before *sensed*. A double pulse it was, like the spell-helm pulse, but hugely stronger, dwarfing those around it like a mountain eagle might dwarf so many pigeons. Tai *sensed* clearly an aura of sheer power to it like nothing he had ever experienced. What manner of being *was* this?

Tai tried to gather his companions away from the entranceway, but the demons moved too quickly, spilling through the portal into the room like a wave. He saw with his world-eyes the glitter of pike-blades and the demon-faces, yellow eyes shining, tusks glimmering palely. Thrusting his companions behind him, Tai *reached* destructively, tearing away their lives so that, shrieking and howling, they died.

But in their midst was the different one.

With his world-eyes, Tai saw: soot-black armour, this one wore, so that it seemed almost a moving shadow in the room's dim light. It had no face at all, just a pale, shining orb; eyeless, lipless.

Tai had seen the like before, long ago now it seemed, on that fateful morning in the High Hills when he and Colby and the rest had been taken. And on the heels of this memory, he *sensed* something else. Between this being and the mutilated thing on the couch pulsed a glowing ribbon of energy.

One of the Lords Veil.

The Veil leaped forward to place himself protectively before the dais, a coldly glimmering broadsword in his hand. 'It seems we have underestimated you, boy.'

Tai *reached*, trying to wrench the life from the Veil as he had from the men-demons.

But, once again, he found himself balked. The sheer hugeness and power of the Veil's double-pulsing energy was beyond his capacity to grasp. It was like trying to handle a huge, slippery stone; he simply could not get a proper grip.

The Veil reeled at Tai's *reaching* but recovered all too quickly. 'We are not such easy fodder, boy.' He padded a few steps towards Tai, dead silent despite the armour he wore, the sword raised dangerously. He moved lightly, with the coiled-spring strength of one of the great hunting cats.

Tai shivered. He tried the trick he had learned through Dreamwalker in Costa's back room in Long Harbour. *Reaching*, he attempted to fling the Veil's broadsword across the room. The weapon shivered slightly in the other's hand, but that was all.

The Veil laughed. 'You must do better than that.' He padded nearer. The only effect of Tai's attempt was that the Veil had both hands on the sword's hilt now. 'I am going to take you apart like a boar at a banquet, boy, piece by bloody piece.'

Tai backed away, helpless. The Veil was simply too powerful. All Tai's new-found abilities failed against such a one.

Tai's companions had not moved at all since the howling rush of the demon guards had been stilled; they were too dazed by the suddenness of events. Indeed, Dreamwalker sat slumped against the wall, hardly conscious it seemed. But now Tai saw Skeefer sidling over, and there was something about the fur-man's look that made even the Veil pause. Tai had never imagined such furious hatred. He *sensed* the mad, violent force of it.

The Veil laughed, gesturing with the broadsword. 'Come, animal. We hold your death too.'

'No!' Tai cried. But too late.

Skeefer launched himself at the Veil, all spitting, mindless fury.

The Veil skewered him easily, opening poor Skeefer up from belly to throat, and flung him away to land writhing upon the stone floor.

'Aieeee . . .' wailed Ree. She dove at the Veil, swarming about him with hapless, intense fury. He swatted her darting form out of the air with the flat of his hand, sending her smashing into the unyielding stone of the wall. She hit with an audible *smack*, leaving a wet, strawberry mark of blood upon the stone, then fell to the floor, an unmoving heap of feathers.

Tai stood, stricken.

'And now, boy,' the Veil said. 'It is your turn.'

Before he could take a step, though, a sound from behind made him whirl lightly. Standing next to the still form of Dreamwalker, Costa was drawing the blade from his cane. The Ratter, knife in hand, began to circle warily towards the Veil.

Costa stepped away from the wall, danced forward nervously, blade up.

The Veil laughed. With a quick, leaping movement, he grabbed Costa's blade in one guantleted hand and wrenched it from the smuggler's hold.

The broadsword came up. Costa cowered away from it.

'Hoi!' Ratter's voice.

The Veil turned. 'So . . .' His featureless face gazed towards the Ratter, who scuttled carefully out of reach.

Tai could *sense* the pleasure all this gave the Veil, neither simply sensual nor spiritual, but some combined strain of both. The wielding of power, the taking of life, the struggle and surge of confrontations such as this. All were as food and drink to the Veil.

Instinctively, Tai *reached* to the Ratter, who still padded about, knife in hand. He, Tai, was the only one of them here who stood any chance against the Veil. He would *not* stand idle and let Ratter die as Skeefer and Ree had.

'Leave me . . . be,' the Ratter hissed at him, his words coming in slow pants as he struggled against Tai's control.

'No,' Tai responded, trying to keep the man back. 'No! He will kill you as he killed the others.'

'Leave . . . me . . . *be*!' the Ratter panted again. 'It's *ye* will kill me. Not 'im!'

Tai backed off, shocked.

Released from Tai's will, the Ratter resumed his padding about, circling the Veil, feinting in and out again.

It was pitiful, the little knife against the great broadsword.

'You are a brave man,' the Veil said. 'We grant you that.'

Tai *reached* to the Veil, trying, once more, to wrench at the pulse of his life-force. But it was no good.

The Ratter sidled up towards the Veil. 'Are ye so ugly that ye has to cover yer face with that . . . mask?' he demanded.

The Veil laughed. 'Is this your idea of subterfuge?'

'Aye,' the Ratter replied. 'Poor thing that I be, this is my idea of subteefooge. Don't ye 'ave anythin' clever to say back? Rat got yer tongue then?'

Tai did not understand what the Ratter thought he was doing. Why this bandying about? The man sidled back and forth, coming close to the Veil and backing off, circling, all the while keeping up a running talk. 'Sure ye must be especial ugly under that mask. And especial stewpid too. Can't think of nothin' to say to a poor soul such as meself?'

'Enough, little man,' the Veil hissed then, stepping forwards threateningly. 'We have had enough of your insolence . . .'

''Ave ye, now?' the Ratter replied. 'Well, then, per'aps it's time I *did* somethin' . . .'

With this, he turned suddenly, unexpectedly, and dived past the Veil to the dais.

'Come away from there!' the Veil cried.

Quick as quick, Ratter reached up and plunged his knife into the belly of the writhing man-form that lay atop the dais.

'No!' screamed the Veil. '*No!*' He leaped forwards, a single great stumbling leap that carried him across the room, knocking the Ratter away before he could strike again.

But then the Veil faltered, clutching at his belly under the armour.

The Ratter moaned, shook his head, which bled from a cut across his brow, and picked himself up off the floor to his knees. His knife was gone out of his hold, but he grinned. '*Got* ye, ye bastard!'

The only response from the Veil was a bestial, inarticulate rumble of rage. He stalked towards where the Ratter knelt, helpless.

Behind the Veil's back, Tai ran to the dias and scrambled desperately atop. He grabbed the writhing man-thing by the throat, choking it.

The Veil whirled, leaving the Ratter untouched, and leaped back. Even hurt as he was, he still moved with impossible agility and speed. Before Tai could so much as flinch, he found the Veil standing over him, legs astride the dais. The sword came up, glimmering coldly.

Tai stared up into that terrible faceless visage, *sensing* the wound in the Veil that Ratter had made, *sensing* the rage, too, and his own death in that rage.

The sword came down, a flashing arc.

The world seemed to slow.

Tai did not wish to die. He did not want to be there as that cold blade came down upon him. He felt his very flesh shrink away from it.

Tai felt a queer, dark sickness take him, as if he were plummeting through a lightless tunnel. Then, with a painful and unexpected *thwack*, his back smacked up against the cold stone of a wall with bruising force, and he found himself seated splay-legged on the floor, gone from the dais in some instinctive, incomprehensible, wonderful manner, and gone from beneath the falling arc of the Veil's broadsword. Gasping, Tai stared as the Veil's blade came down, heavy as any woodsman's axe, through the now-empty air where Tai had crouched.

'No!' the Veil cried. '*No!*' But it was too late. The swordblade bit through the man-thing, severing head from torso in one great blow. With a scattering of sparks, the metal blade *thwanged* against the stone. then all collapsed, blade, armoured figure, writhing man-thing, all.

## XXXV

# Long Harbour

Jonaquil stared, helpless, as poor Egil knelt defencelessly before the two black-armoured, faceless, invincible beings. One of the two raised his broadsword for a final, killing blow. She saw the creature's huge glowing nimbus of light spark and crackle like a great fire. She saw Egil look up, bleak-eyed, seeing his own death in that coldly glimmering blade.

There was nothing anybody could do.

Then, unexpectedly, the faceless ones shuddered, the hands of each going suddenly to his belly. Jonaquil saw the hugely glowing light about them waver, dim, surge up, dim again. They stood transfixed for a long moment, as if hearkening to something far off that only they could make out. Then, in absolute and uncanny tandem, their backs arched and their heads bent back.

'No!' they cried. '*No!*'

Jonaquil saw the trailing ribbons of light that tentacled out from each of the two faceless beings suddenly extinguished. One instant those ribbons of energy were there, glowing and strong, the next they had vanished, leaving naught but two limp husks behind.

All in the square watched, stunned, as the faceless ones collapsed utterly.

Dead silence, then, for long, long moments.

But Egil scrambled to his feet and reached up his axe from where it lay on the ground. Lifting the gory thing, he shook it above his head triumphantly. At his feet lay the two faceless dead.

A great shout went up from the crowd of ragged men. 'Bloodaxe! Bloodaxe! Bloodaxe!' And so crying, they surged upon the stricken man-demons with a renewed and deadly fury.

## XXXVI

# The Miradore

Slumped against the chill stone of the wall, Crane gazed wearily around her. The room was disaster, littered with dead demons, the dais stained crimson-black with flooded blood. By the wall across from her, Costa leaned over the Ratter, helping the grey-bearded man to his feet. Tai stood over Skeefer's sad body, and the sadder one of little Ree.

'Is that it, then?' Costa said hoarsely to the room at large. 'Is it over?'

Crane felt weary beyond measure. She wanted to let go, to slip away into the beckoning dark of the Shadowlands. Almost, she could see that darksome realm looming before her.

She yearned to give in to the Shadowland pull.

Not yet, she told herself. She felt the *pull* upon her, strongly. The cusp-time was not yet finished. The Dream was not yet brought fully to fruition.

'The city,' she said to Tai, her voice a mere whisper. 'We must get back to Long Harbour. Now!'

Tai looked at her quizzically.

'Can thou not . . . *feel* it, man?'

He stood silent for a long moment, as if listening. He nodded. 'I *sense* something.' He reached down his hand to her. 'Are you able?'

Crane nodded wearily.

'What are ye sayin'?' demanded the Ratter. He looked, the poor man, as if he had been dragged backwards through several thorn-bogs.

'It's *over*,' Costa put in. 'That – ' he pointed to the dead man-thing on the dais – 'is killed.'

'Come on,' Tai said.

The Ratter looked at them, stunned. He put a hand wearily to his bleeding head, wanted only rest now, Crane knew, as did she, not more plunging across the Bay in Costa's boat.

'Come on,' Tai repeated. 'Come *on!*' He was feeling it now, she could tell, that urgent *pulling* . . .

Crane tottered to her feet on Tai's arm. The room about her seemed dim. It was the darkness of the Shadowlands creeping into her, she knew. She held it back by sheer force of will.

Not yet, she told herself again. Not *yet!*

# XXXVII

# Long Harbour

Sub-Commander Gerrid stood perched on a rickety wooden stool, hands gripping the bars of his cell window, peering out into the street below. His cell was on the second floor and he could see a fair way, though the thick stone of the window's casement limited his vision to only a slice of the streets below. The streets were full of running men, guard squads pelting along, wounded being carried on makeshift stretchers through the mess. It was chaos.

Gerrid shook his head and cursed. It was mid-morning now, and the fighting had been going on since dawn. Rebels had obviously attacked the city. And they had moved fast! He himself had only arrived from the Palisade the day before yesterday. He had no idea how the fighting in the streets below might be progressing. It infuriated him.

Stepping down from the stool on which he had been perched, Gerrid began pacing the small area of his cell, frustrated and furious. The Lords Veil had not listened to him, had refused even to grant him an audience. All he had suffered in their service, and they had discarded him like some broken tool!

He knew all too well the fate of those the Veils discarded so: the executioner's block.

He looked across at his spell-helm where it lay on the tatty bunk he had been given to sleep upon. They had not even bothered to separate him from his helm. No need. Even spell-helm strength was not enough to break from this prison room. And the helm would be destroyed with him, upon his execution. He picked the helm up, felt the smoothness, the heft of it. Beautiful, treacherous thing. It put him in mind of the torments he had endured to win it. He had had such hopes . . .

All finished now.

Gerrid cursed Commander Chayne for a fool, and himself for a double-fool.

The sounds outside his cell window reached a sudden crescendo of confusion. Something was happening. Turning, he leaped back up on the stool, gripped the cool iron of the window's bars, peered out. Men were streaming down the street in a confused rout.

He cringed inside, seeing it. Where was their discipline? Their pride? How could the Lords Veil's troops have become such a rabble? It seemed to make no sense. Gerrid could see no enemy pursuing them. What was *happening?*

'Ho!' he called out, trying to attract the attention of one of the fleeing crowd. '*Ho!*'

Nobody paid him the slightest bit of notice.

He persisted, yelling until his throat was hoarse. Finally, one man down below looked up. 'What *is* it?' Gerrid demanded of him. 'What is happening?'

The man's demon-face looked pale and haggard. 'It's the Lords Veil,' he said, and paused, as if the next words stuck in his throat.

'Out with it, man,' Gerrid urged. 'Out with it!'

'They're . . . they're dead,' the man shouted up.

Gerrid stared. '*Dead?*'

'Dead!'

Gerrid felt a sickening sense of disorientation take him. The Lords Veil dead? 'How?'

'I saw them die myself,' the man replied. 'Nothing touched them. Nothing! They clutched at their bellies and went down as if they had been stabbed. But *nothing* touched them! I swear it. Some black witchery at work. Cursed rebels have used some black witchery!'

'What about the Commanders? What about Tash, or Sallus? And their Sub-Commanders?'

'Dead. All dead. Or fleeing for their lives. It's over here for us. Do you hear? Over! The rebels are using spell-helm troops against us! And the whole city has risen. There're too many of them. They've defeated us . . .'

Gerrid looked down at the man below him, at the chaos and confusion in the street. 'Get me out of here!' he yelled. 'Get me *out* of here!'

The man only stared up at him confusedly.

'*Get me out of here!*'

The man hesitated, then nodded and disappeared below into the building.

Gerrid stumbled down from the stool. It was impossible! The Veils dead. Commanders Tash and Sallus dead. The rebels using spell-helm troops, as they had at the Palisade. How had it come to pass. How?

It was the end of everything. It was *impossible*! The Lords Veil could not be dead. Could not. The man must be lying . . .

His cell door rattled in its hinges as the outside bolt was drawn back. Gerrid put on his spell-helm and, as the door opened, strode out of the cell. He felt the helm's vibrant strength fill him.

'Tell it to me again,' he commanded the man.

The man repeated it. It was incredible, impossible.

'Two Veils dead, you say?' Gerrid said.

The man nodded. 'And a . . . a third, too, on Hound's Head Isle.'

'A third!' Gerrid said in dismay.

'Men say the Miradore has fallen to some northern wizard. He took the Keep with a band of warriors. Materialized out of air, they did. He killed the Seer Tancred, too, this wizard. I tell you, it is the end for us!'

Gerrid took a long breath, another, trying to assimilate what he had been told. He could not but feel a sense of relief over the Seer's going, but as for the rest . . .

From outside, he heard the sounds of a full-scale rout in progress. Was this how it would all end, troops driven like hapless cattle? Were they to die dishonourably, fleeing for their lives like cowards before this northern rabble?

Gerrid clenched his fists. He was not yet ready for that fate.

'What company?' he demanded of the man who had freed him.

'Lowe's company,' the man said, surprised. 'But Lowe too is dead. Too many are dead!'

The man was so dishevelled that it was impossible to see insignia or marks of rank on him 'Your name? Rank?'

'Pall. Squad Leader.'

'Right then, Squad Leader,' Gerrid said. 'Consider yourself promoted to Company Head.'

The man stared.

'Field promotion,' Gerrid snapped. 'Do you not know who I am?'

The man shook his head.

'Gerrid. Sub-Commander Gerrid.'

'But I thought—'

'It matters not what you thought, Company Head,' Gerrid told him. 'The situation has changed. It appears I am the only one surviving to command.' He strode on ahead, towards the stairs leading down into the street. 'Come,' he called back. 'There is much to be done here!'

For a long moment Pall simply stood there, his face slack. Then a look of enormous relief came over his demon-features. 'Yes, *Sir!*' he said, and followed after Gerrid's retreating back down the stairs.

It took Gerrid long hours to get some sort of order implemented. He shouted commands until his voice became a harsh croak, organized the remaining men into squads and troops, assigned defensive perimeters, saw to the organization of what supplies and food there was, and to care of the wounded. It was late afternoon before things began to approach even a semblance of their usual organization.

And throughout it all, sporadic fighting continued.

The rebels were in solid control of much of the city, including the quays. But Long Harbour was a large, complex place, with too many streets and sideways. Numerous though they were, and with their ranks swelled by the citizenry who had risen up with them, the rebels could still not cover everything, even with spell-helm troops. So Gerrid had managed to create a kind of temporary haven spanning a half-score of blocks in the south-western quarter of the city. But temporary it certainly was.

Sitting at a makeshift field-desk in a ground-floor room of a gutted house, Gerrid sipped at a cup of tepid water and tried to think. This was no war of conquest they fought here. Now they fought simply to stay alive and keep themselves free. They had supplies, food and weapons, but in limited amounts. Water too would prove a problem soon enough. And they were trapped here. At their backs lay the Bay Cliffs, twenty paces of sheer rock leaning out over Harbour Bay. Not very high perhaps, but high enough. Getting men and supplies down would be impossibly difficult. Besides, they had no boats. Escape that way was impossible. South of them, the rebels held the city, blocking off retreat in that direction, as they did east and north.

Their only chance for survival here, it seemed to Gerrid, was to attempt to bore a way through the rebel forces eastwards, flee the city that way, and escape into the expanse of the Wold. They would *have* to win free from this trap they now found themselves in. It was that, or defeat and death.

Evening would be coming on soon. The city was strangely quiet. Fires burned here and there, their light making an eerie radiance in the distance, but neither side could afford to fire the place. Not yet, anyway. Gerrid filed the thought away as a future possibility. If all else failed, they could make a funeral pyre of this entire city. Let that be their monument!

He felt a kind of fierce, hopeless exaltation. He felt like some predatory beast, cornered by hounds, turned at bay. Everything had been stripped from him now, his career, his one time ambitions. But all the intrigue and confusion that had plagued him were gone, too. It was like being flayed alive. But it was also strangely liberating. He was a prisoner no longer. He had men to lead, and nothing left now to fight for but life itself.

He could read the same sentiments in the men about him.

Enough of retreat. They would win free here, or they would die. But if they were to die, then they would do so honourably, weapons to hand, not fleeing like some hapless, disorganized rabble.

He watched the distant fires flicker, and waited. There was no point in delaying overlong here. Time was on the rebels' side. As soon as evening settled in, he and what force remained to him should be off. If they moved quickly and forcefully enough, they just might be able to punch their way through to the city's eastern gates and thence through to at least a chance of safety in the open lands beyond. If not – well, their vanquishment would cost the rebels a high price indeed.

They moved out with no fanfare, slipping through the streets as silently as possible. Gerrid had sent small parties ahead to try and clear the way. If Gerrid could get his force moving quickly enough, they ought to be able to take the rebels by surprise. The rebels were exhausted, and obviously taking what they saw as a perfect opportunity to rest. So much the better.

But Gerrid's force too was exhausted. There were only a few hundreds of them now – certainly far less than what the combined rebels and citizenry amounted to – and of that number, all too few were truly hale and whole. And many of these were encumbered with wounded. Gerrid had given instructions that not a single man left living, no matter how badly hurt, no matter how much a burden to carry, was to be left behind.

They had little choice but to push on and hope.

Gerrid moved at the head of the straggling column. It was difficult to keep any sort of proper order in the darkness, moving through the narrow, twisty streets, but he did his best, keeping runners going up and down the line to pass on instructions. They slowed their advance as they neared the rebel-held positions.

Gerrid called a halt. All was as well as could be expected up to this point. He stood leaned against the dark wall of a building. According to his scouts, a segment of the rebel force were encamped in a large market square ahead. Not enough, his scouts insisted, to resist them. This was it, then. Their entryway to escape. He sent orders down the line for everyone to prepare himself. They formed up in a kind of spear-head formation, the wounded in the rear.

At the spear's point, Gerrid gave the signal. They moved forward through the darkness in a mass, at a slow, jogging run. There was no sound but that of their movement, the slapping of bootsoles on cobblestones, the clanking of gear, the panting of the men's breaths.

They were through and into the square before the rebels were properly aware of them. The point of the spear should have bored through the rebel encampment, the rest following behind. They should have been able to cut their way through.

But Gerrid slowed, stumbled to a halt, his men stopping along with him.

The square before them seethed. The place was lit by a kind of eerie half-light, partly from distant fires, partly from the torches and low-burned campfires the rebels had used here. What Gerrid saw before him was not individual men, but a swirling, confused mass of limbs and stark faces and weapons. Here a pike-blade glimmered in the light, there a face appeared suddenly, mouth opened, only to be gone again in an instant.

In their haste, and in the darkness, Gerrid's scouts had misjudged the numbers here. Misjudged badly. He understood how it might have happened. It did not matter how it might have happened. It was a fatal mistake.

There would be no escape for them from this place.

Gerrid swallowed. One too many mistakes. The final, hard lesson was to be his, then.

So be it.

As if by some sort of strange, mutual, unspoken agreement, the two sides stood facing each other without moving, silent, the rebels in a solid, disorderly mass along the far side of the square, Gerrid's force formed up into a more compact group across from them. Thirty paces of littered cobblestone lay between. The square was silent. Gerrid could hear the pop and crackle of the dying fires, the shuffling of somebody's boot-heel across the cobblestones nearby, the clank of a blade.

Before him, suddenly, he sighted the huge, scar-faced, axe-wielding man he had seen up in the Peaks. The rebel leader. The man stood now, tall and thick as an oak, the great double-bladed axe swinging in his hand like a pendulum. Gerrid remembered that axe all too clearly. The man's face was a mask of grim fury. Silently, he raised the axe over his head.

'Bloodaxe! Bloodaxe! Bloodaxe!' the crowd about him roared.

The man brought the axe down in a sweeping, smashing gesture towards Gerrid and his men. Gerrid braced himself. This was to be it: the final clash. Now there remained nothing but to take as many of these rebels with them when they died.

But then, startlingly, unexpectedly, a voice rang out, high and clear and shrill. A woman's voice.

'Enough!'

The utter unexpectedness of it was such that everybody froze.

From the far edge of the anonymous ranks of the rebels, a figure darted out into the clear space separating the two opposing forces and stood there, arms raised. To his surprise, Gerrid recognized her. It was Jonaquil, the Healer from the Palisade.

The startled silence that had descended upon them all was such that her voice carried clearly across the square. 'Enough dead,' she cried to them. '*Enough*, I say!'

A growling mutter came from the packed rebels. Gerrid shook his head. What madness had possessed this woman?

The scar-faced rebel leader paused, looking askance momentarily at Jonaquil. But his face showed no change from the fury that was in it. The rebels behind him looked as if ready to make their charge.

Gerrid braced himself for it.

# XXXVIII

# Long Harbour

Jonaquil stood on the cobblestones, exposed between the ranks of the two forces. Her heart beat wildly, and, for a moment, she could not get breath.

Her leap forward from out of the crowd of Egil's men had been unthinking. She had seen enough, this past day, of death and hurt. Her Healer's flesh agonized with it still. And more than enough of hate. She could feel it all about her like a live thing beating through the men here, like her own pulse beating in her throat. It sickened her, what these men here were become.

So she had leaped forwards, driven by a revulsion so strong it made her gag. There was no question of her attempting to halt the violence here as she had at the Palisade. The scale of it all was too huge. But something had to be done to stop these men from butchering each other further.

'Enough!' she had cried. '*Enough*, I say!'

She stared about her. Flames flickered and leaped. It was an image from out of the dreams that had been haunting her, this, man-faces and demon-faces in flickering torchlight, contorted with the dark passion of their hate, ranked about her like so many poisonous flowers. An animal rumbling came from the crowded ranks. She half hoped to see the elder woman and the man appear here miraculously by her side, to make the dream come properly true. But no. She stood alone.

She must do *something* . . .

'Enough of death!' Jonaquil called out. It was a lame beginning, but a beginning nonetheless. 'Too many have died already. And for *what?*'

'To free our homeland!' a voice shouted out from amongst the men ranked behind Egil, and half a hundred more roared in agreement.

Jonaquil held her arms higher aloft, gesturing them to silence. 'Your homeland is freed!' she called. 'The southerners are *finished*!'

'Not yet!' Sub-Commander Gerrid shouted. 'Not finished yet . . .'

At this, Egil raised his great axe and the men crowded behind him let out a roar.

Jonaquil felt a rush of terror go through her like a cold wind. Her legs quivered weakly. For a long moment, it was all she could do just to stand there. But she raised her hands to Egil. His face was a hard mask of fury. 'Wait!' she shouted to him over the tumult. '*Wait!*'

Perhaps it was some recollection in him from out of the Woodend days that made him do it, but she saw him hesitate, lower the axe. The roar of the massed men behind him quietened. But it was momentary, only momentary . . .

She turned and faced Gerrid. 'What have you left to fight for, Sub-Commander?'

Sub-Commander Gerrid stared at her, his snarling cat-visage showing no human feeling. His voice carried clear in the quiet that had descended over things. 'You have the right of it, perhaps, Healer. We are like to be finished here. But not yet. While there is breath in us, we will still fight.'

'For *what?*'

'For our lives, Healer. Our lives and our freedom and our . . . *honour.*' He pointed to the ragged crowd of men at Egil's back. 'We will not subjugate ourselves to such as *them.*'

A surge of approval ran through the demon-horde behind him. Demons thumped their war-pikes against the cobblestones, chanting in their throats a guttural battle chant.

'And is there,' Jonaquil shouted, 'no choice facing you here, Sub-Commander? Is it to be death, death, and more death? Is there *no* other choice?'

Silence settled once again at her shouted question.

The Sub-Commander shook his head, gesturing again to Egil and his gathered force. 'I see no other choice, Healer. Do you?'

Jonaquil felt the moment slipping from her. What could she possibly say to turn things here? In desperation, she cried, 'Then change how things are, Gerrid!'

The Sub-Commander laughed outright. 'You talk nonsense, Healer. Get out of our way before you are cut down.'

Jonaquil stared at his unhuman face, breathless, intent. 'Are you so—'

'Enough!' a voice called suddenly, cutting Jonaquil off.

She whirled and saw Egil stride forward. His face was a mask of fury. 'Enough of words. *Words* will never end things here. *They* – ' he hefted his axe, pointing with it – '*They* will not listen to words, woman. They must be destroyed, utterly.'

Egil was panting like a hound, as if all this unaccustomed talking left him breathless. He grasped Jonaquil roughly by the arm and shoved her, stumbling, off to the side and away. '*They* must be destroyed!' he cried. 'Destroyed, I say. *Destroyed!*'

A great roar went up from behind him, and men began to move forwards.

But then, to the amazement of all, a figure appeared suddenly at Sub-Commander Gerrid's side, out of the very air it seemed. The figure was tall, shrouded in a dark cloak, the cloak's hood hiding the face in shadow. Jonaquil had never seen this newcomer before, but she recognized him.

'Tancred!' Gerrid hissed.

'Sub-Commander,' the Seer returned with a mocking half-bow. 'It seems you are in need of some assistance.'

'They said you were killed.'

'As you can see, "they" were wrong.'

Gerrid looked at the Seer uneasily. He had small liking indeed for the man. Even now, knowing that the Seer's powers would make all the difference to the outcome of things here, he could not summon up any enthusiasm.

The square had gone dead silent at the Seer's uncanny appearance. Still, not a soul had moved.

Tancred raised his arms. There was a great whirling of air. The hairs along Gerrid's arms prickled painfully.

Egil stumbled back and away from where he had stood between the opposed forces. The rebels arrayed across the square cowered back with him like wind-blown froth.

But then, 'Tancred!' a voice called out. '*Tancred!*'

Four people came into the square, running: three men and an old woman, the woman so weak she had to be carried by two of the men. Into the cleared space they stumbled. One of them, a young man with a half-healed scar across his forehead, stepped forwards and stabbed a hand towards the Seer. 'Tancred!' he called yet again.

The Seer stared at the newcomers. 'I was two,' he said, 'and now I am one. You will *pay* for that, boy, you and your companions. You have meddled with my designs too often.'

Gerrid felt *power* move the air. The square fairly crackled with it. To all appearances, the Seer and this unlikely young man merely stood there, staring at each other. But underneath that appearance, great bucklings of *something* were taking place. Gerrid felt a stab of nausea go through him and he gagged. About him, all did the same.

And then it stopped, abruptly.

From his knees, Gerrid looked up. Yet more newcomers had appeared. But he had never seen the like of *these* . . .

They were tall, and impossibly thin of limb. Pale-skinned, with huge dark eyes.

Three of them glided across the square towards the Seer. There was something about them that made them hard to see, as if they slipped in some manner in and out of one's vision.

Whatever they were, Tancred recoiled from them. 'No!' he cried. 'Away. Away from me!'

But they only glided closer. 'Thou hast meddled too far, man,' one of them said. And though Gerrid knelt not twenty paces from them, he could not tell which it was had spoken.

'Begone, creatures!' Tancred returned.

'Long and long hath it been since one of humankind disturbed us as thou hast. Thou hast meddled far, man, weaving many false nets, but thou art not the only creature with a *will*. We have woven nets of our own since first thou and thine came to disturb these lands. And now the time hath come to gather those nets in.'

'No!' Tancred cried. 'You cannot! Begone!'

They closed upon him, three pale, spidery-limbed, uncanny creatures, and the Seer screamed. And then, somehow, where three pale and one dark shape had been, there was only empty air.

A stunned hush gripped the square.

Crane quivered, feeling the Dream coming into fruition before her eyes.

The Fey.

She felt stunned that they should involve themselves thus in human affairs, they who lived only partly in the human world. And yet this had the feel of an inevitable conclusion, a final drawing-together of many strands woven together over time.

And so all the Seer's complex meddling had come to this: he had meddled with folk beyond him and it had proved the undoing of him. No more would he be seen in mortal lands, she felt sure of that.

But though the Seer himself might be gone, and his threat ended, events were not finished here.

In the square, the opposing forces were recovering.

The man with the axe shook his weapon over his head. 'Bloodaxe! Bloodaxe!' men roared.

Crane struggled forward. The Ratter and Costa had been supporting her, but she pushed them gently back now and went on alone, tottering, only her stick keeping her from falling face first to the cobblestones under her bare feet.

She felt the Dream a-borning in the moment. This was the cusp. Here. This very moment. All had led to here. She felt the Dream fill her, like a kind of radiance.

There had been too much of death and hatred. It was time for an ending or all would be destroyed. She saw it clearly: like the waves from a great rock thrown into a pool, the effects of this death-struggle would wash out across the whole of the Wold, destroying all.

Crane hobbled across the cleared, cobblestone space between the opponents. The combatants fell hushed, for the Dream-radiance that Crane had felt fill her was grown into light indeed, and before the eyes of the amazed men she glowed like a gentle torch.

Slowly, Crane raised her arms. The radiance about her shimmered. Her hands seemed to light up like candles. She gathered all her remaining strength. 'I say to thee all,' she began, 'that the time for death is *over*. I say—'

'Witch!' a voice cried from somewhere. A knife spun through the air, flashing in the firelight.

Crane stared aghast at the hilt protruding from her breast.

Not now! Not like this! She could *feel* the great Pattern a-borning here. And she was dying too soon . . .

She stared about her, seeing faces staring back. Silence hung over all. Her breast was filled with a great, cramping agony. She could feel her heart's blood welling through the rent the knife had made in her.

Turning awkwardly, she saw the man Egil with his axe, huge and bristling with fury. Above him, Crane's Shadowland-touched eyes could see a faint, hovering figure. It startled her. A long-haired female spectre, swirling about Egil, shrieking silently, mindlessly.

Crane *felt* how it was: trapped, pour soul, trapped between this land and the next, held by her own mindless terrors and Egil's blind love, trapped in a cycle of hopeless hate and vengeance, neither fully of this land nor the other. An iron will, this spectre, but a mind gone with too much pain. Only the agony, the fear, the soul's raw, raging hate . . .

And the poor man, the poor, poor man, his mind gone as hers, trapped no less than her between the worlds.

Crane tried to call out. But it was no use. She was too weak, too hurt. Every halting breath brought a stab of agony through her.

Then, as if a cord had unwound somewhere, she felt herself released. A great, swirling mass of Shadow gripped her, dragging at her like a tidal pool. She struggled, bringing to bear all the skills she had ever known as Dreamwalker. The Shadow tore at her. She felt herself being drawn off, drawn apart, like a clod of earth dissolving in a strong current of moving water. She felt terror come over her at her own impending dissolution. But she resisted it. She knew that the greatest barrier to dying was the fear. The fear made everything terrible. So she ignored the fear, allowed the fear to evaporate. Instead, she focused on the swirling spectre before her.

Where before it had been Egil who was clear and the shape above him faint, now it was that shape which became terribly clear to her and Egil who dwindled. The woman stared out of blind eyes, screaming. Flames seemed to dance about her.

Crane moved. Slowly, with great difficulty, she drew close to the woman.

Trapped in her agonies, in the strength of her own will, trapped in her love for Egil and his love for her, trapped in this torment for an eternal, terrible moment.

Crane put her own insubstantial arms about the woman. 'Let be,' she said in her voice that was no longer a voice. 'It is *over*. Let go. Release. Come with me. *Come.*'

The woman only screamed, tugging to get away from Crane's ethereal clutch.

The pull of the Shadow upon Crane increased. She resisted it. 'Come,' she soothed. 'Let go. Thou cannot stay here any longer . . .'

The Shadow-pull upon Crane was become almost overwhelming. Her strength was fast falling away. 'Come,' she insisted. 'Come with me. Have peace. Let him go . . .'

The woman stopped her endless screaming.

Crane stroked the woman's face, her face that was no longer a face, with hands that were no longer hands. 'Come now. Let go. Come.'

Like a small child, the spirit of the woman buried herself in Crane's arms, weeping.

This was it, Crane sensed, the Dream's final fulfilment.

'Come,' she repeated, beckoning, feeling the Shadow's pull on her irresistibly now. The woman shuddered, like some poor, crippled bird.

'Come,' Crane repeated soothingly. 'Come with me.'

Then, together, they allowed the Shadow to pull them away into the great dark from which they would never again return as they now were.

Tai stared in anguished disbelief at the crumpled body of Crane. A raw flash of hatred filled him suddenly. An old woman, a defenceless old woman!

The trip back from the Miradore burned in Tai's mind: Crane huddled in the boat, sunk into herself, hoarding her strength, the Ratter staring at the heaving sea, Costa silent and grim, bucking a contrary wind all the way to the quays. Through deserted, shattered streets they had stumbled, Crane urging them on in a voice cracked with weariness. And into this square.

And him *sensing* the drawing pattern of it all the time but not, oh not foreseeing *this!*

Standing in the flickering, half-lit, crowded square, Tai shuddered with anger. He would make *them* pay for this! It was time to make an ending.

In his anger, he started to *reach*, to tear away *their* lives once and for all. Now was the time for final retribution. He *sensed* the mass of pulsing intricacies that the gathered forces here formed, searching for the tell-tale, unnatural life-force of *them* in *their* fell helms.

*They* stood massed on one side of the square.

On the other were grouped northern men, his own kind.

To his sudden dismay, Tai found he could *sense* no difference. Each pulsed the same with unnatural, spell-helm violence.

Tai fell back to his world-eyes, confused.

Somehow it was not the gathered combatants that caught his attention. Instead his gaze focused on the huddled, sad form of Crane.

Tai recalled Crane in the Miradore, when the madness of anger had been upon him: 'Violence is a Power that moves in the world,' she had said. 'Violence *breeds*, man.'

Tai looked about him. Glinting blades on all sides, twisted faces, eyes blank and shining with fury in the wavering firelight. Hungering to kill, all of them.

And he remembered Tancred saying: 'Good and evil are a child's concepts. There is only *power*, boy, and those who wield it. Those with power do what they do because they *can*.'

He could not tell from which side the fatal knife might have come. He could distinguish no difference between the two sides; there was the same surge of unnatural spell-helm strength, the same rage to kill on each.

And he, in his new found power, was becoming as they were.

Tai shuddered, stricken by this realization. How had it come to this? He felt suddenly sick of it all. The anger that had lit him died.

Enough of death. *Enough*! He would not become like the Seer, like *them*.

But what could *he* do to stop the two sides from destroying each other?

Too much had happened here this night for him to be able to *sense* anything truly clear now. His earlier struggle with Tancred had torn many things loose. And the Fey . . .

Only partially did he grasp what the Fey had been about. Tancred had woven nets of his own devising through the world, trying to *reach* his will into all. The Fey had felt such, and resisted. But their resistance had been long and slow and subtle, like the weathering of a rock.

And all that had occurred, Tai now realized, had been influenced by the under-currents of the Seer's *willings*, and the counter-influence of the Fey's, like hidden tides drawing men's actions one way or another. And the Fey – deep creatures that they were – had settled patterns in ways he could neither comprehend nor even *sense* in any clear fashion. And under all this was the movement of the Powers through the world, which he was only just beginning to *sense*, so deep were they.

He had not the experience to make true sense of the complexity of this moment.

He could *sense* clear enough, though, the terrible tension inherent in events here, like a too-tightly wound spring, ready to burst itself asunder at the slightest touch.

And he could *sense*, too, that this was a special moment, a moment of balance.

But what could he *do*?

Any instant now, everything would burst around him.

Tai saw Egil raise his axe. The men behind him roared, gathering to fling themselves upon the demon pack across the square.

But then, unaccountably, Egil stumbled, came to a halt. He stared sightlessly about, as if some support had suddenly been wrenched from him. The men around him shifted confusedly, not understanding what was happening to their leader.

For a long, stunned moment, all eyes were upon Egil, on his knees now, head bowed, weeping in great, shuddering spasms.

From across the square a great, triumphant shout went up from *them*.

Tai was in despair, not knowing how to stop the carnage.

And then . . . And then he knew!

He *reached* desperately, with all his strength, tearing at the strange life that animated the spell-helms, but leaving the man-glow intact.

He stood there, panting, drained, staring with his world-eyes now.

Confusion and shouting, men stumbling, crying out.

The helms were dead.

But it was not enough.

To Tai's dismay, men began to adapt. This was battle; nerves were strung too tight, hearts beating too fast. There was too much sheer momentum. Spell-helms were flung aside to land clattering upon the cobblestones. Tai heard the man commanding the southerners shouting instructions. The two sides formed up once more. But they were shaken men now, all of them, no longer filled with spell-helm vigour. They stood, uneasy, casting quick, skittering glances here and there.

Between the opposing forces, all alone, lay the small, pathetic form of dead Crane. Tai walked to the body, drawn, uncertain of what he was doing.

He stood for a moment, mind blank, trying to find his voice, trying to find something to say, staring at the faces staring back at him.

'Out of the way!' somebody shouted. 'Out of the way, fool, or be ground underfoot!'

Suddenly, Tai knew what he had to do. He raised his arms. 'Stop!' he shouted. 'Listen to me!'

For an instant, they quieted.

'I stand here before you unarmed, defenceless. I will *not* move. You will have to kill me first, before any of you can come to grips with your "enemy".' He stared at them, hands out and empty, looking men in the face, feeling a strange strength come over him. 'Which of you will kill me first?'

An armoured man laughed, stepping forwards, war-pike in hand. Tai felt his heart stutter and would have *reached*. But that was . . . wrong here. He *sensed* that suddenly. He must use nothing here but his simpler self. Tai faced the man openly, and the man hesitated.

Suddenly, there was the sound of running feet.

Tai looked round. It was the Healer, Jonaquil. She stood next him, on the other side of Crane's dead body, and took his hand in hers. 'You will have to kill *me* as well!' she cried.

From the edge of the square a grey-haired woman with a knife in her belt came running to join them, taking the Healer's hand.

'Tishta!' he heard the Healer say.

'A friend in need,' the other woman panted in response.

From out of the crowd, Tai saw the Ratter come stumbling. He said nothing, merely took the grey-haired woman's hand in his and stood with them.

Somebody else scrambled out to join them. Costa, it was, and with him, against all likelihood, came old bespectacled William, the Curer.

But no more.

They stood there, hand in hand, a fragile human chain separating the two opposed forces, and the silence deepened.

Egil shook his head groggily. He felt as if some force that had been powering him was gone. He felt bereft. And yet he felt a sense of relief as well, as if the pain from a terrible toothache had finally stopped.

It is over, a voice seemed to say to him. *It is over . . .*

Somebody was weeping nearby.

It was a long, long moment before he realized it was himself.

He felt as if he was coming out of an endless, uncertain dream, a dream of blood and iron and dying. He saw the line of frail figures that stood between the two opposed forces, heard the angry sound of his own men behind him. He looked at the great double-bladed axe in his hand, nicked and dented now, stained with the blood of dead men. Suddenly he felt a revulsion so great it gagged him. With a grunt, he heaved the axe away. It landed with a clatter on the cobblestones. In the silence all about, the noise of its landing seemed preposterously loud.

Slowly, Egil moved forward. The ghost-wails that had haunted him for so long were silent. He felt empty. His body ached terribly, and each step, now that he was emptied of the hatred and the battle-madness, was an effort. He drew near to the human line. They parted, staring uncertainly, making a gap for him, hands out hesitantly for his. Instead, he walked through the line and across to the other side.

Some strange and terrible thing had happened here, Egil realized. His mind was so numbed and clumsy that he had not noticed immediately. His enemies no longer held their accustomed demon-shape. And neither, he noticed, did his own men. What had happened?

Searching, he saw nothing but human faces in *their* ranks.

'Which of you,' he demanded, his voice hoarse, 'commands here?'

'I do,' said one of them.

'You are?'

'Gerrid. Sub-Commander. Commander now of these forces.'

Egil looked at him. 'Come here,' he said, his voice low.

The Sub-Commander bristled.

'Are you frightened?'

With a grunt, Sub-Commander Gerrid detached himself from the line of his men and came forward.

It was strange to face one of *them* and have that one be in simple human shape. 'My wife and son,' Egil said, 'are dead. Your kind roasted them to death in our home.'

Gerrid said nothing.

'I have hated you and yours for long and long.'

Still, the Sub-Commander remained silent.

Egil shuddered, 'But everything seems long, long ago now . . .' He paused. 'Revenge,' he then said, 'does not bring back the dead.'

There was a long moment of silence. The two men looked at each other and the forces ranked behind them waited.

Egil took a step towards Gerrid, held out his hand. 'I say that those standing linked behind me are right. Let there be no more death here.' He looked at Gerrid straight, his hand still out. 'I do not have it in me to offer you friendship, stranger. But it is not what I offer you here that counts. It is what I do *not* offer. I do *not* offer you death. Not any more.'

Gerrid looked uncertainly at Egil's proffered hand. 'How do I know I can trust you?'

Egil shrugged. 'You have trusted me so far to fight against you. When I offered you death, it was a true offer. Why should you not trust me now *not* to fight? This offer is as true as the other.'

'You expect me to believe that these men of yours will simply put away their weapons and let us live in peace? *My* men would obey me. But that rabble of yours? You expect me to believe that the months of fighting, the rancour between us will just *disappear?*'

Egil shook his head. 'Of course not! Things are not that simple.'

'Then what is it, exactly, that you offer here?' Gerrid demanded.

Egil hesitated. 'I am not sure,' he said. 'I do not know what may come of this offer I make to you here. I do not know if there may be a place for you here in the north, or whether you would even wish for such a place. I do not know how many of my men might refuse to honour any vow I may make. I do not speak for all of them. I know only one thing—'

'And that is?' Gerrid asked.

'What have we left to fight for?'

Gerrid studied him. 'Honour,' he said finally.

Egil lowered his hand. He stared at Gerrid for a long minute. 'If that is your final word, Southerner, then so be it.' Turning, Egil walked back to the human chain and joined it, taking up Tai's hand in one of his and Jonaquil's in the other. 'I will not fight you, Southerner,' Egil called to him. 'Not any more. On *my* honour. It is over, do you hear me? For me, it is *over!*'

Silence still hung heavily over everything. Nobody moved.

Gerrid stared. 'I do not understand you, man,' he said, his voice heavy with confusion. 'What you suggest here makes no sense!'

Egil said nothing, merely stood in the line along with the others, hands linked.

'Your words are those of a coward,' Gerrid went on. 'But you are no coward. This I know.' The Sub-Commander scratched at the stubble on his chin. 'I do not understand you,' he finished lamely.

'You do not need to understand me to kill me,' Egil replied.

Gerrid nodded. 'True enough.'

'But I have had enough of death. What is there left to learn from death?'

Silence.

'What have *you* to learn from death?'

Slowly, Gerrid took a step forward, another. He ran a hand tiredly over his eyes. 'I do not know,' he said, with unaccustomed humility. 'Perhaps . . . *perhaps* . . .' He paused, glanced at the massed men on the far side of the square, back at his own men behind him, took a breath.

Gerrid looked hard at Egil. 'You offer peace here. Peace between us on equal terms. No surrender on the part of my men?'

Egil nodded. 'You have my word.'

Gerrid gazed at him, human face twisted in hard thought.

In the square, not a man moved.

Gerrid stepped forwards. Slowly, he held out his hand. 'I do not know what may lie between us in the days to come, but let it be as you say. Let there be no more death between us now. No more death.'

Egil detached himself from the line and took Gerrid's hand in his. 'No more death,' he repeated.

The men crowded into the square stood rigid, uncertain, unbelieving. Then, slowly, a great sigh went up. It was like the sound of the wind in the trees, or the murmuring of a distant ocean. Egil felt a long shiver sweep through him.

It was over.

# PART FOUR

# BURIAL AND BIRTH

# XXXIX

# Outside Long Harbour

Tai stood staring out across the dark emptiness of the Wold. Dawn was not far off. A cold wind blew. He shivered and wrapped his arms about himself.

Beside him loomed the open pit of the grave they had dug into the soil of the Wold. There would be no coffin, no marker. The earth would take the dead back. Soon enough, the only remains would be in the memories of those still living.

Save for the moan of the wind, the world was silent. No birds sang. Tai shivered.

The eastern sky began to lighten.

Tai sighed. Dawn was funeral time. An end and a beginning. A new day. A new life.

A new beginning for the dead, once having passed through the Shadowlands. A new beginning, too, for the ones who lived on without them.

Behind him, Tai heard those gathered here begin to stir. He turned and gazed at them. An unlikely company: men and women from throughout the Wold, southerners, Long Harbour citizens, Dreamwalker's strange folk. Not altogether comfortable with each other yet, not by a long count. Yet there stood Sub-Commander Gerrid, stiff and self-conscious, but respectful as any relative, and next to him stood Egil.

Next to the grave itself, lay the still form of Dreamwalker.

Tai felt his eyes fill with tears. It was grief for the old, wise woman, but it was so many other things as well. So many other dead: his foster-uncle Colby, and Skeefer, and poor little Ree. He had lived through so much, seen so much, and so much of it hurtful. So much passing away. So many endings. He was no longer the innocent he had once been. The boy he had once been had died as surely as had those others.

Crane's body lay on the ground, unshrouded, dressed as she had been when death took her. The earth would have it all. Looking at her, Tai felt the hairs on the backs of his arms and along his neck shiver. Had her death been foredoomed? Had it been the deep patterning of the mysterious Fey that she should die as she had? Had it been the working of the Powers? Tai did not know. He could *sense* no clear pattern of that magnitude.

But through her death, an end had been made. That was clear enough. All here had common cause now, one way or another.

Let that be enough, then, Tai thought.

The dim, silvery light of first dawn lit the graveside now.

'It is time,' Egil said.

Dreamwalker's body was lowered into the grave by her own people. One of them, an old man with only one eye, leaned over the grave and slowly emptied a leather packet of bones over Dreamwalker's body. Tai did not understand what special significance these small bones might have, but Dreamwalker's people bowed solemnly, watching the pale things trickle into the grave.

Jonaquil, the Healer, standing slightly apart, recited the ritual for the dead: 'A scathless journey in the darkness, friend,' she breathed, her voice hardly more than a whisper. 'A scathless journey and a fruitful end. Gone from the world of women and men. Into the Shadowlands . . . to begin again . . .'

The sun crested the eastern horizon, and the silver-grey of pre-dawn warmed to glowing ochre.

The living stood together gazing at the sunrise, each quiet with his or her own thoughts.

It was not just a single human death they mourned here, Tai thought, but rather a way of life. The Wold and its habitations had been all but destroyed, communities shattered. There was hurt and hatred and ruin. Nothing would ever be quite the same again.

He would never be the same again. He had seen the cautious way others looked at him now.

All familiar patterns had been broken.

But there was birth as well as burial here. A chance to put away violence, to bring hope.

It seemed to Tai then that he *sensed* a Power move through them all. His heart beat strongly with it. But it might have been his own wishful thinking. He did not know.

At this moment, staring into the face of the new sun, he did not need to know. It was enough, for now, simply to be alive, to feel the sun's beginning warmth upon his face, the presence of the others all around him, to know that the worst was passed and that, against all expectation and despite all uncertainties, there was a future ahead for them that was not drowned in blood and violence.

It was enough just to be alive and at peace.